"A heart-tugging, slow-burning, second-chance romance . . . This is a couple that I couldn't help but root for."

—*Red Cheeks Reads*

"If you love small-town romances that are rich in scenery and packed with sweetness, heat, and fun and [are] looking for an easy reading escape, look no further."

—*TotallyBookedBlog*

"Filled with emotion, laughter, and loads of sexual tension . . . I dare you to not fall in love with Harper and Rogan!"

—*Nightbird Novels*

"Sweet, sassy, sexy, and sentimental."

—*Harlequin Junkie*

"Second-chance enemies-to-lovers romance at its finest."

—*Bookishly Nerdy*

"I'm a sucker for second-chance romances, and add in the small town and I'm hooked. And who better to give me all the feels with a little humor and a mix of sexiness than Meghan Quinn."

—*Embrace the Romance*

That Second Chance

"With each book I read by Meghan Quinn, I become more in awe of her writing talent. She truly has a gift! *That Second Chance* was simply perfect!"

—*Wrapped Up in Reading*

PRAISE FOR MEGHAN QUINN

The Reunion

"Funny, brilliant, and full of swoon. Fans of *The Family Stone* will adore this book. A must read."
—Kendall Ryan, *New York Times* bestselling author

"Are you a fan of the family dynamics in *Schitt's Creek*? Then you will devour this book. Real, raw, and hilarious. Meghan Quinn at her best."
—Rachel Van Dyken, #1 *New York Times* bestselling author

"I was hooked from the very first page; this book has it all. The drama, the romance, the heat, and especially the humor."
—Laurelin Paige, *New York Times* bestselling author

"This laugh-out-loud romantic comedy was also filled with brilliant romance and surprising depth that absolutely enthralled me."
—Corinne Michaels, *New York Times* bestselling author

"Sweet, hilarious, and delightful, *The Reunion* captivated me from page one."
—Melanie Harlow, *USA Today* and #1 Amazon bestselling author

"Laughter and tears with a heavy dose of romance. Highly recommend to any romantic comedy fan."
—Lucy Score, #1 Amazon bestselling author

"An emotional journey of three siblings finding love and family all over again. Meghan Quinn brings both humor and depth in *The Reunion*."
—Skye Warren, *New York Times* bestselling author

"*The Reunion* is a delicate balance of laugh-out-loud moments and thoughtful tones that will leave every reader wanting more."

—Kennedy Ryan, *Wall Street Journal* bestselling author

"Flawless storytelling of six points of view, three love stories, and one big happily ever after."

—BB Easton, *Wall Street Journal* bestselling author

"The way Meghan Quinn was able to carry humor through the emotional aspects of the story was pure brilliance. Another hit."

—Tessa Bailey, *New York Times* bestselling author

"*The Reunion* is positively gripping, with intertwining story lines and six points of view. I wondered with bated breath what was going to happen next in this fun and witty romantic comedy."

—Amy Daws, #1 Amazon bestselling author

"A Meghan Quinn classic! Rich with her signature humor, clever in the storytelling, and brimming with delicious spice!"

—Lauren Blakely, #1 *New York Times* bestselling author

The Wedding Game

"Readers won't have to be reality TV fans to get a kick out of this fun, quirky rom-com."

—*Publishers Weekly*

That Forever Girl

"A terrific read."

—*Once Upon a Book Blog*

RUNAWAY GROOMSMAN

Other Titles by Meghan Quinn

All her books can be read on Kindle Unlimited

My Best Friend's Ex

Twisted Twosome

The Other Brother

STAND-ALONE TITLES

The Modern Gentleman

See Me After Class

The Romantic Pact

Dear Life

The Virgin Romance Novelist Chronicles

Newly Exposed

The Mother Road

The Reunion

The Highland Fling

The Wedding Game

BOX SET SERIES

The Bourbon series

Love and Sports series

Hot-Lanta series

RUNAWAY GROOMSMAN

MEGHAN QUINN

Text copyright © 2022 by Meghan Quinn

Published by Montlake, Seattle

www.apub.com

Amazon, the Amazon logo, and Montlake are trademarks of Amazon.com, Inc., or its affiliates.

ISBN-13: 9781542035002
ISBN-10: 1542035007

Cover design by Caroline Teagle Johnson

Printed in the United States of America

RUNAWAY GROOMSMAN

PROLOGUE
SAWYER

"She's so beautiful." A cooing aunt swoons.

"Absolutely breathtaking," a mother admits while waving her hand in her face, warding off tears.

"Simon is one lucky SOB," a man says while turning to Simon and giving him a wink.

"Oscar de la Renta in white looks spectacular on Annalisa. Don't you think?" Armie, Simon's brother, says as he nudges me with his elbow, pulling me from my lethal reverie.

"Yeah . . . a real goddess," I say, my voice dripping in sarcasm as I watch my ex-girlfriend walk down the aisle, hand in hand with her father, toward my best friend, Simon Fredrickson.

You read that correctly.

My ex-girlfriend is marrying my best friend.

A large, wet sniff echoes through the illustrious cathedral, which is coated in white from the light-washed floorboards to the vaulted ceilings connected at a forty-foot pitch. A church made in Hollywood Heaven.

I glance over at Simon, who's dabbing at his eyes with a light-blue handkerchief, a tender yet purposeful groom's gift from his bride: a statement that it's not just okay to cry while she walks down the aisle but required, because the cameras will be flashing.

The cameras have not stopped flashing since they were caught together on a boat cruise to Catalina. She was wearing a floral-print sundress, Gucci leather sandals, and her hair in loose curls, while he sported a pair of simple navy-blue shorts and a light-blue button-up with the top four buttons undone. No man undoes the top four buttons of his shirt as casual wear unless his first name starts with Douche and the last ends with Canoe.

The reason I know exactly what they were wearing when they were "caught" is because I read the caption under the picture of their love tryst at least 752 times before it actually processed in my head.

Annalisa Morton, my girlfriend of five years—the woman I planned on marrying—and breakout actress from the wildly popular streaming platform Movieflix, known for starring in wholesome romantic movies, was cheating on me, with my best friend.

Not just my best friend.

But her costar.

Her costar in the movie I wrote for both of them.

Some blogs said I practically wrote the script for their love, and with the undeniable force between their looks and my words, it was bound to happen. I should have been smarter.

Yeah, sure, blame it on the guy who was cheated on.

Couldn't have been the fact that my ex-girlfriend and best friend wouldn't know loyalty if it slapped them in the face with the latest fad drink from Starbucks.

Overnight, the affair erupted, and the world embraced the new couple.

Embraced!

I thought that was a kick in the crotch, until Simon asked me to meet him at the pub around the corner from my beachside apartment and begged me to be his best man at their wedding.

Begged.

Pleaded.

At one point . . . threatened.

Which has landed me in this very spot, staring down Annalisa in a slim-cut silk dress that screams old Hollywood, tears brimming in her eyes as she walks down the aisle toward Simon.

Why not say no?

Why not tell them to fuck off?

Because you see, there is a hierarchy in society we must follow. It goes: God, Hollywood, the president, and then it trickles down from there. At times, Hollywood and God duke it out for the power to make decisions, and more often than not, the greed from Hollywood wins out.

Unluckily for me, the producers of the movie we were all making together, as one big happy family, pulled me to the side and whispered in my ear that if I ever wanted to write in "this town" again, I needed to suck up my pride and do what was best for the film.

With my career in the balance, I sucked up my "pride" and I went along with the romance, acting as if everything was okay.

I smiled gaily when their engagement pictures spread like wildfire.

I gleefully shook Simon's hand when he asked me to be his best man—after the ominous threat, of course.

And I even gave an enthusiastic thumbs-up to a paparazzo when Simon's bachelor party was staged in Vegas.

And now that I'm here, standing at the altar with my sniffling weasel of a best friend, all I can think about is how I'm not sure I can possibly take any more of this fanciful mockery of a union.

When she's midway down the aisle, because Annalisa is living up this nauseating moment, the congregation breaks into joyous applause, as if she's Miss America taking her victory stroll, sash and flowers clutched dramatically to her bodice.

The men next to me clap.

The parents in front of me clap.

The bridesmaids to the right of me tear up and of course . . . clap. Trained actors at their finest.

I'm the only sane person in the building who is looking around, wondering what the hell is going on—until I'm on the receiving end of a sharp elbow jab to the ribs from Armie, accompanied by a ferocious side-eye that can only be described as the embodiment of derisive contempt.

I lift my hands and offer a slow clap, laced in sarcasm.

Thankfully, no one notices the true meaning behind my subtle clap. As long as I'm performing joyful noise, they don't bother considering my intent.

After what feels like half an hour, Annalisa makes it to the altar, kisses her dad on the cheek, and then sucks in a sharp breath as she makes a scene of giving her besotted groom a slow once-over. And because they are expert performers, she turns to the audience—oh, excuse me, *ahem*, friends and family—and gestures to Simon with her bouquet.

"Give our groom a round of applause. Have you ever seen anyone more handsome?"

The best man cleans up pretty well, but who am I to argue with the bride on her wedding day?

Once again, the chapel rings with clapping, and as all eyes are on us, I smile and give Simon a few claps as well while I envision his head between my hands, and instead of clapping my palms together, I'm slapping him right in those floppy, surgically pinned-back ears of his.

The chapel finally calms down, people take their seats in the sturdy pine pews, and the pastor begins his speech.

I tune him out. Not quite in the mood to hear about how the happy couple is the model for a perfect marriage. Instead, I stare down at the light-blue wing tip shoes that expertly match my light-blue Armani tuxedo, Danny Kaye–style.

The shoes bring me back to a time I brought Annalisa to my Boyle Heights apartment, which was littered with friendly drug dealers and ruled by an unspoken agreement—you don't rat us out and we won't murder you in your sleep. It was a deal I didn't mind taking. Annalisa was a struggling actress at the time, so she understood the need for low rent and didn't even think twice about where I lived. Instead, we cuddled up on the futon on my floor and streamed *White Christmas*. I marveled at the timeless story line, and she sighed over the costumes, declaring that one day, she was going to marry a man who wore a suit that matched his shoes. I promised her that on her wedding day, I'd make that happen.

Only . . . at the time, I was convinced I was going to be the groom, not the best man.

"The couple has prepared their own wedding vows," the pastor says with an impressed lilt to his voice.

Of course they have.

Bet they didn't actually write the vows themselves.

I refrain from crossing my arms over my chest and tapping my toe indignantly as they proclaim their everlasting love for each other. This should be *good*.

Simon continues to dab at his eyes—the man must have tear sticks attached to his handkerchief because even though his eyes haven't stopped dripping, his facial expression remains stoic. Wouldn't be the first time he inconspicuously taped a tear stick to his eye. I was the one who introduced him to the magical Hollywood trick.

In grand fashion, Annalisa sets her shoulders back and makes a dramatic display of drawing a folded piece of paper from the depths of her cleavage like a magician pulling a bunny from his hat. The awe that falls over the crowd is exasperating. You'd think she'd just mastered boss-level sorcery from their oohs and aahs.

If they think that's spectacular, they should attend one of my family reunions, where my aunt Suzie utilizes her cleavage like Mary Poppins's carpetbag. Roarick, my brother, still swears to this day that he saw her pull a live succulent from between her "bosoms."

Carefully, Annalisa unfolds the paper and looks up at Simon. One would think for being such a trained actress, she'd memorize her vows. But like everything else, it's all for the show.

I stuff my hands in my pockets, and from over Simon's shoulder, I stare her down. Just waiting to hear what she has to say.

"I can remember the day I first laid eyes on you," she begins.

Yeah, it was at my apartment. Simon came flying in looking like a gnome-size Dwayne "the Rock" Johnson in jeans and a black turtleneck. He'd just finished an off-off-Broadway performance of *A Day in the Life of Zack Morris*, a less-than-titillating "play" that required the hole-in-the-wall theater to refund ticket prices to the audience due to the lead puking across the ten-by-ten-foot stage after an overdose of Sausage McMuffins that morning.

He barged through my door, told me there was vomit everywhere, and then ran down to his apartment, one level below me. Annalisa found him offensive.

"From your beautifully stark black hair."

Dyed black hair.

"To your square, masculine jaw."

Jaw implants; he got them five years ago.

"To your mesmerizing blue eyes."

Okay, those are real and are quite fetching.

"You took my breath away."

A snort pops out of me before I can stop myself. Annalisa's eyes flash to mine, beaming a strong warning to keep it together.

I straighten up.

"I had just started making a splash in the movie business but lacked the confidence I needed to become a true leading lady."

Uh, not the way I remember it. She already had an impressive ego by the time she met Simon.

"And then you walked into my life, like a knight in shining armor, but instead of a white horse and a suit of clanking metal, you were cloaked in a Tom Ford suit and drove an Aston Martin."

"Ha," I say, which catches the attention of everyone around me. Oh shit. "Ha-ow amazing," I say to recover. "Just amazing vows." I lift my hand and give Annalisa a thumbs-up. She returns it with a murderous look.

But come on . . . Tom Ford and an Aston Martin?

What a load of crock.

More like heavily pocketed parachute pants and a 1993 Geo Metro without power steering.

"From a lonely, defeated, and confused part of my life, like a phoenix rising from the ashes, you lifted me up and resurrected me from the smoke and into the heavens."

Jesus Christ.

So basically, I was Satan, strapping her down in hell, only for Simon to come swooping in like a glamorized Tarzan minus the loincloth to rescue her from the pits of purgatory.

I can feel the eyes of family and friends on me, and not because of my not-so-subtle guffaw but because most of these people know the truth.

I'm the reason Annalisa made it into the movies.

I'm the reason Simon got his big break.

And I'm the reason their latest flick was so well received—not only am I now a highly sought-after screenwriter, but I wrote the screenplay that made audiences fall in love with them.

So, the question is, Why am I standing here next to an ex–best friend who was nervous the Botox in his armpits wasn't going to keep him from sweating through his suit on his wedding day, watching my ex-girlfriend heap praise on him—praise the double-crossing nitwit doesn't deserve?

I shouldn't have to stand here, supporting them.

The movie is done.

The press is over.

The audience has gone wild.

There's nothing holding me back. The studio can't offer me any more threats.

I put my time in.

Nothing making me stand at this altar and take this abuse.

So . . .

I decide to leave.

In that moment. I know it's time to go.

I take a step forward as Annalisa stares up at Simon.

Then another step.

And another, which draws their attention.

Annalisa sizes me up with those crystal-blue eyes. "What are you doing?" she says through a clenched smile.

I clear my throat. "If you'll excuse me, I must announce to the masses that I have better things to do than stand through this mockery." Simon moves to the side so he can look at me in absolute horror. Hinging at my hips, I make a graceful bow—because it feels right—and when I straighten up, I lift both of my middle fingers, one for each of them. "I pray to the Holy Spirit that this marriage goes down in flames."

I offer my apologies to the pastor for my straightforward verbiage with a quick wave, then spin on my heel and jog down the aisle while camera phones flash and a cacophony of whispers echo against the forty-foot vaulted ceiling. One particular camera flash—a light so deathly glaring it's like looking directly at an eclipse—momentarily blinds me, making me stumble down the rose-petal-dotted aisle and step on the lace of one of my shoes.

Whoa boy. I nearly fall flat on my face. A litany of curse words flies from my mouth before I quickly regain my balance, courtesy of the second-to-last pew coming to my rescue.

Mentally praising God for the assist, I dip two fingers into the bowl of holy water resting just inside the entryway, throw a peace sign up to the big guy, and then push on the handle to the doors.

Not so gracefully—*thank you, undone shoelace*—I stumble out the cathedral doors as a wave of cameras flash, blocking me from my unscripted breakaway. But their greedy flashes quickly turn into disappointed clicks when they realize I'm not the much-anticipated newly united.

If only they knew the moment they just captured will bring a hefty price when the news hits—the fleeing groomsman. They'll find out soon enough.

Spotting my escape vehicle, I jog down the stairs of the cathedral, only for my untied and ill-fitting shoe to slip off my foot midjog on the second-to-last step. The loss of footwear careens me into the stair rail, and I perform a spin move so epic, the greatest running back of all time would be jealous. Catching my balance, I glance back at the shoe just as Simon comes into view at the top of the steps, an expression of pure murder crossing his eyes.

Yikes, time to go.

Goodbye, shoe.

"Someone stop him!" Simon calls out dramatically, as if I've just stolen his wallet. And I take that moment to book it.

I run—well, hobble on shoe and socked foot—through the parking lot, all the way to my car, trailed by the few paparazzi smart enough to chase after me.

With cameras flashing through my tinted windows, I turn my car on and grip the steering wheel tight with one thing on my mind: time to get the hell out of here.

And just like that, with no plan attached to my lead foot, I drive.

CHAPTER ONE

FALLON

"Please tell me you finally got some white wine in stock," I say, flopping onto one of the many dilapidated barstools in Beggar's Hole, the only bar in the little town of Canoodle, California.

A platinum-blonde pixie haircut pops up from the bar, and Jazlyn, my best friend, wiggles her eyebrows. In my opinion, she looks like the singer P!nk's long-lost twin sister. "Refilled just this morning. I threatened Tommy with no payment and a quick slash to his tires if he didn't have any on his truck."

"I'm sure he thanked his lucky stars he had white wine—you have a reputation for seeing through on your tire-slashing threats."

Jaz winks and moves around the bar with ease, pulling up a wineglass for me—one of twelve she has in stock—and then filling it with wine and seltzer before topping it with a dash of lime.

My mouth waters at the sight.

"Long day?" she asks.

"If you consider wallpapering your hand to the men's bathroom wall while your foot is stuck in the toilet, then yes, I'd say a long day." I bring the drink to my lips and take an eager sip.

"Care to explain how you got in that predicament?"

My eyes meet Jaz's. "One word: Sully."

She holds her hands up. "Say no more." She moves around the bar. "Waffle?"

"Obviously," I say with a roll of my eyes.

She chuckles and heads to the kitchen to put in my usual order of a candied bacon waffle with extra syrup.

Yup, waffles at a bar named Beggar's Hole.

The thing about Canoodle, California, is that we do things our way, and we don't step on each other's toes. Everyone has a place in this town, and we live harmoniously as one big group, population: 2,510, tucked away in the San Jacinto Mountains between two large rock formations that are almost as grand as the terrain that surrounds us. Straddling the famous Harry Balls hiking trail, Bald Nut Rock hangs on the edge of the mountain, offering a steep decline, while Ancient Nads Rock extends high up the mountain, offering a very lifelike depiction of, well . . . a man's dangling bits.

Beggar's Hole is the town's bar, situated on stilts just above Bald Nut, so if you drunkenly fall off the side of the deck, you're tumbling to your alcohol-infused death. Thankfully, since the opening of the historically seedy yet charming bar, there has yet to be a deck-related casualty. Just outside the door leading to the deck hangs a gold-framed chalkboard showing a running total of "days since rock formation death." Currently, the town of Canoodle is sitting on 22,630 days of no deaths. An accomplishment widely congratulated through the whispering streets of our town.

Sipping my white wine spritzer, I turn in my chair, pressing my back against the bar top and crossing one leg over the other while I take in the wonderfully dingy space, only a light hum of classic rock and roll playing in the background. Jaz keeps the music just loud enough to be heard, but not too loud to drown out conversations. The wood-paneled walls have never seen one hint of renovation, but they have acquired fist holes and bent planks, lending the space an eerie but still charming ambiance. The uneven and sticky wide-plank floor resembles the deck of a pirate ship: knotty, splintery, and full of bodily fluids. But, like most of the townspeople, we gladly embrace "the Hole" and retreat here for an evening of spirits and breakfast for dinner.

"Other than papering your hand to the wall," Jaz says, reappearing and resting a giant waffle infused with candied bacon bits in front of me, "how are the renovations coming over at the Cove?"

"Not great," I answer, spinning around again and grabbing a fork. Friday nights are for waffles and wine, an odd combination that somehow works. "I don't know what I was thinking, taking this all on while being Grandpa Sully's sole caretaker. It's a bit overwhelming." I feel a pang as I glance back toward the table in the far left corner, Sully's table, where he's "shooting the shit" with his best pal, Tank, the owner of Village Hardware and Jaz's grandfather. "Today, Sully asked me at least seven times to unload the dishwasher. When I said it was already unloaded, he'd make a grumbly sound, and then I'd walk into the kitchen to hear it running. I stopped it every time to not waste water, but Jesus, Jaz, he's getting worse."

"Have you talked to the doctor at all about the new developments?"

I shake my head. "Between trying to keep the guests at the Cove happy, the renovations, apologizing for the renovations, and stopping the dishwasher, I haven't had time."

"I thought you shut down for renovations."

"After this weekend, we'll be shut down so I can focus on the renovations." I cut into my waffle and gather a large bite on my fork.

"Do you think you need some—"

WHACK!

The door to the bar flings open, adding to the handle hole that's already made quite the dent in the wood paneling.

The bar goes silent as a tall dark shadow emerges from the plank, the bridge that connects the street to the bar.

The figure slowly comes into view, starting with light-blue shoe— yes, shoe, singular; his other foot is sheathed in a light-blue dress sock (which is not the least bit attractive: the shoe, not the sock)—followed by matching light-blue pants, light-blue suit jacket with accompanying vest, white shirt, and tie.

"Beer," the man grumbles as he comes up to the bar and takes a seat on a stool two spaces away from me. "Lots and lots of beer."

Jaz flings a coaster at him. "Does it matter what kind?"

"Nope," he says, reaching into the bowl of puppy chow in front of him. "Odd," he says, lifting up one of the powdered sugar–coated Chex squares before popping it in his mouth.

The few people in the bar immediately begin to chatter again, and I know exactly what they're chattering about . . . the mysterious man in the flamboyant tuxedo.

He might not know it.

But Jaz and I do. We exchange looks while she pours the man a beer from the tap.

"Watcha runnin' from?" Jaz asks, setting the beer down in front of him.

He downs half the beer before setting the pint glass back on the bar top and wiping his mouth with the back of his hand. This one seems to be lacking etiquette—surprising, given the pristine press of his suit pants and the gold cuff links peeking past his suit jacket.

"Who says I'm running?"

Jaz leans on the bar top. "We might be small-town people, but we're not stupid." She flicks the corsage pinned to his suit jacket. "From the freshness of this corsage, to the hold-strong gel in your hair, to the desperate demand for beer, I'd say you either left someone at the altar—or they left you."

Ohh, very observant.

From my position, I can only catch him from my peripheral view, but I can easily note the tension in his jaw as he stares down his pint glass and then lifts it to his lips. After a few seconds of silence, he finally answers: "I ran."

Jaz smacks the bar top. "We've got a runaway groom, folks!" she shouts to the rest of the crowd, which boos him uproariously, chucking a few used napkins his way.

"What?" the man says, shaking his head. "No, I was the *groomsman*."

Jaz pauses. "The groomsman?"

"Technically, best man," he says, finishing his beer and pushing the glass toward Jaz for a refill.

"But you ran from the wedding?" He nods. Confused, Jaz asks, "Did a swarm of bees chase you out? Possibly the fashion police, attempting to slap you with a fine for an abomination of a tuxedo?"

"Something like that," he mutters before shoving more puppy chow in his mouth.

Jaz leaves it at that, fills up his drink, and then comes back to me. She jabs a thumb toward the man. "Seems like someone wronged him."

I take my first true glance at him. Square, muscular jawline, not an ounce of scruff or five-o'clock shadow; laugh lines dancing near the corners of his eyes; blond hair, styled to the right and short on the sides, a hairstyle that could look good on any man. But . . . from the sight of him, something familiar starts to bubble up in my stomach. Recognition.

Why do I know him?

Why is that passive way he speaks so . . . familiar?

"I feel like I know that guy," I whisper, leaning across the bar.

"Really?" Jaz asks. She glances over at him. "He seems like a tawdry dud. Did you see the shoe?"

"I did. Absolutely dreadful. But beyond that, he looks familiar. Like I've met him before."

From his deflated position two spaces over, he turns to us. Fear creeps over me that he heard us talking about him—Jaz couldn't care less, but I have some semblance of social decorum. Though when he asks us a question, I know he didn't hear a thing. "Is there lodging around here?"

Boy, is he talking to the right person. Lodging . . . of course we have . . . GASP!

It hits me.

Those tired blue eyes.

That thick blond hair.

The small crook in his nose.

The man hunched over the bar, inquiring about lodging, Mr. Matchy Pant-Shoes . . . I went on a date with him.

Yes, it's true. I, a sophisticated and engaging woman, went on a date . . . with *him*.

One single date.

A date that lives rent-free in my brain as the worst date I've ever been on.

Now, before you start conjuring up ideas as to why the date went sour, I'm going to set the record straight right here, right now. I am not the reason for such a foul memory. No, I was an absolute delight that night.

But the apparent runaway groomsman, on the other hand . . . he was less than desirable to be around.

"We do have lodging," Jaz says. "In fact, it's your lucky day. The owner of the Canoodle Cove Cabins is sitting right here."

The man turns and looks at me straight on for the first time.

I brace for impact.

For the heat of embarrassed recognition to settle over him.

For him to announce to the bar, with a pointed finger in my direction, that he knows me.

I wince.

I hold my breath.

I grip my fork just a touch tighter, steadying a bite of waffle on the end of the tines.

And then . . .

"Any vacancies?" he asks before bringing his beer to his lips.

His voice is gruff. His posture drained. His eyes glazed over with woefulness.

There's no pointing. No "aha" moment.

Wait . . . does he not . . . does he not recognize me?

I blink a few times, waiting for it to hit him. Waiting for him to smack his palm to his head as realization dawns on him. But his face remains passive, and I realize quite quickly that, just like our date, I'm making zero impression on him right now.

"Uh, yeah," I answer. "We have a few cabins available."

"Perfect." He turns back around and faces the bar, tipping his drink up to his lips. "I'm going to need one."

❖　❖　❖

"Why do you need to talk to me back here?" Jaz grumbles as she looks through the porthole of the kitchen door. "I have customers, you know."

"Jaz, I know him."

"We established you saw some resemblance."

"Yes, but I know from where now." I tug on her arm.

"Okay, delight me with the story."

I glance out the window as well, just to make sure we're clear of eavesdroppers. "We were set up on a blind date."

"Wait. You went on a date with Mr. Matchy-Matchy? The guy who's missing a shoe? Ew, why?"

"He wasn't matching then. Well, I mean, he matched, but not like he is now. He was dressed just regular." I shake my head. "That's beside the point, Jaz." I drop my voice even further. "He didn't recognize me."

"Are you sure? Did he even look at you?"

"Yes. When you told him I own the cabins—which technically isn't true; Sully owns them. But he looked at me, actual eye contact. Trust me, he has no idea who I am."

"Was it a memorable date?" she asks.

"Does it matter?"

"Not really." She taps her chin while looking out the window. "Do you want me to slash his tires?"

17

"No. For the love of God, no."

"Because you know I will. No one wrongs my friend and gets away with it."

"Judging from his Easter-inspired tuxedo, I'm going to guess he's had punishment enough."

Jaz quirks a singular brow to the sky. "So, you're not mad about him not remembering you?"

Am I mad? I mean . . . it's never great to be forgettable, but then again, it's not like I made a strong impact on him during our date. It was evident from the way he ignored me. Mad? No. Indifferent? Yeah, that feels more like it.

"It's not like there was a love connection. He was on his phone most of the time. The only reason I stuck around was because we went to the Golden Star in Palm Springs, and I ordered the steak. I wasn't leaving until I devoured it."

"God, what I wouldn't give to have eight ounces of that meat in my mouth right now." She stares up at the ceiling dreamily. "I don't blame you for sticking it out. Did you even talk on the date?"

"Minimally. It was incredibly awkward. He showed up late, was in a terrible mood, and then grumbled a lot about plotlines and story arcs."

"Is he an author?"

"Uh, I think he does screenplays or something like that. At least that's what he said when we first met."

"I find this all very fascinating. Shall we bring it up to him?" She wiggles her eyebrows.

I grip her arm and stare her in the eyes. "Do *not* bring this up. For the love of God, just let this be between you and me. He's probably passing through. No need to make this more awkward than it needs to be."

"Doesn't seem awkward to me—seems like fun."

"Please, Jaz."

She rolls her eyes and sighs. "Fine. But can you at least reconsider the tire slashing?"

"No," I say, exasperated.

"You know, I don't see why you're protecting him. The guy seems like a doofus. Doesn't know who you are, walked out on a wedding, and he doesn't even know what puppy chow is. An absolute disaster. Why protect him from my sarcastic wit and cunning conversation?"

"Or your knife-wielding skills."

She smirks. "That too."

"Not happening. Okay? I'm not protecting him, just . . . I don't know, not trying to cause any drama where it's not needed. He'll be gone tomorrow, so let's just leave it."

With an annoyed groan, Jaz tosses her arms in the air. "Then what was the point of coming back here if we're not formulating some sort of plan of attack?"

"It was just so I could tell you I went on a blind date with him."

She growls in frustration. "You're losing your edge."

"Blame it on Sully," I say, chasing after her as we head back into the main bar area.

I take a seat at my stool, and Jaz makes me another drink, swapping the one that I left on the counter for something new. She's very cautious about leaving drinks around, especially with passing tourists.

"His nose is crooked," she mutters, handing me the drink.

"I know."

"But he has a lot of hair for a man who has such weary eyes. How old is he?"

"I don't know," I whisper. "Doesn't matter."

"My guess is forties." She taps the bar top. "Hey, Groomy, how old are you? Forties?"

He turns his head. "Groomsman."

"Whatever." Jaz waves her hand dismissively. "Just answer the question."

"What's it to you?"

19

Jaz plants one hand on the bar, the other on her hip. "Because I asked, and unless you want everyone in this bar to turn on you, I suggest you answer the simple question."

He sighs. "Thirty-five."

"Thirty-five." Jaz whistles. "Invest in some eye cream."

He doesn't flinch.

Doesn't even act insulted.

Instead, he picks up his beer, downs the rest of his glass, and then asks for another.

I can barely remember what we talked about the night we went out. I can sort of recall what I wore, what he wore. But I do remember his disinterest, the bleakness in his eyes. That hasn't changed. That's something I will forever remember—because I felt the same exact way.

That was the night I found out about Sully.

That was the night I made the executive decision to abandon my life in Palm Springs and move up to the mountains to help my grandpa with his rental cabins.

I left everything behind. The date was a mere formality.

I wasn't present. Neither was he.

There was no connection.

Just like right now, as he sits a few feet away. There is no pull, no cosmic force shoving us together.

He just happens to be a runaway groomsman who stumbled into my town.

Nothing more.

❖ ❖ ❖

"I told you not to give him that last beer," I grunt, walking the last few steps into the lobby of the Cove and stumbling under my new guest's weight.

"I wanted to see if he'd fall off the back of the deck," Jaz responds as we deposit him on the old western-style couch just across from the check-in counter. He smiles up at us and offers a wobbly thumbs-up.

"Well done, ladies."

Ugh, men are exhausting.

"Let's just get him checked in so I can get to bed. The last thing I need to do is take care of two grown men."

"Technically, Tank is taking care of Sully tonight," Jaz says. I shoot her an annoyed look, and she chuckles. "But I understand what you're saying."

I walk behind the check-in counter and wake up the early-2000s computer with a shake of the corded mouse. It takes a few seconds, but the screen blinks on, and I open up the registration log. It was the one thing Sully was always adamant about: taking down notes, making sure reservations were set. He noticed early on that he had a tendency to forget—and forgetting a reservation in a small mountain town where you run the only lodging other than house rentals is not a good way to conduct business.

"Do you have mountain views?" the man says, attempting to button up his light-blue tuxedo.

"The entire town is a mountain view, dumbass," Jaz says, leaning against the counter.

"It's dark, how the hell am I supposed to know?" He gestures drunkenly to the wall.

"I suggest you stop talking to him before you lose your cool," I mutter. "Not worth it." Directing my attention to . . . what's his name again? Sean? Sam? "I'm going to need an ID and credit card."

He digs his less-than-dexterous hands into his pockets—struggling uncomfortably—and then fishes his wallet out, only for it to land on the floor.

He leans back on the couch, breathes a heavy sigh, and then . . . passes out.

Jaz and I both stare at his unmoving carcass.

"Uh . . . is he dead?" Jaz whispers.

"I can't be sure," I answer wearily. "Poke him."

"Ew, I'm not poking him. You poke him."

"I can't have my DNA on him. We have history—I could be considered a suspect."

Jaz rolls her eyes. "Your history is one blind date where he ignored you. I barely consider that history."

"It's enough to get me questioned."

"Jesus," Jaz huffs, making her way to the umbrella stand next to the back door leading to the cabins. She picks up an umbrella and positions herself in front of . . . hmm, Silas? Steven maybe?

With two hands, she taps . . . Spencer (?) on the knee with the tip of the umbrella.

He doesn't move.

"Oh God," I whisper, leaning over the counter now. "What if he's dead?"

"That would not be good for business. We'd have to do some *Weekend at Bernie's* recon work. Stick him in front of Spirits and Jerky, make it seem like a natural death-by-sidewalk-type thing."

"Poke him again." I jab the air with my finger. "See if rigor mortis has set in."

"It doesn't work that fast, you idiot." Jaz takes a step closer and pokes his chest.

We hold our breath.

And then . . . nothing.

"Oh my God, he's dead. He's really dead." My voice rises in panic, and I look closer. "I can't see if his chest is moving. Is it moving? Check his pulse."

Jaz shakes her head as she takes a step back. "That's where I put on the brakes. There's no way I'm about to touch a dead person. Sorry."

"Uh, you'll have to touch him if we're sticking him in front of Spirits and Jerky."

"That's what tarps are for—body dragging."

"What is wrong with you?"

"Me?" She points to herself. "What is wrong with *you*? We should've just left him at his car, but noooooo, you thought it would be kind to bring him here . . . where he has *expired*!"

"He was looking for lodging," I say, moving my way around the counter. "I thought it would be better to help him here instead of letting him get back in his car. I didn't know he was going to . . . shut his eyes forever here." I press my hand to my forehead. "I mean, is he really, you know . . . ?"

"Dead?"

"Yeah, that. Is he? I can't see through that stupid suit. This is getting ridiculous. We need to check his pulse. Call an ambulance."

"And tell them what?" Jaz says, growing serious. "That we carried a drunk man to your lair, where he just happened to die? I have a record, Fallon. This does not look good on me."

"It's not my fault you've made it a hobby to go around and slash tires."

"I'm a vigilante!" She raises her fist to the air.

"Dear God, this is getting out of control. For the love of everything holy, just feel for his pulse." I shove her toward the couch.

"Ew, no way. You do it. You're the former nurse, and the one with a romantic involvement."

"It was one blind date."

"Still, you are more attached, and bringing him here was your idea. I touched him with the umbrella! I did my service; now it's your time."

I shake my hands while jogging in place. "Can you at least be ready with the hand sanitizer?"

"That I can do." She drops the umbrella and snags the bottle of hand sanitizer from the counter next to the computer. She holds the bottle out in front of her, legs spread in a sturdy stance and one finger on the nozzle, ready to attack. "Okay, I'm ready. Touch him."

Mentally preparing myself, I convince my brain that I'm not about to touch a dead person, that in fact, I'm just touching a man who is sleeping. I slowly inch toward him. One scoot at a time until I'm hovering over him. Slowly—wincing the entire time—I reach down to his lifeless wrist and press two fingers to his skin—

"Mashed potatoes!" he yells, sitting straight up. I fall back on my ass and scream bloody murder.

"Satan!" Jaz yells, squirting him with the hand sanitizer.

I scoot backward, crab-walk-style, until I'm far enough away to catch my breath after the heart attack he just gave me.

His inebriated eyes land on me, and he slowly wavers in his seat, bobbling to and fro as he stares down at me. Languidly, he holds up his index finger and says, "One plate, please." And then he collapses back against the couch.

Frozen in fear, we catch our breaths and then calmly distance ourselves a little more.

"I think it's safe to say he's not dead, just very drunk," I say with relief as I stand from the ground and brush off my hands.

"With some ghost possessing him, maybe the owner of that suit. It can't be new—has to have been dug up from somewhere." Jaz picks up the umbrella again and gradually runs the tip along his shin. "Looks like old fabric to me."

"Stop stroking him with the umbrella, and hand me his wallet so I can get him checked in and then get him the hell out of here."

Jaz fetches the wallet from the ground and tosses it to me. She holds the umbrella up to him like a sword, probably warding off any more abrupt pleas for mashed potatoes, while I flip open the old, torn leather of his wallet. My eyes land on his ID and his name.

Sawyer.

Ahh, see, I knew it began with an *S*.

It takes me a few minutes, but once he's checked in, I grab the key to cabin eight—it offers a wonderful mountain view, because I'm nice like that—and together, Jaz and I lift his arms over our shoulders. We drag him to his cabin and dump him on the bed once we've unlocked the door.

Jaz tosses his wallet at his passed-out body and then catches her breath. "You couldn't have picked a closer cabin?"

"He asked for a mountain view."

Her eyes flash to me. "I hate you."

"I know." I sigh. "But hey, at least we can say we did a good deed. He's safe in his cabin, and no one robbed him."

"So you think," Jaz says, holding up a twenty-dollar bill between her fingers.

"Jaz," I scold, reaching for it, but she stuffs it in her torn-up jean shorts. "Call it a bellhop tip. Now if you'll excuse me, I have a man waiting for me at my place."

"What?" I laugh. "Who?"

We walk out of the cabin, and I lock it up with my spare key so no one can get in—just in case, since we're pretty much crime-free here—and Jaz ruffles her hand through her hair. "That marine I met two years ago—he's on leave and drove up for some fresh air."

"Wait . . . Hunky Hakeem is waiting for you back at your place?"

"Yeah, and he sent me a picture of himself spread eagle on my bed, so your attempt to be Mother Teresa has put a dent in my fun."

"You should have told me."

"And let you take care of *that* yourself? No. I might have a wicked soul, but my heart still has some good in it. Couldn't have let you go about that alone." We make it back to the main office, and she heads toward the front door. "I'm assuming since there isn't much rush on your end, Peter isn't headed up here this weekend? You're usually prep-ping and primping, getting ready for him."

I shake my head. "His shift ends on Sunday. He's coming up Monday."

"Well, at least you have some entertainment until then." She nods toward the back cabins.

"The less entertainment, the better. Have fun with Hakeem."

"Oh. I will." She winks and then takes off.

I lock the door behind her, turn off the vacancy sign, and shut down the main office before heading upstairs to the residence quarters.

Fridays are usually my favorite days. Peter, my boyfriend, travels up here from a long shift at Palm Springs General Hospital's emergency room. Sully spends the weekend with Tank, giving me a break, and I can just take a deep breath. But the disturbance from the runaway groomsman has put a kink in my plans to relax.

At least I can go to bed knowing he and his terrible suit will be heading out of here tomorrow.

Chapter Two

SAWYER

"Death," I mutter as I stare back at myself in the bathroom mirror. "Absolute death."

Bloodshot eyes with very large bags underneath them.

Hair a complete mess.

Dry, cottony mouth.

And clothes completely askew.

I woke up this morning with no knowledge of where I was, how I got there, or what happened the moment after I sat down at Beggar's Hole and had a drink.

All I know is that my wallet is still with me—minus twenty dollars—and my keys and phone were still in my pocket, hence the reason my left leg is in an immense amount of pain. Sleeping on keys—wouldn't recommend it.

I grip the yellow laminate countertop and take a few deep breaths. Jesus.

Yup, this is a hangover at the age of thirty-five. Walking the line between life and mortality.

I push my hand through my hair and head back into the quaint cabin's main living quarters. The olive-green carpet has seen better days, the worn-down oak furniture squeaks, and the curtains are tattered near the hem. I wouldn't quite label the space as seedy, but it's getting close. One more stain on the floor and it could qualify.

This is what we would call an exposition in the screenwriting world. A quick rundown of my demise, the background of where I've landed, and well-placed scenery to draw up an image in your mind as to how I've absolutely, without a doubt, hit rock bottom.

Look around, this is it—this is what a sorry excuse for a man looks like.

Dressed in a powder-blue suit, drool encrusted on his face, bloodshot eyes, and . . . wait, am I only wearing one shoe? I search the cabin—slowly—and while I'm on my hands and knees, becoming one with the rank olive-green carpet, memory strikes me hard in the head.

I sit back on my heels and let out a deep sigh.

I left the shoe on the stairs of the church.

Yup, I pulled a flighty Cinderella moment while barreling down the steps.

My phone buzzes in my pocket, startling me to my feet. I pull it out and see my brother's name scroll across the screen.

With a groan, I lie down on the bed, put the phone on speaker, and then rest the phone on my chest.

"I'm on the verge of death," I answer.

"You sound like it." Roarick's baritone voice fills the quiet space. "Tried to forget last night, I'm assuming."

"Yeah, something like that." I think back to the moment I dashed out of the wedding. The whispers. The stares. The light gasps as the church doors slammed behind me. "Dude, last night—"

"I can't believe you walked out on the wedding."

I pause and slowly sit up, picking up the phone and bringing it to my ear.

"How do you know that? Did I text you?"

"No," Roarick answers cautiously. "Dude, it's trending everywhere. You're the runaway groomsman. Someone took a video of you flipping off Annalisa and Simon and turned it into a GIF. The lack of care in your expression really screams, 'I don't give a fuck.'"

I press my fingers into my brows. "Shit. Is it bad?"

"I mean . . . depends on what bad is to you."

"Roarick . . ."

"Well, let's see, you're all over the news. The shot outside the church was my favorite. Missing shoe, stumbling down the stairs in a light-blue tux. With your blond hair, you truly looked like a modern-day Cinderella."

"Not fucking funny."

But he doesn't care. He still chuckles. "Annalisa claims you ruined her wedding. Simon swears there were no ill feelings between you two and states he even asked your permission to date her—"

"Bullshit."

"Yes, I'm aware, just telling you what they're saying. The press is eating it up as the biggest thing to rock Hollywood since talking pictures, and then, of course, the clever trolls on the internet have replaced Julia Roberts's head with yours on the movie poster for *Runaway Bride* and changed the title to *Runaway Groomsman*. It's pretty convincing. I might have snorted when I saw it."

Remember when I was talking about rock bottom? I thought I'd hit it.

Nope, this is it.

"Fuck," I say, flopping back on the bed again as a wave of nausea overtakes me. "This is not good."

"It doesn't seem like it is. It actually seems quite bad."

"You're not helping," I groan.

"I didn't call to help; I called to be the lucky person to check up on you, and hopefully deliver the radiant news about your public oopsie."

"Can you not call it that?"

It's bad enough I was slighted by my best friend and ex-girlfriend—and am negatively trending as a result. I don't need my brother calling it a "public oopsie."

He chuckles. "Seriously, though, are you okay, man?"

"No." I breathe out while I smooth my hand over my forehead, willing the pounding of my headache to let up for at least a second. "Having a public meltdown wasn't necessarily something I wanted to engage in. But, hell, I lost it yesterday. I bottled up the deceit, the pressure from the studio, put on a smile, and I thought I could get through the obnoxious fanfare until they started their vows. It was such a load of crap that . . . hell, man, I snapped."

"In grand fashion too."

You could say that. This wouldn't be half as big a deal if it didn't involve America's favorite couple—yeah, it pains me even thinking that, but it's unfortunately true. And because we're dealing with a drama-obsessed diva who believes her big toe should have its own Instagram handle, this is going to be blown way out of proportion, with my name dragged through the mud.

Sure, I flipped them off at the altar, *but* I was also the one who was wronged, so I should get a pass, some compassion.

There should . . .

But I think we all know, given Annalisa's impeccable ability to cry on cue, that's not how the public will perceive the mishap.

"Do Mom and Dad know?"

"Oh yeah, they know," Roarick says, and I hear the laughter in his voice.

"Are they mad?" I wince. Yes, I might be thirty-five, but I still seek out my parents' approval like I'm a twelve-year-old overachiever.

"Mom's worried about your mental health, and Dad was more concerned about the sloppy form of your middle finger."

"There's no proper form for flipping someone off."

"According to Dad, there is. He showed me this morning when I dropped off doughnuts before hitting the fields."

Our family owns a 180-acre vineyard. White grapes, the best in Southern California, as my dad likes to say. He also says we don't make wine—we grow grapes. They provide grapes to some of the most sought-out wineries in Southern California. Recently Roarick has taken over the duties of running the vineyard, giving Mom and Dad more time to relax—and apparently practice the art of flipping someone off.

"I'm sure he'll give me a lecture about it at some point."

"He's already working on his presentation, which involves a slow-motion video. I think you'll be impressed with his camera angle," Roarick says. "So . . . what are you going to do now?"

"I don't know. I'm sure that Annalisa and Simon are soaking up all the limelight, which of course makes my life a living hell."

"Oh, from the brief interviews I've seen, your apartment is definitely swarmed—lots of paparazzi camping outside."

"Yeah, there's no way I'm going back there right now." I glance around the cabin, taking in the quiet space—only the distant sound of a cricket chirping outside fills the air.

"Where are you now?"

"Uh . . . someplace called Canoodle."

"Canoodle? Wait, isn't that up in the San Jacinto Mountains? I think Mom and Dad like a wing restaurant there. They stop whenever they're driving back to Palm Springs after visiting you."

"Yeah, that sounds familiar. I stopped here because I saw a bar as I was driving and found the idea of drinking myself into oblivion very appealing."

"Understandable. I'm sure any other person in your shoes—well, shoe—would have done the same. Although, from the sounds of it, it seems like you drank the entire bar."

"Feels like it." I heave a sigh. "I'm in some cabin right now. I have no idea how I got here."

"Dude, that's terrifying."

"Tell me about it. It's a very unsettling feeling, waking up in an unfamiliar location with no idea how I got there. It was also unsettling when I couldn't recall where I left my other shoe. But none of that is nearly as terrifying as going back to LA right now."

"I think you're right. Going back to LA is basically serving yourself up on a gold platter to the snarling, hungry wolves also known as the entertainment press. Why don't you come down to the vineyard, hide out for a bit?"

I shake my head, even though he can't see me. "I'm not sure I can deal with Mom and Dad right now. The relentless joking from Dad, and Mom's incessant need to hug me to her . . . *bosom*, is not something I can stomach."

Roarick chuckles. "I did walk in on Mom hugging a picture of you to her chest this morning. It might be smart to steer clear."

I stand from the bed and walk up to the window, where I part the curtain. The sun shines through the glass, a beacon of searing, head-ache-inducing light, blinding me for a moment before my pupils adjust but offering little relief. Despite the garish glow, I take in the stunning view—a calm lake stretched out tranquilly in front of my cabin, sur-rounded by soaring, pine-covered mountains.

The first thing that comes to mind: peace.

Next thing that comes to mind: escape.

No one will find me here.

This might very well be the perfect place to lick my wounds.

I take a deep breath, and a tightness in my chest—which I haven't even noticed until now—loosens.

Yup, I may have just drunkenly stumbled into a safe haven.

"You know what? I think I'll actually hide away here for a bit."

"In Canoodle?" Roarick asks, obviously dumbfounded. "The wings are good, man, but are they really that good?"

"Better than going back to my place or dealing with Mom and Dad."

"Do you even have any clothes with you?"

I glance down at my tuxedo pants and blue, dirt-stained sock. "Uh, about that . . . think you want to do your brother a favor?"

"No."

"Roarick . . . please."

He sighs. "What do you need . . . ?"

❖　❖　❖

I really should have thought through my retreat from the church, at least for a second, before I started driving away, because making the walk of shame to the front office in this powder-blue tuxedo and one matching shoe takes a huge shot at my barely present pride.

This right here . . . this is rock bottom.

I know I keep saying that, but the situation continues to burrow deeper and deeper into rubble.

Before I left my cabin, I adjusted my dowdy button-up to look somewhat presentable by rolling the sleeves to just below my elbow and tucking in the hem. There was nothing I could do about the color of the pants or the singular shoe other than own up to them, so I pushed some water through my hair to flatten out the mussed-up strands and then exited the cabin.

Being in the mountains in the middle of July, the heat beats down on you as if you're walking on the surface of the sun, and the added one mile of altitude doesn't do much for the blistering temperature. Reprieve is only found under the shade of the towering ponderosa pines and California black oaks. But despite the overhang of their limbs and the lightest of breezes, I still feel the scorching pain of my hangover beat through me with every hobbled, uneven step I take toward the main office.

I make my way down the cracked cement walkway, past a broken bench that rests in front of the pristine blue lake, and open the door to the main lobby, which is covered in peeling varnish. This place has seen better days.

The bell rings above my head, and when my eyes adjust to being inside again, I take in the half-renovated space. Olive-green carpet matches the carpet in my cabin; the leather and wood furniture sports tears and nicks, making the couch practically unusable; and the wall to the right of the fireplace is half papered and half stripped down to its drywall.

Not a great first impression.

Then again, have I looked in a mirror? It's not like I have a lot of room to talk.

"Be right there," a feminine voice calls from above. My eyes follow the sound of her voice to a staircase behind the counter.

I make my way to the check-in counter and take note of the computer that must be from the nineties. And behind it rests a printer caked in a thick layer of dust, making me believe it doesn't even work at all. But what has really snagged my attention is the sign resting on the countertop in front of me.

Welcome to the Canoodle Cove Cabins. Sully, my grandfather, is the owner of the cabins but has been diagnosed with middle-stage Alzheimer's. Please be patient and kind while we navigate through renovations and his care. Thank you.

Well, that would explain the wallpaper.

"Hello, can I help?" A woman steps out past the wall that shields the staircase from view, and when her eyes land on me, her shoulders straighten, and she slows down her steps. "Oh, how did you sleep?"

"Uh, fine," I say uneasily. She recognizes me, but I have no idea who she is.

But I kind of wish I remembered because, wow . . . she's, uh . . . she's incredibly pretty.

Her long chestnut-brown hair is pulled back into a thick ponytail. Her eyes are devoid of any makeup, but her thick black eyelashes make her ocean-blue eyes stand out against the beautiful heart shape of her face. On her right cheek, a small yet pronounced freckle sits simply in the crevice of her dimple. And as she walks up to the counter, I catch the chipped red nail polish on her nails, something Annalisa would never let happen, and yet I find it endearing.

She moves a stool behind her and takes a seat. "Glad to hear it. Frankly, when you passed out, we weren't sure if you were dead or not."

Great, *she* saw me drunk? Of course she did, because that's how life works. Already down on your luck, and life comes barreling in with a sense of humor, thinking, *Why not embarrass him in front of the attractive cabin owner?* It's bad enough I'm attempting to show an ounce of pride while wearing one shoe, but knowing she saw me in my intoxicated state just makes things that much worse.

"I, uh, I passed out?" I ask, scratching the back of my neck, trying to play dumb, because that makes the situation better.

Jesus, Sawyer.

She leans her arms on the counter and nods. "Oh yes. Right there on that sofa." She points to the threadbare sofa. "That was after my friend Jaz and I helped drag you here from the bar. It's a hefty walk." Drag me? Oh fuck, that explains the dirty sock. "Thankfully, we shoved you in the back of Jaz's truck and only had to walk you from the parking lot, and then, of course, to your cabin."

Mm-hmm, yup, cue the bout of sweat that lacerates like razor blades of embarrassment down my back.

"Shit. That's, uh, that's humiliating. I'm sorry."

She shrugs. "Jaz took twenty dollars from your wallet as a tip."

Well, that adds up.

"I noticed it was gone. Hell, I feel like I owe you guys more."

Her head tilts to the side, and I fidget under her stare.

Does she know?

Does she know who I am?

Does she know that just over twelve hours ago I flipped a bride and groom off at the altar?

Roarick said my public "oopsie" was trending, so if she has any sort of social media, there's little doubt that she knows why I'm here and who I am. If the inebriated state I was in last night doesn't say it, then the powder-blue suit gives me away.

"It was a lapse of judgment," I hear myself say under her clear blue gaze.

She folds her hands. "What was a lapse of judgment?"

"Leaving the church like that. I should have just—"

She holds her hand up, halting the onslaught of what was going to be a very emotional and awkward confession.

"I have no idea what you're talking about, and there's no need to divulge anything." She moves to her ancient computer and wiggles the mouse, probably to wake up the screen. "We all have our bad days. I'll just get you checked out of here. I'm assuming there were no damages?"

"Checked out? Oh, I was actually looking to stay longer."

Her eyes flash from the computer up to me. "Staying . . . uh, staying longer?"

"Yeah." I rap my knuckles on the counter. "Looking for a bit of an escape right now." Since she has no idea why, I don't dare go into details. "How much for a long-term stay?"

"Long, uh . . . long term," she says, her eyes blinking rapidly as she stumbles over her words. "How long term are we talking?"

"Not sure," I answer. "At least a few weeks." That should give some time for the news to die down.

"Oh wow, okay." She glances at the computer. "Well, we're in the middle of renovations, so we might not be the best place to stay. We're actually closing down for a bit so guests don't risk getting hurt. There are some rental houses around town that might be a better option."

"I don't need a house. The cabin is just fine. And I've been around my fair share of renovations. If you're worried about me getting hurt"—I hold my hands out, showing off my wounded pride—"pretty sure it's not going to get any worse than this. I'll sign a waiver if you need me to."

Silence falls between us as she stares at me, unmoving. Not a word, just . . . staring. A few blinks.

"Uh, is everything okay?" I ask.

"Yes, oh right, sure." Her eyes go back to the computer. "I, uh, am just thinking. Let me check here." She clicks around, and I lean against the counter, my eye catching the still-dark screen. With forced nonchalance, she reaches under the computer monitor and turns the screen on. It lights up. "Just checking a few more things." A.k.a. waiting for the computer to come to life. "It seems like we have the space, but we won't be quiet, you know."

"Like I said, I'm used to construction," I say. I press my palm to the counter. "So, are we all set here? Do you need my card, or is it still on file?"

"Yeah, it's on file." She looks up at me. "Are you sure you want to stay here? We have a lot going on."

"I can see that." I glance around at the chaotic room. "But I'm sure. Keep me booked. I'll let you know when I'm ready to leave."

I push away from the counter and am headed toward the door when I remember—breakfast, clothes, some necessities, maybe finding my car.

I turn back toward her. "Uh, is there a place where I could find some clothes? Maybe a toothbrush? A matching pair of shoes?"

Her eyes land on my pants and then travel back up to my face. I really wonder what this random stranger must think of me.

"May the Forest Be with You?"

Huh?

"Uh . . . and also with you?" I ask, because not sure what she's really saying.

She chuckles, but it sounds forced, nervous. "No, that's the name of the souvenir shop here in town. They have clothing in the back. Then the Pine Pantry is our grocery store—it'll have everything you need as well. Your car is still at the bar, so you're going to have to walk, but Strawberry Lake is the center of town, and everything else is laid out in one big circle around it. If you go out the front, just turn right and follow the loop. The shop will be on the right, the bar right up on the left after Nine Juan Juan Tacos, and right past the gazebo, you'll see the Pine Pantry. Follow the circle around, and you'll be back here at the cabins."

"Cool." I nod. "Thanks." Sounds simple enough.

Without another word, I head out of the lobby and onto the not-so-busy sidewalk of Canoodle, California. Time to shed this suit and forget about yesterday's dimwitted choices.

❖   ❖   ❖

"Do you happen to have anything that doesn't have 'Canoodle' written on the butt?" I ask the store clerk, holding up a pair of men's sweat shorts. I just need something for today—Roarick will be bringing me my things tonight—but there doesn't seem to be anything in this store that doesn't beg strangers to "canoodle" my ass.

"Unfortunately, that style is a bestseller for us, so we keep that in stock. Sorry," the old lady whose feather-gray hair runs all the way past her backside says, eyeing me. "But dare I say, it's better than what you're currently wearing."

I smile at her, despite the jab. "I guess anything is better than this suit, right?"

"An abomination," she says before turning away and heading back to the counter.

Not a fan.

Noted.

I grab a pair of black sweat shorts with red writing on the butt and then sift through the shirts to find my size in a black shirt with *May the Forest Be with You* printed across the chest, and under it, *Canoodle, California*. That will do. And lucky for me, they also sell sandals, so I don't have to hobble around in one shoe. And for being ten dollars and made with tawdry materials, they're actually pretty comfortable.

I change in the dressing room, remove the tags, roll up my clothes, and then head to the front, where I hand the old lady the tags to purchase.

"Typically, we prefer the customers to wait to remove tags until we can confirm payment."

"Trust me, I'm good for the bill." I hand her my credit card.

She just stares at me. "Why on earth should I trust you? I know nothing about you, except that you have a penchant for ruining people's weddings."

Ahh, well, that's the reason for her disdain.

And here I thought I was going to go undetected. Looks like my luck has run out.

I lean forward. "Technically, she was supposed to marry me."

"Ha!" the lady says, snapping my credit card out of my hand. "In what universe? Simon Fredrickson is a legend among men—you are merely a man with a crook in his nose."

The fucking nerve.

My hand goes to the small bump on the bridge of my nose, a childhood souvenir from when I fell off my scooter and ran my face into a set of concrete stairs.

As a screenwriter, I'd classify my nose as a charismatic quirk that distinguishes me from the rest. Something memorable that makes me not entirely perfect so viewers can relate to my imperfections.

But our dear shop friend here apparently lacks the sophistication to understand the kind of interesting impact an imperfection can offer an appearance.

"Adds charm," I say through clenched teeth.

"Not the kind of charm that would win over Annalisa Morton." Her chin tilts up with her futile insult.

And of course her antipathy only skyrockets my self-consciousness.

"I'll have you know we dated for five years before she cheated on me with Simon." Yup, I went there.

She finishes ringing me up and hands me a receipt. "Dear boy, if you are going to stay in this town, it would be best if you didn't start spreading lies."

Spreading lies?

She thinks I'm the one spreading lies?

My teeth grind together.

My hand curls out of frustration at my side.

And then I realize . . . what's the point?

This old hen is stuck in her ways. No matter what I say, she's going to trust what she reads on the internet over what I say.

Time to move on.

I take the receipt from her and refuse a bag. "I hope you have a wonderful day . . . Uma." I squint at her name tag. With a final tight smile, I leave her store, letting the door slam shut behind me.

I hope Uma finds herself with a nasty dose of canker sores today. Yup, I'm inwardly attempting to hex an old lady while wearing the word "Canoodle" on my ass.

Do we need to have another conversation about rock bottom? Or can we just agree—anything beyond this point is just me firmly situating myself in my own grave?

Rolled-up clothes in hand, I head over to the Beggar's Hole parking lot, where I spot my car.

I have no recollection of this small town from last night, nothing beyond the neon sign in the bar window reading **BAR** in bold red. It caught my attention, and the rest was history.

But now that I'm here in the daylight, the entire town comes into frame, from the shadowing trees to the pristine landscaping along the sidewalks. The buildings give off an old western feel with their false-front architecture and rising facades that shield the gable roofs behind them. The sides of the buildings are either peeling and worn or covered in chipped brick. Despite the signs of aging, the fronts are kept in immaculate condition, with crystal-clear four-pane windows and delicately designed storefront names—with the exception of Beggar's Hole.

And at what I'm assuming is the entrance of the town—given the passing of traffic—rest two large rock formations that seem to cradle it in their stony warmth while sweeping pines stretch toward the sky, offering a dreamy, whimsical escape.

It's quite breathtaking. So breathtaking it makes me forget Uma's judgment, or at least not care about it too much.

When I reach my car, I unlock it and toss my clothes into the passenger side. I should really offer up the suit and button-up shirt to some campers for kindling—I can't imagine ever wearing them again.

I pull out of the gravel parking lot and drive the short distance to the Pine Pantry, which looks more like an old saloon from the outside rather than a grocery store. A two-story facade, square false front, with an elaborate cornice detail running parallel to the roof. Not your average grocery store, that's for sure.

Once my car is in park, I hop out and head right into the nicely air-conditioned space, where I'm transported back to civilization. From the outside, I'd almost believe I'm waiting for Clint Eastwood to step up next to me, loaded gun in hand, only to ask me if I feel lucky . . . *punk*.

Answer would be no.

Not in these shorts.

Chapter Three
FALLON

"How is lover boy?" Jaz asks, strolling into the main lobby. She's wearing cutoff jean shorts with paint stains splattered over every inch and an old Wynonna Judd concert T-shirt that she turned into a crop top. I remember the day we went to see Wynonna in concert. We were in high school and begged Tank to take us. He said no, several times, but the day of the concert, he waved tickets in front of our faces as a surprise and was subject to our terrible singing all the way to Anaheim and back. Jaz bought a T-shirt, and I bought a mug that I've sadly lost along the way.

"Can you not call him that?" I shout-whisper.

She glances around the empty room. "Why are you hissing at me? His car is gone—he left."

"Uh, he might have left your bar, but he's taken up residence here."

"What do you mean?"

"I mean . . . ," I drag out, "he's staying longer than we anticipated. Much longer."

"Seriously?" she laughs. "The luck you have. Isn't that just perfect. An old flame, shacking it up in your cabin."

"He's *not* an old flame." I set down the roll of wallpaper I've been attempting to match up. If I wasn't so dedicated to Sully's plan to renovate, I'd have given up on this entire endeavor weeks ago, but guilt is driving me to see through the plans he sketched out in his notebook, so here I am, papering the lobby walls in a black-and-white buffalo plaid design. "He came in here this morning all chipper, looking for some permanent, yet temporary, residence."

"I don't think that's a thing."

"It's a thing," I shoot back. "I booked his cabin indefinitely after I attempted to convince him to stay somewhere else."

"And he wanted to stay in this palace?" Jaz asks, her arms spreading wide. "I can't imagine why not. This is what I call living in luxury."

"You're not helping."

"Do I ever?" she says with a smirk.

"You did last night."

Jaz flops down on the threadbare couch and dangles one leg off the side while she sifts her hand through her hair. "You caught me at a weak moment."

I take a seat in the chair next to her and prop my feet up on the coffee table. "I'm annoyed."

"You're giving off that vibe. Is it because Peter didn't drive up last night?"

"My life doesn't revolve around a man."

Jaz snorts. "Literally your entire life revolves around a man."

"Not a man *romantically*," I clarify.

"So why are you annoyed? Because the blind date is sticking around?"

I pick a piece of lint off my shorts and flick it to the side. "I mean, sort of. Like, move on, man. Why are you sticking around here?"

"Have you not paid attention to the internet this morning?" Jaz asks.

"No, I'm not sucked into social media like you."

"Maybe you should be sucked in just a little." She pulls up her phone and taps away on it before turning the screen toward me. "Your friend walked out on the biggest wedding of the year."

I sit forward and take the phone from her. The title of the article is "Runaway Bride Groomsman: How Sawyer Walsh Single-Handedly Destroyed a Fairy Tale He Created."

Under the title is a picture of him, flipping off the bride and groom, right there at the altar.

"Oh my God." A small chuckle pops past my lips. "That's kind of psychotic."

"You think?" Jaz says as she pulls out her trusty switchblade, which she keeps in her pocket at all times. "That's not even half as bad as what I did when Brad cheated on me." Oh, Brad, I can still remember the cold fury in Jaz's eyes when she caught her boyfriend cheating on her with an out-of-towner. Let's just say Brad had an awfully hard time leaving town—not just because his tires were slashed, but because she'd also ripped all the soles from every single pair of his shoes.

I eye her. "This is different; this . . . this is a mental breakdown."

"Oh yeah. It's easy to see why he's staying here. Lover boy doesn't want to go back home and face the media storm he created. You should watch the interview of Annalisa and Simon. I've never seen anything so . . . absurd, but God, I couldn't look away. The tears. The hitch in her voice. The drama. Honestly, it feels like a soap opera and I'm waiting for the next episode."

The door to the lobby opens, sun rays blinding us momentarily as Sawyer walks in carrying a shopping bag and wearing Canoodle-themed clothing. Seems like he found the souvenir shop.

"Oooh, maybe we'll get our next installment right now," Jaz says, flipping her switchblade open.

"Hey." Sawyer lifts his hand. "I found the stores and my car. Thanks."

"Sure," I say as he continues to walk toward us. "Glad you were able to get out of that suit."

"The *town* is glad he was able to get out of it," Jaz says. "Next time you plan on crashing a bar, wear something that isn't going to offend everyone's eyes."

Sawyer glances over at her. "You look familiar."

"I should." She sits up and flips her blade shut. "I helped carry your sorry ass here."

"Jaz, be nice."

"I am," she says. "I could say a lot worse."

True, she could. She has absolutely zero filter.

"Well, then I owe you a thank-you," Sawyer says sincerely. "I appreciate you two looking after me last night. I realize I could have been in a really bad spot, and instead of just leaving me outside, you brought me to a safe place for the night. I'm indebted to you."

"I'm glad you see it that way," Jaz says, folding her hands together.

Before she can start listing off all the things she'd like in return for her good deed, I say, "It's what we do in Canoodle: look out for people. No need to say thank you."

He glances at me, making direct eye contact. Up until this point, I've avoided looking him in the eyes. Instead, I've danced around his face, pretending to look at him but focusing on the crook of his nose, or the thickness of his hair, or even the slight wrinkle between his eyes.

But now that our gazes meet, I feel . . . nothing.

Well, that's not entirely true. I feel sorry for him—seems like karma has caught up to him, and now he's having to deal with it.

Looking away, he clears his throat and opens the bag in his hand. "Well, it's not much, but the girl at the Pine Pantry said that all the locals like these cookies." From his bag, he pulls out a twenty-four-pack of the strawberry shortbread tart cookies that Jaz and I are obsessed with.

Before he can offer them to us, Jaz snatches them out of his hand and rubs the top of the container, eyeing Sawyer. "I prefer knives as a gift, but I shall accept these cookies." She points a finger at him. "Don't think this wins me over, though. I still think you're a douche."

Douche might be extreme.

Then again, I bet if he turned around, "Canoodle" would be plastered over his ass—a bit of a douchey clothing choice. It's not a good look on anyone, but it's better than the suit he was wearing previously.

Aw, and look, he found some footwear. I wonder if he thinks things are looking up for him.

The expression on his face is a mix of humor and confusion. "Let me guess . . . you saw the news?"

"Hard to miss," Jaz says, popping open the container and taking a cookie out. She crosses one leg over the other. "Why go to the wedding if you're just going to flip off the bride and groom in the middle of the ceremony? Pretty cold, if you ask me."

Look out, Sawyer: a strawberry shortbread cookie is not going to mellow out Jaz.

"There's a lot more to the story than what I'm sure the media is letting on." He shifts on his feet, looking extremely uncomfortable.

"Well, we have nowhere to be—please, entertain us." Jaz gestures with her hand, giving him the floor.

Wanting to spare him—not because I care about his feelings or anything like that but because he doesn't need to be hanging out with us—I decide to cut in before he can start his story.

"We actually have a lot to do and don't have time to chitchat," I say. "But if you need anything, Sawyer, just call or ask. Enjoy your stay."

He turns toward me, and I can see a hint of hurt in his eyes. I'm not sure if it's from my dismissal or the mention of the wedding, but either way, I'm not going to dive into it. We share an awkward history, and even if he doesn't remember it, I don't care to spend much time around him. Though I keep insisting to Jaz that everything was fine during our date, it's still embarrassing that one, he ignored me, and two, he doesn't recall who I am at all. I don't need to be reminded of that every time he's around.

"Yeah, I'm sure you're pretty busy." He glances around the empty, quiet lobby. "But just wanted to say thank you. And, uh, I didn't quite catch your names."

"I'm Jazlyn," Jaz says, her mouth full of cookie. "Everyone calls me Jaz, but I'd prefer you call me Jazlyn since we're not on a friendly basis, despite the cookies. And that ray of sunshine over there is Fallon."

Sawyer's eyes meet mine, and his brow furrows as he observes me for a few beats.

Does he recognize me?

God, I hope not.

"Does she look familiar?" Jaz asks, obviously reaching.

"Jaz, shut up," I say through clenched teeth, making her smile and take another bite of her cookie.

"Should she look familiar?" Sawyer asks, confused.

"Ooof, digging yourself quite a grave, Julia."

"Julia?" he asks as I stand from my seat and start ushering him to the lobby's back door.

"Yeah, you know, Julia Roberts from *Runaway Bride*. I think it fits you nicely."

I push him toward the door. "Ignore her—she has a vendetta against the world. Have a great stay." I open the door and bump him with my hip, sending him outside and slamming it shut behind him. "Jesus, Jaz, what the hell is wrong with you?"

She heaves a heavy sigh. "What? We finally have some drama in this town. Why can't I eat up the moment?"

"Because I don't want him knowing we went on a blind date. I just want to drop that, okay?"

"Why not? You could have fun with it."

"I have better things to do with my life than mess with someone who's just going to pass through town. I need to focus on getting this wallpaper done before Sully gets back from Tank's and before Peter arrives. I'd appreciate it if my friend would help me, but if you're not going to help, take your half of the cookies and leave."

She groans and stands from the couch. Silently, she walks over to the wallpaper and starts matching it up. While she's doing that, I prep the wall and gather the tools we'll need.

We work in silence until Jaz says, "You mentioned taking half of the cookies—so you want nothing to do with him, but you'll take his gift?"

I glance up at her from my crouched position. "I might want nothing to do with him, but those are strawberry shortbread cookies. I'm not an idiot, Jaz."

Her laugh echoes through the small space, and together, we finish papering the wall.

CHAPTER FOUR
SAWYER

Roarick: Almost there. You owe me.

I stare down at the text from my brother and bounce my knee up and down.

I've been restless ever since I looked at the headlines on Page Six.

I told myself not to.

That the media's contorted narrative was just going to paint me in a bad light and do nothing but infuriate me.

So, I stayed away.

Instead of doomscrolling, I took a walk around Strawberry Lake.

I marveled at the giant, vaguely phallic rock formations that sandwich the town. Gray granite crests with smooth, sheer faces and rounded tops that make climbing almost impossible. Any attempt would be asking for trouble.

I fed a duck a piece of bread out of the kindness of my heart, only to have him demonically chase me around before I was able to find a branch to shoo him away with. He put up a decent fight, making it clear he's the alpha of the lake. Given the snap of his beak, I took him seriously.

After that, I'd had enough nature for the day and retreated to my cabin, where I opened the crossword puzzle book I purchased at the Pine Pantry and solved three puzzles—only checked the answer key five times . . . per puzzle—and when I couldn't take it anymore, I opened the browser on my phone. At first, I told myself it was to check the latest acquisitions, see what's selling around Hollywood, but then . . . somehow, I wound up searching my name.

And there it was. Plain as day. A picture of me, sporting devil horns as I flipped off the bride and groom, who of course wore the faces of two people inserted into a horror flick. There I was, spitting satanic fire at the soon-to-be betrothed, while the "innocent" bride, sheathed in white, stared back in utter horror. If I was an outsider looking in, I'd immediately think, *Wow, that guy is actually the worst.*

Worst best man ever.

Man of honor? More like man closely related to Lucifer.

Clear as day, there is no doubt that the picture is damning.

But the article that followed?

Brutal.

They used words like jealous. Green with envy. Jaundiced with greed for the spotlight.

Jaundiced?

They couldn't have found a better word?

The negative headlines and devil horns are bad enough, but to use jaundiced? That's just a kick to the dick while a man is down.

My phone rings, and I half expect it to be Roarick, telling me he's here, but when I see my agent's name scroll across the screen, I can physically feel my scrotum crawl up inside my body.

Fuck.

Knowing Andy, he's not going to stop calling me until I answer, so might as well get it over with.

"Hey, Andy," I answer, taking a seat on the bed.

"Sawyer. How are you doing, man?" Sarcasm drips from his voice, heavy and thick. Yup, I'm about to get an earful from him.

"Do you even have to ask? I think you've read how I'm doing."

"I'd like to hear it from you, actually."

"Considering I didn't have to finish listening to Annalisa's bogus vows, pretty good, thanks."

"Sawyer." His stern voice booms through the phone, and I wince. "Do you realize the kind of damage you've done?"

"Damage? I wouldn't call it damage. It seems like Annalisa is getting more publicity and media attention than she ever imagined. My guess is she's booked on every news outlet to tell the story for the next month."

"I mean damage to your career—you're the one I care about, not them," he practically yells. I knew he'd be upset, but not this upset.

"Oh." I scratch the side of my head. "Well, hopefully not much damage."

He sighs. "I've already received calls from Movieflix's execs. They are not happy. How can they possibly have their top screenwriter, the man who writes the most poetic romances ever to hit the screen, destroy a wedding in real life? It goes against everything you write about."

Very valid point, and once again . . . damning.

"Hey, I offered them those thrillers to diversify—it's not my fault they didn't want those pitches. This whole debacle would have been great advertisement for an upcoming thriller, suspense film. 'Groomsman goes on murdering spree at wedding.' Tell me that doesn't sell fast."

"It does!" Andy shouts. "But you're not known for thrillers, Sawyer. You're known for romance, for intricate, small-town stories that touch the heart. That's what people want from you, and this little stunt you pulled is not sitting well with them."

Yes, it is what people want from me. Prior to Annalisa cheating on me, I'd take an article I found while scrolling through the news, a human interest piece on, let's say . . . a sibling reunion, and twist the narrative into a story line that interweaves three story arcs about each sibling finding love in their own lives. It would be zany and heartfelt, a movie that would leave viewers weeping with joy.

But the deceit in my life has torn down my lovey-dovey, romantic heart. These days, I'm ready to kill off the bride and groom within the first scene, making sure they never get their happily ever after.

Does that mean I'll never write romances again? Of course not; they're my bread and butter. But excuse me while I take a fucking minute to gather myself.

"Please," I groan. "This has to be helping in some way. There's no doubt the media attention Annalisa and Simon are receiving is great for their movie."

"Yes, but media is catching wind that you're the one who wrote the screenplay, and Movieflix is having a hard time spinning the story to make their best screenwriter not look like a bitter curmudgeon. They need to maintain credibility with your movies, but your temper tantrum is not helping."

"It wasn't a temper tantrum," I say. "I just . . . hell, Andy, I couldn't take it anymore. From the very beginning, I was told to suck it up, to not care about the fact that my girlfriend cheated on me with my best friend . . . in the public eye. I was supposed to act okay with it. I was told to put on a smile and be the charming best man. And I did that. I tried. I pushed away all the hurt and anger for the good of the movie. But standing up there, listening to her lies, I couldn't take it anymore. And I snapped. Do I regret it? Maybe a little, but I'm also glad I finally stood up for myself."

Andy lets out a sigh. "It wasn't the time to stand up for yourself, Sawyer."

Growing frustrated, I stand from the bed and start to pace the length of the cabin. "Andy, you have children, so tell me this—if one of them was hurt, if their heart was broken, if the person they thought they were going to end up marrying cheated on them, would you be able to just sit back and tell them to suck it up?"

He's silent, and I know I've struck a chord—if anything, Andy's a family man.

We met in a coffee shop on Venice Beach. I was attempting to write a screenplay while working my odd construction jobs to pay the bills. Andy found me scribbling in my notebook on an off day, writing down notes of all the people who walked by, consuming different character traits, the way couples interacted, the way they touched each other, the looks in their eyes, making note of every interaction I saw so I could better understand the bond between two people. Andy said while I was watching them, he was watching me, fascinated with how I studied human nature.

After an hour, he came up to me and asked if I was a writer. We got to chatting and developed a solid relationship from there. We worked on some movie ideas I had, and he guided me to a few classes that helped me hone my craft. Then . . . we sold my first screenplay. We've worked together ever since.

I know him like a brother. Which means he should know me just as well.

"Set aside the business for a second," I say to him quietly. "And look at the situation as a father, as a brother . . . as a friend. I didn't do this to fuck over anyone, I just . . . hell, Andy. I lost it."

"Yeah . . . I know," he says softly. "I could see you starting to snap going into the wedding weekend. I thought you were going to be able to hold it together, though."

"Clearly I didn't," I say with an exhausted chuckle. "Fuck, how bad is it?"

"Bad."

"Does the studio care that I was the one who was cheated on?"

"I hate to say it, but they're going to protect the actors first. Though they did acknowledge this hasn't been easy on you."

"Oh, that's kind," I say sarcastically. "So, what now?"

"Well, you're still under contract with them."

"Yes, I'm aware."

"And they're not walking away from that. They gave you a fat chunk of change, and they won't let you just sulk away. You'll have to meet the demands of their contract."

"Of course not. What do they want?"

"They're formulating a plan now and will be in touch, but until then, they want a pitch from you—and not a thriller. They want what they paid for. If you can't deliver, then there are going to be severe consequences. Not just monetary consequences, but career-changing ones. Movieflix holds the market right now—you're in a cushy position, and they know it. So, if you want to continue to work with them, you'll need to blow them away."

"You've got to be fucking kidding me," I say, stomach dropping. "Can't they offer some sympathy or understanding for what I've been through? You know, since they basically made me put my feelings to the side and act like nothing traumatic happened to me."

"I think they would've been willing to do that, but now that you've caused this shitstorm, that option is off the table."

Fuck.

I've worked so hard to foster this relationship with Movieflix. I've done everything they've ever asked of me—meeting deadlines, working with up-and-coming screenwriters as a mentor, and setting aside my feelings for the betterment of the company—and they're willing to just toss me to the side? As if none of that matters?

Then again, I did cause a media shitstorm, and they're cleaning it up.

And even though it pains me that they'd be willing to just drop me, to ruin my career over a public meltdown, I can understand. I wouldn't want to lose that relationship, or destroy any future opportunities I could garner from working with them.

So, it looks like I'll start thinking of screenplay ideas.

I scrub my hand over my face. "Of course." I glance up at the window in time to see Roarick making his way up the trail leading toward my cabin. "Listen, my brother is here—"

"Where is here, exactly?"

"Now, *that* I'm keeping to myself. I need some time away, some time for things to settle before I head back to LA."

"Well, while you're hiding out, come up with your next big idea, because I think it's the only thing that's going to get you back in their good graces. You don't want to piss off Movieflix, Sawyer."

"I'm aware," I say as Roarick knocks on the door. "Thanks, Andy, and I'll talk to you later. Keep me updated on everything." Without saying bye, I hang up and toss my phone on my bed before I open the door for Roarick.

He takes one look at me and snorts. "Nice shirt, man. Really embracing the small-town vibes."

"It gets better," I say as I turn around, bend at the waist, and wiggle my ass in front of him.

He throws his head back and laughs as he steps into the cabin. "Oh shit, you look like a sorority girl in those things. I didn't know men wore shorts with words on the butt."

"Apparently they do in Canoodle." I help him with the bags and set them down on the bed. "Thanks for bringing this stuff up for me. Were there still reporters outside my apartment?"

"Oh yeah, elbowed a few people. They kept asking where you were, and when I left, a few followed me—that's why it took me so long. I had to lose them before I drove up here, so you owe me."

"I don't have much to offer at the moment besides a broken career, bad press, and . . . sweat shorts that say 'Canoodle' on them. Want those?"

He glances down at my shorts and then back up at me. "I mean . . . they do look comfortable."

"You would really take the clothes off my back, the one shred of dignity I have left?"

"Technically, they're off your legs, not your back, and yes, I'm your little brother—I'm supposed to kick you while you're down. I wouldn't be doing my job if I wasn't."

"True." I take a seat at the small wooden dining table that rests right under the cabin's front window. "How are Mom and Dad?"

Roarick leans back on the bed. "Worried. I told them you were just going through a midlife crisis and would be out of it soon."

"I'm thirty-five. I wouldn't quite call this a midlife crisis."

"Thirty-five is old."

"You're thirty-three, you idiot."

"Yes, still a spring chicken, but you're an old rooster with his gobbler dangling off his beak, barely hanging on."

"I don't think it's called a gobbler."

He smirks. "It is in my head."

I roll my eyes and go to my suitcase to start unpacking. I unzip it, and the first thing I see is a large box of condoms. "What the hell is this?"

Roarick shrugs. "A considerate addition to your list. You don't know who you might meet up here, and with the way you're advertising your rear end, they might come in handy."

"You're the absolute worst, you realize that?"

"Not the kind of thank-you I was hoping to get after all the trouble I went through." His brows lift.

"Sorry, you're right." I hold the box up to him. "Thanks, I guess. Toss those in the nightstand. Don't believe I'll use them, but at least we can all rest assured that if I do happen to have sex in Canoodle, it will be protected."

"No baby mamas allowed." Roarick puts the condoms in the drawer. "So, what's your plan? Just hole up here until you think the coast is clear, or until someone else causes a scandal and you can resume life again?"

"Pretty much."

He nods. "Solid idea. And it's nice up here. Very . . . forest-y. Fresh air. Big rocks. An old western town. And hey, there are ducks on the lake. That's neat."

"Don't feed them. They'll end up chasing you around, looking for more with their little snappy beaks."

"You seem to be speaking from experience."

"I wish I wasn't," I mutter as I pick up a pair of jeans and quickly change into them. "Want to grab something to eat?"

"Something to eat . . . or something to drink?"

"Both." I whip my Canoodle shirt off and change into a plain black T-shirt.

"Aw, I thought that shirt was cute on you."

"Fuck off."

He laughs, and together we take off toward the bar.

❖　❖　❖

"I think the look in that duck's eyes will be branded in my mind forever," Roarick says as we take a seat at the bar. "I've never seen anything so scary."

"See, I told you. That's not a short-necked swan."

"Maybe that's why he's not happy. The short neck."

"Possibly," I say as Jazlyn walks from the kitchen into the bar area. When she sees me, she rolls her eyes but still comes up to us.

"What do you want, Julia?"

"Julia?" Roarick asks.

"Don't ask," I mutter. "Can we get two IPAs?"

Unmoving, she eyes me and then looks to the side at Roarick before returning her gaze to me. She nods toward Roarick. "Who the hell is this?"

"My brother, Roarick. Roarick, this is Jazlyn. People call her Jaz, but I'm not allowed to."

Roarick chuckles and holds out his hand. "Well, Jazlyn, it's a pleasure to meet you. I'm a friend of anyone who can put my older brother in his place."

In the blink of an eye, Jazlyn turns from stone to a puddle of mush.

The furrow in her brow flattens.

Her frown morphs into a smooth smile.

And her body language screams . . . *interested* as she leans on top of the bar, showing a hint of cleavage as she takes my brother's hand.

"*You* can call me Jaz."

Of course he can.

If I were to extract my emotions and observe their interaction from the screenwriter's perspective, I'd consider this a possible meet cute moment. It doesn't necessarily pack the punch of, let's say, meeting in a foreign country—you're only wearing a towel when you're startled by an angry Scot in your cabin rental. Nor does it have the same sort of tension that we'd see from two characters who meet on a DIY wedding-competition show when one assumes the other is a coffee-fetching production assistant, which instantly sparks an enemies-to-lovers trope that sets up the entire story line.

This is subtle.

The making of a secondary story arc.

Nothing high concept enough to base a screenplay around.

Looks like I need to keep thinking on those ideas.

"What the hell is he doing?" Jaz says, pulling me from my thoughts.

"He does that," Roarick answers. "He drifts off, daydreams, has conversations in his head. Plotting, usually for his next screenplay. I've gotten used to it."

Jaz leans over the bar and flicks me in the forehead with her index finger. "Well, stop it. It's freaking creepy, Julia." With that, she grabs two pint glasses and starts filling our drinks.

I rub my forehead. "Shit, that hurt."

"I'm really curious about where this whole Julia nickname came from. I mean, you've been here for twenty-four hours, and you already have a nickname? You work fast, man."

Jaz hands us both coasters and then sets an IPA on each before drying her hands with a towel. "*Runaway Bride*. Julia Roberts plays Maggie in the movie. Just seemed fitting."

"I told you, I was the groomsman."

"Oh, I know. I read all the blogs this morning, but still, Julia fits." She sets a menu between us. "We serve breakfast for dinner. Let me know if you want anything." With that, she strides toward the end of the bar, where she leans forward, grabs an old man by the back of the head, and plants a large kiss on his cheek.

"Wow, she's . . . something else," Roarick says, staring off at her.

He's interested.

I can see it in the way he twists his beer on the bar. The far-off look in his eyes. And the smile that tugs gently at the corner of his lips when he glances down at the menu.

Love at first sight. Could be a thing. Could base a story around the—

"Dude, are you listening to me?"

"Huh?" I ask, looking up at him.

"Jesus." He shakes his head and turns back to the menu. "What is wrong with you? You're never this bad."

I glance at the menu as well and see a breakfast burrito that I guess would pair okay with my beer. Who serves breakfast at a bar?

"Andy called right before you arrived. He said Movieflix wasn't happy with what happened at the wedding—you know, since their screenwriter basically took a shit on love."

Roarick brings his beer to his lips. "I can see how that might not go over well."

"So, Andy is doing damage control, but in the meantime, they want a new screenplay idea, and they're not going to settle for anything other than romance."

"What if you don't send them an idea?"

I consider the question. "Overall career suicide, and I'd be penalized."

"Like . . . money?"

"Yes. Isn't that what makes the world go around?"

"So, you're trying to come up with an idea?"

"I mean, doesn't seem like I have a choice. I know what I'll be doing while I'm up here."

"What better place to plot than in a town called Canoodle. Screams romance, demon ducks and all."

I chuckle, and the door to the bar opens, grabbing my attention for a moment. Fallon walks in wearing a black sundress that falls just above her knees, curving around her bodice and flaring at her waist. Her hair is pulled into a low bun, and she's . . . she's holding a man's hand.

Huh, did not see that coming.

Muscular, but at least a few inches shorter than me, he waves to a few locals and smiles when Jaz yells, "You made it up here!"

"Hey, Jaz," the man calls out. "Can we get two waffles?"

"Coming right up," she says as I watch Fallon walk the man to the back of the bar, onto the deck that overlooks a forest of towering trees. He pulls her chair out for her and kisses her lightly on the shoulder before taking a seat across from her. He reaches across the table and takes her hand in his.

Fallon leans in and smiles while he says something to her.

"Hey, isn't that Fallon?" Roarick asks.

"Huh?"

"Fallon, that's her, isn't it?"

"Wait, how do you know who she is?"

Roarick turns to me, disbelief written over his face. "Are you kidding me?"

"Does it look like I'm kidding??"

"Dude." He groans. "I thought you were staring at her because she was the one who got away, but you don't even recognize her?"

"What the hell are you talking about?" I ask.

"That's Fallon Long."

"That means nothing to me."

"It should. You went on a blind date with her."

"No, I didn't."

"Yes, you did," Jaz says, popping out of nowhere. "And you ignored her the whole time." She shakes her head. "Such a Julia."

And then she takes off, two drinks in hand.

"Wait . . . what?" I ask, trying to understand what the hell is going on.

"Do you remember when I was casually dating Samantha before she moved to Florida?"

"The nurse?" I ask.

"Yes. It was a few months after Annalisa cheated on you. We wanted to get you out of your funk and thought a blind date could help. You were in Palm Springs to get away, and so we set you up with Samantha's friend Fallon." He jabs me in the arm. "You took her out."

I took out Fallon? I wouldn't forget that. Even from the limited interaction I've had with her, she's made an impact on my memory, especially when those wandering eyes connect with mine.

"No fucking way—I would have remembered her." I shake my head in disbelief.

"Clearly you didn't," Roarick says just as Fallon looks up in my direction. The joy on her face quickly falls before she turns to her date again. "Yeah, and it looks like she realizes you didn't recognize her."

"Yup, she totally does," Jaz says, materializing on the other side of the bar again.

"Jesus, where are you coming from?"

She leans in close and whispers, "Your nightmares." *Christ.* With a smile, she faces Roarick and gently reaches out to trace her finger over the back of his hand. "Have you decided on anything to eat tonight?" Her voice is laden with innuendo, and I can see Roarick's mind racing with possibilities.

"What's good?"

"Come in the back, and I'll show you."

For the love of God.

"Can you not hit on my brother, please? He's here for a night, and I'm kind of going through a crisis," I say.

Jaz gives me a scornful once-over. "And how is that my problem?"

"She has a point." Roarick playfully smiles.

"Dude, loyalty."

He rolls his eyes and huffs. "I'll take the meat skillet."

"And I'll have the breakfast burrito, no tomatoes."

"Extra tomatoes, got it," Jaz says, snatching the menu from between us and walking away.

"Why do I have a feeling your burrito will be more like a pile of tomatoes wrapped up with a sprinkle of cheese?"

"Because she hates me."

"I don't blame her. You don't remember going out with her friend, and she doesn't seem the type to let that go."

"Not so much." I glance back at Fallon, guilt gnawing at me. "I seriously went out with her?"

"Yeah. I remember Samantha saying you were on your phone most of the date. Fallon got a free meal and left."

"Shit," I say softly. "I was not in a right frame of mind after Annalisa cheated on me with Simon. If I can't even remember the date, I can only imagine the way I acted."

"Not great."

"And she was the one who helped my drunk ass last night—hell, she works at the cabins. No wonder she's been short with me."

Roarick chuckles. "Isn't karma a crazy bitch?" He elbows me. "Hey, there's your story. Angry cabin-rental worker who had to help the drunk lush to a cabin after he didn't recognize her. Smells like the perfect meet cute. Think of the possibilities."

"Trust me, no one is going to want to watch that story arc play out."

I glance over my shoulder at Fallon again. She's smiling intently at her date, her plush lips painted a light pink, making her porcelain complexion look innocent but enticing all at the same time.

I ignored *her*?

Jesus, I'm a dumbass.

I must have been in a really bad place—because sitting here at the bar, I'm finding it really freaking hard to ignore her now.

Chapter Five
FALLON

"Do you know where my running shoes are?" Peter calls out from my bedroom.

"I think they're under the bed," I say while I finish cutting up a strawberry in the kitchen.

"Found them," he announces before appearing in the kitchen, where he walks up behind me and wraps his arms around my waist. "I'm going for a run." He kisses my neck.

"I made you a yogurt parfait," I say. "Want me to stick it in the fridge for you for when you get back?"

"That'd be great."

He releases me and takes a seat on the couch, where he puts his shoes on. I turn toward him and lean a hip on the counter. "Thank you for finding the time to come up and visit me—and for switching your shift around in the first place so you could come up early. I know your schedule is tough and this isn't easy. I wish I could make more of an effort to meet up with you in Palm Springs, but things are . . . crazy."

"You don't have to thank me or explain," Peter says as he double knots his shoelaces. "When we first started dating, he'd just been diagnosed, and you were already preparing to move here. I knew the challenges, and if you ask me"—he stands and walks over, pulling me in close to his chest—"I think we're doing a pretty good job navigating them together. It will get better, you know, once we figure out where this relationship is going." He winks, and I can't help but wonder what he means. This isn't the first time he's mentioned the future, but now is not the time to get into it.

"I think so too." I smile up at him.

He places a chaste kiss on my lips. "I'll be back in about an hour. Doing the Harry Balls Trail."

"Your favorite."

"For the name alone." He winks again and then takes off down the stairs.

I finish up the parfaits and place his in the fridge before taking mine down to the lobby, where I sit at the check-in desk. Not that we have anyone checking in, but we do have one guest.

I got a good portion of the wallpaper hung yesterday before Peter popped into the lobby, surprising me with a bouquet of flowers and his handsome smile. Jaz was gone by the time Peter got there, so he convinced me to put the work down, take a shower, and get ready for date night. I couldn't say no to that, especially since Sully was still with Tank, so I took advantage of the grandpa-free time.

We had such an amazing night last night, even though I felt Sawyer's eyes on me from time to time. I was able to block him out and enjoy my time with Peter. Which was a relief, because the long distance has put a palpable strain on our relationship—we ended our last phone call with some unspoken tension simmering between us.

The back door to the lobby opens and . . . speak of the devil.

"Good morning," Sawyer says with a light wave of his hand.

He's sweaty, fresh from what looks like a run or a workout. A black tank top clings to his sweaty torso, and even though I am currently taken, I can't help but notice his sculpted arms and the obvious contours of his pecs through the sweat-drenched fabric. I hate to admit it, but he's an attractive man.

It's funny, because when I first met him on our blind date—that he doesn't remember—I wondered why this extremely handsome copy of Alexander Skarsgård who happened to be a fancy Hollywood screenwriter would want to date an ER nurse like me. But now that I've seen him at his lowest of lows, drunk in a powder-blue tuxedo and missing a shoe, I've lost all sense of intimidation.

To me, he's . . . just blah.

Despite the nice pecs.

And the eye-catching smile.

Blah.

"Good morning," I say, turning to my trusty computer to look busy.

"Uh, would I be able to get a towel? My brother stayed with me last night and used both mine and the spare this morning."

I hop off my stool and move to the back office, where we keep extra housekeeping supplies for situations just like this. I grab a few towels and then drop them on the counter for him.

"There you go." I pick up my parfait and take a large spoonful, keeping my eyes on the computer screen in front of me.

"Thank you." He walks up to the counter but doesn't take the towels. I brace myself, afraid he has more to say. "I, uh . . . ," he continues, "I was informed last night that we have a past I don't quite recall."

My spoonful of yogurt and a strawberry slice pauses halfway to my mouth. I turn toward him. "Jaz told you?" I'm going to wring her neck.

"No." He shakes his head. "My brother did, actually. He recognized you. Apparently, your friend Samantha, who he was dating at the time, set me up with you."

Oh, that's right. I forgot she was dating Sawyer's brother.

"Yes, that's true," I answer, unsure of what else to say.

"Well, I want to tell you that I'm sorry for not recognizing you and for the way I treated you that night. I was—"

"No need to explain anything," I say. "Seriously, we all have our bad dates. Not a big deal."

"But you seem mad at me," he says, an apologetic look on his face.

"I'm not mad." I shrug. "Just indifferent, I guess."

He nods. "So, I guess that means you're not going to be my first friend in Canoodle."

God, when he says it like that, it makes me feel bad, but then again, what's the point? He's not staying here forever. He's temporary, and we clearly don't mesh well.

"Not sure we have what it takes to be friends," I say, trying to be delicate as possible. "Plus, Jaz really doesn't like you, so, that's an issue."

"She probably hates me a lot more since I didn't let her take Roarick back to her place last night."

"Yeah, I'd avoid Beggar's Hole for a while if I were you."

"After the burrito I got last night, which was loaded with tomatoes that I didn't want, I'm going to take that advice." He grabs the stack of towels. "Well, thanks. Have a good day."

He sulks away, and a part of me actually feels bad for the guy.

He's hiding away to avoid all the media attention, he's clearly going through something, and he's looking for a friend. Refusing to help someone in a predicament isn't like me.

But I have enough going on in my life. I don't need another project.

I need to focus on the cabins and Sully.

Those are my top priorities—oh, and making time for Peter.

❖ ❖ ❖

"How is our baby girl?" my dads say into the phone when I answer their video call.

"Who's that?" Sully asks as he grumpily sits in his recliner, whittling away with his knife into a piece of wood I found and knew he would like.

"It's Dad and Papa," I say while I point the phone in his direction.

"Hey, Sully," they both say when they see him on the screen. Sully grunts something unintelligible and goes back to his stick.

Tank dropped him off an hour ago and looked absolutely devastated, his usually jolly, mustachioed face drawn into a deep frown, and while Sully went up to the residence, he pulled me to the side and told me it had been a rough day. Sully had kept asking for his wife, Joan, and couldn't understand why he was still at Tank's house when all he wanted was to see her.

The first time Sully asked for Grandma Joan, who passed away six years ago, I was gutted. I wasn't sure how to respond, how to tell him that she was gone. It took me by surprise, and I ended up sobbing myself to sleep that night.

When I decided to help my grandpa out and move up here, I wasn't fully prepared for what that would entail. I figured since I was a nurse, I'd be able to care for him, but I didn't quite think about the emotional toll it was going to take on me. The move has weakened me; it has damaged my spirit in a way. Growing up, I'd visit Sully and Grandma Joan at the cabins, and it all seemed so . . . magical. An escape full of beautiful memories. But now, the rose-tinted glasses have been removed and the magic has been swapped out with harsh reality—my grandpa is not well, and the cabins are not what they used to be. And it all rests on my shoulders.

I take the phone back to my room and shut the door quietly, knowing Sully's not in the mood to have a conversation today.

"He having a bad day?" Dad asks, concern heavy in his voice. Dad—Izaak, if you're one of my friends—is Sully's son. They have a beautiful bond, just like I have with my dads. Very loving. Sully, although a grumpy gruff of a man, is so loving when he sees Dad. Always kissing him and hugging him and telling him how much he loves him. Sully's diagnosis has been really hard . . . for everyone.

"Yeah, he just got back from Tank's. He was asking for Grandma Joan. I hate days like this."

"I know, kiddo," Dad says, glancing at Papa. "You know, we were thinking that maybe we should reconsider those homes we were talking about."

The homes that were created for people in Sully's position, a place they can go when taking care of them gets too difficult.

I shake my head. "No, he'd be miserable. At least up here, he gets to be with Tank; he gets to be around people he knows, in the town he loves. We can't pull him from a place that gives him stability. Not yet at least."

Papa—or Kordell to everyone else—chimes in, his deep chocolate eyes filling with tears. "But you can't keep living like this, Fallon. We can see the stress you've taken on. The renovations alone are too much, and we know that the cabins aren't doing well." According to my dads, the two of them met in college . . . at church, where they were good boys who never did anything bad and waited until they were married to engage in anything sexual. The real story, from what Sully has told me, is that Dad met Papa at a gay bar in college. They bonded over how they were both wearing fishnet shirts and their nipples kept poking out. Ever since that magical beginning, they've been inseparable, and Papa has been a solid sounding board for Dad as he navigates through Sully's health.

"Wait . . . the cabins aren't doing well? What are you talking about?" I ask as Papa's words sink in.

My dads exchange a glance, and when they look back at me, I can see it in their faces, the bad news that's coming.

"Since we've been managing the finances for Sully, we've noticed there haven't been many bookings at the Cove recently. It's been hard to pay the mortgage and your paychecks." Papa gives me an apologetic look. "We've been paying you from our personal account."

"What?" I ask, sitting up. "You've been giving me money?"

"There isn't enough money in the Cove bank account to pay you a decent wage, Fallon," Dad says. "You need to make a living somehow."

"Not with your hard-earned money," I protest. "We can stop renovations, save some money until we get more reservations."

"You and I both know you're not going to get bookings when you're still in the middle of renovations, not with the vacation properties taking over." Why does Papa have to make so much sense?

"We just got a long-term booking this weekend. Guy who's staying for a few weeks." It's measly cash compared to a sold-out facility, but it's something.

"Just one?" Dad asks.

"Yes, but that's better than none."

"Fallon, I know that you want to hold on to this, keep the cabins going for Sully, but there comes a time when you need to face reality. This isn't working. You're young, you have a life with Peter, and I think it's time we sell the cabins so you can come back to Palm Springs to live your life again."

I look away from them.

How could they possibly even consider selling the cabins?

This is where I grew up during the summers.

This is where I've had some of the best memories of my life.

This is where Sully's life is.

I can't imagine just . . . giving up because things are tough. Not only would that destroy Sully, but it would absolutely gut me. I came up here for a reason. To carry on the legacy that my grandparents built together.

I shake my head. "No, we are not selling. We aren't going to let someone else take over the Cove. This is our home, just as much as it is Sully's."

"You might not have a choice," Dad says. "If we can't pay the bills, we're going to have to sell."

Panic rips through me. They're serious. Of course they're serious; they wouldn't bring it up if they weren't. Which means . . . we're in a lot of trouble.

"Just, give me a few weeks, okay?" I plead. "We just got done papering the walls in the lobby. We're coming along with renovations." They give me a look that says they don't believe a word, and, yeah, maybe we aren't coming along, but I don't need to admit that. "I have some things to do around the cabins, and then I'll have Jaz take professional pictures of the place so we can roll out the new website. Just . . . trust me. I can bring Sully's vision to reality."

"While taking care of him?" Papa asks.

"The town is helping with that. I have more hands on deck than you think," I say. "Please, please don't take this away from me yet, okay? I'll never forgive myself if I don't try to see this through, give it my best shot."

Dad sighs. "We need more reservations, and we need them quickly."

"I know. The new long-term guest will be helpful, and, uh, we'll work on the others. Just give me a few weeks—I promise I'll turn this around."

"I don't like this for you," Papa says. "I want you to be happy. I want you to live your life."

"This makes me happy," I say, tears welling up in my eyes. "This is my life. I made a commitment when I decided to move up here. And I made a promise to Grandma Joan. I was going to take care of Sully, through thick and thin. Just because we're hitting a bit of a roadblock doesn't mean we give up. Please, just a few more weeks."

Papa nods. "Okay, Fallon. But you promise you'll tell us if it's too much?"

Thank God. That's all I need, a few more weeks. I can get this done. I know I can.

"I promise."

"And we plan on coming up there soon. We have some meetings down here in Palm Springs, but we want to see our little girl. We miss you."

"I miss you too," I say. I glance toward the doorway, where Peter is leaning against the woodwork. "Hey, I'm going to take off. Peter's here, and I want to spend as much time with him as I can before he has to leave again."

"Don't let us keep you. Tell that boy we said hi and that we miss him."

I turn the phone toward Peter, and he lifts his hand in their direction. "Izaak, Kordell, good seeing you. Let's plan for a lunch sometime soon. We can chat about the girl we love."

"Sounds like a plan," Dad says. I turn the phone back, and he says, "Fallon, he is such a catch."

I roll my eyes. "He can still hear you."

"I know."

I blow them kisses. "I love you, talk soon."

When I hang up, I drop the phone on the bed and lean back on the mattress. Peter comes up to me and places his hands on either side of my face, leaning down. "Did you hear what I said?"

I play with the collar of his shirt. "That you love me?"

Oh, I heard it.

And I heard it the first time he said it.

The second.

And all the other times he's said it as well.

And it is always followed by my awkward silence.

Because for some reason, I can't find it within me to say it back.

I don't know why.

I'm not sure if it's because I'm stressed, because I'm still skeptical that he'll wait around for me, or because I'm just trying not to get my heart broken, but I can't seem to muster up the proper response.

"Yeah, that."

I smooth my hand over his face. "I did. It was very sweet."

And just like every other time I don't utter those three little words back to him, his face falls and it rips me in half, seeing that I can hurt him like that. He leans down and presses a kiss to my nose. "I'm going to take a shower. Sully's getting ready for bed."

"Okay. Thank you. I'll get him in bed, and then we can maybe hang out on the balcony, play some cards?" I ask, feeling awkward.

He nods. "I'd like that."

With that, he takes off. I stare up at the ceiling for a few moments, unable to move, my thoughts racing.

How on earth am I going to get these renovations done?

Bring in more people to the cabins?

It's been an uphill battle for Sully ever since Vrbo and Airbnb became so popular. Small mom-and-pop places like the Cove have taken a huge hit, while vacation homes have rocketed to the top.

I can remember when this place was in its heyday.

Sully and Grandma Joan had a weekly schedule of activities. Candle making, guided hikes, basket weaving, and horseshoe tournaments—and that's not even scratching the surface. I can't remember the last time I heard the clank of a horseshoe hitting a throwing target. Slowly, over time, the activities faded away, the late-night storytelling around the campfire ended, s'mores night no longer existed, and then the business started to diminish, just like Sully's health.

And I can pinpoint the moment activities and the magical feeling of the cabins began to fade—it was when Grandma Joan caught pneumonia. She passed away soon after, and Sully never recovered from the loss. As he became consumed with mourning her death, the landscaping started to overgrow, the paint started to chip on the moldings, and, before we knew it, the pristine cabins that were once a coveted travel destination fell to the wayside.

And then he became sick, losing memories and pieces of himself, falling into his own state of disrepair—unable to execute the renovations and plans he'd laid out in his notebook.

That's when I stepped in. When the Alzheimer's diagnosis came, I lay in my bed in my Palm Springs apartment and made the decision to help. To give up my career to be there for the man who'd given me a beautiful escape when I was a child. After we buried Grandma Joan, I stood at her grave and told her that no matter what, I would take care of him for her. I would take care of their legacy. I stared up at the ceiling and said goodbye to my life in Palm Springs, realizing it was time to make good on that promise.

I owe it to him, and to Grandma Joan, to bring this place back. To make it better than before. And if it means killing myself over the renovations to make it happen, then I'll do it.

Canoodle Cove Cabins will be restored to its former glory, even if it means giving up everything to make it happen.

Chapter Six
SAWYER

Roarick: Annalisa and Simon were on Good Morning Malibu this morning. The tears she shed could have filled a glass.

Sawyer: Seriously? It's been a week. Shouldn't this be over?

Roarick: Dude, this will be going on forever if Annalisa has her say, but Noely and Dylan, the news anchors, were not buying It. You could see the skepticism on their faces. They said they were fans of your work and Noely started to ask if you guys were dating beforehand, but before she could finish, Annalisa let out this huge sob and walked off the set, saying she couldn't talk about it anymore.

Sawyer: Remind me to send flowers to Noely and Dylan.

Roarick: Might be smart. Noely was all over the internet a few years ago—she's the one that found love on that blind date app, Going in Blind, remember that?

Sawyer: I can barely remember my fucking ATM pin at this point.

Roarick: No shit, look it up, could be a good article of inspiration.

Sawyer: I'll pass.

Roarick: Oh really . . . so then, any billion-dollar movie ideas come to mind?

Sawyer: No, and you texting every day about it is not helping.

Roarick: Just making sure you're staying on task.

Sawyer: Not necessary.

I set my phone down on the overgrown grass next to me and stare out at the lake—far away from the ducks. The pines and Douglas firs lining the shore reflect off the surface of the lake, blocking my view of the clear mountain water.

I can't remember the last time I just sat somewhere and took a moment to think, to soak up the silence, other than the odd distant car that drives by or the laughter of a child.

It's as if I've pressed pause on my life and everything else is swirling around me, moving along, but I'm at a standstill, observing. If I weren't being bombarded with emails asking about the "run-out," then it would almost feel like the days before I sold my first screenplay. Before I met Annalisa.

My phone buzzes again. Well . . . at least I had some peace, for a second.

Roarick: Have you seen Jaz again? Did she mention me?

Jesus Christ. Doesn't he know I am trying to be one with nature?

Sawyer: No and . . . get a life, man. You met her for a second.

Roarick: Have you ever heard of love at first sight?

Sawyer: Doesn't exist, doesn't work well as a plot point either. You're better off with unrequited love.

Roarick: Love at first sight does exist. I swear, when I saw her, I felt my heart skip a beat in my chest. Hey, use that as a line in your next screenplay.

Sawyer: Too cheesy. Also, you're not experiencing love at first sight. It's lust.

Roarick: Maybe a little of both. I still can't believe you didn't let me go home with her.

Sawyer: Dude, she Is *insane*. I told you that. She breeds the kind of crazy you want to stay far, far away from.

Roarick: You're just saying that because she doesn't like you.

Sawyer: No, I'm saying that because I saw her pick her teeth with a switchblade at the bar, which screams "crazy."

Roarick: Crazy hot.

Sawyer: You need help.

I set my phone back down and stare out at the lake, trying to understand why it's called Strawberry Lake. By no means is it shaped like a strawberry, nor are there any strawberries in the area. I know because I've walked its perimeter at least half a dozen times by now. And it's not red, not red at all; there are no strawberries, not even a hint of a bush, so frankly, it's very—

"Who sits on the grass when they could sit on a bench?" a gruff voice says behind me, jerking me from my thoughts and startling me where I sit. "Christ, you look like a flea jumping in dog's fur like that."

"Sorry," I say, turning around. An elderly man stands over me, a sprinkle of white hair on the top of his head, little strands that waffle with the breeze. Deep-set wrinkles line his forehead and run along his mouth and the corners of his eyes, forming the perfect frown. A frown that is currently aimed in my direction. "You startled me."

He gestures toward me. "Serves you right for diddly dawdling on your phone when you have a perfect view of a lake in front of you. Kids today don't understand when the best things are right in front of them." His checkered button-up shirt is tucked into high-waisted jeans that reach past his belly button, held strategically up by two-inch-thick red suspenders, offering him a decent set of high-waters. His white tube socks reflect brightly in the early-morning light, and his worn black rubber-bottomed shoes create a stark contrast. He's the ultimate grouch, a side character in a movie whom you can't help but love because you know a heart beats behind all that annoyance.

"I was actually just contemplating why they call it Strawberry Lake. Do you have any clue?"

"Because, you jack wagon, this damn place used to be full of strawberries before humans came and civilized it." Jack wagon, huh? Don't hear that insult too often. I make a mental note to use it in a script.

"Oh, well, that makes sense."

"Of course it does." He gestures to the bench that I didn't bother sitting on. One side is laid out completely on the grass, broken and dilapidated. The other side still stands, but it's splintered and barely holding up the length of wood it offers as a precarious seat. Weathered, sun-soaked wood—it's seen better days. "How did you break this?"

Break it? Me? Dude, that's been broken for a while.

"I didn't break it—it was already like that."

"Bullshit." He kicks the dilapidated bench seat. "I walked by this bench this morning, and it was fine. So, what were you doing? Jumping around on it like an idiot?"

"No, sir, it was broken when I got here," I say, confused.

He holds his shaky finger up to me. "Don't toy with me, boy. This bench was perfectly fine. I sat on it just yesterday with my best girl, Joan, while we stared out at the lake. And now I find you here, and it's broken."

I glance down at the weathered wood, which has clearly been broken for years. I glance back up at him . . . and then it hits me.

The sign in the lobby.

Please be patient and kind while we navigate through renovations and his care. Thank you.

This must be Sully.

Treading carefully, I say, "You know what, you're right. I broke it." I pat my flat stomach while standing. "Too many beers last night. If you direct me to the right place, I'd be more than happy to fix it myself."

"Damn right you will," he says. He lifts his hand and points to the east. "Village Hardware is just down the road. Tools are in the shed back there." He gestures to a peeling shed that's nearly invisible behind an overgrown rhododendron. "I expect this bench to be fixed by tonight. Understood?"

I salute him. "Yes, sir. I'll get right on it." I pocket my phone, and we part ways as I go back to the shed, to assess the kind of tools we're working with here.

Before I made it big as a screenwriter, I moved to LA and worked a few odd jobs until I met Harmer, a genius contractor. He took me under his wing and taught me everything he knew about construction, and together, we'd renovate houses around Hollywood. It paid the bills and gave me enough so I could start saving up, just in case the screenwriter thing didn't work out. I even met Simon through Harmer. We'd lament about the show business world while hammering nails by hand. Then I met Andy at the coffeehouse . . . and everything changed.

But I've kept the skills close to my heart, enough that I have my own setup at my parents' house, and whenever I need a break from LA, I pack up and go to the vineyard in Palm Springs to work on the old kayak I've been attempting to build for a few years now. Mom and Dad never touch it, though Roarick will send me the occasional selfie standing next to it and holding a saw, but every time I go back home, I construct a small piece of it here and there. Someday the kayak will have its maiden voyage, but until then, I can at least fix the bench.

I pop open the old shed's rusted-out door and run straight into a spiderweb when I step inside.

"Fuck," I mutter, swatting at the air. With no light in sight, I take my phone from my pocket and turn it on, illuminating the dark space, finding only a small toolbox in the right corner, a few piles of wood, and a very old, rusted saw.

Huh.

With my foot, I flip open the toolbox and bend down to examine it. A hammer that's missing the actual hammer part, one Phillips-head screwdriver, and a few nails.

Well, this won't do.

We're going to need to update this toolbox.

I leave the shed and look back at the main lobby. I recall Fallon doing some wallpapering—maybe she has some tools. Then again, from her prickly attitude, I can tell there's no way in hell she's going to let me fix any benches.

She has too much pride and too much disdain for me.

No, this is a task that's best accomplished alone. Unannounced.

Resolved to keep Fallon out of this, I head down the road to Village Hardware.

A few tools are all I need.

Fixing the bench will give me something to do and possibly help alleviate any stress Sully might feel over seeing his bench, his and Joan's special spot, fall apart. I don't know much about Alzheimer's, but I can't imagine the unsettling feeling he must have when something familiar isn't the way he remembers.

The walk to the hardware store isn't very far at all, just down the street, past the Strawberry Fields Diner and the Whistling Kettle— both places I haven't visited yet. Since I picked up groceries at the Pine Pantry, I haven't needed to go out for provisions.

But I'm sure the microwaved grilled cheese sandwiches I've been making myself are going to get old pretty quickly.

When I reach the hardware store, I push through the door and run right into a very tall, very burly man. He's covered in tattoos, and his long, flowy white hair and white mustache are so perfectly combed that I wonder if the man even eats.

Compared to my six-foot-two stature, he still has a couple inches on me, so when I stumble backward, he steadies me at the shoulders.

"You okay there, son?" he asks in the deepest voice I've ever heard. I mean, this man gives James Earl Jones a run for his money.

"Yeah, sorry, didn't see you there."

"Hard to miss me." He holds his hand out. "I'm Tank."

Yes, yes he is.

"Sawyer," I say. "Nice to meet you."

"New around here?" he asks.

I gesture my thumb behind me. "Staying at the cabins for a few weeks. Thought I'd stop in for some tools to fix a bench."

Tank slowly nods. "A bench, you say?"

"Yeah." I scratch the top of my head. "Ran into, uh, Sully, back there." Tank nods in understanding. "He was upset about a bench being broken. Figured I'd alleviate that pain for him."

"He used to sit there with Joan every morning and enjoy a cup of coffee while they spoke about the upcoming day. I know the exact bench you're talking about."

"He was upset that it was broken. I, uh, I saw the sign in the lobby." Tank nods again. "I thought since I'm not doing much, I could fix the bench. You know, so he's not upset when he sees it."

"Thoughtful of you," Tank says in his burly voice. "Do you know how to fix a bench, son?"

"I do," I answer. "I have quite a few years of construction under my belt, especially woodwork."

"Well then, let me lead the way to what you'll need."

We spend the next ten minutes going over the different tools I want to work with, opting out of the electric tools and going with the simple things. They're less expensive, and there's something gratifying about skipping out on power tools and putting your own muscle and grit behind a saw that you have to work yourself. We also pick out some wood that will last through the heat of the summers up in the high altitude, along with a stain that will work nicely with the other benches around the lake.

Tank doesn't say much while he helps me shop, just offers suggestions while guiding me around his hardware store. I observe him the entire time, taking in the tender way he picks up his tools, the way his weathered and cracked fingers drag over the wood as he speaks about it. From his exterior, he's intimidating, a personality I'd use in a screenplay as a bruiser, someone to get the job done. But this man's anything but that. He's patient, quiet, speaks when he wants to make a point—and he's gentle. A positive light to show there's still moxie in this small town.

My supplies now in hand, Tank drives me back to the cabins in his truck and helps me unload the supplies near the shed. When everything's unloaded, he turns toward me and places his large hand on my shoulder.

"What you're doing is awfully kind. I appreciate it." His timeworn green eyes offer a softness to his rough appearance.

"You're, uh . . . you're welcome," I say awkwardly, not sure I need the praise. If anything, it gives me something to do, something to keep my mind off the nightmare of Annalisa and Simon.

Once Tank takes off, I go back to the dilapidated bench and start taking some measurements.

Time to get to work.

❖   ❖   ❖

I lift the hem of my shirt to my brow and dab at my forehead before taking another look at the bench. Damn, it's hot out.

It took me a few tries to remember what the hell I was doing, but once I got the dimensions correct in my head, I went to work, never once stopping. I measured, I sawed, I sanded, I nailed. I did this on repeat until the bench was completely fixed. I was even able to preserve some of the original wood to keep the memory for Sully and Joan. Now it's time to sit on it and make sure it's sturdy before I stain it.

Knowing this is a big moment, I turn and take a seat, hoping I don't fall through and right onto the grass. As I lower myself, I hold my breath. When my butt hits the wood and holds firmly, I lower all my weight on it and crack a smile—my first in what feels like a lifetime.

I've still got it.

I drape my hands along the back of the bench, pleased with myself.

Would you look at that—a bench. Pride swells through me. The simple task of rebuilding a bench is making me burst into a smile as I drum my fingers over the wood. Sometimes, when I'm immersed in writing a story, attending endless editing sessions, and going through my demanding work schedule, I forget about the simple pleasures in life, like building something with my own two hands.

Up until now, I didn't realize just how much I needed this.

"I've been watching you all morning," a familiar gruff voice says behind me.

I turn to find Sully wearing a scowl, though the creasing in his face feels gentler. Not as harsh as this morning, when he was reprimanding me for breaking his bench. God, he's the perfect secondary character—the type of grumpy guy everyone secretly roots for and cheers for in the end.

"You did that all wrong." Sully points at the bench.

I glance down at it. "How so?"

He walks up to me and presses his hand to the back of the bench and gives it a shake. It doesn't move. Solid, ha! He then moves to the front and kicks one of the legs—once again, unmoving.

Sorry to say, Sully, but this softened screenwriter still has it.

He grumbles something and then moves to the front of the bench and takes a seat.

"It's uncomfortable," he finally says, crossing his arms and resting them on his small belly.

"Do you want a pillow?" I ask.

"Do I look like a man who sits on a bench pillow?" Insult laces his voice, and I hold back my chuckle.

"No, sir, you don't."

"It's uncomfortable because your craftsmanship is subpar."

Uh-huh, sure. I don't believe a word of it, but for his sake, I agree with him.

"Very subpar," I say. "It's shocking that two grown men are able to sit on the bench together and it doesn't fall apart."

Sully turns and looks me up and down, his perusal a tad frightening. Even though I can characterize him in a second as a teddy bear inside, I still wither under his glower. The man has life experience; he receives a degree of respect from this town—you can see that just talking with Tank—and from our few interactions, I can tell that he's not someone you want to mess with. But I don't falter under his stare.

I don't look away. He seems like a man who'd respect that. And when he then turns back to the lake, I can tell I've made the right decision. "I like your snark. Keep it coming." Then, with a groan, he stands from the bench and motions to it. "Don't leave an unfinished product—be sure to stain it and then follow up with my granddaughter, Fallon, in the lobby. She'll be able to pay you for your time."

Sully takes off, and I smile to myself, keeping my eyes fixed on the lake.

Did I just make my first friend in Canoodle?

I think I did.

CHAPTER SEVEN

FALLON

"Two deep breaths, and then flow into cobra," Jaz says in her calming yoga voice.

Every Friday, before the weekend crowd shuffles in, Jaz holds a yoga class at Beggar's Hole, out on the deck. She spends the morning pushing the chairs and tables to the side, cleaning the floor—the only clean floor in the joint—and then laying out yoga mats. It's first come, first served. Attendees have to sign up on the corkboard next to the bar, and only ten spots are available because that's all she can fit on the deck. It's peaceful, and the best way to de-stress after a long week. I have a permanent spot.

"Back into downward dog, and then walk your hands to your feet. On your next breath, lift and bring your hands up and over your head, and then down to heart center." She lets out a long breath. "Now go fuck up shit this weekend."

Everyone claps, and we all slip our shoes back on as we wipe down the yoga mats and roll them up while Jaz rolls a cart around the deck, collecting the supplies.

"Great class, Jaz," Dolly, the owner of Barber Streisand—the local salon—says as she walks by. "And Fallon, maybe next time, you can bring that hunk of a doctor around to join us."

"If he can get up here early enough, I'll for sure bring him," I say.

"Is it just me, or does he seem to get beefier every time he drives up here to visit you?"

"He's been working out a lot," I answer. And I've noticed. He's starting to get definition in his abs, and his arms look like absolute boulders, especially with his shorter stature. Hunky doctor is correct.

"It shows." Dolly winks. "See you around, ladies." I'm waving to her just as Faye, Dolly's archnemesis, comes up to us.

"That is so inappropriate of her," Faye hisses, disgusted. "To ogle your boyfriend like that, positively despicable. That woman has no notion of keeping it in her pants." I nearly snort. "Have you seen her lurking around Village Hardware? She has an eye for Tank. Harlene was telling me that she overheard Dolly telling Tank how she wants to comb his mustache for him." Faye clutches her pearls—yes, actual pearls. She drapes them over the turtleneck she wears to yoga every Friday. "The audacity. Could you ever imagine asking a man if you could comb his mustache?"

"I asked a man the other night if I could sit on his face, so combing a mustache feels G rated in comparison," Jaz says. Faye clutches her pearls harder and lets out a humph before stomping off, clearly horrified.

"Jaz, why did you have to say that to her? Now she's going to be in a tizzy for the rest of the day."

"She's too much for me." Jaz brushes her off with a wave of her hand. "Someone needs to take the stick out. Maybe Tank can do the honors, since she has such a crush on him."

"I don't know if she does. I think she just really, really dislikes Dolly."

"No, Faye's been pining after Tank for years. That buttoned-up widow wants the bad boy, but she's just too scared to admit it."

"Maybe," I say. "Hey, do you have a second to talk something over with me?"

"Only if you help me with chairs and tables after."

"Don't I always?"

"Yes, but I'm worried that one day my brash attitude is going to scare you away, and you're not going to want to help me anymore."

I chuckle. "If I've stuck around for, what . . . twenty years? I'm pretty sure I'm not going anywhere. You might scare me at times, but I know that deep down, you mean well. You're stuck with me."

"Just the way I like it—a clinger." She smirks, and together we move one table, only to sit down at it.

I pull my notebook out of my bag and steady my nerves. "My dads called me the other night."

"How are my two favorite gay men? Still living their best sixties-era life in Palm Springs?"

My dads own several properties in Palm Springs, all with a classic sixties Cali theme. Specializing in midcentury modern decor, they've added clean lines and bold colors to all their properties. We're talking terrazzo flooring, split-rock fireplaces, gilded hanging lamps, and raspberry-colored swan chairs. They've preserved the golden era and are starting to finally see success with renting out the properties to anyone searching out the nostalgic feel of Palm Springs in its heyday. It's a bittersweet success, though. They've been able to capitalize on the Airbnb boom, the same trend that's taking Sully out of business.

"They are," I say. "But they didn't call with good news."

Jaz's face falls. "Is everything okay with Izaak?"

I know exactly what Jaz is thinking. My dad Izaak is paralyzed from the waist down and has suffered from health complications as a result.

"Yes, nothing like that," I say. "But they did call to tell me that the Cove is running out of money, and if I don't turn things around quickly, they're going to have to sell."

"*What?*" Jaz shouts. "No way, they can't sell. Sully would be devastated—hell, the whole town would be devastated."

"I know, but they don't have much of an option. They've been paying me out of their own account."

Jaz winces. "That's not good. What did you say?"

"I told them to give me a few weeks to turn things around. If I can just fix at least the front lobby and a few cabins, I can get the new website up and running and book some more reservations. You know? We have all the materials—I just need to find the time and help to do it."

"Yeah, I see where you're going with that." She levels with me. "But have you forgotten *you're* the one who has to renovate?"

"I know," I say, shifting uncomfortably. "Which is why I thought I'd break it down to the musts, to things I know how to do, to at least make the place . . . look prettier until I can afford the help. Small projects here and there. Little touches that can build up to bigger things. I know how to paint. The floors can't be too hard, right? I don't want to even think about electrical, that can wait, but new paint and floors and assembling furniture—those are things I can do."

"Yeah, those tasks seem simple enough. Do you think it will make the kind of impact you need?"

"It has to. I literally have no other plans. This has to work."

"Okay. What can I do to help?"

I smile. "And that's why you're my best friend."

She reaches out and takes my hand in hers. "That's what friends are for—to help you with renovations and slash people's tires when they wrong you. Which, I'll have you know, it's taken a lot out of me not to slash Julia's tires. Tempting, very tempting."

"Well, I'm glad you've been able to control yourself. There's no need to slash them. I told you, I'm fine with everything. It's not like we had a deep connection. Honestly, I feel nothing toward him."

"Well, just say the word. If he pisses you off, I can be there in seconds, ready to bust through some thick rubber."

I snort, enjoying the image despite myself. "How about you help me paint this weekend? I need to paint the dark wood in the lobby white. Once that's done, we can replace the floors and then just decorate. I already have tons of ideas for how to make the space more modern but still keep the mountain feel."

"You know how much I hate painting—I prefer demolishing things. Do you need me to take a sledgehammer to anything?"

"Not at the moment," I answer. "But I'll be sure to keep that in the back of my mind."

"That's all I ask."

❖　❖　❖

"Sully, dinner is ready," I call out.

When I don't hear anything, I walk downstairs to find him. "Sully . . . dinner."

I look around the lobby and the office, but there's no sign of him.

Panic sets in. He's always around here when it's close to dinner. I frantically search the main lobby area one more time.

"Sully . . . where are you?" I call out as I exit the building and turn down the winding path to the cabins. I push past a few overgrown trees and jog down to where the lake opens up on the property. I glance around, my heart pounding.

That's when I see him.

Sitting on a bench.

But not just any bench, *his* bench.

The bench that was broken just a few days ago, that's been broken for years now.

Confused, I hurry to the edge of the lake. "Hey, Sully, I was looking for you."

He doesn't look at me but instead pats the bench next to him. "Sit, dear granddaughter."

Unsure where his head is, I take a seat, and he wraps his arm around me, pulling me into his familiar scent of mint and Irish Spring soap, a smell I always find comforting.

"What a beautiful lake, don't you think?" he asks, his voice lacking its usual harshness.

"Yes." I lean into him, uneasy but also soaking up the moment. "It's always been the prettiest lake, in my opinion."

He doesn't answer right away, letting the light breeze pass while watching the water lap at the shoreline. The imagery in my head of this moment feels so real, but in my place beside him, Grandma Joan is cuddling into his chest, one hand resting on his checkered shirt, the other curled around his back. Sully would lean his cheek against her head and quietly hum his favorite Glenn Miller tune.

"If you listen carefully enough, you can almost hear the light breeze trying to push through the water," he says, his voice so sweet, so consoling.

We sit there, listening. And he's right: if you let nature take over and truly listen, you can hear the most extraordinary sounds. Like the ruffle of leaves from a bird landing on a branch. The distant buzz of a bee searching for pollen, and, of course, the breeze caressing the waves on the lake.

"The bench— did you fix it?" I say, after a few peaceful moments. I'm too curious not to ask. Also, I need to know if he somehow stumbled across the tools he should no longer be using without heavy supervision. A few months ago, I found Sully downstairs, attempting to cut some wood. In the middle of sawing, he had a lapse in judgment and ended up cutting the back of his hand. I rushed him to the emergency room, beside myself with worry. Seven stitches later, I spoke with his doctor, and we both agreed that hiding the tools would be in his best interest.

"Did I fix the bench? No, your contractor did."

"Contractor?" I ask. What the hell is he talking about?

"You know, Grandma Joan won't be happy with the angle of this seat back. I told him it wasn't comfortable, but he didn't listen and stained it anyway."

Color me utterly confused. I didn't hire a contractor.

I want to ask him what on earth he's talking about, but it's getting late, and Sully has a strict bedtime schedule. Sleep is one of the most important things when it comes to Alzheimer's, and if we stay on routine, he can usually have a decent night's sleep, which leads to a healthy day. So instead of getting into it, I direct him back to why I came out here in the first place. "Dinner's ready, Sully."

He rubs his stomach. "Good, I'm starving." He leans over and presses a kiss to my forehead. "I love you, granddaughter."

And just like that, tears well up in my eyes, and I squeeze my grandpa back. I can't remember the last time I heard him say that, not to mention offer me this type of affection. "I love you too."

"Thank you for taking care of me."

It's rare, getting moments like this with him. His lack of lucidity drives him to forget who I am sometimes, and although it's painful, I understand. But this bench . . . this bench has always been where he's felt comfortable, so I shouldn't be too shocked he can open up here. He can remember who he is, right here, where some of his best memories were created with his girl, Joan.

"It's my pleasure," I reply, soaking in this moment with him, committing it to memory, because I'm not sure how many more we'll get.

CHAPTER EIGHT

SAWYER

"Hey you, what are you doing just lazing about?" Sully calls out while charging toward me in those unmistakable suspenders.

I sit up from where I'm sprawled across the lawn in front of the bench—one of my favorite spots, because it's far from the ducks but still has a great view of the mountain and the rock formations.

"What do you mean?" I ask as he reaches me, a pinch in his brow.

"We aren't paying you to sit by the lake and look around for four-leaf clovers," he snaps. "Get to work." He tosses his hand to the side.

"Oh, I was unaware there was more work to be done." After yesterday, I assumed any need for my handiness was over and done with.

"Of course there's more work to be done. If we want to get ready for opening season, then we need to get this property ready," Sully insists. "Which means you need to move your ass."

I glance down at my blank notebook page. The only thing written is *Noely, Going in Blind*, but I scratched that out quickly. I can do better than steal a love story from a news anchor who tried to defend me. Since I haven't gotten anywhere on the idea front, it won't hurt me to lend a hand again, especially since I got so much joy out of it yesterday. So, I stand up and tuck my notebook under my arm. "What do you need me to do?"

"You can start with those picnic tables over there." Sully points down the hill to an area with overgrown grass and weathered picnic tables. "Do you really think anyone is going to eat at them with all that chipped wood? People don't come here to get slivers in their asses. Sand them down and repaint. I expect to see them all finished by day's end."

Day's end? Shit, I'd better get to work, then.

With that, he turns on his heel and charges back toward the main lobby, arms pumping at his sides. For such an old man, he has quite a pep in his step when he's angry.

I chuckle to myself and consider asking Fallon if she wants me to tackle the picnic tables, but I know Sully has a point. I haven't sat at the tables yet, and it's because they're in desperate need of some sanding and a paint job.

So . . . I head back to my cabin, change into my work clothes, and then make my way to the hardware store. This time, I don't run into Tank at the door. He's standing at the counter, hovering over a catalogue, and I give a quick wave as I walk up.

"Back for more?" he asks.

"Picnic tables. Need to sand them down and repaint."

"Looking for an electric sander?"

I shake my head. "Nah, I think I want to do this by hand. I like the feel of the hard work."

"You're a better man than me," he says. "Let me get you what you need."

He takes me to the back and helps me pick out some sandpaper, sanding block included. I might not want an electric sander, but I know a block will help immensely.

"Sully believes I'm a contractor—I honestly didn't think he was going to remember me."

"He hasn't completely lost his short-term memory. But he does get confused a lot. He probably associates you with the bench. It's very near and dear to him, so he most likely has it in his head that you fix things."

"That makes sense," I say as we walk toward the paint section. "I have no idea what color to pick."

"Red," Tank says without giving it any thought. "Sully and Joan always liked red picnic tables on the property. They enjoyed the pop of color against the natural woods."

"Then we'll go with red."

When we reach the counter, I pull out my wallet, but Tank holds up his hand. "Your money's no good here."

"Tank, I can pay."

"I'm aware what you can do, but I said your money isn't good here. You're helping out my friend; therefore, you don't pay. Got it?"

"Are you sure?"

"Don't make me kick you in the ass," Tank says, voice lowering to a threatening tone. Jesus, if I didn't know any better, I'd think he's related to Jaz.

"Okay." I pocket my wallet. "Got it."

Once again, Tank drops me off back at the cabins, and I get right to work.

Sanding.

And sanding.

And sanding. The summer heat consumes me to the point that I have to go back to my cabin and change into a pair of shorts.

I return to the picnic tables and begin sanding again.

You'd think I'd regret not going with an electric sander, but I like the feel of the hard work on my body. I like the physical labor, exerting my body to the point that I feel like I might collapse. I like the fact that while I'm sanding, I get lost in the grain, in the vibration of grit against the wood, in the rough sound filling the space around me. I like that my mind doesn't wander, that I can block out the reality of Annalisa and Simon's deceit, and the looming demand of another screenplay. I can just . . . disengage.

But shit, it's hot.

I set the sandpaper down and reach behind me to pull my shirt off. I fold it into thirds, lengthwise, and then I stuff it in the back of my shorts, letting it hang there as I twist my hat backward to pour some water on my face. But when I reach for my bottle, I realize I'm all out. Damn it.

Knowing there's a bottle-refill station in the main lobby, I make the trek up the hill to the lobby and push open the door. I step inside to find Fallon and Jaz painting the dark woodwork that spans the length of the front wall.

"Why is this taking forever?" Jaz complains when she turns and spots me. Her eyes fixate on my bare chest and then float up to my face. "Well, would you look at that, Julia has muscles. I was not expecting that."

"What?" Fallon asks, turning as well, paintbrush in hand. When she sees me, her eyes immediately dart away. "Oh, uh, hi. Do you need something?"

I hold up my bottle, even though she's not looking at me. "Just need to refill my water."

Jaz, on the other hand, has no shame in checking me out. "What do you know, he has defined abs. I never would've guessed. What else are you hiding?" Her eyes fall to my crotch. "Anything . . . special?"

"Jaz," Fallon scolds. "Stop that."

"What? I can't stand here and appreciate a male specimen when I see him? You know, you can look at him—it won't burn your eyes. Look at his nipples; they're a great size."

"Uh, thank you." I move to the water-refill station to the right, feeling oddly flattered. The last person I'd ever expect to grant me a compliment is Jaz, so even though she's talking about my nipples, I'll take it.

"I wasn't really talking to you," Jaz says, clearly catching her mistake: paying me a compliment. "Just making general commentary. I still don't like you."

"Good to know," I say, trying to be as casual as possible. I refill my water, feeling Jaz's eyes on me the entire time.

"You must do a lot of push-ups, don't you?" Jaz asks.

"What's it to you?" I shoot back at her, making her eyes narrow.

"Are you giving me sass?"

"Does it feel like I am?" I face her and take a sip from my water bottle.

"You are." She points at me. "Watch it: you don't want to mess with me."

"Maybe I do," I say, trying a new approach with Jaz. Maybe she'll respect me more if I don't act like a complete pushover.

"I wouldn't." Fallon speaks up, her eyes still avoiding my topless torso. Me, on the other hand, I can't say the same. Those ripped jean shorts look fucking good on her. "Now enough of this—we have to get this painting done. And since that stupid spray-painter thing won't work, we need to get a move on."

"Why won't it work?" I ask, pulling my eyes from the way her jeans hug her ass.

"We don't need you butting in with your immense screenwriting knowledge." Jaz shoos me away with her hand. "I'm sure you can maneuver your way around a plot twist, but that isn't quite helpful with what we're doing."

Ignoring her, I walk up to the paint gun and take a look at it. Within a few seconds, I diagnose the problem.

"You don't have the nozzle set up right." I make the proper adjustments.

I turn it on and spray the wall. The white paint comes out in a perfect sheet across the wood. With a satisfied smile, specifically directed at Jaz, I hand the spray gun to Fallon, who is finally looking at me, appreciation in her eyes.

"Oh my God, thank you," Fallon says, excited. "You just saved us so much time."

Jaz eyes me. "I don't like that you knew how to do that," she says. "Are you some sort of wizard?"

"No, but like you said, I'm hiding things. You might just have to dig a little deeper to find them." I give them a sturdy salute. "Good luck with your painting."

Content with putting Jaz in her place, I leave the lobby with a smile on my face and head back down the hill to the picnic tables, where I find Sully sitting on one of them, testing it out.

"There you are," he says. "I thought you were taking a nap."

I shake my head. "Just filling my water back up."

He motions to my chest. "What happened to your shirt?"

"I was hot."

"Well, this is a family facility—put it back on. You don't see me taking my shirt off, do you?" He snaps his suspenders against his chest.

"That I don't." I reach behind me and pull my shirt from my shorts, then put it back on. The cotton fabric already feels stifling. There is a very, very cold shower in my future.

"And wear your hat the way it's supposed to be worn, bill forward."

I twist my hat back around. "Sorry about that, sir. Is that better?"

He scans me again. "Yes, now, hand me some sandpaper—you missed some spots."

Knowing damn well I didn't, I hand him some sandpaper anyway, and together, we sand the picnic table. My strokes are fast, labored, getting the job done, while Sully takes it slow, deliberate with each stroke.

"You're going to throw your back out going that fast. Enjoy the moment, the calmness of the paper running against the grain of the wood."

Since I'm almost done, I decide to slow down and join him in his pace.

"See, enjoy it," Sully says, his shaky hand running along the wood.

"You're right. This is nice."

"Are you working on any other projects in your own time?"

"I am," I answer. "I've been working on a kayak for a few years now. I've been building it from scratch. It's taken me a really long time, especially since I don't get to work on it very often at all."

"A kayak." He nods, the gruffness in his voice easing. "That's quite the ambitious task. Lots of curves."

"Yes, it's been a challenge, but rewarding."

"Maybe someday you can float it on Strawberry Lake. We don't get many boats out there anymore."

"Why is that?" I ask.

"Can't be sure, might be the new mayor."

"Do they not like boats?" I chuckle.

"Doesn't like water." Sully looks me in the eyes. "It's a damn cat."

Confused, I look behind me and then back at him. "What's a cat?"

"The mayor."

"Huh?" I ask.

"The mayor of this town is a cat."

"A cat? Like . . . meow?" Why did I just say "meow"?

But it makes Sully laugh as he nods and then sands in between the table's cracks.

"An actual cat. The damn thing is the fattest animal I've ever seen. Spends all day sleeping on a silk pillow and only removes itself during feeding time. A ridiculous load of crap, if you ask me."

"Wait, so an *actual cat* is the mayor?" Sully nods. "How?"

"Canoodle opted out of local government, and as a novelty, they hold elections every four years. The competition is always between dogs and cats. Personally, I think the entire thing is a joke."

"Adds to the quirk of the town," I say.

His bushy eyebrows draw together. "You think this town is quirky?"

"I do," I say. "It's the type of town that you'd find in a movie. A small town in the middle of nowhere, surrounded by trees and full of local charm. Quirky townspeople, fascinating store names, a cat for a mayor . . . it's the classic setting for a romantic Christmas movie." I've written about a town like this a time or two as a screenwriter, especially back when I was working with Lovemark, the network known for its sweet, romantic movies. This is the kind of location they're looking for—a place where people can escape their troubles.

Huh . . . that's exactly what I'm doing. If I didn't know any better, I'd think I'm living out my very own troubled story line, although if that were the case, where's the heroine who's supposed to step in and help me realize my worth?

My mind immediately falls to the one single woman I know in town—at least I think she's single—Jaz. I shiver from the thought. Terrifying. That would be absolutely terrifying.

"Romance?" Sully asks. "Are you a romantic man?"

I dig a little deeper into the cracks with the sandpaper. "I used to think I was, until my girlfriend left me for someone else." I'm ashamed to look Sully in the eye. There's something about his stoicism that makes me feel weak at the mention of Annalisa.

Sully doesn't respond at first. The scrape of sandpaper against wood fills our silence, and then, after a few minutes, Sully clears his throat. "I was cheated on myself."

Sully . . . cheated on? I don't believe it. I can tell from the green in his eyes and the strength in his jaw that he was an attractive man in his younger years. And despite his surly disposition, I can see his kindness resting just beneath the surface.

"That doesn't seem possible."

"Even the most handsome of the bunch can be unlucky in love," Sully says with the smallest of smirks. "But I have to admit, even though it hurt, it was a blessing in disguise—after I was cheated on, I moved here, to Canoodle. I used every last penny in my account to build these cabins."

"You built these?" I ask, taking a look at the craftsmanship. Designed to look like mini log cabins, they're finished in a light oak with black metal gable roofing. They're very quaint. "You did an incredible job."

"Thank you," he says softly. He's been so talkative, so chatty, that I wonder if today is one of his more lucid days. He seems to be very clearheaded, very in tune with his thoughts—I'm curious what he was like before Alzheimer's grabbed ahold of him. There's no doubt in my mind I'd still want to be sitting here, with him, sanding an old table and just chatting. "It was when I was picking out furniture that I met Joan." His eyes drift off toward the lake. "She sold furniture—hand-made pieces and antiques—and she was the most beautiful woman I'd ever seen. The lightest blue eyes that tore right through my heart. Brunette with the prettiest curls. She captured me. In an instant, I knew this woman was special—and I needed to spend the rest of my life with her. I told her about the cabins, and she came by to look at them. It was a drive, since she was living down in Palm Springs, but she made the trek up the mountains and helped me pick out furniture and bedding for each of the rooms. It took a lot of convincing, but she finally went out on a date with me, and I never looked back."

"That's beautiful," I say. Reminds me of a classic Nicholas Sparks romance. A blue-collar man making the most of what he has, impressing not with his wallet, but with his work ethic, his charm, and his caring heart. "So, the cabins, this property . . . it's like the beginning of your love story."

He nods. "It was. It was what brought us together, and not a day goes by that I don't miss her. That I don't see her around here. These cabins were a part of her." Sully looks up, a twinkle in his eye. "And I *romanced* her. This old guy had quite a few tricks up his sleeve."

"Oh yeah?" I ask, even as I feel a pang, realizing my suspicions were correct—Joan has passed. "Like what?"

Sully sets his sandpaper down. "That's a story for a different day. I trust you can clean this up?"

"Yes, sir."

"Good. Meet you out here tomorrow to paint." With a parting nod, he gets up and leaves.

I watch him as he retreats to the bench I rebuilt, where he takes a seat and stares out at the lake, the sun setting behind the mountains, bringing in the perfect magic-hour illumination—a filmmaker's dream, ambient light. From a distance, I can see his mouth moving, as if he's talking, but I can't quite hear him from where I sit.

His arm is draped along the bench, though, and I just know he's wrapping his arm around Joan, talking to her as the sun begins to set. And I'm not sure I've ever seen anything more romantic in my life. Because even though Joan is gone, she's still in his heart, and the man continues to love her, ache for her, include her in his life.

That's the kind of love movies are written about.

That's the kind of love I want in my life.

Not a roller coaster of drama, like I had with Annalisa. If I truly give it some thought, that relationship wasn't based around a deep appreciation for each other, but rather a common goal—of making it in show business. There wasn't a foundation between us. There wasn't friendship.

I think about what Sully confessed, how he retreated to Canoodle after he was cheated on and found solace here, among the trees, in the deep lake and solitary mountains. Makes me wonder . . . will I find the same solace?

I stare up at the dimming night sky.

You know, I think I might have already started to find it.

❖   ❖   ❖

"So, what were your famous moves?" I ask Sully as he calmly paints a picnic table, being very careful with his strokes. The vibrant red of the paint put a large smile on Sully's face when I opened the can and revealed it to him. He asked how I guessed what color he'd want, and I told him Tank at Village Hardware had offered some help.

"Famous moves?" Sully asks, clearly confused.

Oh. Right. He might not remember all of our conversation from yesterday.

"The moves you made to romance Joan."

"Ah," he says, a sly smile now passing over his lips. "Well, she was a tough shell to crack at first."

"Why was that?"

"Because she wasn't into me. Not that she didn't find me attractive. Back in my day, I was what they called a hunk."

"I believe it," I say. "You still are."

"I prefer you not stick your head up my ass—it's not comfortable." I let out a loud laugh as Sully continues. "She had a boyfriend at the time."

"Really?" I ask. "Huh, I didn't see that coming."

Sully dips his paintbrush in the can and strokes the wood carefully. "His name was Earl. He owned a rock company."

"A rock company? Like, geodes?"

Sully chuckles and shakes his head. "No, landscaping rock."

"Oh, that makes sense." I laugh.

"They were high school sweethearts, Joan and Earl. She was very much attached to him, and I respected that, though it was easier said than done at times. When I first asked her out and she told me she had a boyfriend, I was crushed." Sully sets his brush down and reaches into his pocket. He takes out his wallet and fidgets around with it until he pulls out a worn, yellowed picture and hands it to me. "That's my Joan."

Despite the discoloration of the photo and the wrinkle that travels the length of the right side, I can easily see how beautiful Joan was. As a screenwriter trying to paint a picture, I'd describe her hair as rag curls, silky without a strand out of place, and her eyes, despite not being able to see their color, seem kind, loving. And of course, even in black and white, I can tell there's bright-red lipstick on her heart-shaped lips.

"Wow, she's beautiful."

"She is, and she's aged with grace," he says. "When you go to get your payment, you'll see what I'm talking about. She makes the best snickerdoodle cookies. I think . . ." He pauses, and my heart sinks as his eyes glaze over. I'm losing him. "I think there are some in the oven right now."

In an instant, I watch his lucidity disappear, only for confusion to cross his face.

He sniffs and glances over his shoulder. "Yes, there are . . . there are some in the oven."

This right here, watching a man so full of life, so full of stories, fall into a fit of uncertainty—God, it's heartbreaking, especially since I know there are no cookies in the oven, no Joan in the lobby.

But I don't want to make the situation worse, so I go with it. "That's great. I love snickerdoodles. Maybe I'll stop by later for one—after I finish these tables, of course."

He nods, then takes the picture from my hand and stuffs it back in his wallet. For a second, I think he's going to resume our conversation, but when he doesn't pick up his paintbrush again and stares off at the lake behind me, I know I've lost him.

Unsure of what to do, I continue to paint and try to bring him back to the present. "So, Joan was dating Earl?"

Sully clears his throat. "Yes, I, uh . . ." He glances back again. His jaw worries back and forth, his hand now shaking in front of him. "I think, I, uh, I think I should go check on her." He taps on the table with his knuckle and cautiously rises, his eyes wandering, his sense of direction clearly confused as he carefully looks around to gain his bearings.

He doesn't recognize where he is. I can't imagine how frightened he must feel.

I need to step in.

"Uh, you know, I have to go to the lobby for some more water for my water bottle. Can I walk with you?"

"Yes, sure." He nods but doesn't move, so I set my paintbrush down on the paint can top. I grab my almost-full water bottle and start walking toward the lobby. "Ah, yes," he says, pointing in the right direction. "Right this way."

"Thank you," I say, even though I'm leading the way.

"Are you enjoying your stay?" he asks, his voice changing from that of the grumpy storyteller to the ever-happy host.

"I am," I say. "The cabins are beautiful."

"Thank you. Did you know I built them?"

Yes.

I don't want to lie to him, so I say, "You did a wonderful job. I can really see the fine detail you put into them. The joints you cut out are excellent."

He chuckles. "Almost lost a finger cutting those."

"I can imagine."

We make it up to the lobby, and he pats me on the back. "Enjoy your stay." He opens the door for me, and we walk into the lobby to find Fallon touching up the paint job she was working on yesterday. Jaz isn't here this time, but Fallon's boyfriend is instead, crouched down by the baseboards, paintbrush in hand.

"Hey, Sully." The boyfriend stands. "How are you?"

Sully freezes and looks to Fallon. It's written all over his face—he has no idea who that man is.

"Sully, you remember Peter," Fallon says.

"Oh yes, Peter." Sully doesn't move, but just raises his hand at him. Confusion still clouds Sully's eyes, and he turns to Fallon. "Where is your grandma Joan? I want to check on her."

Fallon's face falls, and in that one expression I can feel her grief, sense the heartache she carries for not only losing her grandma but repeatedly having this conversation with Sully. Instead of emotionally withdrawing, though, she sets her shoulders with courage and walks up to him. "Why don't I take you upstairs, and we can talk." She turns to Peter. "Can you finish up for me?"

"Sure, sweetie," he says as Fallon disappears upstairs with Sully, her hand gripping his arm the entire time.

When they're out of earshot, Peter lets out a deep breath. "Did you run into him outside?"

When I realize he's talking to me, I clear my throat. "Oh yeah, we were chatting. He seemed to get confused about where he was, so I helped him back here, figuring that would be pretty safe."

Peter nods. "Thank you. He sometimes forgets where he is, so I'm glad you were there to help him." He holds out his hand. "Peter."

The steadfast boyfriend.

The type of character thrown into a story to throw the viewers off, especially when he's a good guy, when there don't seem to be any warning signals, nothing telling the viewers there's a possible mean streak in him that could shake things up. That could . . . wait, what am I talking about? This is playing out in my head as if Fallon is the heroine of whatever romance is simmering in my head.

But . . . my pitch could be about a small-town girl with a boyfriend who flies in and out of town on the weekends, and during the week, she starts to fall in love with someone else . . .

No. Too complicated.

I give Peter's hand a shake. "Sawyer. I'm staying in one of the cabins."

"Oh, nice. For how long?"

"Uh, probably a few weeks." I scratch the back of my neck. "Kind of giving myself a little escape from real life at the moment."

"I can understand that. What I wouldn't give to have a brief escape with Fallon right now." He shakes his head. "Sully is a full-time job."

Not sure why Peter is telling this to a perfect stranger, but I just nod along. "She seems to do a very good job with him."

"She does." He nods as well. "Anyway, I should get back to painting." He holds up his brush. "Have a good stay."

"Thank you." I fill up my water bottle and then head out the back door to the picnic tables, which I soon finish painting. The entire time, I can't get the picture of Joan out of my head.

Or Fallon's fallen expression.

CHAPTER NINE

FALLON

"Why doesn't Tank have Sully this weekend?" Peter asks as I join him in bed after checking on Sully one last time.

"He has a motorcycle club meeting. They're once a month, and I don't want Tank missing those. I know how much they mean to him."

Peter is leaning against the white wooden headboard, and I'm tucked up against him as he rests his laptop on his lap so we can watch my new obsession, old episodes of *I Love Lucy*.

"I didn't know he was part of a motorcycle club—I mean, I guess with one look at him, you could assume that, given the constant leather he wears, even in the heat."

"Yeah, it's a good break for him. Just like I get a break, he needs one too."

"Maybe next weekend, we can go somewhere—you know, on a real break. I'm sure Jaz wouldn't mind keeping an eye on the cabins for you. We can spend a long weekend in Palm Springs or even go down to San Diego, or Temecula. Spend a weekend in the wine country." He kisses the top of my head.

What is he even talking about? Just this afternoon I was telling him about my never-ending to-do list. Does he really think I can take a break right now?

"I would love to, Peter, but right now is not a good time. We're kind of in a crunch to get these renovations done."

"Sweetie, you've been working on the renovations for a while; they'll still be here—"

"That's the thing," I say, turning toward him. "They might not still be here."

"What are you talking about?" Peter shuts his laptop and turns toward me.

"I mean, I spoke with my dads, and the cabins aren't doing well. We're badly in need of income, and until I finish these renovations, I can't bring any in."

"What happens if you don't finish them?"

I stare down at my hands. "Then we have to sell."

"Really?" Peter says, and there's no mistaking the hope in his voice. "Fallon, that's great. You could sell and then come back to Palm Springs. I've been looking at the different facilities in the area for Sully, and I have a friend who works at this great—"

"Peter, I don't want to sell."

"What?" he asks, a pinch in his brow. "Why not?"

"Because this is where I grew up, this is where I have so many memories of Sully, of Grandma Joan. This is my second home, and I can't imagine giving it to someone else, someone else who very well might tear down the cabins Sully worked so hard to build. I can't do that to him. To me."

"But Fallon, this is too much for you. Renovations on your own while taking care of your grandpa? How is that fair to you?"

I feel like very few people would understand where I'm coming from. Hell, my dads don't even understand, but they support me. This is more to me than just helping out my grandpa; this is about preserving the legacy my grandparents left behind.

Every summer, without fail, my dads would drive me up here—not because they wanted time away but because I begged them to let me spend those weeks with my grandparents in the mountains, where I'd go on hikes with Sully, or bake snickerdoodles in the kitchen with Grandma Joan. They'd hold a cabin just for me and Jaz, where we could pretend to be guests and stay up until the late hours of the night just talking and goofing around. This place, this town, holds my fondest memories, and these cabins are more than just a place to stay; they were dreamed up by Sully, perfected by Grandma Joan.

There's magic here in the Cove, and I'll do everything in my power to make sure the magic stays with us, here . . . where Sully and Grandma Joan fell in love.

"I'm not looking for anything to be fair, Peter," I say. "I'm looking to do what's right. And if that means sticking around to make sure I did everything I could to hang on to this property, then I'm going to do it. How do you not know that about me?" That's an even more important question, because I've told him countless times the meaning behind the cabins.

"I do." He lets out a deep sigh and takes my hand. "I'm sorry, I just . . . this has been hard, only seeing you on the weekends. Coming up here, not having private time with you. Not being able to relax with you. Seeing you work yourself until you're bone tired. Your mention of selling just got my mind going, seeing that there could be relief in the future."

"I know, I'm sorry—"

"You don't need to apologize," Peter says, pressing his hand to my cheek. "You are incredible, doing this for your family. I'm sorry that I just got frustrated. I love you, Fallon, and I want to be able to have you more often than the weekend."

I swallow hard.

Those three words ring through my head all over again.

Bleeding through my bones, and yet, they don't spur on the same reaction.

They don't spur anything at all—other than unease.

I look up at him. "I know this has been hard on you, Peter, and I can understand if it's too much—"

"It's not," he quickly says. "It's not too much, and I'm sorry if I made you think that it is. Just a momentary lapse into frustration." He takes a deep breath and cups my cheek. "This is not too much for me. You are worth it."

I can't keep meeting his gaze—looking into those eyes brimming with love feels . . . overwhelming. Instead, I curl into him and allow him to hold me tightly while he kisses the side of my head.

"Do you want to watch *I Love Lucy*?" I ask.

He shakes his head. "No, I'm kind of over it. Let's just talk."

"Oh, okay." I stare up at the ceiling. "What do you want to talk about?"

"Maybe a future trip we can take when you're in a good place with the renovations. Somewhere we can go and just be us—not us, Sully, and the cabins."

I know he doesn't intend his words to sound mean, but how can he not see that those things are a part of the person I am? If you get me, you get Sully, you get the cabins, you get this small town. How does he not see that?

And should I be worried that he doesn't see that?

Or am I just so tired, so overwhelmed, that I'm overthinking this? Probably the latter.

I need to relax, enjoy this moment with Peter—maybe I'm asking a lot of him, and I need to indulge in these fantasies, if only for a night.

"Um, let's see, ever been to Las Vegas?" I ask.

He chuckles. "Now, I like that kind of thinking."

❖ ❖ ❖

"Okay, floors next?" Jaz asks, hands on her hips as she stares down at the pile of flooring that we've been storing in the lobby's back room—so that on the off chance someone does come by, looking for a reservation, they won't run into the boxes."

"Yup." I tap the boxes with my toe. "I watched at least four YouTube videos last night on how to put together these floors. I think Peter was annoyed with me. He seemed agitated when he left this morning."

"Uh, yeah, you spend the night watching DIY floor videos when he's only here a few nights. You should have been boning."

"Ew, can you not say it like that?"

"What?" Jaz shrugs. "It's true. The man is a beefcake—you should be spending every moment you have together in the sheets."

We do . . . but we just don't do *that* all the time.

"It's hard to do that when I'm constantly tired," I say, and Jaz slowly spins toward me.

She's chewing a piece of gum, twirling it around on her finger—*gross*—as her eyes widen. "Wait, do you mean to tell me you don't have sex with him every night he's here?"

"It's kind of hard to have sex when I'm tired and Sully's constantly shifting around on the monitor."

"The baby monitor you have on him?" I nod. "Turn it off and fuck your boyfriend. Jesus, Fallon, what's wrong with you?"

I take a seat on the pile of boxes. "God, I don't know." I bite the inside of my cheek. "I still haven't told him I love him, and I feel really bad about it. I think I'm just messed up in my head right now. I'm emotionally unavailable for anything other than taking care of Sully. And with the pressure of keeping the cabins, getting them up and running . . . it feels impossible to tap into those feelings, you know? Because if I tap into them, I tap into all my other emotions, and I can't afford that. I'll break down if I actually try to think about how I feel."

Jaz walks up to me and places her hands on my shoulders. "I love you, Fallon. But Peter is right: you're carrying too much. He's a good guy, but if you don't give him the attention he deserves, it's going to be too late."

"I know."

"And do you want to lose him?"

I bite on my bottom lip and shake my head. "No, I don't think I do."

"Then why don't you go call him, just check on him, and I'll get started ripping out the carpet in the lobby. I could use the moment to myself to get out some aggression."

I chuckle. "Okay."

Wanting some privacy, I take my phone and walk out the back of the lobby, to the property. I take a deep breath, savoring the fresh breeze coming up from the lake, then dial Peter and bring the phone to my ear.

It rings twice before he picks up.

"Everything okay?" he asks.

"Yes," I answer, feeling like absolute crap. "I'm sorry, Peter."

"Sorry for what?"

I walk along the path toward the lake. "For not being a good girl-friend. You drive up here every weekend, and I put you to work. We, uh, we don't, you know . . . do it every night, and I—"

"Fallon, I'm going to stop you right there. I don't drive up to see you every weekend just to have sex. I drive up to see you, to spend time with you, and if that time is spent painting the lobby, then that's how we spend our time."

"You seemed irritated this morning, and I wasn't sure if it was because, you know . . . we didn't do anything last night."

"I mean, would I have wanted to make love to my girlfriend last night? Yeah, I would have. But you don't owe me anything. I want you to have sex with me because you're in the mood, because you want to. I'm more than happy just snuggling." Regret hangs heavy in his voice. "I also understand that you have a lot on your mind. I'm sorry if I seemed irritated, but I'm not going to lie, I was."

"I know and I'm sorry. This was my fault." I head down the stairs that lead to the back of the property, the overhang of the ponderosa pines providing shade from the already-beating sun. "I shouldn't have been watching those videos last night."

"How about this," he says. "When I get up there, we do whatever you want to do. If it's renovations, then we work on those, but after eight o'clock, it's my time, and we do what I want." His voice deepens, and I can hear the innuendo.

I chuckle. "I think that's fair." I stop and stare out at the lake. "I'm sorry, Peter."

"I know, sweetie. And I'm sorry I left without talking to you about how I felt. I didn't want to put more on your shoulders. But I'm glad you called."

"Me too."

"I love you," he says.

I squeeze my eyes shut.

"I'll, uh, I'll see you next weekend. Okay?"

"Yeah." He sighs. "See you next weekend, Fallon. I'll call tonight."

"Okay."

And then we hang up. Even though that conversation cleared the air, I can't shake this nagging feeling of unease in the pit of my stomach—it's stuck there and won't come out, won't free itself. And I have no idea how to make it.

Taking a deep breath, I'm turning to go back to the lobby when something from the corner of my eye stops me. A flash of bright red, just over the peak of the hill.

Curious, I move closer, and as I make my way up and over the hill, I stop dead in my tracks. Many years ago, Sully and Grandma Joan laid down stone under some of the largest trees on the property, fastened lights along the branches, and stuck picnic tables under the trees. It was the perfect spot for a picnic, for small gatherings, and one of my favorite places on the property.

Over time, the tree branches drooped, the lights stopped working, and the picnic tables became chipped to the point that you couldn't sit at them anymore.

But what I'm staring at right now is not the familiar run-down picnic area.

The crowded slate stones have been cleared, the rock scrubbed clean of any moss and buildup. The picnic tables have been sanded and repainted a bright red—Grandma Joan's favorite color. And the stringed lights no longer hang from the trees but instead are hanging from poles that have been cemented into the ground, giving them the proper sturdy base that they need to weather the winter storms.

It looks . . . magical.

How on earth?

I glance around, looking for a construction crew, for anyone who could have possibly pulled this off, but when I see no one in sight, my confusion only deepens.

I take a few minutes to let it wash over me and soak in the beauty of this spot, the same place where Grandma Joan used to take me to teach me how to cross-stitch. I never became as proficient as her, but the memories of her patiently directing me flood me all at once.

And a tear falls down my cheek. It feels like it was only fifteen minutes ago, the afternoon Grandma Joan and I brought a basket of cookies and lemonade out to these tables and gabbed about Leon Johnson, my high school crush. She reached across the table and told me I shouldn't have to wait around for a boy to like me. I remember her words so vividly, the way she comforted me when I said he wouldn't dance with me at spring formal. It was the first time I heard her call someone a nitwit. But it definitely wasn't the first time we fell into a laughing fit. How have fifteen years gone by since that day?

The memory feels too real. Too palpable, like it's happening right now. I turn away.

No.

I can't get emotional.

Not right now.

Not when there is work to be done.

Getting lost in memories won't help me. But I do need to find out who made this happen, because I owe them a huge thank-you.

I walk back to the lobby to find Jaz slashing her knife at the carpet while heavy metal plays in the background.

"Take that," Jaz says, pulling at the old green carpet. "And that."

"Jaz!" I call out over the music.

She turns to me and smiles, knife held aloft, like she's in a slasher movie. "Come join me—this is very therapeutic."

"Did you do something to the picnic tables?"

"What?" she calls out over the music.

I reach for the Bluetooth speaker and press pause. I point to it. "We will be playing something . . . less murder-y."

"Cat in Heat is a great band if you give them a chance."

"I will never give a band named Cat in Heat a chance." I set the speaker down. "I asked if you did anything to the picnic tables."

"The ones down by the trees?"

"Yeah," I say.

"No, why? Did someone break them down? A sledgehammer to that old wood might be doing them a favor."

"No, they're, uh . . . they've been sanded and painted. The entire picnic area had a makeover. Slate rocks are cleaned, lights restrung. Overgrown trees cut back and pruned. It looks . . ." I swallow back my emotion. "It looks like it used to, like when I'd go down there with Grandma Joan—"

"And cross-stitch," Jaz finishes for me.

"Yeah. You didn't have anything to do with it?"

"No." She wipes at her forehead with the back of her hand. "I'm kind of knee deep in helping you with the lobby and running the bar. I wish I could have pulled that off for you, but it wasn't me."

I glance up at the stairs. "It's not Sully, is it?"

"No way." Jaz shakes her head. "I'd like to think that he could handle a project like that, but you saw him when he tried to repair the fence; he just doesn't have the mental capacity to take on repairs or construction. He forgets what he's doing."

"Yeah, I know." I kick at the carpet. "The bench that Sully likes to sit on is fixed as well. I wonder if my dads sent someone up here to get some work done and forgot to mention it."

"That's probably the truth, actually," Jaz says. "But ask them later, because we're on borrowed time."

She's right. We are, so I push the picnic tables to the back of my mind and tackle the carpet with her.

❖ ❖ ❖

"Push."

"I am pushing," Jaz grunts.

"Push harder."

"*You* push harder," she yaps right before she falls to the floor and takes a rest. "We should have cut it into pieces. I told you one giant roll would be too much for us."

"I thought you just wanted to slash the carpet—I didn't know there was a point behind it." I join her on the floor, our rolled-up old carpet half in the front lobby door, half out.

"I did want to slash something, but there was also a point to it. Want me to call Tank? See if he can round up some hands to help us?"

I shake my head. "I don't want to bother him."

Just then the back door to the lobby opens, and Sawyer walks in, sweaty, shirtless, and looking slightly dirty, water bottle in hand. How much does this guy work out?

I swear, every time I see him, he's sweaty, shirtless, and needing a refill on his drink.

Granted, he has an impressively lean body, so his hard work is paying off, but sheesh, doesn't he have anything else to do? Maybe write another movie or something?

He stops and takes us in, his eyes falling to the carpet and then rising back to us. "Need some help?"

"No," I say, waving my hand. "We're good."

"Are you insane?" Jaz asks. "As much as it pains me to ask Julia for some help, we need it. And look, he has muscles, muscles we could desperately use right now."

"I don't mind," he says, putting his water bottle down and walking over to us. He examines the rolled-up carpet and hops on top of it, walking the length until he's outside and jumping off the end. "You're stuck on some uneven concrete over here. I'll pull from here, and you push. Ready?"

"You really don't have to help," I say. I know what an outsider looking in must think—*Uh, hello, lady, take the man's help*—but it feels weird. For one, he's a guest, and guests shouldn't be helping with anything when it comes to the cabins. But two, we have an awkward history. I know we spoke about it, and he apologized, but I don't know . . . I just don't want him thinking I need help—though it's evident I do. There's something about saving face in front of a person who blatantly didn't think you were important enough to spend an evening with.

"Yes, he does need to help," Jaz counters. "It's the least he can do, since we didn't leave him out in the elements the day he arrived. Now stop being stubborn, and let him help us."

Sawyer peeks his head up and smiles at me. "Yeah, Fallon, stop being stubborn and let me help you."

"Hey." Jaz points a finger at him. "I want it to be known, we are not becoming friendly because we happen to agree on one thing."

He holds his hands up in defense. "I wouldn't even consider it."

"Good. Now that we have that established, let's get this musty carpet out of here."

Even though I don't want to rely on Sawyer for help, I scramble to my feet, and on three, Jaz and I push while he pulls. In seconds, the carpet is out of the main lobby and settled in the corner of the parking lot, ready for Tank to pick it up later this week and take it to the recycling plant.

"Thank God that thing is out of the way," Jaz says. "Good job, Julia. Now we just have to lay down the floor before the bar opens tonight. No biggie."

"We have a lot to do," I say to Sawyer, ready for him to take his sweaty body and leave. "Thank you for your help."

He glances at the lobby and then back at us. "Do you need some assistance?"

Jaz holds up her hand. "I think two incompetent people is better than three—we're good."

"Who says I'm incompetent?" Sawyer asks.

Jaz props one hand on her hip and gives him a slow once-over. "You're telling me your frilly Hollywood ass can lay down some floor?"

"You can do anything if you put your mind to it," Sawyer says with a smirk.

"Ugh, you're annoying." Jaz moves past him into the lobby and then starts cleaning up all the carpet staples.

I turn to Sawyer. "We, uh, we got it handled. I watched some YouTube videos, and Sully will come supervise us in a few."

"Okay," he says as we walk into the lobby. "But if you need help, you know where to find me."

"Thank you—but just enjoy your stay. Uh, we have some picnic tables on the south end of the property that might be an inspiring place for you to write—you know, when you're done with your workout."

A slow smile plays at his lips. "I'll be sure to check it out. Thanks."

When he turns away to refill his water bottle, my eyes travel the length of his back, the contours of his muscles that run all the way down to the light curve of his ass. Just above the low-riding waistband of his shorts are two dimples that catch my attention more than they should. They're subtle but just pronounced enough to make me wonder, for an insane moment, what it would feel like to run my fingers over them.

When he's done refilling, he doesn't bother turning back around to say goodbye. Instead, with the palm of his hand he pushes against the back door and exits—the whole time, I watch the ripple and pull of his back muscles.

"Stare a little longer, why don't you," Jaz says, startling me.

"I'm not staring," I say as I spin back around toward her, but I can feel a blushing stain on my cheeks.

And Jaz notices it.

She scoffs. "Okay . . ."

Jaz: How's the floor coming along?

Fallon: Why did I think I could do this? I know nothing about renovating a house, let alone laying down floors.

Jaz: That bad?

Fallon: After you left, I had to tear up an entire row because I didn't install it correctly. I'm about to throw in the towel.

Jaz: Take a break, come grab a drink. We can start again tomorrow.

I glance at the clock. Seven at night. I have two more hours to actually get some of the floor down, two hours before I pass out in my bed. If I want to finish up these renovations—and get those reservations—then

I need to finish this. Taking a break isn't an option at this point. I need to push and keep pushing when I think I can't push anymore.

Push through the frustration.

Push through the sore hands.

Push through the fact that I really have no clue what the hell I am doing most of the time.

Fallon: Thanks, but I'm going to try to figure this out.

Jaz: Have you had dinner?

Fallon: No. Not yet.

Jaz: I'm going to call up Rigatoni Roy and send a pizza your way. Sausage and onions?

Fallon: You're the best, thank you. How's Sully?

Jaz: Hanging with Tank and the boys. He's in his element. Really happy, actually. Tank was telling me he's seen a noticeable change in him lately, like he isn't grumpy all the time.

Fallon: I've noticed the same thing. I'm happy he's having fun. Okay, back to work.

Jaz: Want me to see if someone can take over the bar so I can come help?

Fallon: No, I'm good. Might be better if I try to figure this out myself. I have a bunch of cabins that need new floors as well, so I better get the hang of it. I'll talk to you later.

Jaz: Okay, pizza is ordered.

Fallon: Thank you.

I set my phone down and scan the new flooring. Sully picked it out from a few samples I showed him. At first, he didn't understand why we needed new flooring, but when I showed him his design book and the renovations he had wanted to make, he understood. It's pretty, some natural-looking grains on a luxury vinyl flooring—it's extremely durable and the latest fad in construction. But if you don't know what you're doing, it's a pain in the ass to attempt to install. "You can do this, Fallon," I whisper just as Sawyer walks into the lobby, sweaty once again and ready to fill up his water bottle.

Talk about revenge body.

It's the only reason I can think of for why he'd be working out as much as he is—to get back at Annalisa and Simon. A droplet of sweat rolls down the front of his chest, between his pecs that are lightly sprinkled with trimmed hair, and then down his stomach. Peter is starting to develop abs, and I know it's something he's been working on—but Sawyer . . . I'm pretty sure the man was born with definition, because there's no looking for them; they're in your face, plain as day.

"Hey," he says, looking at the two pathetic rows of flooring. I'm sure anyone else would be much further along by now. "How's it, uh, going?"

"Well, you know, it's going." I attempt casual, like this is how I intended the floors to be installed . . . one plank every hour. I nod toward his bare chest. "Enjoy another workout?"

He glances down at himself and then back up. "Yeah." He leaves it at that. It almost feels like there's more behind that "yeah," but he's not sharing, and there's no way I'm willing to ask. He walks up to me, and I expect to smell sweat, but I'm consumed by the fresh soap scent clinging to him. How is that even possible? "Seems like you have a good two rows done."

"Yeah, I had a third, but messed it up and took it out."

He nods. "Well, I'm available if you need some help."

"Oh, that's okay—"

"Fallon." He gives me a knowing look. "Let me help you. You clearly want to get this done tonight or else you'd have called it a night already. I've laid down quite a few floors in my lifetime. We can have this done in an hour and a half."

I don't want his help.

I don't want him seeing me like this—pathetic.

Helpless.

Lacking ability.

I want him to see me as a well-put-together woman, the kind of woman he should have paid attention to on our date. I know I say I'm over the whole blind date thing, and I am, but that doesn't mean I don't want him to see me thriving and regret, just a little bit, the way he treated me, to maybe even see me as the one that got away.

Sitting in the middle of subflooring, planks of wood scattered about, doesn't necessarily give off that kind of vibe.

I want him to just go back to his little workout world and leave me alone, but . . . God, I'm desperate. If I finish this floor tonight, that'll mean I can move furniture back in and start redecorating. Then I can take pictures and add them to the website. So much comes down to these damn floors.

Would it be so terrible if I had him help me?

Yes, it would be terrible. Not that it's a competition, but I feel like I have the upper hand in our nonrelationship. Seeing him wasted and having to drag him through the cabins, passed out, really gave me that edge. Asking him for help . . . well, that would put us on an even playing field.

But God, look at this place: there's no way I'll finish this tonight—I'll be lucky if I can get at most another two rows done by myself.

I roll my teeth over my bottom lip as I take in a deep breath.

Crap . . . am I really going to ask him for help?

I said I'd do anything to keep these cabins . . .

"You really think we can get this done tonight?"

"Easily."

He seems so confident, like he truly believes we'll be able to get this done. And for some inexplicable reason, I believe him.

I'm so desperate at this point to move these renovations along that I'm willing to believe anything.

"Well, if you don't mind, I could use some help. I can take some nights off your bill as compensation."

"Don't even worry about it. Gives me something to do other than sulk in my cabin." He picks up a board. "Shall we?"

Sulking in his cabin? Maybe that's why he's always shirtless and working out.

"I guess so."

Sawyer takes charge and puts me at the saw. He calls out measurements, and I cut the boards before handing them off to him and then watching in fascination as he lines them up and snaps them in place. He works fast, laying them down, hammering the grooves into place, and moving on to the next. In a few minutes, we've expanded to two more rows, a two-person assembly line that works flawlessly.

"Wow, you were right: we could get this done pretty fast."

"Just have to have the right person at the right job." He winks.

And that one wink is like an aphrodisiac as it makes my heart skip a beat. A feeling I wasn't expecting at all, a feeling that is incredibly unsettling.

"Uh, yeah," I say awkwardly. *Get it together, Fallon. It was a wink, not like he called you beautiful or stripped you down nude.* "It helps when you're not fighting over what music to play either."

He chuckles. "You mean that heavy metal stuff that I heard blaring from the lobby earlier wasn't your choice?"

"I prefer for my ears not to bleed when I listen to music." I adjust the safety glasses on my face before cutting a piece of flooring. Sawyer swiftly moves on his knees, grabs it, and lays it down.

"What would be your choice of music?" he asks.

"My first choice would be the best of the fifties. But Jaz would cut her ears off before listening to that."

"Fifties, huh?" Sawyer asks. "There's some beautiful nostalgia to listening to music from the fifties. The era where the electric guitar boomed, Elvis became king, and doo-wop revolutionized jazz and the blues. And it still sounds so innocent, even though I'm well aware there's nothing innocent to the era. But you can't help but feel how pure it is."

Wow, he knows his music—wasn't prepared for that kind of answer. I guess I just assumed he was into writing and that was it. What a one-dimensional assessment. Clearly, he'd have other interests.

"The fifties also meant the death of the classic crooner—a loss Sully didn't take lightly. But anyway, Jaz vetoed my selection rather quickly when I asked Alexa to shuffle my fifties playlist. It doesn't help that the first song she played was an old twangy country song."

Sawyer winces. "Yeah, you're not going to win over anyone with that choice." He hands me the measurements he needs on a piece of paper—we've found that's easier than him saying them out loud, which was getting confusing. While I cut, he starts lining up the next row. "When you're not listening to the best of the fifties, what are you listening to?"

I bite my lip. "The best of the sixties."

He chuckles. "So, you're a classic kind of listener."

"Jaz and Peter both think I need help. I don't know, I just grew up listening to it here at the cabins with my grandparents, and it feels wrong to listen to anything else, you know?"

"Makes sense. It's more than nostalgic for you—the music, the lyrics actually mean something."

"Yeah," I say, feeling weird because . . . am I actually having a conversation with Sawyer? A legit conversation. I'm not sure we've ever had one of these. And I'm actually enjoying it.

Not only are we having a conversation that doesn't involve being overly polite just to move on with our day, but he actually gets me—and that freaks me out. The man who once found his phone more interesting than me can now understand my music choice in just a few minutes. I'm not sure what to think about that.

"What would you be listening to?" I ask.

He snaps in a few boards. "I tend to go on artist binges, not necessarily by genre or era."

"Okay, so who are you bingeing right now?"

He shakes his head. "I can't tell you that."

"Why not?"

He hands me back the piece of paper. "Because it's embarrassing, and I think I've embarrassed myself in front of you enough for a lifetime."

"What music could possibly be embarrassing?" I glance at the paper and cut more boards.

"Trust me, it's embarrassing."

"Try me."

Still kneeling, he looks up at me from his spot on the floor. I watch him waver between telling me and not telling me, but then he lets out a resigned sigh. "Wilson Phillips."

A snort pops out of me, and I cover my nose. "Wilson Phillips, as in the all-female pop group known for singing 'Hold On'? They have more than one song?"

He narrows his eyes. "That's offensive. Of course they have more than one song."

"Uh-huh, and how many times a day do you listen to 'Hold On'?"

"Enough," he answers, avoiding my gaze. I let out a shocked laugh.

"How many?"

He lifts from the floor and walks toward me, a smile playing at his lips. "At least five." A loud laugh falls past my lips as he rests his hands on the table where I've laid down my saw. "Do not tell Jaz that—it's bad enough she calls me Julia."

"Oh . . . there's no way I can't tell her. I'm sorry in advance."

"I'd like to say you're cruel, but in a weird way, I understand your need to share. It's not the kind of information you can hold close to your heart."

"It is not," I say. "It's something that needs to be passed around. Vital information."

He takes a sip from his water bottle and then removes the wood from my saw table. "I should have never said anything."

"No, you shouldn't have. But I preyed on the weak, and I'm not even upset about it."

"I can tell from the wide grin on your face." As he walks back to his spot on the floor, he twists his baseball cap around so it's backward on his head and sticks the pencil he's using up into the hat, on the side of his face, as he snaps more boards in.

While he's crouched on the floor, my eyes wander to the corded muscles in his forearms, the way they ripple with every board he puts in place. I don't recall Sawyer being this . . . muscular on our date. Then again, I don't recall much of him that night.

He looks so at ease with what he's doing. I know he said he's done this before, but I wasn't expecting for him to be so quick, so efficient. I also wasn't expecting him to be this easy to talk to. When I said I could use his help, I was mentally prepared for another silent night from him, but when he started asking questions, bantering back and forth with ease, I immediately felt comfortable. Color me surprised.

We'll be done tonight, and that is a huge weight off my shoulders. It means I can move forward with finishing the lobby and then start on the cabins. Just one step closer to saving everything.

I hate to admit it, but . . . letting him help was a great idea. Who knows, maybe I'll be able to pull through these renovations a lot faster than I expected.

❖ ❖ ❖

Fallon: <picture> Floors are done.

Jaz: What the actual hell? Holy shit, Fallon. What kind of wizardry did you do to pull this off?

Fallon: Julia walked in and asked if I needed help. Turns out, he's pretty good at laying floor down.

Jaz: Wait . . . Julia did that?

Fallon: He did.

Jaz: Oh, look at him being useful. Why is that irritating?

Fallon: I found it irritating too. I think it's because we saw him at his worst, so we expect him to be that same guy, drunk and barely able to walk.

Jaz: That feels right. Wow, so what does that mean for tomorrow?

Fallon: New furniture assembly and decorating. Bring your camera so we can take pictures.

Jaz: Done. I'm impressed. Maybe next time I see Julia, I'll ease up a bit.

Fallon: Oh, get this, his current music binge is Wilson Phillips.

Jaz: Scratch that, there's no way I can't give him shit for that.

Fallon: He's expecting it.

Chapter Ten
SAWYER

"Where are you off to, boy?" Sully calls out as he heads down the path toward my cabin.

I twist my hat so it's sitting properly on my head—don't need to be yelled at again. "Headed off to get some breakfast, then the hardware store."

"Where are you going for breakfast?"

"Uh, I was just going to grab something at the Whistling Kettle."

"A muffin isn't going to get you through the manual labor I have in store for you today. Let's go to Strawberry Fields." He takes me by the arm and pushes me toward the path between the cabins that leads out to the main street.

"Uh, are you sure?"

"Yes, that's where I was headed anyway. The boys are meeting me there."

"Okay, if you don't mind me imposing."

"Would it be imposing if I told you to come? Stop making a fuss and walk."

"Sure thing," I answer, holding back my smile.

I'm pretty intrigued at the prospect of breakfast. I haven't explored many of the restaurants here because I've been too exhausted to do anything other than eat a few protein bars before passing out.

And this morning, I knew I needed a change from my usual protein bar. My body is aching. I spent all day yesterday cleaning up the horseshoe pits. They were overgrown with grass and weeds, and it took a trusty sharp-edged shovel to cut through the grass. When I went to go get more water, I didn't expect to see Fallon by herself, attempting to install the lobby floor. There was no way I could go pass out in my cabin, knowing she was attempting that on her own, so I stayed.

And now my knees and back are screaming at me.

Looks like doing renovations at thirty-five is very different from doing them at twenty-five.

"What kind of food does Strawberry Fields have?" I ask, trudging beside him down the pine tree–lined path.

"Regular food. Why?" Sully asks.

Okay . . .

"What's your favorite thing to order?"

"What's it to you?" Sully looks over at me as we step onto the sidewalk that runs parallel to the main road.

There is absolutely no traffic this morning, not a single car as we cross the street. The town is one giant circle, with Strawberry Lake at its center. I've learned you either have a business on the outside circle—the other side of the road—or the inside, which is where the cabins are, offering guests a beautiful lake view. Most of the eateries are on the outer circle. Behind them are either a forest of pines or sheer, deadly cliffs.

"Just trying to think about what I should get."

"That's what menus are for."

Well, there goes my attempt at a conversation.

We walk the rest of the way in silence, and when we reach the diner, Tank and a man I don't know are standing outside, waiting.

Sully gives them a wave. "Hope you don't mind I brought Phil with me." Sully motions to me.

Phil?

Is that what he thinks my name is?

"Phil, nice to meet you," Tank says as he shakes my hand. "I'm Tank and this is Roy. He owns Rigatoni Roy's, the best Italian restaurant in the mountains."

Rigatoni Roy, your quintessential animated Italian man. What do I mean by that? Imagine what every Italian restaurant owner in the movies looks like. Round, short, with a large black mustache that extends past his rosy cherub cheeks. That's Roy, but instead of black hair, his is peppered with gray.

He's what I'd call a zany side character who brings some comic relief to intense situations. A character who adds to the dynamics of the world-building, really pulling readers into the small-town feel.

"Nice to meet you, Phil."

"Pleasure is all mine."

"Enough with the pleasantries." Sully pushes past us and enters the diner with Roy. "I'm hungry."

I start to follow, but Tank stops me with a hand to my shoulder. "Did you tell him your name was Phil?"

"No." I shake my head. "Who the hell is Phil?"

Tank nods slowly. "His brother, who passed away quite a few years back." Tank pulls on the back of his neck. "Just go with it."

"Are you sure? Shouldn't we correct him?"

Tank twists the end of his mustache. "Probably, to help him understand better, but I just don't have it in me. I know Fallon spends her time telling him the truth, but he's . . . he's my best friend; I can't watch the heartbreak in his eyes. The sadness. I know there aren't many more months I might have with him, so I keep it simple and just go with what he's saying."

"Understood," I say. "I guess I'm Phil."

I'm not entirely comfortable with pretending to be someone I'm not, but then again, Tank is his best friend, and he knows what's best for Sully—who am I to try to step in and make a change to what works for them?

"Thank you," Tank says in a gruff voice, and then we walk into the restaurant, only for me to stop dead in the doorway, my body refusing to take another step toward the horrifying sight in front of me.

What the actual living . . . hell.

Wall to wall, the restaurant is lined in floor-to-ceiling shelved cases, stuffed full of troll dolls.

The old nineties trolls.

The ones that will give you nightmares with their bulgy eyes, gem belly buttons, and fetus-like fingers and toes. With tall hair in every color of the rainbow, their scrunched faces are twisted into identical, spine-tingling grins that can freeze even the hardiest of souls into a Popsicle of fear.

I'm pretty open-minded when it comes to my flavor of decor, but I can tell you right now, this motif is not working for me.

Concern is etched on Roy's face as he sidles up next to me. "It's shocking at first," he whispers, "but as long as you don't look them in the eye, they won't haunt you in your sleep." He claps me on the back and directs me toward the booth in the back of the diner where Tank has taken a seat with Sully.

Easier said than done. When their eyes follow you as you walk, it's hard not to look at them . . .

Roy gestures for me to slide into the booth first, but I shake my head, staring at the troll-encrusted wall. "I can't sit next to those things." There's no way in hell I'm going to be trapped in the booth. I'm going to require a slick exit—an old one-two step straight to the door.

"Afraid they'll break through the plexiglass and try to eat your food?" Roy asks with a smile.

"Yeah," I answer honestly. I can see it now: I'm midway through my breakfast and feel a little tappity-tap on my arm, only to find the one wearing clown pants standing like the devil on my shoulder, grinning.

Fuck. No.

Roy lets out a good, hearty laugh—the type of laugh that I know is his signature—and then he slips into the booth, his rotund belly sliding along the table. I slide in after him, but instead of looking around the diner, getting a feel for it, like I normally would for world-building research, I keep my eyes focused on the menu.

"What's wrong with you?" Sully asks.

"The trolls freak him out," Roy answers.

"Oh, for crying out loud. They're dolls, Phil. You're telling me you're afraid of some little dolls?"

Yes . . . yes, I am.

I swallow hard. "No, just, uh, shocked is all. I wasn't expecting the restaurant to be decorated like this when I walked in. Doesn't give off the troll vibe from outside."

"Faye has been working on this collection for years," Tank says. "She's going to open a museum in the back and charge admission."

Who the hell would pay to see more of this chilling display?

"There are more trolls?" I ask.

"Boxes," Roy says. "She's a fanatic. It's not just dolls but memorabilia as well. I like that she collects them. Shows her freaky side." He waggles his eyebrows and twists his salt-and-pepper mustache. I nearly throw up in my mouth.

"Hello, sirs," a woman says as she sidles up next to us, pen poised on a piece of paper. Wearing a floral-print peasant dress, she looks like she was plucked from the nineteenth century and plopped in the middle of this mountain town. Her thin gray hair is in a loose bun on the top of her head, with little wisps framing her face, while silver-framed glasses sit perched on the tip of her nose.

She could easily pass herself off as an angry schoolteacher, the one in the story who puts everyone in their place while wielding a wooden ruler—a unique character who doesn't have much of a role in the main plot other than to pop in with little anecdotes here and there.

But her straitlaced, buttoned-up appearance appeals to me in a storytelling kind of way, and I make a mental note to remember her. If I weren't sitting with Tank, Sully, and Roy, I'd pull out my phone and make notes—just like I used to when I first came to LA.

Huh, when was the last time I had the urge to write something down like that? A characteristic that sparks a thought in my head? Not in a while, that's for sure. Wow, I might actually be getting back—albeit slowly—my writing mojo.

Perhaps later today, after I help out Sully, I'll write down a few notes about the weathered waitress . . . as for the troll restaurant, I'll save that for the thrillers I have stored away. But this lady brings a lot of character to the table herself. She's a curmudgeon behind the counter, but she just might be a useful source of knowledge when it comes to love.

Hmm, just like Sully.

"What would you like?" she asks, running her tongue over the corner of her mouth.

"Good morning, Faye," Roy says, leaning close to me and batting his eyelashes.

He smells like garlic.

And tomatoes.

The man is a walking Italian dish.

Wait . . . *this* is Faye?

I give her one more once-over. This is the troll lover? Never in my wildest dreams would I picture the crazed troll collector to be a background actor from *Bridgerton* serving up hash browns. The owner in my mind would be a flamboyant woman with neon-colored hair—two inches of roots due to not having enough time to get to the salon—with the wardrobe specifically plucked from *Back to the Future Part II*, Marty McFly rainbow cap and all.

"Good morning," Faye says, chin held high.

"Have you met Phil?" Roy asks, nudging me with his shoulder.

"I don't believe I've had the pleasure of meeting our newest resident." She curtsies. "Pleasure. I'm sure you're finding your new dwellings satisfactory." Not sure I've ever met someone so proper—with a freaky side to them.

"I am," I say. "Thank you—"

"Enough with this wishy-washy conversation," Sully says grumpily. "Faye, the usual." He hands his menu off.

"The usual for me as well," Tank says, following suit.

"And me," Roy says, and then all eyes fall on me as if they expect something from me, as if I shouldn't even bother looking at the menu either.

Cautiously, I say, "Uh . . . the usual for me as well."

Tank offers me a nod of approval as Faye takes my menu.

"Very well. I'll be back shortly. Gladys will be around with coffee." With a curt nod, she takes off.

"What's the usual?" I ask, looking around the table with trepidation.

Tank smiles. "You'll see."

❖　❖　❖

I'm going to throw up, right here, at the table. For all the trolls to see— and I know their eyes are on me. I can feel them.

There is no way in hell I can eat this last bite.

I can't possibly fit it in my stomach. This measly one-inch-by-one-inch piece of pancake.

But as I stare down at the last bite on my fork, I feel all three men watching me carefully to see if I'll "buck up" and join them in finishing their plates, a show of respect to the cook.

But . . . fuck, I really don't think I can. I can feel my breakfast at the base of my throat, waiting to come back up any second.

Let me paint you a little picture. "The usual" is not usual by any circumstances. When Faye came over with our plates, it was as if she unloaded a truck, and a wave of plates fanned out across our table. Two large pancakes, two scrambled eggs, two links of sausage, two pieces of bacon, two pieces of ham, hash browns, two slices of buttered toast with a side of jam, and a cut-up banana.

When my plate was set down in front of me, Tank tapped my plate with his fork and shot me a knowing look. "You're expected to eat all of that."

And he wasn't kidding. Sully watched me intently to make sure I took down every last bite. How he did it, I have no clue. I didn't think old people could eat that much, but he shoveled it down no problem. Meanwhile, here I am, sweating, bulging at the waistline of my pants, and ready to curl into a ball on Roy's lap and cry myself into a food coma.

Roy lifts his dirty napkin to my face and blots my forehead. I don't have it in me to care.

"There, there, newbie. Take deep breaths. You'll make it through this."

I really don't think I will.

"Oh, for crying out loud," Sully snaps. "Stop being dramatic and take the last bite."

Please, Jesus . . . God . . . anyone who wants to listen to me, don't let me throw up on this table, just let me get through this last bite, say some goodbyes, so I can quietly embarrass myself behind a dumpster. Just not at this table, with these men, who I know won't let me live it down.

With a deep breath, I take the last bite as a wave of sweat breaks out on the back of my neck.

Chew, man.

Just chew and breathe.

When I finally swallow, Tank says, "Welcome to the breakfast club." He says that as if it's an accomplishment. Gluttony at the troll parlor feels more like a punishment.

I can guarantee you, this is not a club I want to be a part of—not if I have to order this every time.

I take a sip of water and am setting my glass down just as Faye rips the check off her pad and sets it on the table. Tank picks it up and then offers it to me with a smile. "Newbie buys."

And before I know what's happening, Tank is getting out of the booth, as well as Sully, and Roy is pushing at me to get up as well. I slide out, allowing Roy to leave, and when I sit back down—because Lord above, I need a second before I start moving—they all look down at me with a smile.

"Thanks for breakfast, Phil." Roy claps me on the back, shooting my body forward and my face inches away from my cleaned plate, where only a faded streak of egg yolk mixed with syrup remains. My stomach gurgles.

Please . . . not here, anywhere but here.

"See you around," Tank says. And together, they stride past the rows of demonic trolls and out of the diner, leaving me to grip the table with both hands and pray to the breakfast gods that I can hold it together.

I glance down at the check, and my eyes nearly bug out of their sockets. Over one hundred dollars.

What the actual hell?

Not that I can't afford it, but I'm sitting in the middle of the mountains, in an old western false-front building surrounded by troll dolls— isn't the food supposed to be cheap in a place like this?

The decor *screams* cheap.

"Stiffed you with the bill?" Faye says. "You must have really made an impression for them to do that." She pats me on the shoulder. "I think you made some friends. Welcome to Canoodle."

And then she walks away to top off some more coffee mugs.

If this is what friendship is in Canoodle, I'm not sure I'm ready for it.

❖   ❖   ❖

Bugs drone through the still, scorching air as I collapse onto the grass and stare up at the overhang of pine trees, providing me much-needed shade.

It's so freaking hot today.

I tamp my right hand around the grass, looking for my water bottle, and when I find it, I open the top and squirt myself with water that I filled up about twenty minutes ago. When I walked into the lobby earlier, I found Fallon and Jaz on the floor, assembling furniture. When I asked if they wanted help, Jaz told me to turn up Wilson Phillips and beat it—while Fallon shot me a somewhat apologetic look.

I took that as a no.

While I filled up my water bottle, I heard Fallon hiss at Jaz to be nice, and as I started to leave, she called out a thank-you for the offer. Perhaps I made some sort of an impact last night. I don't need to be best friends with her, but I do want her to know I'm a good person, that I'm not the narcissistic man she once met in Palm Springs at the Golden Star.

I hate leaving a bad impression on people, although . . . isn't that what I did at the wedding? Everyone there got the worst impression of me ever.

And so did the world.

I squirt my face with more water when my cheeks heat up at the thought of what I did.

Now that I've had a moment to cool down from Annalisa and Simon's dramatics, I'll admit that what I did was embarrassing. Something I'd write about but never do. It's the kind of exit I'd write into a scene to hook the audience, to get them invested in the outcome, but nothing I'd ever do in real life.

So why did I do it?

Fed up?

Couldn't take it anymore?

Jealous of the fact that I was supposed to be the one who proposed to Annalisa, not Simon?

Like I said before . . . I completely snapped. All the pressure, the hurt, the anger, built up to the last moment, and instead of acting like the professional I've always prided myself on being, I chose the low road. What I thought was a moment of justice has only tarnished my reputation. Audiences and execs are only hearing one side of that story, after all. And that side is pretty damn damaging.

And now I'm trying to navigate through the repercussions.

Andy emailed me yesterday, asking me about ideas for my next pitch. I tossed him another thriller about a zombie groomsman who disrupts his ex-girlfriend's wedding, bites the best man, and together, they turn the entire wedding party into a zombie platoon, taking Hollywood by storm. Andy told me to stop fucking around.

I don't know, it felt like a good idea at the time. I told him there was romance in it, unrequited love between the zombie groomsman and the woman trying to kill him and save the world.

Still didn't work.

It's not like I don't enjoy writing romance, because I do. There's something so special about coming up with a meet cute and making it unique. About building a loving relationship through friendship. Or turning an enemies-to-lovers scenario into a truly beautiful love affair. I've always been a romantic—thanks to my parents, who taught me to love the idea of love by setting a beautiful and caring example with their marriage.

But it's hard to write romance, to write anything, when you feel so . . . lost.

"Always lazing about," Sully says, cutting through my thoughts.

I didn't even hear him approach.

I lift up from my spot on the grass and prop myself up on my elbows.

"Just letting the cement dry," I say. "Should be done tonight."

Sully walks around the horseshoe courts and examines them.

Two horseshoe courts with pits in dirt and grass in between. They've been cleaned up by yours truly to reveal their true rectangular shape. What I thought was going to be an easy project turned into an absolute nightmare because I spent a decent amount of time chopping into the overgrown grass and re-forming the pits. And because it was all so old, I had to redo the iron rods in the ground, reinforcing them with cement that I had to wheel down with a janky wheelbarrow. It took a lot more effort than expected, and now that the poles are set, I'm ready to call it quits.

"Looks decent," Sully says. "But what about the benches?" He gestures to a pile of wood I dumped off to the side of the courts.

"I plan on tackling that tomorrow," I answer.

He glances up at the sky and then down to his watch. "Plenty more time in the day to get these done."

Yeah, but after using every ounce of strength I had to consume that breakfast and then trying not to throw up while I whipped the wheelbarrow around the property, I'm completely toast.

"Not sure I have much left in the tank," I say.

Sully's eyes narrow. "Balderdash. You're young, now get to work. I'm not paying you to sit around."

Technically, you're not paying me at all.

Which doesn't matter to me. Not in the slightest. I've enjoyed keeping my hands busy. It's kept my mind off the negative press—just this morning, before breakfast, Roarick sent me an article claiming I'd been plotting to ruin Annalisa and Simon's wedding for the entire engagement. If that were the case, I'd at least have had a confetti cannon in my back pocket, ready to shoot off as I peaced out. And even though I'm grateful to focus on something other than the wedding and my screenplay, I'm ready to pass out. Last night's hard work, accompanied by a hellish breakfast and hard labor this morning . . . I'm toasted.

But I can sense that Sully is not going to let up, so I get up and walk over to the wood pile. I let out a deep breath. "What kind of benches are you thinking?"

"A bench, what is there to think about? You sit on it, there is a back. Simple."

I nod. "Okay, so like the ones around the lake."

"Yes," he says, and then the gruffness eases up as he adds, "like the bench my Joan and I sit on."

"Not a problem," I answer. "Do you, uh . . . do you want to help?"

He glances at the wood and then back at me. I can see some confusion in his eyes, but then he clears his throat. "I'll supervise and assist when needed."

Sully is a proud man, and I can sense that he wants to do this, to build, to work with his hands, but I also think he's confused and doesn't remember exactly what to do. I need to guide him but at the same time convince him that he's the one guiding me.

"Okay, so six feet long, correct?"

Sully lifts his chin. "That's correct."

"Okay, cool." I squat down to the wood and start moving the pieces around, then take out my measuring tape and start to measure the length. To my surprise, Sully gets down on the grass with me, and he holds the tape measure at one end. We spend the next few minutes measuring everything out before I pull out my trusty handheld saw and start cutting, my muscles aching the entire time.

"Joan helped me build a bench once," Sully says. "It was the first fight we ever had."

I chuckle. "Were you dating then?"

Sully shakes his head. "She was still with Earl at the time, but she was up in Canoodle, helping with some furniture. I asked her to help me with a bench, and she obliged. She thought I meant moving it, not building it. She was upset because it was a bench in one of the cabins, and she wondered why I didn't just buy it from her."

"Why didn't you?"

"Because." He smiles. "I thought that it could be a good project to do with her, something that would help us get closer." He chuckles. "I've never seen her so red in the cheeks, frustrated with me because I wouldn't let her do any of the cutting."

"Why not?" I asked.

"Because it was with a saw just like that." He points to my saw. "She was wearing a dress, and I didn't want her to get all sweaty. I knew she had a date later that night with Earl. Even though I really liked her, I respected her relationship and knew she'd be upset if she wasn't perfect for her date."

"So, you told her she wasn't allowed to use the saw, I'm guessing."

He nods and looks out toward the trees, his eyes wistful, daydreaming.

"She was furious with me. Asked if I thought a woman couldn't handle a saw."

"What did you say? Did you tread carefully?"

"Do I look like a man who treads carefully?"

I laugh. "No, but I wasn't sure if you eased up for Joan."

"I did not. I told her a woman like herself couldn't handle the saw."

"I can't imagine that went over well."

I finish cutting the last board and hand Sully a piece of sandpaper. Together, we sand down the raw edges of the wood.

"It didn't. She stormed away, and I chased after her. I apologized and told her I was protecting her. She shot back that she didn't need my protection, and I realized she really didn't. She is a very strong woman, you know."

He talks about her in the present tense, and it punctures my soul. I can't imagine living day in and day out, thinking the love of your life is still alive, only to find out she isn't. It would be devastating. Especially for Fallon, who has to break the news to him. Talk about a strong woman. Fallon must have learned it from Grandma Joan.

"She's very much like Fallon," Sully says, as if reading my thoughts. "You've met my granddaughter, right?"

Boy, have I.

I met her when I was not in the right mindset.

I was reacquainted with her when I was absolutely wasted.

And last night, I finally was able to converse with her, unguarded, without Jaz tormenting me. I got to experience a true moment with Fallon, and ever since I said good night to her—an awkward wave as I strode out back to my cabin—all I can think about is the dreamy smirk she wore when I told her about Wilson Phillips, or the gentle way she asked if I wanted to share the pizza that Jaz had delivered, or her genuine laugh that still seems to ring through my ears when the breeze dies down and the trees around me still their rustling branches.

I nod. "I have met her. She is very headstrong, determined."

Funny.

Loving.

An old soul.

"And beautiful." Sully looks up at me.

I swallow hard. "Yes, beautiful."

Really fucking beautiful. And that's not a lie. Fallon is quite beautiful. A natural beauty with her flawless skin and pouty pink lips that turn down when she's irritated, upset, or just thinking. But her looks aren't the only thing that make her beautiful in my eyes—it's her endless bravery for taking on the daunting task of redoing the cabins while caring for her ailing grandfather.

"You should ask her out on a date," Sully says.

I sputter out a cough.

"Um, she has a boyfriend—Peter."

Sully pauses, his eyes moving back and forth. "Ah, right. Peter," he says, and it's almost convincing.

After my first interaction with Sully, I fell down the internet rabbit hole, and from what I've read, people with Alzheimer's will at times pretend to know something, just to avoid the confusion, but they really have no idea what's going on.

From Sully's reaction, I can gather that's what's happening.

"They've been dating for a bit?" he asks.

"Uh, I think so." I shrug. "Not sure of the details."

He nods. "Well, if they break up, you should ask her out."

"Not sure I'm her type." I pick up another board and start to sand the edges.

Sully looks up at me and tilts his head to the side. "You might be right. Your crooked nose might not be what she's looking for."

It's not that fucking crooked. Jesus!

In Hollywood, they call it character. Haven't they heard of Owen Wilson?

Not everyone can be perfect.

I take a deep breath. "Well, good thing she has Peter then, huh?"

"I guess so. Although . . ." Sully nudges me with a piece of wood. "I do find you entertaining. I very well might like you better."

That puts a smile on my face.

I like you too, Sully.

I like you very much.

CHAPTER ELEVEN
FALLON

"Wow, it looks good in here," Sawyer says, walking into the lobby. "I love the pops of red."

"Thank you," I say, still surveying the sitting area that I just finished decorating.

The furniture took much longer to build than I was expecting, but once I remembered that I could use the electric drill to make things easier, that sped up the process. Jaz had to leave while I was building the last chair, but by then, we'd already hung a few pictures on the wall and some plaster taxidermy deer heads over the fireplace. Two black ones, a white one, and a red—they look modern, but cute, and a bit rustic at the same time.

The pictures we hung are shots Jaz took of the property, in black and white to go with the aesthetic. There's also a wedding picture of Sully and Grandma Joan sitting on their bench, looking out over the lake. I made sure to hang it so it's the first picture guests see when they arrive.

The red rug brings a vibrant pop of color against the neutral furniture and beautiful new floors while brightening up the space and tying everything together. When Sully walked in a half hour ago, he didn't say a word—just wrapped his arms around me. It brought tears to my eyes, knowing I was able to do this for him. The sleepless nights and long days were all worth it for that one moment.

"I'm sure you must be exhausted," Sawyer says.

I nod, acutely aware of my aching shoulders and sore back. "I'm going to eat and then pass out on my bed."

"Seems fair." He glances at me. "I, uh, I was headed to Beggar's Hole for a bite myself. Do you want to walk over together? Clearly, you don't have to eat dinner with me, but you know, if you want company walking over."

I'm too tired to even put thought into my answer. "Sure. Let me just run upstairs to change my shirt. Be right back."

"I'll clean up these boxes for you," he says.

"Oh, don't worry about that. I can do it later."

"Fallon, you're exhausted. It's no problem." He starts breaking down the furniture boxes and piling them on top of each other. I have no energy to fight him. I let it happen as I head up the stairs and go straight to my bedroom, where I catch a glimpse of myself in the mirror.

Dear God.

I look like a wretched witch.

My hair is barely hanging on to the ponytail it's in, my shirt is drenched, and there are pools of sweat under my arms.

Wow, Fallon, really attractive.

Not that I'm trying to look attractive in front of Sawyer, but I feel like there's a basic human standard I like to maintain. Given the fact that he's in a pair of khaki shorts and a clean white T-shirt, sporting a backward hat, I'd say he's living up to the standard and I'm failing spectacularly.

I move around my bedroom and bathroom quickly. I wet a towel—yup, that's the level I'm at—and wipe at my face, chest, and armpits. I fish out a clean shirt from my dresser, a simple Town of Canoodle shirt, and then I grab a baseball hat and slip it over my head, only to pull my hair through the back and tie it into a messy bun. Feeling slightly more human, I apply some lip balm and deodorant, then slip on my Birkenstocks and call it a day.

I'm about to head down the stairs when my phone beeps in the back of my jean shorts. I pull it out and see a text from Peter.

Peter: Not sure I can make it up this weekend. They need me to cover Bill's shift since his brother just passed away. I'm sorry, sweetie.

I feel a pang of regret as I take a seat on my bed.

Fallon: I understand. I can't say that I'm not disappointed though. I really wanted to make last weekend up to you.

He types back right away.

Peter: Trust me, I wanted nothing more than to see you this weekend. Let me see what I can do, okay?

Fallon: Okay, but I understand if you can't.

Peter: I guess it would be too much to see if you can come down here?

Fallon: I wish. I have twelve cabins to renovate. I promise though, soon. Once this is all over.

Peter: Holding you to that. I love you, Fallon.

I squeeze my lips together and type him back.

Fallon: Have a good night.

I pocket my phone and then head down the stairs to the lobby, where Sawyer is finishing up with the boxes and stacking them up against the wall near the door.

"Wasn't sure where you wanted these."

"That's actually perfect, right there. Thank you."

"Not a problem." The deconstructed boxes start to fall, and we quickly push them against the wall, shimmying them in at a better angle. "That should do it." He chuckles and then presses his hand to the top of his hat—that's when I notice his hands.

"Jeez, what happened to you?" I point.

He brings his hand into view and takes a look at it. Scrapes and cuts line the backs of his hands and his knuckles. When he turns his hands over, I gasp at the multiple blisters along his fingers.

"Oh my God, Sawyer. Is that from last night?"

"Nah," he says, stuffing his hands in his pockets. "Just some work I've been doing." He's very evasive, avoiding eye contact. He nods toward the door. "Ready to go?"

"Yeah." But I don't move; instead I stare at him, curious at his reaction. "Do you want any Band-Aids or anything? We have a first aid kit."

"I'm good. They're just some nicks. I'll be fine." He pushes the door and holds it open for me. Deciding not to push him, I walk through, catching a whiff of his soap, which reminds me how he can be a sweaty mess to look at but still smell fresh. I don't think I've ever met anyone like that. "So, are you happy with how the lobby turned out?" he asks as we make a right and head north toward Beggar's Hole.

"Very happy. Sully, my grandfather, actually came up with how it should be decorated. He's always loved red because it was the color my grandma Joan loved wearing. So, he wanted to make sure there were pops of red everywhere for her. He also loves plaid, so the wallpaper was his idea too."

"Surprising, it's very modern."

"I thought the same thing, but he's been watching shows on the DIY channel and told me that wallpaper is the new thing, so we worked on finding some that he thought would work."

"I like the buffalo plaid," Sawyer says, nodding thoughtfully. "It's fresh but also has a mountain feel to it, like Paul Bunyan's greeting you when you walk in."

I chuckle. "I never thought of it that way, but you're right. And of course, the floor came out so well—thanks again for the help on that."

"Not a problem. Gave me something to do."

"You keep saying that," I say, "but aren't you working right now? I thought I heard Jaz mention you had another movie under contract for Movieflix."

"She did, did she?" He raises an eyebrow. "Is she reading up about me?"

"When I say you're the most exciting thing to happen to Canoodle in a few years, I mean it."

"Aren't small towns supposed to be full of gossip and drama?"

"You'd think," I say, "but the biggest drama around here is when the mayor is elected every four years."

"Cat or dog, right?"

"Yup. It's a bloodbath. Not only is it the highest praise you can receive, to have your animal elected the mayor of the town, but you and your animal also get to live in the mayor's house. The best part is it has a pool, *and* it's the only place in town with one."

"A pool would feel pretty good right about now. I'm surprised the Cove doesn't have a pool."

"Sully planned on one." I let out a sigh. "He actually wanted to put one in that looked over the lake but never had the money for it."

"Shame, it would be a huge perk. There have been days where I've considered diving into the lake out of pure desperation."

"Yeah, not allowed. It's why the water is so clear—because we don't let anyone in it. It's just for the ducks and fish—and boats, twice a year, when we let them out on the water."

"Only twice a year?" he asks.

"Yup. Beginning of spring and end of fall. Canoodle is very adamant about preserving the natural habitat."

"I can tell," he says, glancing up at the trees. "It's why it's so beautiful here. But the cutthroat fight for the mayor's house makes sense. I'd adopt a pet just for a shot at the pool."

"Jaz swears she's going to do just that every time the election comes up because she wants to spend her summer days floating in the pool." I shake my head, half-exasperated, half-amused.

"When's the next election?"

"In a year. She has some time, but not too much. If she wants to make a name in the pet-owning community and make it seem like she adopted an animal out of the kindness of her heart and not just for the election, she needs to do it soon."

"I'm guessing she'd be a cat person."

I laugh. "Yup. She doesn't want an obedient dog, willing to please the minute you walk through the door. She wants a cat with a mean scowl—and ideally a penchant for flipping people off as they walk by."

He lets out a chuckle. "Sounds about right."

Together we cross the main street that circles around the town and walk up to Beggar's Hole. The parking lot is jam-packed, and as we head down the plank to the front door, the boisterous laughter from inside filters into the still night air.

"Wow, looks busy," he says.

"Which means Jaz is probably ready to toss herself off the deck. She likes the business, but she doesn't like to be run ragged."

Sawyer holds the door open for me, and I step inside the dimly lit bar, music thumping from the jukebox. Lo and behold, the place is stuffed full of people. The only seats left are two stools at the corner of the bar.

Which means . . . we'll have to sit next to each other.

And that knowledge shoots a bolt of anxiety through me. It seems so stupid, since we spent all last night laying down a floor and even sharing a pizza, but this feels different. This feels more . . . intimate.

The seating is in a corner. The stools are bumped up next to each other. And there will be eyes on us. Jaz's eyes. Not that she has anything to be concerned about. Sawyer is . . . well, he's not really a friend; he's just an acquaintance. Do I think he smells good right now? Of course. And do I think he looks charmingly handsome with a backward hat and a light shade of scruff on his jaw? I'd be dense not to. But I have a boyfriend who I . . . uh, who I care for very much. So, there's nothing to worry about. There's nothing wrong with eating a meal side by side.

"I hope you don't mind eating near me," I say. "Seems like there are only two seats left."

"Company could be worse," he says as we walk around crowded tables and over to the empty stools. Jaz spots me as we take a seat, then lets out a loud sigh as she walks over.

"Gather up some bail money—someone's getting stabbed tonight." I wouldn't expect Jaz to say anything else. And don't worry; she won't actually stab anyone. She sets down a coaster and then looks over at Sawyer. "What's Julia doing here?"

"We walked over together," I say with a pointed look, trying to make sure she knows it means nothing. Absolutely nothing.

But she's in a mood today—the busy bar has clearly frayed her nerves.

"You walked over together?" she asks, brows raised. "What is this? A friendship now? First the floor, now you're eating together?"

"We're not eating together," Sawyer says. "Just parallel to each other. And I wouldn't dream of starting a friendship with Fallon. Not

151

after the way I treated her on our blind date. I'm quite aware that I'm lucky she's even talking to me. This is merely a coincidence. No bond has been formed."

See, entirely platonic.

"Uh-huh," Jaz says, looking between us. "Answer me this—on your walk over, did you make each other laugh?"

Guilt swarms me, which is ridiculous. Sure, we had a conversation, and yeah, I laughed. A mere chuckle, nothing knee-slappingly funny that would make me buckle over.

"Aha!" Jaz points at me. "You did laugh."

"He said something funny." I shrug.

Jaz crosses her arms on top of the bar and leans forward. "It's Julia, for fuck's sake, Fallon. What could he have said that was possibly funny enough to laugh at?"

I glance at Sawyer and then back at my friend. "We were talking about the mayor elections and how you'd adopt an animal just for a chance to get into the mayor's mansion."

"Facts," Jaz says.

"And he guessed that you were a cat person. It made me laugh."

"Cheap laugh," Jaz declares, pushing off the bar. "It's obvious I'm a cat person. I want to work for an animal's love; I don't want it handed to me the minute I walk through the door. I want to spend an hour looking in every crevice of the house for my animal, only for it to hiss at me. That's the kind of animal I want."

"Sounds magical," Sawyer deadpans.

Jaz holds up her hand. "Your commentary is not needed. Just tell me what you want so I can move on."

"Waffle and some water," he says.

"Water?" she says, raising her brow. "When did you turn into a square?"

"When I had to be carried to a cabin by two women."

Jaz smirks. "Aw, my favorite memory of you, Julia." She turns to me. "Same as usual?"

"Yes, but no beer. Cranberry juice, please. I'm exhausted, and a beer is not what I need."

"Beer was created for exhausted people. That's what the term 'sitting down with an ice-cold beer' is for." She looks between us. "You don't come to a bar to not order alcoholic beverages."

"No, I came for the waffle," I say.

"Same," Sawyer adds.

"Okay, freaks." Jaz turns around and heads to the back of the bar to put in our order.

"Does she ever hold back?"

I shake my head. "Never."

"Well," he says, after a moment, his gaze pointed forward. "I guess I'll leave you be."

He stares down at his hands, and I can't help but chuckle. "You're seriously going to sit next to me and not talk? You don't think that'll be more awkward?"

"Just trying to give you your space is all," he responds. "I know you don't want to be friends, so, you know, I'm preventing that from happening."

And now I feel like a jerk. When I said I didn't want to be friends, it was because seeing him again put me in a weird place. I really wasn't mad about the whole blind date thing—I guess more embarrassed than anything. No one likes to be forgettable, so being around him brought back sour feelings from that night. But now that he's staying in Canoodle longer, and since I've gotten to know him a little more, the thought of talking doesn't seem so bad.

"Well, we don't have to become friends, but we can hold a conversation."

"I don't know," he says. "I can be pretty friendly. I don't want to sway you toward friendship." The charm in his voice eases the tension in my shoulders.

"I have a strong hold on my emotions. Trust me, you're not cracking the shell of friendship," I tease.

"That confident?" he asks.

"That confident."

He turns in his stool and faces me. "Okay, then let's have a conversation."

"Okay. What do you want to talk about?"

He shrugs. "Anything."

I give it some thought, and to be honest, I am curious about one thing . . .

"How's the fallout from the wedding?"

He winces. "Man, I shouldn't have said anything."

"We don't have to talk about it," I say quickly.

"Nah, it's fine. It's better to talk about it than to bottle it all up, I guess. And my brother can only hear so much of my bemoaning."

"Ooooh, bemoaning, it has to be good."

"Let's just say, things have not been going well. The media is eating up Annalisa and Simon's sob stories, to the point that I saw they were offered a spot on a TV show to throw a whole new wedding, one that isn't disrupted by their best man. I think it's called *Wedding Redo* or something like that. Movieflix, who I'm under contract with, pretty much thinks I'm Judas at this point. They're holding me to my contract of giving them another movie script, but they refuse to let me pitch any genres other than romance."

"And I'm assuming romance is the last thing on your mind at the moment."

"Very true. But they aren't letting up, so I've been trying to come up with some ideas. I'm falling short, though, and the ideas I do come up with all end up with a murder twist, so that's not great."

"Jaz would love it."

He chuckles. "I'm sure she would." He lets out a deep sigh. "It'll come to me at some point. Ideas always do, especially when I least expect them, and they're usually environment driven."

"What does that mean?" I lean forward, my curiosity getting the better of me.

"Meaning I get my best ideas from observing the people around me. My big movie break actually came from a small town in Maine called Port Snow. I was visiting my aunt in Pottsmouth."

"Pottsmouth? That's a name of a town?"

"Yes, very unfortunate, and she was telling me about this gift shop, the Lobster Landing, that has the best fudge on the East Coast. She told me I had to try some, so we took a short drive over to Port Snow and spent the day there." He smiles at the memory. "We sat by the harbor and had crab-cake sandwiches from a food truck called Jake's Cakes, picked up some famous mustard from the local deli, and then we ate way too much fudge from the Lobster Landing while we both sported a lobster claw oven mitt. It was a great day. But when I was there, I saw Lovemark was filming a small-town romance at a big white manor that was tucked away, practically hidden in the trees surrounding the town. I was fascinated and started researching when I got home. I found out that Port Snow is really popular for small-town movie locations—and then an article popped up, and I came across the Knightly family."

"Who are they?"

"They own the Lobster Landing. But there was this rumor spread around town that the four Knightly brothers thought they were cursed while down in New Orleans on a boys' trip."

"What kind of curse?"

"A love curse."

"For real?" I snort.

"Well, they believed it was a love curse. Not sure how real it was, but just from going there and learning about the town, I developed a story based off the brothers and sold it to Lovemark. It was my first big movie deal."

"Ah, I see what you mean by environment. Was that your first movie?"

He shakes his head. "I wish it was."

"You say that as if your first movie wasn't so great."

"It wasn't." He pulls on the back of his neck. "My first one was about finding love on Mars. An astronaut fell in love with a martian."

"Stop." I feel my eyes widen. "That's not true, is it?"

"Unfortunately, it is. I don't know how it sold or how it was green-lighted, but it's probably the most embarrassing piece of film ever made, and I resent that it's on my IMDb page. At one point, a few years ago, a bunch of college kids found it and blasted it on social media, and it became a drinking game."

"A drinking game? How was it played?"

"Uh, every time the martian panted over the astronaut, they had to drink."

I chuckle. "Was there a lot of panting?"

"The martian put a dog in heat to shame."

"Oh God," I say just as Jaz drops off our drinks, but she doesn't stick around because someone else is calling her. "I can proudly say I will probably never watch that movie."

"I prefer it's never seen again."

"What happened after that?"

"I wrote a few scripts that were picked up but were never green-lighted, and then I struck it big with Lovemark. After the Port Snow script, I went into some other lighthearted romances, Christmas stories that are incredibly predictable but always fun to watch. And after that, I wrote a script based off a DIY wedding show. The maid of honor and the best man duke it out for their siblings and end up falling in love. Sold it to Movieflix, and they signed a five-movie deal with me."

"And now you're on movie number five?"

"Yup. Trying to figure out my hook for it." He grips his water glass with this thumb and index finger and gives it a small twist on the table, his eyes cast down.

"I'm sure it'll come to you."

I don't want to say that hearing his story makes him seem more . . . human in my eyes, but it does. He's slowly unraveling from the ruthless date I once spent an evening with and is now showing vulnerabilities and human characteristics. It's doing a number on my guarded idea of him.

I want to continue to think he's an ass. That he's too busy for conversation because he's buried in his phone. But that's not the case at all. He's engaging. He's ambitious, and that ambition only reminds me of myself. And that's scary because I can relate to him. Beforehand, I would keep him at arm's length, claiming nothing in common, but now, there's *actual* potential for friendship.

"It better, or I'm totally screwed." He lifts his glass of water and brings it to his lips, so I awkwardly do the same. When he sets his drink back down, he asks, "So, what are you doing next on the renovation list? Or are you all done?"

I sigh, the weight of it all settling over my shoulders. "I wish I was done. Not even close. Next, we're tackling the first cabin. I have to add a fresh coat of paint, new floors, change out countertops and light fixtures and new bathtub fittings, and then of course furniture."

"And you're doing that for all the cabins?"

I slowly nod. "It feels impossible to get done in such a short amount of time."

"How short?"

"A few weeks," I answer. "I just need a few cabins done, and then I can open up reservations while I work on the others. Hopefully get more visitors than the occasional runaway groomsman." I give him a pointed look that makes him chuckle.

"And you're doing this by yourself?"

"Jaz is helping when she can—she was telling me just yesterday, before she had to leave, that she thinks Tank is bringing his motorcycle club up here one weekend to help, but he hasn't been able to nail that timeline down yet. So, until then, I'll be tackling it all."

"Let me help you."

Could you imagine?

Sawyer and me doing renovations together? What an odd twist of fate that would be.

He did do a good job on the floors in the lobby, but there's no way I could even remotely consider asking him for help. Not when he's a guest, and not when . . . well . . . not when we're not friends.

"Oh, that's not necessary. I can manage. Plus, you have a movie to think about."

"I can think about the movie while I help you."

I shake my head. "No, that's really okay. I can handle it. But thank you." We sit there awkwardly for a few seconds, so I add, "Plus, Peter, my boyfriend, will be able to help on the weekends."

"Weekends are two days—I can help all week."

"No, really, it's okay," I answer, even though a small part of me wants to say yes. I bet with his help we could really work fast, but then I'd have to pay him, and I can't afford to pay anyone. Free labor is the kind of help I need. Like help from Jaz, from Peter, from Tank's friends.

Also, I'm not sure spending that much time with Sawyer is a good idea. The appalling first and second impressions I have of him are wearing off with every moment I spend with him. And I'm starting to think he's actually not so bad.

Possibly a good person.

A fun person.

So, yeah, Sawyer is not an option.

Through the bustle of the bar and patrons demanding their drinks, Jaz appears and drops off our waffles. "I almost put tomatoes on your waffle, Julia, but decided to spare you."

"Thank you?"

"You are more than welcome." She taps the bar in front of him. "Hear from your brother recently? Has he asked for my number?"

Sawyer glances up from his waffle, looking nervous. "He has, actually."

"Really?" Jaz asks, leaning forward with interest. "Did you give it to him?"

"Uh, remind me of the day you gave me your number, because I don't recall you ever did."

Jaz pulls a pen from behind her ear and picks up a coaster from the bar. She jots down her number and hands it to him. "I expect contact within forty-eight hours. If I don't hear from him, I'm coming for you." She slips her pen back behind her ear, winks, and then takes off again.

"That's terrifying," Sawyer says before putting the coaster in his pocket.

It is, but that's Jaz.

Watching her work this hard, though, right after helping me with renovations, makes me realize just how lucky I am to live in a town like Canoodle, where friends will do just about anything for you.

"How did you two meet?" Sawyer asks, bringing his gaze back to me.

"She's Tank's granddaughter. Do you know Tank?"

"Oh yeah," Sawyer says, eyes bright in the dim light. "I've already met him, and you know, I see the family resemblance."

I laugh despite myself. "Yeah, and Sully's best friends with Tank. We had no choice but to become friends when we were kids. I'd come up here a lot, especially in the summer, and spend the weekend with my grandparents while my dads would go on 'short-term love trips,' as they liked to call them."

"Love trips." Sawyer chuckles. "If I ever have another relationship, I think I need to call our getaways love trips." He cuts into his waffle and takes a bite. "Sorry if this is offensive, but since you have two dads, does that mean you're adopted?"

"I don't find that offensive." Am I pleasantly shocked that he's asking personal questions? Yes. Didn't think we'd get to that point, ever. "And yes, I was adopted. My birth mom's from Idaho, and she got pregnant with me on prom night—typical. She didn't have the means to raise me and wasn't ready, so she put me up for adoption. My dads applied through a local adoption agency and were picked."

"Do you still have contact with your birth mom?"

"Not really, no. Last I heard, she's living in Idaho still, married with two kids, but I haven't felt the need to meet them. I know other people would probably want to know that side of their life, but I really don't need to. I'm content just keeping that in the back of my head."

"I can understand that. I think I'd feel the same way as you." He takes a large bite of his waffle. I glance over and catch the way his strong jaw works as he chews, before my eyes travel to his neck when he swallows. "So, growing up with two dads in Palm Springs? How was that?"

His question startles me back to my waffle, and I stare down at the nooks as they gather maple syrup. *Jesus, Fallon, stop staring at the man.*

"Uh, well . . . I went to some of the best themed parties of my life."

He chuckles. "I didn't want to stereotype, but I could imagine the kind of shindigs they put on."

"Not at all. My dad and papa easily throw the best parties. My friends growing up always looked forward to their end-of-the-school-year bonanzas. Jaz would come down as well for them. Always the best food, the best decor, and *RuPaul's Drag Race*–level costumes. I missed their summer ball this year, and I'm still trying to mentally get over the FOMO."

"What was the theme?"

"'Let's get intoxi-gay-ted.' You were supposed to bring your favorite cocktail recipe, serve up a flight, and then there was a blind vote for the winner. The Swamp Sipper took home the prize."

"The Swamp Sipper?" He winces. "Dare I ask?"

I shake my head. "All I know is dry ice was involved, and it was a crowd-pleaser."

"What was the prize?"

"I'm glad you asked," I say, biting into my waffle, loving the sugar dots Jaz adds to the batter. I have a sweet tooth, and the fact that I can satisfy it at dinner does everything for me. "They throw this summer bash every year, and a contest is always part of it, so a coveted trophy goes from household to household. A medal of honor, if you will."

"What is it?"

"A spray-painted gold-and-glitter dildo nailed to a block of wood."

Sawyer nearly chokes on his waffle as he coughs out a laugh. I give him a solid pat on the back while he takes a sip of his water.

When he's settled, he says, "I was not expecting that answer, but that is freaking amazing."

"And of course there's a large group text for the winners to show off pictures of the trophy every year. I've never won. Neither has Jaz, and it really has taken a toll on her self-confidence. You can't even mention it to her—she gets so upset."

"I would be upset too if I owned a bar and couldn't win the glittery gold dick for a year."

I laugh out loud, and Jaz's eyes snap my way from across the bar. Her expression isn't angry, more curious than anything, but I know she's going to drill me tomorrow. With her disdain for Sawyer, I can't imagine her liking me sitting next to him at the bar, sharing a conversation, and *gulp* laughing. In my defense, as you can recall, there weren't any other seats.

"Do your dads come up to visit often?"

"Not as often as I'd hope. I love it here in Canoodle. When I was younger, it was my second home, and now that I live here permanently, I can't imagine being anywhere else. That being said, it's not super handicap friendly. My dad is paralyzed, from the waist down. So, when he comes here, he has a hard time getting in and out of some of the buildings around the Cove and in town. It's a problem Sully had been addressing before he, uh, got sick. Since the buildings are so old, they weren't necessarily up to today's code, but we've been working on it."

"You know, now that I think about it, the whole right side of the street of the town is raised on a hill—every store is only accessible by stairs."

"Yup," I say. "That's an old mountain town for you. At the Cove, we do have a handicap-accessible cabin off to the side of the main residence that we don't ever use for guests. Sully started building it for my dad but never was able to finish it. The bones are there, though—just needs the last touches."

"Where do your dads stay when they're here?"

My cheeks flush from embarrassment. Dad has never complained to Sully or me about how hard it is to get around, but we've witnessed it, and Papa has made a few comments here and there. It should not have taken this long to fix things. "We convert the back office into a bedroom. It's not ideal, but it works. I know it's one of the reasons they're not up here often—the whole setup is uncomfortable."

Sawyer's quiet, and I wonder if he's judging how little I can accommodate my own father.

"They said they'll come up to help maybe in a week or so," I hurry to add. "So, that's good at least. I miss them a lot. Before I moved up here to help Sully, I'd have Sunday-night dinner with them every week. They'd make an elaborate four-course meal, and I'd bring dessert. Some of my favorite times."

He pushes a piece of waffle around on his plate. "I wish I spent that kind of time with my family. They own a vineyard just outside of Palm Springs. My brother helps them, so they're always together, and since I need to be close to LA, I always feel like an outsider when we get together—not that they treat me like one."

"I felt like that every time I came up here after being gone for a while, but then the awkwardness always faded away after a bit."

"Same." He finishes off his waffle and leans back in his stool. "This night turned out to be better than I thought."

"Oh yeah? What did you think was going to happen?"

He brings his water to his lips and takes a sip. Once again, I unapologetically watch as his Adam's apple bobs with his swallowing. The thick column of his neck contracts, fascinating me, pulling me into a trance. *What's wrong with you, Fallon? Swallowing is not sexy.* I should not be fascinated by a man drinking a glass of water, but God, I am. It fascinates me. He fascinates me.

"I thought I was going to take a quiet walk to the bar, dodging the demon ducks—"

"Oooh, experience their snappiness?"

"Day one. I've steered clear of them ever since. Then I figured I'd come here and get harassed by Jaz the entire night while picking tomatoes out of my meal. Instead, I've had a delicious waffle sans tomatoes and a great conversation. But don't worry," he says quickly. "I don't think we're friends or anything. Just . . . acquaintances."

I hold back my smile.

"Good, wouldn't want to give you the wrong impression."

"Trust me, you aren't." He winks, just a flick of his eyelid, but from that little movement the strangest thing happens to me—my stomach does a crazy somersault. My skin breaks out into a sea of goose bumps, and my body fills up with this urgent need to let out a very large, very unflattering sigh of contentment.

What on earth is happening to me?

My cheeks heat up, and I look away from him as I try to mentally process why he's giving me all these new, tingly feelings. Why is he so different from what I expected?

Why does he have to be funny? Kind? Interested?

Why can't he be the man I met at the Golden Star?

Why does he have to complicate things? Because that's what it feels like. The last thing I need right now is complicated, and yet, when I look back up at him, I can't help but smile at just how adorable he looks sitting next to me.

❖ ❖ ❖

Jaz: What the hell was going on tonight?

Fallon: I'm exhausted, Jaz. I just want to go to bed.

Jaz: No way in hell. You need to explain yourself.

Fallon: Explain what?

Jaz: You were blushing. I saw it. And I saw the way you were looking at him.

Fallon: I was not. And it was hot in there, everyone's cheeks were red.

Jaz: You are a liar, and you know it. Do you like him?

Fallon: What? Are you insane? First of all, I have a boyfriend. Second of all, I barely even know the guy. How could I possibly like him?

Jaz: Oh, I don't know, he's insanely attractive, kind, and tall. Not to mention he makes you laugh.

Fallon: Uh . . . I thought you didn't like him.

Jaz: I don't, but let's call a spade a spade. Sawyer is a catch, and you would be a nimrod if you didn't think otherwise. So . . . are you attracted to him?

Fallon: I love you, but you've lost it. Go to bed.

Jaz: You've lost it!

Fallon: Okay . . . see you tomorrow morning.

Jaz: Yeah, you WILL. Because I expect you to explain yourself.

Fallon: If that's the case, don't bother coming.

Jaz: Ha. Nice try. I'll be bringing breakfast to lessen the blow. See you bright and early.

CHAPTER TWELVE
SAWYER

The sidewalks are quiet around me, only the whisper of a breeze crossing through the pine trees as I glance over my shoulder.

Feeling nervous—probably because I'm trespassing—I casually grab the knob on the cabin's front door, squeeze my eyes tight, and, on a hope and a prayer, I turn it.

To my delighted and grateful surprise, the door is unlocked, so I push through into a dusty, vacated cabin. Dust whooshes into the air, and I cough a few times as I reach for a light switch and flip it up, illuminating the space. Fallon was right—needs a bit more work, not much, though.

It took me a second to find the cabin meant for Fallon's dad, since it's truly tucked in the back in its own little grove of pines, but when I did find it, I knew it was meant for him. I could already tell the door was wider, and there are the makings for a ramp, but the planks haven't been nailed in yet. Inside, the cabin is just like mine, but the walls are white on the inside rather than a natural oak. The floors are a white-washed gray color and are a little more than halfway installed, while the moldings and furniture are on the finished side. I glance in the bathroom and notice that tiles and flooring have been installed—thank God—but plumbing fixtures are still in their packaging. The cabin really is almost done. Timing is key, and I feel an ache of sympathy that Sully got sick when he did because I'm sure it pains him that he wasn't able to finish this for his son.

Taking in the unfinished products and the supplies already there, I'd say it needs a day's worth of work. I can knock out the floor quickly and attach the baseboards and molding no problem. Touch-up paint will take a second to dry. Fixtures won't take long. And it looks like the planks for the ramp are already cut—they just need to be nailed into place.

Yeah, I can easily get this done in a day.

I survey the rest of the space, making sure I don't miss anything, and that's when I come across design plans hung on the wall behind a mattress that's leaning against it. Since the windows are covered in sheets, blocking most of the early-morning light, I reach for my phone and turn on the flashlight to get a better look.

The bed will go in the middle of the room, with a red carpet underneath. I glance around and spot a rolled-up rug in the closet, along with bags of bedding. I gratefully check those off my mental list. Next to the rug are two lantern-style wall sconces. Where do those go? I turn back to the design and notice they're supposed to go on either side of the bed. I adjust the king-size mattress some more and see that the wall has been prewired. Thank God. I can work with electric, but it's not my favorite thing. Installing a sconce is not a big deal, but prewiring . . . yeah, no thank you.

I step away from the design plan and take in the space one more time as anticipation flutters through me. This will be easy, even with how sore I am. And it will be worth it. Hearing Fallon speak of the unfinished project last night nearly broke me. Not only could I hear the disappointment, the embarrassment in her voice, but it was also written all over her face. And the way she spoke of her dads, how much she missed them, and knowing this is blocking their ability to see each other more . . . I need to finish this.

But first things first: I need some water, and then I need to fetch my tools from the shed.

Water bottle in tow, I exit the cabin and walk along the pine-covered pathway toward the lobby. It's early, so the sun is still cresting over the rock formations, adding a pink glow to the sky. I can see why Fallon loves it here so much—it's absolutely breathtaking.

"What do you mean you have to leave?" I hear Jaz say as I step inside. "Are you lying to me?"

The door shuts behind me, and both Fallon and Jaz look up, eyes widening.

"Oh, there he is . . . the home-wrecker."

"Jaz, stop," Fallon moans.

But she doesn't; she takes a step forward. "What were your intentions last night?"

Well, good morning to them as well. Christ. I wasn't expecting to be interrogated this early.

"Uh, to eat dinner," I say, frankly frightened by the crazed look in her eyes.

She closes the space between us and pokes me in the chest. The surprised look on her face from the impact of her nail against my muscles almost makes me smirk. But I'm not a dumb man—I know a smirk will only piss her off—so I hold back.

Jaz gathers herself, huffing and straightening up. "So, you mean to tell me that you had the purest of intentions last night?"

I glance over at Fallon, who's massaging her brow with her fingers, clearly already bruised and battered from Jaz's verbal onslaught.

"I have no idea what you're talking about," I answer.

"So, you weren't trying to hit on my friend?"

"Jaz, please," Fallon says.

"You weren't trying to take a second chance at love? Because let me tell you something, *Julia*, you had your shot with Fallon, and you blew it."

"I'm so sorry," Fallon says. "Please ignore her."

I look between them, my confusion rising. Uh, as far as I know, everything was innocent last night. No one crossed the line. It was a night involving waffles, nonalcoholic beverages, and strictly platonic conversation. So where is this coming from? I surely hope I didn't do anything to make Fallon believe otherwise. "I was hungry last night. I wanted a waffle, so I went to your bar. Fallon happened to be going at the same time. My plan was to sit alone and drum up ideas for my next script, but the place was packed, which forced me to sit next to Fallon. It would have been weird if we didn't talk. So, I talked to her. There were no other intentions involved. I understand she has a boyfriend, a pretty chill guy, actually, so trust me when I say I don't intend on doing anything to jeopardize that. I know what it feels like to be cheated on—I wouldn't do that to someone else."

Jaz straightens up, a dignified lift to her chin. "Checks out." She turns back to Fallon. "So do you want apple-cinnamon or blueberry?" She walks over to a bakery box resting on a nearby table and flips it open.

"Seriously? You're going to act like you didn't just insult me?" Fallon asks. "Or insult Sawyer, for that matter?"

"You act as if I have any sort of ability to control my filter. You should know better by now."

"Jaz, you owe us an apology. That was completely inappropriate."

Jaz sighs and pulls a muffin out of the bakery box. "I'm sorry if I was rude, but I'm also concerned. I saw the way you were looking at him, the laughing . . . it made me think you were interested."

Not the impression I got.

But I did enjoy her laugh.

I loved her smile.

And it was nearly impossible not to bump her playfully with my shoulder or even lean closer.

But I held it together, because like I said, she has a boyfriend.

"I wasn't looking at him any certain way," Fallon shoots back, her voice growing angry.

Jumping in, I add, "I, uh, I didn't notice any certain looks. We even stated that we weren't friends, just acquaintances."

"Okay." Jaz pulls the muffin wrapper down. "Just want to make sure nothing's going on. You know, for Peter's sake."

"You don't need to worry about Peter," Fallon says. "I have that under control. Now, if you'll excuse me, I have to take Sully down to Palm Springs for the day."

"You really are leaving?" Jaz asks.

"Yes, I told you, I forgot he had appointments today, so I have to take him down there, and then we're having dinner with my dads. I won't be home until late."

"Are you meeting up with Peter?"

Fallon's eyes flash down. From the droop in her shoulders and silence, it's obvious she's hiding something.

"Did you even tell him you were going to be in Palm Springs?" Jaz presses.

"I didn't." Ahh, there it is. "But I'll text him and invite him to dinner."

"Uh-huh." Jaz moves toward the entrance of the lobby. "You do that, you text him." She turns and points at me. "Your brother texted me—you're lucky you did something right, Julia." And without another word, she strides outside, muffin in hand, switchblade sticking out her back pocket.

Seriously . . . she's terrifying.

And yeah, the minute I got back to my cabin, I sent Roarick her number and told him he'd better text her, at least to keep my balls intact. But he was grateful to get her number, so . . . something is going on there.

When the door shuts, Fallon lets out a deep sigh. "God, Sawyer, I'm so sorry about that. How embarrassing."

"Don't apologize," I say. "It's really fine. She's just being a friend."

"An annoying, obtrusive one." Fallon flicks the top of the bakery box. "Do you want a muffin? There are three in here."

"That's okay, I don't want to take your muffins."

"I'm offering you one. It's the least I can do after that embarrassing conversation." She grabs the box and brings it over to me. "Blueberry or apple-cinnamon?"

"Which one is your favorite?" I ask her.

"Apple-cinnamon."

"Blueberry it is," I say, taking one out. "Thank you."

"Thanks for putting up with Jaz."

I set the muffin on top of the water jug. "You know, some people might think that offering a muffin would be a sign of friendship," I tease.

"Some might think that, but that's not the case here. Just a nice cabin owner, offering their guest a morning muffin. Nothing more."

Fuck, she's cute.

Just talking to her like this, going back and forth, brings a lightness to my life I forgot I was missing.

"Right." I finish filling up my water bottle. "Because we couldn't possibly have anyone thinking that we are friendly."

"Precisely, but also because . . . we're not friendly."

"Nope, not even in the slightest."

I smile.

She smiles.

And then the door flies open, making both of us startle and jump in place. Sully walks in, and his eyes meet mine. "Phil, there you are. Tonight, horseshoes. I'm going to show you how a real man plays."

I can feel Fallon's eyes on me, questioning, wondering what the hell Sully is talking about.

"Uh, sure."

"Sully," Fallon says, stepping in. "The horseshoe pits aren't in commission right now."

"Yes, they are, I was just down there. Brand new."

I can see the look of concern on Fallon's face—she must think he's having a nonlucid moment.

"They are," I say, helping Sully out. "All cleared out; they look great."

Fallon frowns. "What are you talking about?" she whispers.

I don't want to tell her I was the one who cleared them out. For some reason, I like moving around the Cove, getting work done undetected. I like being a mystery to Fallon—part of me thinks if she found out I was the one helping, fixing all the things Sully wants fixed, she wouldn't let me do it anymore. And doing renovations has been freeing, cathartic, a way for me to reconnect with myself. The pressure of Hollywood can be so demanding, and it's easy to lose yourself. And for all my success, I know I've lost pieces of myself over the years. Being here in Canoodle, speaking with Sully, working with my hands again, experiencing the sheer loyalty and camaraderie of a small community—it's given me a new start. I'm not ready for it to end just yet.

So, I opt for bending the truth. "Yeah, I was down there on a run, and they look perfect. Told Sully I would challenge him to a game."

"What?" she says, confused, and turns to Sully. "Can you go to the bathroom? We're going to leave for Palm Springs soon."

"I'm not a child. I know when to go to the bathroom," he huffs.

"Then go now—it's a long trip down the mountain." With that, she takes off toward the back door. I follow her, pulled forward by a force I don't really understand.

She charges down the path, between the cabins, and to the play yard, where, over the past few days, I've fixed the horseshoes, cleaned up the landscaping, added some benches, and even built a wooden scoreboard for the two courts.

"What the actual hell?" She plants her hands on her hips, looking around. "Who's doing this?" she mutters under her breath. She walks up to the pit and runs her hand over the smooth, stained bench. "It's . . . perfect."

"Yeah, looks pretty good," I say with a slight shake to my voice. *Please don't ask if it's me doing this. Please.* "So, yeah, Sully and I will break it in tonight."

"We won't be home until late," she says, looking up at me. "Maybe tomorrow." She walks over to the scoreboard and plays with the point system. "I'm asking my dads about this."

"About what?"

"About all of this." She sweeps her hand around. "I think they hired someone to go around and fix things. Did they think I wouldn't notice? I just want to know who it is."

"What, uh, what else did they fix?" I ask, playing dumb.

"The picnic table area, Sully's bench, now this. And I think I saw some mended fences down by the road as well."

She did. I tackled those the other day. Took a few seconds.

"It means a lot to me, seeing the Cove being transformed like this. I want to be able to say thank you, to show how grateful I am for all the hard work. And I also don't like things happening without me knowing."

Well then, she might not like what I have in store for today.

But that's not going to change my plan. She's going to be gone all day, which gives me plenty of time to finish the cabin.

She looks down at the time on her phone and groans. "If I want to make it to Sully's appointments on time, I need to get going. Lord knows he's going to have to pee when we're driving." She glances at me. "Enjoy your muffin; sorry about Jaz—if you want to stay somewhere else, I completely understand."

I chuckle. "I'm fine. Safe drive." I offer her a wave as she smiles lightly over her shoulder and then jogs toward the main lobby.

When she's out of view, I take a seat at the bench overlooking the horseshoe courts and undo the wrapper from my muffin. I take a deep breath, savoring the piney mountain air. The calm before the renovation storm.

I smile to myself.

This should be fun.

❖   ❖   ❖

"This is not fucking fun," I groan into the phone while lying back on the floor I just finished.

"What the hell are you doing?" Roarick asks.

"Renovating a cabin."

"Why?"

"As a surprise."

"A surprise?" Roarick asks. "Uh, correct me if I'm wrong, but aren't you supposed to be writing a screenplay summary? Not renovating a cabin."

"I'm coming up with ideas while renovating."

"I see, and what exactly are these ideas you're coming up with?"

I lift my water bottle to my mouth and take a large sip, wetting my very dry throat. "Oh, you know, ideas."

"Name one," Roarick challenges.

"Uh . . . troll collector falls in love with local Rigatoni Roy. They join forces and make a museum out of pasta and trolls."

"What . . . the . . . actual . . . fuck? Please for the love of God tell me that was a joke." When I'm silent, he goes off. "Sawyer, you can't possibly think a movie about someone who collects trolls and some Italian food Ralph—"

"Rigatoni Roy."

"Whatever, you can't possibly think that is an idea that's going to be greenlighted."

"There could be potential."

"There is absolutely zero potential behind that idea. Seriously, dude, what's going on? You're never this dried up for ideas. You always seem to have something in your back pocket."

"I know, I know. It's just been, I don't know . . . hard. I guess I haven't really tapped into that part of my brain lately, because when I do, I think of Annalisa and Simon, and that's the last thing I want to think about."

"Why? Are you still in love with her?"

"What? No. That ship has sailed. There's not a fat chance in hell I could ever be in love with her again. I've seen what she's capable of. I've seen how fake she is. When I first met her, she was down to earth, kind, a hard worker, and ever since she became famous, that's all she cares about. She's all image now, and I don't think that'll ever change."

"Attention can be a dangerous thing," Roarick says. "For a lot of people, it's their downfall if they don't know how to professionally handle it. Instead of using the attention to be for good, it becomes the downfall in their career."

"So far, Annalisa's riding high on her attention—her career is far from falling."

"Trust me, she'll have a downfall. It's bound to happen with attention seekers, because once that attention starts to fade, they're so desperate to get it back they wind up doing something off brand, something that will ultimately take them out."

I think of all the other actors who've done just that, who were once in Annalisa's shoes. "Yeah, I think you're right."

"I know I am. I've seen plenty of celebrity downfalls, and you know how wine people gossip. Working at the vineyard, I've heard from different wine labels who come to the farm, going on and on about the latest celebrity hosting they just did. It will happen. Just be patient."

"I don't want her to have a downfall," I say quickly.

"Bullshit," Roarick laughs.

"I'm serious. I wouldn't want to see that."

"So, you're telling me that if in the news tomorrow you see that Annalisa posted some tasteless story on her Instagram and people started revolting against her, you wouldn't take a little joy in that?"

"Maybe a little," I answer honestly. I can't lie—I know I'd feel just a slight sense of justice.

He laughs. "That's right you would. Everyone enjoys the downfall more than the rise. But that's beside the point. If you're not in love with Annalisa, what's the big deal? You've moved on, you said your piece with your middle fingers on an altar of a church; what more could you want?"

"I don't know, it just feels . . . sensitive, I guess. I'm not feeling super romantic at the moment."

"Then get romantic. Maybe ask Jaz out on a date."

That makes me actually guffaw. "I think we'd both rather jump off the back of Beggar's Hole than go on a date with each other. Plus, seems like you two are talking . . ."

"We are. Just wanted to test you, see if there were any feelings there."

"Trust me, the only feelings I have toward Jaz are pure terror."

"I don't see why; she's a breath of fresh air." My brother has been spending too much time with the grapes. "Is there anyone else you can ask out?"

"Honestly, I don't get out at all. I've been busy with renovations."

"That's right, and why exactly are you doing those again?"

I stand from where I've been sprawled out on the floor and start picking up the trash that I've thrown around the space. "Because it keeps me busy, keeps my mind busy."

"And Fallon is okay with you just . . . working around the cabins all the time."

"About that . . ." I feel myself flush. "She, uh, she kind of doesn't know it's me."

"Wait, she doesn't know you're doing renovations? How does that work?"

"They've all been in the back of the property, and she hasn't noticed me doing anything. Sully's been guiding me. I don't know, it's been nice. And then she saw some of the work I did. Man, you should have seen the smile on her face. She was so happy."

The phone goes silent.

"You there?" I ask.

"Yeah, I'm here."

"Why are you being silent?"

"Just thinking."

"What are you thinking about?" I ask.

"Uh . . . how you're totally falling for the cabin owner. Dude, there's your story. Wayward traveler stops in small town to get away from the fame and pressures of Hollywood—and falls in love with the kind, humble cabin owner. That is totally something you'd write."

"First of all, I'm not falling for her. Second of all, I feel weird basing a story off this town."

"Why? You're the one who always says you need to be immersed into your environment to write a story. Well, here you are, immersed. Use it."

I shake my head, even though he can't see me. "Doesn't feel right. These people have been nice to me—I don't want them to think I'm taking advantage and using them for plots."

"Are you talking about the people of the town, or are you talking about Fallon in particular?"

"She's part of the town, isn't she?" I ask.

"She is . . . she's also really pretty."

"Fuck off with that shit, man."

A hearty laugh echoes through the phone. "Come on, you can't tell me you're not kicking yourself just a little for not paying attention during your blind date. I honestly don't know how you could ignore her, let alone not remember her."

Yeah, I'm still trying to process how that happened.

All I can remember around that time in my life is that I wasn't in a healthy mental state. I was trying to finish up a project, Annalisa was messing with my head, I was dealing with Movieflix; it just . . . hell, nothing was working for me. I never should have gone on the date in the first place.

"Can we move past Fallon?"

"Why are you getting so touchy?"

"Because . . ." I trail off, at a loss.

"Because why?"

"Because . . . I don't want to talk about her."

"You know, your refusal to talk about her leads me to believe that you really do want to talk about her, but you're afraid of what you might say if you do."

"What?" I ask, getting a headache from just that sentence.

"What cabin are you renovating right now?"

"Uh . . . one in the back of the property. Why does that matter?"

"Because it does. She doesn't know, right?"

"Right," I drag out.

"So how did you know it needed renovating?"

What the hell is he getting at? "She mentioned it last night when we were eating dinner. She said this was the cabin Sully was trying to finish so her dads would have a place to stay. Her one dad is paralyzed, and it's the cabin they were making handicap accessible for him. Sully couldn't finish it after he got worse, and her dads don't come up to visit as much—"

"Dude."

"What?" I ask.

"You had dinner with her last night?"

"It's not what it seems," I say, feeling myself get defensive. "We just happened to be sitting next to each other. We didn't go out to dinner together."

"Still, you talked. She told you about her dads' cabin, and now you're renovating it. I hate to say it, Sawyer, but I think you like her."

"I barely know her well enough to like her," I protest.

"Doesn't mean you're not interested. Tell me this . . . does your heart race when you see her?" When I don't answer right away, because honestly, it races like a goddamn horse, he continues: "I hate to slap you with the truth, bro, but I think you have a thing for Fallon."

My jaw clenches in frustration as I survey the cabin I've been working on today.

I'm not frustrated by Roarick's accusations. I'm frustrated because somewhere, subconsciously, I think he might be right.

I don't know much about Fallon, but I do know she's selfless. She's strong. She's caring. And she's loyal, an attribute that I don't see too often where I live. Her relationship with Sully intrigues me. Her need to preserve the place she's so fond of tugs at my heart. And her boundless determination is—unfortunately—a turn-on.

Not to mention, her smile captivates me, her laugh feels like a warm hug, and it's so simple to get lost in her eyes when she looks at me.

So yeah, maybe I might have a small, very tiny, almost unseeable thing for Fallon, but it's nothing I would ever act on because she has a boyfriend.

Because she doesn't even want to be my friend.

Because I had a shot, and I blew it.

There's nothing more to be said on the topic.

Fallon is off limits.

Chapter Thirteen

FALLON

"Papa, the spinach tapas were out of this world," I say, patting my mouth with my napkin. "If I had more time to make dinner for myself, I'd be making those every night."

Papa clutches my hand in his and beams. "Good thing I made extra and froze them for you to take back to Canoodle."

"Seriously?" I ask.

He brings the back of my hand to his mouth and gives it a kiss. "Always want to make sure our baby girl is fed."

"You treat her like a toddler," Sully grumbles off to the side. He wasn't too pleased with seeing the doctor today. He kept muttering about needing to help Phil. I brought up the confusion to the doctor, but Sully tested better than he was previously, which . . . honestly threw me off. As the doctor said, it's impossible really to predict what's going to happen to someone with Alzheimer's, which feels very true in this moment.

But it's concerning that Sully has not only brought up Grandma Joan many times these past few weeks but also his brother. I thought that was going to be a red flag that he was getting worse, but apparently, he's showing great progress in other avenues. His recollection of what time of the year it is, his past, his present, they were almost entirely on point. So . . . God, I don't know.

I've just about hit my limit when it comes to this disease. I wish there was a magic button that would help me understand. That would help me look inside Sully's brain and see where he's coming from, but I don't have that luxury. No one does.

All I can do is go off what the doctor is saying, and he's saying that we should keep up what we're doing.

That's the thing, though: I don't know what we're doing.

I don't know what's changed.

"I recall you making several batches of cookies and freezing them so I could take them back to college," Dad says to Sully as he wheels himself back from the kitchen, a tray of drinks on his lap. He hands a water to Peter, who's sitting on the other side of me.

"Thank you, Izaak," he says.

"I don't recall a thing," Sully says, popping another spinach tapas in his mouth.

Dad laughs and wheels over to Sully. He places a kiss on his arm, and like always, Sully leans down to Dad and kisses his head. Sully might be a grump, but he's a very loving man, and it shows.

When Dad was eighteen, he was driving around Palm Springs with his friends, feeling invincible, and, of course, not wearing a seat belt. They were T-boned when they ran a red light, and Dad was thrown from the car. He was lucky he wasn't killed that night, but ever since, Sully has been incredibly protective of Dad. The cookies were not an exaggeration. I remember Dad telling me about the weekly visits Sully would make to UC Riverside to check up on him, make sure he was settling into college life. After the first few months, Grandma Joan put an end to it and changed it to once a month.

"My mom would send care packages to me when I was in medical school, but it never consisted of homemade cookies," Peter says.

"What was inside of them?" Papa asks.

"Cup of noodles."

Dad and Papa both cringe while I chuckle.

"Oh, an abomination," Dad says.

"I'm so sorry that happened to you," Papa adds.

Peter holds his hand to his chest. "Thank you. It was a rough life, but someone had to eat those noodles."

We all chuckle, and as my dads joke around with Peter, I can't help but think how well he fits in with my family. He cares for Sully, he jokes with my dads, he makes as much time to see me as he can, and yet . . . it feels like something is missing, but I can't quite put my finger on it.

"Fallon, did you hear me?"

"Huh?" I ask Dad.

"The renovations, how are they coming along?"

"Uh, I've been meaning to talk to you two about that." I twist my glass of water on the table. "When were you going to tell me that you hired someone to help?"

Dad and Papa exchange confused glances.

"What are you talking about?" Papa asks.

"The person who's been helping around the property. You know, the bench, the picnic tables, the horseshoe pits—when were you going to tell me about them?"

Papa crosses one leg over the other and looks over to Dad. When he shrugs, Papa says, "Honey, I have no idea what you're talking about. We didn't hire anyone."

"What?" I ask. "You didn't hire anyone?"

"No, we didn't. Why, are those areas cleared up?"

"Not only cleared up, but they're . . . they're immaculate. Better than I could ever imagine." I turn to Peter. "Did you hire someone?"

He pushes his hand through his hair. "I kind of wish I did, because that would certainly guarantee me some brownie points, but it wasn't me, sweetie."

More puzzled than ever before, I turn to Sully, who is gnawing on a toothpick. "Did you hire anyone?"

"Why would I hire anyone when we have Phil working on things?"

"Sully," Dad says softly, "Phil passed away a few years ago." He places his hand on Sully's shoulder. "I'm so sorry."

"I'm well aware Phil died," Sully says. "I'm talking about the other Phil."

"What other Phil?" I ask, and then it dawns on me. "Wait, are you talking about *Sawyer*?"

"Who's Sawyer?" Sully asks.

"The man who's been renting a cabin," I say. "Tall, blond hair, wears a backward hat."

Sully grumbles. "I tell him all the time to wear it like a normal human."

"Wait." I set my drink down and turn toward Sully. "Are you telling me that Sawyer is the one behind all the renovations?"

"You mean Phil," Sully says.

I try to hold back my frustration. "Yes, Phil. He's the one who's doing the renovations?"

"With my supervision, of course." Sully picks at his front teeth. "If it weren't for me, that boy would be absolutely lost. I do appreciate his use of regular tools. He refuses to use power tools."

That could explain why I haven't heard anything.

"So, you and . . . Phil have been doing these jobs around the property?"

"Yes," Sully confirms, and I sit back in my chair, completely . . . shocked.

I think back to all the times Sawyer came into the lobby to refill his water, all sweaty and even dirty at times. He wasn't exercising, like I assumed—he was doing work around the Cove. He was fixing Sully's bench. He was sanding and painting all the picnic tables, turning that entire area into a dream escape. And the horseshoe pits . . .

I can't . . .

I don't think I can quite comprehend the kind of gesture . . .

My throat chokes up, and my eyes fill with tears.

"What kind of work has been done?" Papa asks.

Throat tight, I glance up at my parents. "The picnic table area is all refurbished, all the tables painted brilliantly in red, and lights are strung around on poles." I swallow back my emotions. "The landscaping is cleaned up too. It's beautiful, just how it used to be when Grandma Joan and I would go down there." I wipe at my eyes. "Sully's bench—"

"Which still feels uncomfortable," he mutters.

"Has to be better than a pile of wood," Dad says with a smirk.

"And the horseshoe pits have all been cleaned and fixed, and he built a scoreboard and benches." My eyes water from the thought of all the work he's put in. The cuts and scrapes on his hands, the blisters. That was from his work. The work he's done selflessly.

"I helped paint the scoreboard," Sully says, startling me from my thoughts.

I grip Sully's shoulder lovingly. "You did a great job," I say, and then something hits me. "Wait, you've been helping him this entire time?"

"Yes, that's what I said. The man seems lonely," Sully huffs out. "To keep him busy, I've told him all about Grandma Joan while we work. Seems to be a romantic, that one."

Peter shifts uncomfortably next to me. "Romantic?" he asks.

Sully nods and points at Peter. "Yes, I'd watch out if I were you."

Oh God.

"Sully," I chastise, and then turn to Peter. "Trust me, nothing to worry about."

"Has he flirted with you?" Peter asks, his face full of concern.

"No. Not at all. I barely even talk to him." Technically not true as of recent events, but the last thing I need is a jealous boyfriend.

"Then why would he be doing the renovations without you knowing?"

Great, great question.

"Because I told him to," Sully says matter-of-factly.

This all feels like too much to take in. The man I thought was horrible, who I wanted nothing to do with, is the one behind the mystery renovations. Not sure I can handle Sully while I process all of this, I turn to Peter. "Can you, uh, take Sully to the back and play cards with him?"

"I'm not an invalid," Sully says as he pushes away from the table. "Just tell me you want me to leave so you can talk about me." He pushes his chair into the table, grabs his plate, and brings it into the kitchen before stomping out to the backyard, the door shutting harshly behind him.

"Should I go out there with him?" Peter asks.

"Do you mind?"

"Not at all." He places a kiss on my cheek and stands from the table.

Once we're alone, I turn to my dads, "The doctor was telling me that Sully seemed more . . . lucid. He asked what we were doing to help slow down the progression of his symptoms, and I told him nothing new." I look between them. "Do you think it's the work he's been doing around the Cove?"

Papa crosses one of his legs over his knee and grips his shin. "You know, I was reading about how a fulfilling activity could actually help slow down the process. Sully has always enjoyed working with his hands. We took away his tools because it was too dangerous for him to do alone, but under supervision, I can see how it would be cathartic."

"He's right," Dad says. "I read the same book. But we weren't sure what would keep him busy that wouldn't keep you busy as well. Seems like this Sawyer is a godsend . . . on many levels."

I glance off toward the backyard, where I spot Peter sitting next to Sully. "I can't believe Sawyer didn't say anything to me."

"Do you have a rapport with him?" Dad asks.

"Sort of. He helped me with the lobby floor—God, I should have put it together then. I've just had such a one-track mind lately. He knew exactly what he was doing and finished the floor in no time. And then we had dinner together the other night."

"Dinner?" Papa asks, raising his brow.

"Not like that. We just happened to sit by each other at the bar. We didn't go out or anything. But we've talked a bit and—" I bite my bottom lip. "We kind of went on a blind date before I moved up there. It was horrendous—he didn't even remember me when we ran into each other again. But that doesn't matter, none of that matters. I should probably, I don't know . . . probably tell him to stop."

"Why would you do that?" Dad asks.

"Because he has a life of his own. Because he's a screenwriter and probably has better things to do than fix up the Cove. To be bossed around by an old man with Alzheimer's."

"But he has to be doing it for some reason—maybe ask him before you tell him to stop," Dad says.

"I agree. Get to the bottom of it first, because for all you know, he needs the work just as much as Sully does, and I think we've established it's helping Sully." Papa smiles. "We love you, baby girl, but sometimes your stubborn pride can get in the way. You have this need to prove to the world that you can do things on your own. It's okay to ask for help."

"It really is," Dad says as he rolls over to me and takes my hand. "And also, be careful . . . Peter is a good man."

"I know he is."

"And he loves you," Papa says.

I nod, something in my stomach clenching. "I know."

"As long as you know." Dad grips my cheek and kisses it. "Love you."

"Love you too," I say.

After we clean up and I load up the car with a very tired Sully, who is already starting to drift off, I stand outside my car, waving goodbye to my dads as they retreat into the house. Peter steps up to me and grips my hips, pulling me close as he presses a kiss to my forehead.

"I wish I didn't have to say bye right now."

"I know. But I'm glad you were able to have dinner with us, especially on such short notice."

He chuckles. "Luckily I didn't have a big workload today and was able to make it work." He moves his hands up to my ribs, and I feel my body light up under his touch. "This weekend, can I take you out to dinner? Maybe Rigatoni Roy's? Just you and me. We can dress up for each other, I can hold your hand, and we can walk around the lake."

"I'd like that a lot."

"You would?" he asks, insecurity flashing through his eyes.

"Yes," I say, sliding my hand to the back of his neck and pulling him in close. I press my lips to his, and he gently pushes me up against the car window, deepening our open-mouth kiss.

When he pulls away, he heaves a sigh of relief. "Okay, I'll see you Friday night."

I kiss him one more time. "Friday night."

He drags his thumb over my cheek. "I love you, Fallon."

I smile at him, and instead of answering him, I kiss him one more time before getting in my car. He holds the door open, and once I'm settled and buckled in—Sully lightly snoring in the passenger side—he leans in. "Drive safe."

"I will." I wave. "Bye."

"Bye." He shuts the door, and as I pull out of the driveway, he stands there, hands in his pockets, watching me drive away, while guilt consumes me.

❖   ❖   ❖

Luck was on my side when we got back to Canoodle. Sully startled awake, so I didn't have to try to help him into the residence, holding him tightly under the arm like I usually do. Instead, he walked himself back inside, and I followed with our spinach tapas and put them in the freezer while he got ready for bed. I helped him into his bed, set up his monitor—which he hates—and then turned on his fan to make sure he was comfortable.

"Are you good?" I ask him now.

"Yes, thank you," he says softly. "You're a good granddaughter. I love you very much."

"I love you too, Sully," I say.

When I go to shut the door, he says, "He's a good man."

"Peter?" I ask, pausing and turning back.

"No," Sully grumbles. "Phil. I like him a lot."

"Oh . . . I'm glad."

"He'd be a great husband—think about it."

I hold back the roll of my eyes. "Okay, good night, Sully."

"Good night."

I shut the door behind me and consider getting ready for bed, but I know there's no way I'll be able to sleep until I talk with Sawyer and ask him about the renovations. So, phone in hand—which notifies me when Sully is detected on his monitor—I head down the stairs and out the back of the lobby toward the path that leads to the cabins. I spot his immediately and notice the lights are off.

Hmm, if he's already sleeping, I don't want to bother him. Although a small part of me wants to bang on his door, just to get the conversation over and done with, but I know that wouldn't be fair to him, since he seems to be working so hard.

With a resigned sigh, I'm turning back to the residence just as something in my peripheral vision catches my attention. I glance to the right, and through the throng of pine trees, I glimpse a flicker of light coming from the handicap-accessible cabin.

Curious, I head down that way, stepping carefully between the dark trees, my stomach churning with nerves as I wonder why that light is on. I draw closer, and the light gets brighter and brighter until I clear the pines and turn the corner—only to stop dead in my tracks.

The ramp to the cabin is finished, handrail and all.

No . . .

He didn't.

Did he?

The door is open, so I walk up the ramp, which feels wonderfully sturdy under my steps, and peek past the open door. My breath catches in my chest.

Sawyer is hovering over the bed—which is centered in the middle of the room, not against the wall—struggling with a fitted sheet.

But that's not what's making my heart beat rapidly in my chest.

It's the finished floor.

The installed moldings.

The beautiful sconces shining bright with new light bulbs.

It's the clean, put-together room that has been languishing, unfinished, for months now.

"Come on, you fucker," Sawyer says as the fitted sheet snaps up from the mattress.

"Need help?" I ask, stepping into the doorway.

"Jesus fuck!" he yells and startles backward, the fitted sheet bouncing into a ball on the mattress. "Christ." Hands on his hips, he takes a deep breath. "You scared me."

"I can see that." I smirk, finding it quite funny that this large, good-with-his-hands kind of man can be so easily startled. I glance around the room. "Sawyer, what . . . what have you been doing?"

He looks down, the guilt clear on his face. "I, uh, I thought that you might want a place for your dads to stay." He shrugs as if that's the end of the story. But it can't possibly be the reason.

"Why?"

He scratches the back of his head. "Because you were sad they don't come to visit, and I wanted something to do."

"The bench, horseshoe pits, and picnic tables weren't enough to do?"

His cheeks brighten with a blush as he glances away. "Those were side projects."

I take a step closer, my body warming with every inch I draw closer to this man. "Why didn't you tell me?"

"Didn't think you'd let me if I told you." He shrugs again. "Honestly, it wasn't my intention to do all of the projects. I was out near the lake, working on ideas for my next screenplay, and Sully asked me why I broke the bench I was lying next to. I told him I didn't, and he called me a bullshitter."

I let out a low chuckle. "Sorry about that."

"Don't be. I remembered seeing the sign in the lobby about his Alzheimer's, so I kind of just went with it. Told him I was sorry and that I would fix it. So, I did."

My heart lurches in my chest.

"From there, he asked me why I hadn't fixed the picnic tables, so I started working on those, and he joined me. I don't know, it was nice talking to him and just listening to his stories about your grandma Joan. It was nice to talk to someone real. The work was hard, but spending time with Sully has been the real joy."

My heart vibrates against my rib cage.

Thump. Thump. Thump.

The sound so loud that I can barely hear him over the beat of my own pulse.

"I'm sorry if I overstepped."

He's sorry? How could he possibly feel sorry when he's done so much for me, for my family . . . for Sully? No one, and I mean absolutely no one, has ever done anything this kind for me. And all the air in my lungs escapes as I realize right here, right now, that Sawyer has made a significant impact in my life.

He has touched my heart in a way I'm not sure anyone else could.

"You . . . you didn't overstep," I say, my voice cracking as my emotions flood over.

Grateful can't begin to describe how I feel.

I'm indebted to this man.

"You have been very kind. And this . . ." I motion to the cabin. "It's . . ." A tear slips down my cheek.

"Shit," he says and then closes the space between us with long strides. He's only inches away from me, and as he reaches up to wipe my tear away, I feel a warm contentment in his touch. "Don't cry, Fallon. I'm sorry."

I shake my head. "Don't apologize; these are happy, grateful tears. I'm not upset with you."

He puts his hands in his front pockets and scrunches his shoulders. "Okay."

The inches between us turn into a foot as he takes a step back, a step I want to protest. I want to reach out, pull him in close again. I . . . God, I want to thank him a million times over. I want to cry . . . sob into his shoulder. Show him just how grateful I am.

But instead, we awkwardly stand there, staring at anything but each other. I can feel the air grow thick as I try to figure out what to do, what to say.

I know, technically this gesture has nothing to do with me and everything to do with Sully, but still, by association, it makes me feel like I'm not the only one who truly cares about this place. That I'm not carrying the burden of the cabins' success all on my shoulders. This is a stepping-stone, a break I needed toward the progress of reopening.

"I don't know if you realize how in over my head I've been," I say after a few moments of silence. "We haven't really been booking reservations because of the renovations, and it's been hurting the business. Trying to take care of Sully and fix the cabins, it's . . . well . . . it's been overwhelming."

"It's a large project to undertake, especially if you don't have much experience."

"I have none."

He rocks on his heels. "Well, I have a bunch. I was a contractor before I started writing movie scripts. It's what I did to pay the bills while I was trying to sell an astronaut martian romance." I let out a dry laugh. "Let me help you, Fallon. I know what I'm doing."

"That's obvious, given what you've done with this space alone." I take it all in, how the room is bright with the white walls, but it has the little touch of pewter gray in the accent wall and moldings. The red rug across the newly installed floors. I can even see he's installed the plumbing fixtures in the bathroom. "It looks like a total dream in here, like an oasis in the trees. But I can't ask you to help."

"You're not asking—I'm telling you I want to."

I shake my head. "Sawyer, you've already done so much."

"I want to," he says, a hint of desperation in his voice. "Please don't take this away from me, Fallon." His eyes connect with mine, and I feel a hitch in my breath as I try to hold it together. "I need the escape. I need the companionship. The real conversations. This is just as much for me as it is for you."

"Why do you keep saying 'real conversations'?" I ask.

"I hate to say the cliché, but when you're wrapped up in the world of filmmaking, you don't always stumble across real people. For over a year, I had to pretend like I wasn't affected by my best friend's choices, by his betrayal. Every interaction I had felt artificial. The only outside source I had was my brother, but even then, I didn't see him in person. So, talking to Sully, even talking to you and"—he chuckles—"Jaz, it feels real. It doesn't feel fake."

"I can see that, especially with Jaz." I twist my hands together. "Well, I feel guilty having you do all of this work with me. It's a lot."

It's so much, and I know I would feel guilty, but in the back of my head, the words I'm saying are just a cover-up, because I want his help.

I want to spend more time with him. I want to be that person he can count on for loyalty, for . . . friendship.

"Then, how about this—you're in charge of dinner. I'll work all day, and at night, you just provide a meal, and it can be as simple as a ham sandwich. You already have to feed Sully, right? So just attach me to that, and we can call it even."

"That doesn't seem very even," I say, raising a brow.

"I know, I know, your cooking is probably worth way more, so I'll be forever grateful."

"I didn't mean it that way." I chuckle.

He winks and then whispers, "I know." He holds his hand out to me. "How about it? Deal?"

I look at his hand and then back up at him, doubt filling me. "You're going to regret it."

"Promise you, I won't. I haven't regretted one thing yet."

"But I'm difficult, and so is Jaz."

"I've worked with worse." He sticks his hand out farther. "Come on, Fallon, take the deal."

I'd be stupid to not take it. I could really use his help, especially since he has experience. And more than anything, I want to save the cabins for Sully. I would do just about anything—pride be damned.

Before I can stop myself, I grab his hand, and we shake. "Deal."

"Good choice." He releases my hand and then goes back to the sheet. "Think you can help me with this godforsaken sheet?"

"Making a bed is something I'm quite good at."

"Maybe you can teach me a thing or two."

"Easily." I lift up the sheet. "First things first: you don't have this positioned the right way. See this tag? It says 'top bottom,' meaning it can go at the head of the bed or the foot."

"Mistake number one." He laughs. "See, this is a working relationship that is beneficial to both parties. But don't worry, I won't get any crazy ideas about us becoming friends."

There he goes with that charming smile.

"Good, because I could see how this new partnership could be construed as a budding friendship."

"People from the outside, if not well informed, could possibly see the potential for friendship, but we'd never let them confirm, because before word could spread, we'd squash any rumors."

I shift the sheets under the mattress. "I'm considering making T-shirts for us that specifically say we're not friends."

"I hate to put extra work on your plate, but I think that might be a very good idea."

I glance up at him and smile. "Then it's settled. Working together, but not friends."

"It's settled." He winks and reaches for the flat sheet as I feel my pulse skyrocket all over again.

Thump. Thump. Thump.

And just like that . . . I find myself letting Sawyer into my life.

Chapter Fourteen
FALLON

"Uh, what is he doing here?" Jaz asks, pointing at Sawyer as he takes a seat at our table in the Whistling Kettle.

Sully is at Village Hardware with Tank, hanging out, and I called Jaz to have breakfast with me to go over the plan of attack for reservations. When I suggested Strawberry Fields to Sawyer, he gripped his stomach and shook his head, begging me anywhere but there. When his face paled to a dangerous shade of chunder, I knew there was a story behind the pain in his voice, and I have every intention of getting to the bottom of it.

"Maybe we should have some coffee first," I say to Jaz. "Before we get into all the details." I slide a cup of coffee toward her—dark roast with half-and-half; she's pretty simple. "There, there, drink up."

She eyes the cup. Then she eyes me.

Skepticism shines brightly through her pupils, testing me. *What are you about to put me through?* is the message creasing the soft anger lines in her frown.

"What did you put in this?" She lightly jiggles the mug at me.

"Nothing," I say while I push Sawyer's cup of coffee toward him. Dark roast as well, but one packet of sugar, no milk. I, on the other hand, need a caramel macchiato—I like the jolt of caffeine, but my infant stomach needs the dairy and sugar to ease the bitterness of the coffee. Unless these two want to see me moan and groan, wailing on the floor for the sweet release of death.

"Thank you." Sawyer grips his cup and brings it up to his mouth, blowing on the liquid before placing his lips on the rim.

"You're welcome."

Jaz, on the other hand, she's silent, looking between us . . . stewing with fierce observation, ready to pounce with her diatribe of disapproval. Instead of picking up her coffee, she folds her arms over her chest and leans back in her chair. "What the hell is going on here?"

Bristly with fangs poised at the edge of her lips, ready to be unleashed, she drums her fingers on the table, like a best friends Morse code, demanding I explain myself . . . immediately.

But "denial" is currently my motto, so with a flick of my finger, I pop open the pink carryout box in front of me. "Cinnamon bun? Apple fritter?" And then I lean in close to Jaz and wiggle my eyebrows. "Blueberry fritter . . ."

Her vehement stare slides back, and a distinct interest pulls at her brow, raising her hairline as she peeks into the box. There it is, resting in all its splendor, the distinguished sugary affair that has swept the townspeople of Canoodle into a sugar-induced orgy.

The blueberry fritter.

Created by Helena.

Duplicated by her staff in droves.

And approved by Miss Daphne Lynn Pearlbottom, the mayor of Canoodle.

The blueberry fritter has swept our tiny nation of mountain locals, and Jaz is no exception.

"Goddamn you," she says, reaching into the box and grabbing the blueberry fritter. She's tended to stay away from the hard-to-come-by baked good as much as possible since last year, when she had an addiction. It got to the point that she consumed a fritter a day for a month.

She ended up cursing herself and spent a great deal of her mornings reluctantly lacing up her sneakers and running the Harry Balls Trail in order to work off the extra calories.

Like an unhinged animal, freshly released from a stifling cage, she rips into the fritter with a considerable bite. Satisfied, I watch her melt into her chair. It's just her and that fritter now.

I must say, so far, this is going well.

I turn to Sawyer and offer him the box. "Fritter or cinnamon bun?"

"I had a protein bar, I'm good."

Or so I *thought* it was going well . . .

Eyes blazing, Jaz snaps up, the wrath of all the gods splayed across her face. Her finger morphs into a steel rod of destruction as she jabs our shared table with such ferocity that I'm tempted to check for earthquake recordings.

"You listen to me, and you listen to me good," Jaz snarls. "That protein bar you claim to have snacked on earlier—it means nothing to you in this moment. As far as you're aware, you're ravenous, and the only thing that can even make a dent in your insatiable appetite is a freaking pastry. So, take your undermoisturized hand, reach into that box of goodness, and grab a breakfast treat, because there is no way in hell we're going to sit here, two women with a penchant for baked goods, and chow down on pastries while you're over there marveling at your self-control while tasting the remnants of your protein bar in the back of your teeth. Oh, hell no. Pick up a GD pastry and eat it."

Face twisted in fear, Sawyer blindly reaches into the box and grabs the first pastry he touches, not bothering to even look.

"That's what I thought." Jaz leans back in her chair with a satisfied smile.

And here I thought I'd tranquilized her with a fritter.

Not so much.

Once they're both settled, breakfast in hand, I hand out napkins. There's no point in engaging in conversation right now. Jaz is three fingers deep into her fritter, while Sawyer nervously chomps away, never letting the cinnamon bun stray three inches from his mouth while keeping one eye on Jaz the entire time. Not disturbed by Jaz's outburst—wouldn't be the first time she's lashed out over pastries—I take a bite of my fritter, letting the light bustle of the café and bakery fill our silence.

The purpose of the baked goods—to ease the daily annoyance raging through Jaz. I need the sugar to soak into her veins before I begin the conversation about why we're all here today, munching over a table that is really designed for two people.

Borrowing a little more time, I turn to Sawyer. "From your ignorance about the pastries in this fine establishment, I'd assume you haven't been here before."

He glances around the airy, sun-drenched space and shakes his head, drawing my gaze to the blond hair starting to curl under the edges of his hat. I've caught myself studying his hair, and the color seems to be natural, washed out from spending hours in the sun. It's the kind of look women pay hundreds of dollars to obtain. "I've only been to the to-go window for some coffee, but never inside. Reminds me of a building you'd find in Portland. Rustic but modern—doesn't really go with the rest of the town."

Insightful. I've never been to Portland, but I've seen pictures, and I can see the resemblance.

"Helena did some renovations last year—ended up breaking a main water valve in the process, and had to replace pretty much everything. It wasn't pretty, but she was thrilled about the prospect of new floors."

Sawyer glances down at the white pine floors and taps his toe, the dull thud an example of their sturdiness. "Solid. They're really nice. I also like the admiral-blue color of the cabinets combined with the black-framed windows and black hardware. Much better than the troll disaster next door."

"Ha," Jaz says, her mouth full of fritter. She punctuates her outburst with a lick of her icing-coated finger. "Finally, something we can agree on. Faye has a problem, and no one seems to have the balls to tell her."

"Have you?" Sawyer asks.

Jaz's eyes narrow into slits. "Of course not. The woman wields a frying pan like Rapunzel in *Tangled*. I like my face—I don't need it smashed in by cast-iron cookery."

"Has she been known to hit people with a frying pan?" Sawyer asks in horror. Jaz and I both nod.

"She got Tank really good once," I say. "Broke his nose."

"What did he do to warrant a broken nose?"

"Told her she should have lined up the trolls in rainbow order," Jaz answers. I can tell she's starting to warm up, which is just what I wanted. I knew the sugar would kick in at some point.

Sawyer picks at a piece of his cinnamon bun. "I thought the same thing when I went in there with Sully and the boys. Missed opportunity."

And *the boys*?

He says that with such familiarity that I truly wonder how blind I've been to this man. Blind enough to not realize he's formed a friendship with my grandpa, conducted massive renovations around the property, and established relationships with *the boys*.

"You went to Strawberry Fields with Sully?" I ask, surprised to hear this. Although I shouldn't be too surprised—it seems like they've started a little bromance behind my back.

"Yup, with Sully, Tank, and Roy."

"Roy, he's a gas." Jaz smirks. "Did they make you get the usual?"

Sawyer's lips thin in indignation. "Yeah, and they made me not only finish the smorgasbord created for Jesus and his disciples, but they also made me pay the entire check."

Both Jaz and I laugh. That's not a cheap bill, nor is finishing "the usual" an easy feat. I've seen Sully take an hour to consume the entire thing, having to take a few breathing breaks in between. I've also seen him do the sign of the cross before diving in, praying for a smooth recovery after consumption. Devouring "the usual" is an unspoken tradition in Canoodle, an Olympic sport not for the faint at heart. "Did your stomach want to burst after?" I ask.

"Let's just say it was not a good day for me." He brings his fist to his mouth and slowly shakes his head, the memory clearly too punishing to conjure up.

"But you finished?" Jaz asks.

Sawyer lowers his fist and nods. "I did. I didn't think there was any other option."

Jaz raises her eyebrows, impressed. "I respect that, but I still don't like you."

"Fair," Sawyer replies.

Grabbing one of the napkins I handed out at the beginning of the meal, Jaz blots at her mouth, clearing away any stray remnants of her fritter. She sips her coffee. Smacks her lips, and then looks between me and Sawyer. "Now that you have me hyped up on sugar and coffee, are you going to tell me what the hell is going on here?"

Looks like her patience has worn out, and I only have so much time to work with the sugar overload before it wears out and she morphs back into her usual demonic Tinker Bell self, fluttering around town, sprinkling glass shards and stardust on people.

I reach into my bag and pull out my notebook and a pen. Looking between the two of them, I take a deep breath. "Sawyer's going to help us with the renovations."

"Oh, for fuck's sake." Jaz tosses her hand up in the air. The exact reaction I was expecting. If she wasn't sugared up, her switchblade would have most likely been flipped open and thrown like an axe across the room—straight into a wall. "Because he was able to lay a floor down once? I don't think we need Julia disrupting our solid workflow."

"Jaz, first of all, we don't have a solid workflow, and secondly, he used to be a contractor. We could really use his help."

"Uh-huh, and have you seen any of his work?"

"He's the one who fixed the bench, picnic tables, and horseshoe pits," I say with a lift of my chin.

At a snail's pace, Jaz turns her head so she's looking Sawyer in the eyes. I mentally prepare myself for whatever is going to fly out of her mouth. She might be sugared up, but she's still unhinged. With a tilt of her head and a careful poise to her shoulders, she asks, "You're the one who fixed Sully's bench?"

The mixture of fear and satisfaction contradict each other in Sawyer's eyes. "Yeah," he says, his voice strangled.

She lightly draws circles on the table, emulating a mob boss calculating when he will strike with his bazooka. *Kablam-o*, rocket to the face. No mercy, the stovepipe has spoken. "And you were the one who did the picnic table area? The same area that made my friend cry because she was so happy to have the spot where she used to cross-stitch with Grandma brought back to life?"

Well, she didn't have to mention the crying aspect. Jeez. My cheeks flame.

Sawyer glances at me. "You cried?"

"Not relevant," I answer, looking away.

Jaz shifts, crossing one leg over the other, an undeniable power move that keeps her in control of the conversation. "And you're the one who fixed the horseshoe pits that Tank was raving about the other day?"

"He was raving?" Sawyer asks with a smile. "That's good to know."

"Don't you dare smile at me." Jaz jabs a finger at him. The gesture shoots Sawyer back in his chair, and he blinks a few times.

And here's my cue to step in. "He's very good. He also refinished the handicap-accessible cabin for my dads." I open my phone to a picture of the cabin that I took this morning.

Dubious, Jaz takes my phone with a roll of her eyes and stares at the picture for no longer than five seconds. She gently sets the phone down and slides it back to me on the table. As she keeps her eyes on Sawyer, her lips twist to the side for a moment. "I don't like you."

And here I thought the proof of his work was going to open her mind, help her see Sawyer from a different angle. But the girl knows how to hold a grudge.

"But . . ." She pauses. "Unfortunately, you do wonderful work." Sawyer cautiously smiles. It flits between a nervous pull at his lips and a frown, his lips performing a cancan of expression as he tries to read Jaz. "This pains me, but fine, he can help us."

Not that she had a choice in the matter. But having her grudging approval will make the whole process much smoother.

She points a finger into the air. "But this doesn't mean we're friends, you hear me?"

Sawyer brings his cup of coffee to his lips. "Don't worry," he says over the rim. "Fallon and I established last night that we're not friends. I wouldn't expect any less from you."

"Good." Jaz flips my notebook open with one finger. "Now that we have all of that established. What's the plan?"

A delightful compromise to a very unpredictable union. Julia the Runaway Groomsman, forgetter of my face, blind date disaster, now assisting us in the makeover of Canoodle Cove Cabins. I take a deep breath. "Well, it's time to tackle some cabins."

❖   ❖   ❖

"Oh my God, there's a mouse turd in your hair," I say, pointing in horror at Jaz's platinum-blonde locks.

"What?" she shrieks. Like the Tasmanian Devil, she spins in place, screeching. "Get it off. Get it off."

Arms flailing, she transforms into a blur, a whirl so strong that no proper defense could subdue her thrashing jazz hands or her chest-high knees. She spins, she ducks, she dives around the outside of the third cabin we're working on.

"Don't just stand there." Her scream is decibels too high, one octave shy of only being audible to dogs. "Get it out. Get it out. Get it out!"

I approach across the grass with caution, my glove-clad karate-chop hands my only defense. "I can't when you're flailing like that. Stop moving."

"If I stop moving, the turd will implant itself."

"That is not a thing!" I yell, swatting at her head with my work glove.

"I saw it on the Discovery Channel."

"You clearly were not paying attention." I swat again, but she dodges my glove. "Jaz, stop moving so I can help you."

"Ahhhh!" she screams, shaking her hands over her hair. "Why is it still—"

Thwack.

Plop.

Jaz stills as if she's been struck with a bullet, straight to the heart. She blinks, her expression dazed, and then, like a freshly cut pine, she timbers down to the grass. In shock, I glance up to find Sawyer standing over her, pillow in hand, looking just as shocked as me.

Did he just whack her with that pillow?

From the way his hands shake as he stares down at the confused Jaz, I'd say yes.

Fear steals my breath as I stand ramrod straight, anticipating the worst. A cacophony of threats, brimming on Jaz's tongue, ready to be unleashed. I can feel it.

May the forest be with you, Sawyer; hell hath no fury when it comes to Jaz.

With a shake and a shudder, Jaz gains her bearings as she recovers from a brutal TKO, her opponent a simple cotton-filled headrest.

My hands twisting in fear, my gaze flits between her and Sawyer. Sawyer stands still, pillow lowered, stunned that he just walloped Jaz across the noggin. Jaz, a worthy adversary, grapples to regain her composure.

After a few moments of silence—and an array of nervous swallows—Sawyer clears his throat. "Uh, the turd has been extracted from your hair . . . via stuffed fabric bag." He holds up the pillow. "And, uh, I would be willing to smack you again, if you ever find yourself in another predicament such as this."

Ooooh, I hate to be crude, but my butt clenches as I await the impending outpouring of unbridled acrimony.

The air stills.

The birds flee from the trees, sensing Hades splitting the ground and erupting like lava to the earth's surface.

And, in the far-off distance, a baby's wail breaks through the stark silence.

Do you smell that? Homicide lurks around the corner. The victim? A six-foot-two, ignorant outsider attempting to claw into the good graces of our town's demagogue.

Her eyes meet his.

Her lips part.

I pray for the children in the town, hoping they aren't exposed to Julia's shrill cry of defeat . . .

Here it comes . . .

Brace yourself . . .

WINCES

"Thank you," Jaz says, calmly.

Rationally.

And I'm not sure if I should check her pulse or be frightened for my life.

"Thank you?" I ask, and I don't know why. Maybe because for the last half hour, Jaz has been doing nothing but complaining about ripping carpets from the three cabins we're working on. Yes, perhaps during our first cabin, we might have run into a cockroach that was so large that it actually waved its little leg at us from the corner, startling us to the core.

And maybe in the second cabin, we stumbled over a series of carpet stains that could have either come from a waterfall of coffee that was never cleaned properly or . . . a covert murder of a woodland creature. Either way, I thanked the renovating gods for the gloves on my hands.

So yeah, fecal matter in the hair after unearthing a mouse nest in cabin three, I guess it qualifies for a reality check.

"These carpets have drained me of my disgust for Julia," Jaz says, defeated. "And it's only been an hour." She looks up at me. "Was Sully cleaning any of these cabins?"

"I guess not as well as he should have been. I'm surprised we don't have any bad reviews. With the amount of foreign matter we've found while tearing the carpets out, you'd think there would be a few unhappy customers."

"Then again, everyone always loves Sully," Jaz says, still sitting on the grass. "You can't compete with his grumpy charm." She lets out a deep sigh. "You can't hate me for what I'm about to say."

"Say what?" I ask as Sawyer sets the pillow down and walks back over to the cabin, probably thanking his lucky stars he just skirted death. Head drawn down, he continues to feed the carpet through the cabin door. He doesn't seem to ever stop.

"I can't possibly help out anymore until I take a shower and confirm that all fecal matter has been removed from my hair."

Even though being down a set of hands won't be ideal, I can appreciate her need to bathe. If the shoe was on the other foot, I would be ducking my head under a hose, washing my head with the high-powered garden nozzle.

"I understand." I reach down and help her to her feet. "Do you think you'll be back?"

"I'll bring lunch. Tacos from Nine Juan Juan work?"

"That works for me." I call over my shoulder: "Sawyer, tacos for lunch—you good with that?"

"Yup," he says with a grunt as he pushes the carpet out of the cabin and onto the grass.

"I should help him."

Jaz puts her hands on my shoulders. "Godspeed."

She takes off, her power walk rivaling Sunday mall walkers getting in their steps for the day.

I walk through the now-cleared doorway and into the cabin, where Sawyer is on the floor, pulling staples from the ground with a pair of pliers. "Can I help?"

He holds out an extra set of pliers to me. "Here you go. Be diligent, and make sure you get all the nails and staples out. Easier to do it now than when you're laying the floor."

"Oh, so you mean like how you had to pluck staples from the lobby floor—you don't want to do that again?"

He glances up at me. "Exactly."

I get down on my hands and knees. "Should I start on the other side of the room or next to you?"

"Next to me. We can sweep together—that way we don't miss anything."

I sidle up next to him and immediately feel the heat pouring off his body. It's a hot July day up in the mountains, and the sun beats through the dusty cabin windows. The demanding labor he's already put in today seeps through the fabric of his cotton shirt, and I can sense he needs to pull his shirt off from the way he keeps adjusting his sleeves, pushing them up and over his shoulders.

Should I tell him it's okay if he wants to take his shirt off?

Might come off a little voyeuristic. Probably should just let him decide on the fate of his shirt.

"You nearly skipped death with Jaz, you know that, right?"

He keeps his eyes on the floor, his intense work ethic shining like a beacon, guiding me through the muddied waters of this renovation. "I'm aware."

"From your stiff shoulders and the worried curl of your lips, I'm going to assume you were prepared for the worst."

"It's why I lowered the pillow over my crotch; at least there would be minor protection from her impending blow."

"Very smart. Covering the crotch could have possibly saved you a severe puncture wound to the scrotum."

"An unfavorable result." He pauses his hands and turns toward me. "Has she done that? Punctured someone in the scrotum?"

"No comment."

He shivers, his entire body convulsing in one giant wave of fright.

We spend the next ten minutes working in tandem, gripping staples, pulling, and depositing in a cup. The sound of our work has a rhythm that by no means would win or be nominated for a Grammy, but the echoing of our labor offers encouragement as we make it to our last section of the cabin.

I've considered many topics to use as conversation starters.

Like . . . I heard you flipped off the bride and groom. Was it difficult pulling off a double bird?

And . . . do you regret walking out of the wedding; do you wish you twerked your way out instead?

Not to mention . . . do you ever yearn to find your missing blue shoe?

But Sawyer is the first to talk as we crouch in the corner of the cabin, toward the door. Almost done. "I know we're not friends, but maybe we can fill the silence with something."

"What do you have in mind? I can pull up some invigorating tunes from Cat in Heat."

"For the love of God, don't." I let out a low chuckle as he shoots me a thoughtful look. "Do you miss the demands of being a nurse?"

Huh, I wasn't expecting him to ask that question. I didn't even think he remembered that I was a nurse. He must have dug deep into his memory bank to pull that one out, especially since he didn't even recognize me or remember our harrowing date in the first place.

"Sometimes," I answer. "I worked in the emergency room, and although it came with long hours, it kept me on my toes. Problem-solving, but with knowledge that I have stored away. With taking care of Sully, I feel completely out of my wheelhouse. And even though I'd come here every summer and help out around the cabins, I still feel like I don't know what I'm doing most of the time. Being uncomfortable seems to be my new normal now. So, yeah, I miss it sometimes, but I wouldn't go back, not when I have these days left with Sully, even the ones when he's not fully lucid."

"I would probably feel the same way in your shoes," he says, dropping a handful of staples into our shared cup depository. "I would want to spend as much time with my family as I could."

"I do miss my friends."

"And Peter probably."

"Yes . . . of course. And Peter," I add, feeling a swift stab of guilt. What the hell is wrong with me? Why wouldn't I mention him first? A nervous sweat breaks out along the back of my neck. Peter 100 percent should have been my first thought, but he wasn't. He wasn't even my second thought. Possibly not even my third. If I am completely honest, the list of what I miss would go dads, friends, Palm Springs pools . . . Peter. Yikes, that revelation isn't settling well in the pit of my stomach.

Trying to ignore my ineptitude at being a loving girlfriend, I opt to change the subject. "I also miss some of the crazy stories me and the other nurses would share."

"Crazy stories, huh?" The smirk that pulls at the corner of his lips kicks me right in the chest. It's all I can do to not fall backward into the pile of rolled-up mouse-poop carpet.

"You, uh, wouldn't even believe me if I told you some of these stories." I sit up from my crouched knee position. "Emergency room in Palm Springs, the celebrity getaway. Boy, do I have stories."

Joining me, he sits up on his heels as well. "Why don't you entertain me, then?"

Entertain him . . .

Immediately, my mind reels with stories that would make him laugh.

A retelling of my very first period and the very heartfelt haiku my dads wrote for me about becoming a woman.

My energetic dance performance at my third-grade talent show featuring the musical stylings of Stevie Wonder singing "Isn't She Lovely" as I hopped around like a dainty fairy.

Perhaps a somber breakdown of the day I lost my virginity to Joel Eaglewash, and how he cried into my breasts afterward for a solid five minutes while mumbling how happy he was. I can still feel the river of his emotions cascading down my cleavage.

Honestly, all blind date material I should have thrown at him. Maybe then he would have remembered me.

"You okay?" Sawyer asks.

"Oh yeah, sorry." My cheeks flame with embarrassment. God, I hope I wasn't offhandedly performing my third-grade dance while in my reverie. "How about a water break?"

"As long as you tell me at least one emergency room story."

"Deal." After standing up, I grab our waters from the windowsill and bring them over to where Sawyer is resting against the wall now.

I sit next to him and hand him his water. He uncaps it, tilts his head back, and gulps. I get lost in the way his throat contracts as he swallows once again, the contours hollowing and adjusting to his consumption. Apparently, I'm a throat girl now.

What does Peter's throat look like? It annoys me that I can't think of it, that I can't picture if it's all . . . contract-y while he drinks as well.

When Sawyer lowers the bottle, I quickly look away so he doesn't catch me staring. Instead, I sit there, rigid, desperately trying to conjure up images of Peter drinking water, his throat contracting in a sexy way, but all I can think of is the time he drank his Bloody Mary too fast and the red liquid careened down his neck, making him look like a victim in a slasher movie. Not the same thing.

Sawyer nudges me with his shoulder. "So . . . ?"

"Yeah, emergency stories." I take a sip of my water and clear my throat. *Get it together, Fallon.* "So, there was this Oscar winner—"

"Name?" Sawyer asks.

"Sorry, privacy laws."

He snaps his fingers in disappointment. "Damn it."

"I know, but you might be able to figure it out. Oscar winner, young, came into the emergency room because he was reenacting a scene from his latest film for his friends and wound up . . . getting a crystal stuck up his nose. It took three doctors and two nurses as well as a large pair of forceps to get it out."

"Ooof, that hurts."

"And after all was said and done, he claimed that he had no idea how it got up there, but he would like the crystal back because it was expensive. Later on, he was exposed on one of those gossip websites, showing a video of him snorting the crystal."

"Jesus." Sawyer chuckles. "Can't fathom snorting a crystal on a lazy Saturday."

"I don't think many people can." I nudge him back with my shoulder. "What about you, any kooky celebrity stories? You're the one who works in the entertainment biz."

"Other than a crazed ex-boyfriend walking out of a wedding?"

"In your defense, it was entirely unfair for them to ask you to be the best man. Fourth groomsman in line at least."

He smiles, and it's absolutely as devastating as his smirk from earlier. He might be a lousy person to go on a date with, but he sure does have that killer Hollywood gleam about him.

"At least," he says softly. "But crazy stories? I don't have many, other than the usual prima donna–type stuff. I haven't had the privilege of being on every movie set, so I'm sure I've missed out on some epic meltdowns."

"Such a shame. Your next endeavor should be writing a book, a tell-all of the behind-the-scenes fodder you've accumulated over the years. That book could fly off the shelves . . . lickety-split."

Lickety-split? I can't recall a time in my life when I've ever used that phrase.

Ever.

"Lickety-split?" Sawyer chuckles. Of course he picks up on it.

Going with it, I snap my fingers in the air. "Like that. Everyone loves a good dose of gossip. As long as it isn't their downfall, that's all they care about."

"True." He lets out a deep sigh and rests his bottle of water on his leg. "I wonder what people are saying about my downfall."

"I have some articles saved if you want to see. My favorite was how they claimed you were paid handsomely by the wagering sharks in Las Vegas to cut out on the wedding, extra if you made a scene. The article claimed you were rewarded with two million dollars and a bedazzled coin purse as a bonus." I turn to him. "Can I see the coin purse?"

He laughs so loud that the sound fills the empty space, consuming the air around us. "Wow, I'd love to live in a world where you can write absolute lies with no repercussions."

"Wait . . . so there's no coin purse?" I playfully ask.

"I'm sorry to be the bearer of bad news, but I have no bedazzled coin purse in my possession."

"It's not in your possession, but that doesn't mean it wasn't a thing." I raise my brow in hope.

"It's not a thing."

"Damn."

Chuckling, he bumps me with his shoulder again. "Call me crazy, but do you think we're becoming friends?"

"Where would you get that impression?" I ask, even though I can feel it. The lightness between us, the joking, the easy camaraderie. Sawyer—when not on a blind date and buried in his phone—seems like the kind of guy everyone wants to be friends with. The people pleaser. The do-gooder.

"You're acting friendly toward me. I'm guessing if I was trapped under a rock, you wouldn't walk by and take a video, but actually call for help."

"Stuck under a rock, that's your example?" I ask.

"It's embarrassing that, as a screenwriter, I couldn't come up with something more . . . death defying."

"Like . . . if we were doing a trapeze act together, I wouldn't necessarily let you fall to your death—I would *consider* catching you."

"Or if I was deathly allergic to cilantro, and you saw a fleck of green on my taco, you'd slap it out of my hand before I could ingest the poison."

"Not sure if I'd slap it out of your hand, but I'd *consider* slapping it out of your hand."

"Ah," he says with a nod. "So, does that mean if I was still stuck under the rock, you wouldn't call someone for help but rather . . ."

"Consider calling someone," I finish for him.

"So then . . . not friends."

"Afraid not, but this water break was a delightful respite."

"It was. But the floors aren't going to take care of themselves."

"Unfortunately." I stand and offer my hand to him. He glances at it for a brief moment before grabbing it and letting me help him to his feet.

He eyes me with his cornflower blues, a color I've written off as boring, but today, they carry an extra glint in them. A knowing one. A glint so strong that it almost conveys a message. A message of victory.

Well, that won't do. If he thinks he's won me over, that he's about to start a beautiful friendship with me, he's sadly mistaken. I'm an iron maiden, emotionless, with no room to cultivate any new friendships. This shop is closed. No vacancy.

Move on.

There will be no friendships allowed.

"Stop looking at me like that and get to work." I turn on my heel and bring my water bottle back to the windowsill, all the while trying to eliminate his hopeful gaze from my mind.

❖　❖　❖

"What on God's green earth is going on in here?" Sully yells from the doorway, startling both Sawyer and me as we finish installing the last of the floorboards in cabin number three.

"Sully," I say loudly as my breath tries to catch up with my heart. "Goodness, you scared me."

"Scared *us*," Sawyer says, one hand gripping his chest, the other gripping the wall next to him.

"You ripped up perfectly good carpet." Sully taps his foot on the new white pine flooring. The flooring he chose when we were at Village Hardware—grumbled over all the options for half an hour before settling on the one he'd chosen first. "This looks cheap."

If Sully were any other person, I could easily see myself pouncing on him. We've been laboring over these floors for the last four hours, and one single criticism will tip me over the edge of pleasant to snarly jaguar, ready to claw out an eyeball.

But since Sully is my grandfather whom I respect and admire greatly, and he has Alzheimer's and clearly doesn't recall the renovations we spoke about, I tread carefully.

I move over to the design plans hanging on the wall near the door, the ones Sully drew and signed so when he does forget, I can show him exactly what he approved. I point to the papers. "You came up with all of these changes, down to the decor—with notes of red throughout the cabins to represent Grandma Joan."

Sully stalks up to the plans and studies them closely. I can see the confusion rippling across his face as he flips through the pages, looking over the samples as well as the color palettes. My heart aches as he tries to understand the approval he's made to all the changes. I can't imagine what it's like to be in his brain, to be so utterly confused and unaware of your surroundings. To still be living but lost in time, unaware of who you are or what's happening in your everyday life.

He slips on a mask of indifference as he shuts the plans against the wall.

He doesn't remember.

He doesn't even recall any of the choices he made, but he's the poster child for "fake it till you make it" because he grips his hands behind him, rocks on his heels, and says, "Everything looks in order."

This is easily my least favorite thing he does—acting like he understands when he really has no clue what's going on. I know it's a defense mechanism because he's a proud man. I know it's painful, confusing, and heartbreaking for him that he goes through these moments in his day where he can't recall anything.

His eyes land on Sawyer, and he straightens up. "Fallon, why don't you introduce me to your boyfriend."

Oh boy, it's a really bad day.

"Sully, this is Sawyer. He's helping with the renovations. Peter is my boyfriend."

Sully glances to the side. I can tell he's attempting to draw up any recollection of Peter.

"Right, right," he says with a nod. "Well, Sawyer, if you ask my granddaughter out on a date, just know she really likes flowers. Daisies."

Grandma Joan liked flowers . . . daisies, to be exact.

I turn to Sawyer and give him an apologetic look. "I'm going to take him back to the residence. I'll be right back."

"Take your time," he says softly. "I'll finish up here."

I quietly thank him and take Sully by the arm. "I saw there were new episodes of that *Renovation Nation* show you like. Why don't we get you something to eat so you can sit down and enjoy?"

He doesn't say anything, but instead he lets me guide him up the sidewalk to the residence. Halfway there, he stops and faces me, his expression crestfallen. "Where's Joan? She was supposed to make dinner. I think she's mad at me."

My heart snaps, and I attempt to hold it together. I slip my hand into Sully's, our palms touching as I bring it up to my heart and carefully say, "Grandma Joan passed away several years ago, Sully."

His eyes fill up with tears.

His lip trembles.

And his hand shakes in mine as his other hand drags up to his chest, clutching it in disbelief. "Not my Joannie," he says, nearly crumbling to the ground.

Despair falls over us like the descending dark of the night, a blanket of sorrow offering no comfort, only pain.

"I'm sorry, Sully," I say, my voice cracking, my emotions getting the best of me.

This happens maybe once a week— me reminding Sully how he lost the love of his life, and every time it seems to grow harder and harder to break the news. Maybe because every time, I watch him handle the news with more and more anguish. The frown lines in his face have grown deeper. The tears in his eyes fall heavier. And the gasp of breath he takes when he hears the news has become more substantial.

"Do you want me to take you to your room?" I ask.

Solemnly, with a tear sliding down his crestfallen face, he nods.

We spend the rest of the walk in silence. When we reach his room, he does exactly what I know he's going to do. He sits on his bed, feet dangling off the edge of the white woven comforter that has seen many years, and carefully reaches over to his nightstand, where he picks up a framed picture of Grandma Joan.

His shaky hand passes over the glass, and tears crest over his eyes and down his worn cheeks.

Heartbreaking. It's the only way I can describe it. Truly heartbreaking.

Sully and Grandma Joan had the kind of marriage people write about, built on a foundation of friendship and grown through loyal and trustworthy love. They had their fights and their moments where everything wasn't beautiful, but they also respected each other and shared an unmatched, undying love. Sully worshipped the ground Grandma Joan walked on and did everything up until her last breath to make sure she was always happy, cared for, and loved.

Seeing him grieve constantly, over and over again, is taking a toll on me.

It's absolutely wrecking me.

"Sully," I say on a shaky breath, taking a step toward him.

He clutches the frame to his chest, his toughened hands trembling. His eyes are cast down, his tears staining his blue khaki pants as he sniffles. "I'd like to be alone."

Like he always wants, and I always respect his privacy, even though all I want to do is wrap him into a hug and tell him how much I love him.

"Okay. Let me know if you need anything."

I know he won't.

I know he'll stay in his room, clutching this picture.

I know he'll open his box of love letters he's kept from Grandma Joan and read them over and over again until he falls asleep.

And I know tomorrow, when he wakes up, he'll forget all about the sorrow he experienced the night before.

I quietly exit the room and remove my phone from my pocket. I open the monitor app and set the notifications so I'll be alerted if he leaves his room . . . just in case.

And then I lean against the wall and catch my breath as my racing heart seems to take up all the space in my chest.

CHAPTER FIFTEEN
SAWYER

Fallon didn't come back right away.

Nor did she come back within an hour.

We are treading close to two hours since she left, and all I can think about is how badly I want to check on her. And on Sully.

The look on his face, the pain, the disorientation—I don't think I've ever seen anything more devastating. In a very short amount of time, Sully has clawed his way into my life and has settled right in my chest. I've never had the kind of relationship Fallon has with Sully, and I know I'm not strong enough to be in her position, the sole caregiver of someone with Alzheimer's. Just being this close to Sully—which, in reality, isn't too close at all—is difficult.

Since Fallon never came back and there was still plenty for me to do, I picked up the paint gun—after tarping everything that shouldn't be painted—and started painting cabin number one. The spray easily transferred to the drywall, covering the worn-down beige. Fallon and Sully wanted to preserve the exposed wood beams lining the cabin's front wall, so I made sure to tarp those well—I'd hate to get any paint on the natural wood.

As the white hits the wall, I picture what the finished product will look like. A natural cabin feel, but with floors that match the exposed wood, making the whole space bright and cheery. The darkness that creeps into the cabin at night with the beige walls, olive-green carpet, and heavy natural wood furniture can be quite overwhelming—trust me, I know from experience—but these new plans will still give visitors a mountainy atmosphere while staying in a space that's more modern and appealing.

Just as I'm finishing up the last wall, the plastic tarp shielding the doorway parts and Fallon steps into the cabin. She's no longer in her work clothes, but rather a pair of blue cotton shorts and a simple *Canoodle, California* shirt. Her hair is wet and braided into two long french braids, and her face has a freshly scrubbed dewy glow.

She looks . . . cuddle-able.

Annnd I've never said that word before in my entire life.

"Sawyer, I'm so sorry," she starts, anxiety written all over her face.

"Hey, no need to apologize." I set the paint gun down.

"You didn't have to keep working. I assumed once you finished the floor, you'd call it a night."

"There was more time on the clock; figured I might as well keep moving forward. I hope that's okay."

"Of course it's okay." But the look on her face tells me another story. She worries her lip as she takes in the freshly painted room, her arms folded across her chest.

I take a step forward and bend at the knees to look her in the eyes. "Are you okay, Fallon?"

When she looks up at me, tears fill her eyes. She shakes her head. "No, I'm not."

Didn't think so.

"You know what, let's get out of here," I say, taking her by the arm. "I can clean up in a little bit."

"I can help—"

"What you can do is follow me." I guide her gently and part the plastic for her. When we step outside, I'm immediately hit by the stark darkness of being in the middle of the San Jacinto Mountains. I've been so cooped up in these cabins with the lights on that I failed to recognize just how dark it's gotten.

The trees have turned to deep shadows, wavering in the background, their branches barely bristling in the light breeze. Solar lights line the pathway along the cabins, illuminating the sidewalk in a pale yellow. And up above, in a clear night sky, stars shine impossibly large, as if trying to replace the missing sun as they glitter above us.

I bring her over to Sully's bench, and we both take a seat. I drape my arm along the back and turn toward her. She brings her legs up to her chest and clutches them close as she stares out at the unmoving lake. The demon ducks are most likely getting their beauty rest, so they'll be refreshed when they wake up in the morning, ready to terrorize innocent people.

I doubt Fallon wants to talk about what happened back there with Sully. If I were her, I'd want a break, to escape for a second, so instead of asking her if she wants to talk about it, I take a different approach.

"I thought I was going to marry Annalisa," I say. "I met her on my first Lovemark set. She was an extra at the time and very grounded. She had raptor tendencies, but I assumed they were normal."

"Raptor tendencies?" Fallon chuckles and looks over at me. Just what I wanted: to extract her from her thoughts and focus on something other than Sully.

"Yeah. She could be very sweet, but when something went wrong, she'd turn into a different person. Her jaw would unhinge, her teeth would grow into these fangs with bloody points, and then, when you weren't expecting it, she'd strike like a raptor, going straight to the jugular, only to leave you bloodied and full of regret on the floor."

She studies me, her eyes searching me, then turns away with a laugh. "You sure do have that creative bone. The overexaggerating is spot on."

"You can't be a writer and not overexaggerate," I say. "In order to portray a mood, a feeling, an action, you have to be able to draw up a picture of intensity inside the reader's mind. Overexaggeration is key."

"You say that as if you write books."

"I've dabbled," I say with a shrug. "But I have a problem painting a pretty picture."

"You just painted a beautifully bloody picture in my head."

I chuckle. "When I was trying to be a screenwriter, I took this creative writing class to help me expand my knowledge, offer me a different perspective. It was helpful but infuriating at the same time, because all I wanted to do was write dialogue, but my teacher was adamant about me slowing down and really visualizing the story for the reader. 'Set the scene . . . set the scene,' she'd constantly say. Drove me fucking nuts. At one point, when reading her notes—she wrote 'Set the scene' one too many times, and I threw my paper across the room and screamed, '*You* set the scene!'" I chuckle again, remembering how it felt to want to pull my hair out. "It was not my finest moment, especially since when I threw the paper, it knocked over a cup of coffee and spilled all over my floor."

"See what happens when you throw temper tantrums?"

"I'd like to say I learned my lesson, but . . . well, my latest temper tantrum is trending still."

"At least this temper tantrum had more finesse than throwing a piece of paper. A well-executed bitch fit."

"Bitch fit?" I raise my brows. "How dare you accuse me of acting bitchy."

"Have you watched the video?"

The humor in her voice tells me my strategy is working. Self-deprecation: always a winner when trying to pull someone out of a funk. Because they don't think about how dreadfully horrible their life is, and for just a moment, they only focus on your lack of ability to function like a normal human. It can be entertaining and boost morale sky high.

Hey, at least I'm not as bad as that guy.

I might be suffering, but check out the baggage he's carrying. Woof.

"Does it look like I'd spend my time lying on my stomach across my bed, legs kicked up in the air, enjoying a video of me acting like an ass on repeat?"

She scrunches her fingers together. "Maybe a little."

"Clearly you don't know me at all . . ." I look her in the eyes. "I wouldn't kick my feet up in the air."

She laughs and turns toward me.

Yup, I'm killing it at this whole "helping her forget her sorrows" thing.

I'm also finding it quite hard not to get lost in her expressive eyes. Even in the semidarkness, they suck me in, clawing at me, begging to stare, especially when they're full of tears, because all I want to do is help remove the anguish lacing them. I want to bring a smile to her eyes. I want to show her that even though she's wading through muddied waters, she still can laugh, she still can enjoy the small things like sitting on a bench, under the stars with a nonfriend . . . laughing at his expense.

"You say that, but how am I supposed to know for sure?" she asks.

"Do I need to show you how I'd watch a video of me throwing a temper tantrum?"

"It would be preferred." She smirks.

For that little kick up of her lip, I'd do just about anything at this point. A smile from her feels like the soft opening of a brilliant sunset, sending a breath of renewed air into your lungs.

So, I slither from the bench and onto the grass, draining out of my seat like molasses, which makes her laugh out loud. I reach out a hand to her. "May I use your phone as a prop?"

"Of course."

I take her phone and lie flat on my back before spreading my legs as far as they will go—this boy needs some yoga in his life because the hips are tight—and holding the phone up above my head. With my free hand, I cover my eyes and then part my middle and index fingers, offering a small window to my demise. I wince and then . . . freeze.

Fallon's laugh is probably one of the most beautiful sounds I've ever heard as it rings through the silent night, filling me with an undeniable joy.

"Why are your legs spread like that?"

"You don't want to know."

"I do," she says, staring down at me.

I sit up on my elbows and look her in the eyes. "I easily get sweaty, so proper air flow is important when watching degrading videos of myself."

"Oh my God," she says, cringing.

"Told you, you didn't want to know."

From her reaction, I think I can guarantee she'll never forget that comment. Any possible chance that things would be romantic between us—in an alternate reality where she didn't have a boyfriend, wasn't attached to a buff man named Peter—just flew out the window. She'd never be able to look at my crotch the same.

For the record, I'm not an overly sweaty person.

I sweat the normal amount.

If I work hard, there will be sweat, but if I'm just sitting at the desk, writing, I'm not breaking out in a sweat, needing a fan to blow a breeze up my lower region, Marilyn Monroe–style, just to cool down.

Although no doubt it would feel good . . .

"For the love of God, close your legs." Fallon laughs, but I just attempt to spread them wider.

The attempt falls short.

Very short.

And before I know it . . . I feel a snap.

"Oy, my groin," I say, clutching my inner leg and rolling to the side. Fallon's laugh is even louder.

See? Self-deprecation.

Works like a charm. Just wish I wasn't clutching my (sweaty) groin in front of her.

*It's not really sweaty, I need you to understand that. But, you know . . . overexaggeration . . . *

"Call the medics . . . oh wait!" I sit up. "Nurse Fallon, report to the grass—your patient popped his groin out of its socket."

"That's not even a thing." She pushes at me with her toe. "And there's no way you're my patient."

"I don't claim to be an expert on medical terms, but I do know good bedside manner when I see it, and nudging a patient with gnarly troll toes is not a proper way to conduct yourself."

Her eyes widen with silent laughter, the corner of her lips curling up in shock. "I don't have gnarly troll toes."

I grip the spot on my leg where she pushed me with her foot. "Say that to the bruise forming on my thigh." I snap my fingers over my head. "Proprietor, proprietor, there has been an obvious case of abuse on the property. I'd like to speak with management."

Fallon's feet drop to the grass, and she crosses her arms at her chest. "I'm the manager and proprietor. What is your complaint?"

I roll to face her. "Your medical staff is unhelpful, your management lackluster, and this grass needs to be mowed because the blades are making my legs itchy."

Hands clasped together, she leans forward. "Your complaint has been received. Please give us seven to ten business days to respond."

I fly off the grass and to my feet in mock protest. "Seven to ten business days? That's outrageous."

She leans back on the bench now, arms still crossed, her expression playful in the moonlight. "Your sweaty crotch is what's outrageous."

"Hey," I say, pointing at her. "That was said in confidence. Don't you dare throw it in my face like that."

"I didn't sign a confidentiality agreement. For all I know, your dripping balls are fair game."

The guttural laugh that erupts out of me could possibly wake up the entire town of Canoodle. "They're not dripping, Jesus." I wipe at my eyes.

"How do I know what's going on down there? You toss an idea in my head, and now my mind is whirling. Temper tantrums, sweaty balls, legs kicked up while lounging—"

"I told you they weren't kicked up; I showed you with spread legs."

"I prefer to envision them kicked up, but I have to say, you're not painting a pretty picture for yourself."

"What about all the relentless labor I've put into the Cove—does that not account for anything?"

"The pulled-groin antics eclipse the hard work, sorry."

I slowly nod and take a seat next to her. "In an odd way, I accept this."

She chuckles. "Is your groin really hurt?"

"Nah, I think I just spurred it alive." The moment the words leave my mouth, I try to backtrack. "Not like . . . that kind of alive. You know. Not like a boner or anything like that."

"Didn't take it that way, but you should be very grateful Jaz hasn't been here for this entire conversation."

"Does that mean you're not going to tell her?"

"Oh no, she's going to know about every little detail of this interaction."

"I wouldn't expect anything less at this point."

Silence falls between us as the sound of the lake lightly lapping against the shore takes the place of our banter. And as we sit here, in each other's company, I feel my heart beat faster than it ever has. The woman beside me is untouchable, and yet I feel my palms grow sweaty being this close. I have a burning need to look over at her, stare into those eyes, push the wisp of hair that keeps crossing over her cheek behind her ear. In the warm embrace of this moonlit night, I realize I made a huge mistake.

A giant one.

Probably a mistake I will regret for quite some time, if not ever.

Ignoring Fallon on our blind date will go down as the stupidest thing I've ever done.

Not falling in love with Annalisa.

Not accepting the offer to be Simon's best man.

And not flipping them off at the altar.

Nope, allowing Fallon to slip through my fingers—now that was a colossal mistake.

I'm realizing that with a force as strong as an attacking army invading enemy territory as she cocks her head to the side and lights up my world with the simplest of smiles. A smile so small that if I wasn't paying attention, I might have missed the shift of her lips. But it's there, and hell, it's sweet. It's beautiful. It's intoxicating.

I feel the grip of that smile tighten around my chest, constricting, causing my pulse to pick up, my lungs to work harder.

"Thank you," she says softly, and my breath trips over the beat of my own heart. Her eyes connect with mine. Getting lost in her gaze is so easy. "For helping me forget for a moment."

"Does that thank-you possibly mean we've stepped closer to the label of friends?" I say, trying to keep the mood light.

"Why would you push your luck like that?"

"Desperation to make a friend?" I offer, the confession partially true.

She eyes me and then stands from the bench. "We're possibly closing in on the friends thing."

I stand as well. "You know, I woke up today thinking, today is going to be a good day." I step in close, and even though I know I shouldn't touch her, I reach out and push that wisp of hair behind her ear. "It was a good day."

My finger trails over her skin longer than it should. I'm not a dumb man; I know she's off limits. I know the way it feels to have someone step in on your relationship. But hell, I needed this moment with her. This calm, quiet, endearing moment.

Just the one touch.

Just one night where I can look her in the eyes and for a second forget that she has a boyfriend. Forget that I let a good thing slip past me when I should have held it tight.

Her eyes search mine. They're not frantic, they're not confused; they're just trying to understand, and I don't blame her, because I'm trying to understand as well, this pull that I feel toward her. Does she feel it too? Does she feel like I'm the ground and she's gravity, the irresistible force bringing us together?

I take a breath. No, I need to keep that pull at arm's length. I can do that—it's for the best.

"It was a good night," she replies, and then, to my utter shock, she steps in close to me and wraps her arms around me, squeezing me tight. "Thank you, Sawyer."

Fuck . . .

And here I thought I could keep my feelings for her close to my chest, locked away so she'll have no idea that I want her in my life, more than just friends.

But with her arms wrapped around me, I'm not sure I can keep my feelings monitored. Not like this.

Not feeling how perfectly she fits into my hold.

How soft and warm she is.

Or the smell of her lavender shampoo filling my head with nonsense. The kind of nonsense that will get me in trouble.

But because I'm helpless, because I'm a pathetic man who has no will when it comes to this woman and her gentle touch, I wrap my arms around her and squeeze her tight. "Any time, Fallon."

For a brief second, her hand travels up my spine and back down before she releases me. If I wasn't desperate to soak up every moment of this interaction, I would have missed it, but because I'm obsessed with her touch, I felt it. The comfort. The warmth. And as she takes a step back, my body turns cold, empty.

With more distance between us, she says, "You can take tomorrow off if you want."

Take some time off? How could I? Not after realizing how petite yet strong she was in my arms, not after savoring the way her laugh vibrated through my chest or feeling the sparkle of her smile to the very marrow of my bones.

No.

Like an addict, I need more. I want to be around her. I want to get to know her better.

Despite my bruised knees, my aching back, and my blistered hands, I'll continue to work if it means getting to spend a portion of my day at her side.

With Fallon.

I stick my hands in my pockets. "Do you really think I'd do that, take a day off?"

"No," she answers honestly as our gazes connect. And in a flash, something passes between us. I'm not quite sure what it is; understanding perhaps? She needs this just as much as I do. "But thought I'd offer anyway."

"Thanks for the offer, but I'm here for the foreseeable future, so get used to me being around."

❖   ❖   ❖

Andy: It's been just over two weeks, and you've sent me nothing. Do I need to be concerned?

I stare down at the text, my fingers poised to reply, but reply with what?

Instead of coming up with a screenplay idea, I've been renovating an array of cabins for free.

Rather than doing the job I'm paid for, I've been secretly catching glimpses of a girl I once went on a blind date with.

In lieu of acting like a professional, I've been following the direction of an old, grumpy man while covertly falling for his unattainable granddaughter.

The truth doesn't read well for me, therefore no need to respond.

I toss my phone on my bed, because if I don't see it, then it's not a problem, right?

Denial is a beautiful thing.

Since I stayed up late last night cleaning up the cabin we were working on—a clean workplace is important to me—I slept in a little longer than I should have this morning, given the workload we have on the docket for the day. But hell, even after waking up a half hour later than I should have, I'm still struggling. Every muscle in my body is sore, my eyes are blurry with sleep, and my groin . . . yeah, it freaking hurts. I know I told Fallon I was fine, but after I finished cleaning up, I realized that was not the case. I attempted to ice it in the confines of my own cabin last night, but I knew there was no chance I didn't hurt it while trying to make Fallon laugh.

And I was right.

It's sore.

Everything is sore.

Even my fingernails.

And yet I'm dressed, baseball hat on my head, deodorant applied, and I'm ready to make something of this day. I take one last deep breath and gaze out my window, savoring the view—the placid lake, the soaring rocks. Despite the text burning a hole in my phone, my mind is clear, peaceful.

If I've learned anything during this time away from the hustle and bustle of the movie industry, it's how to appreciate the small things, like the chirp of a bird, the rustling of leaves, and the importance of a small community of unconditional love—even if that community contains a diner full of nightmare trolls.

Hoping Fallon has coffee ready, I exit my cabin and make the short walk along the pathway to the first three cabins. The sprinklers were on this morning, leaving a moistened glow to the grass that has led to the accumulation of water along the path. The sun is already cresting through the trees, blinding anyone who attempts to be awake at this hour. And even though I know it's going to be a scorching day, it's cool this morning, calm before the heat storm.

I stroll up to the second cabin, and voices filter outside from the open door. When I come into view, I'm greeted by Fallon and Jaz, sitting on the floor, baked goods sitting in the middle, with three cups of coffee, steam drifting from the tops. I'm drawn to the sweet nectar of caffeine, and my body propels itself forward. Uncomfortably—thank you, groin—I take a seat with them on the floor and reach for my coffee.

"Is everything okay?" I ask when they don't say a word.

"Everything's fine," Fallon says.

But Jaz must have had an extra shot of espresso this morning, because she shoots me a smirk. "Glad you were able to grace us with your presence, *Julia Dripping Balls*."

My eyes shoot to Fallon, who's covering her face, a light chuckle shaking her shoulders.

"I can't believe you told her," I hiss. I knew there was no way in hell Fallon wasn't going to tell Jaz about our conversation last night, but it's fun to pretend to be mad.

I'm just hoping she skipped over the part where I pushed her hair behind her ear. Possibly skimmed over the hug; definitely didn't mention how I stared down at her adoringly.

"How's the groin this morning?" Jaz asks, bringing her coffee up to her lips.

I sit up tall. "Could use a massage—you willing?"

The smallest of smirks passes over Jaz's lips. "I'm quite good at massaging groins."

"Given your temper, I'd assume you could really work out some knots."

"I can work a lot more out of a man than some knots."

"Good God," Fallon whispers.

"Well then, what better way to start the day than with a groin massage from my least favorite person in town."

"Least favorite?" Jaz quirks her brow. "You're telling me you like Faye, the troll collector, more than me?"

Seeing how far she'll take this, I set my coffee on the ground next to the pastry box and lie down on the floor. I spread my legs and fold my hands behind my head, getting into position. "You and Faye are technically tied, but you might be able to sneak past her with these expert fingers you claim to have."

I've never been someone to back down. I actually enjoy pushing people to see how far they'll take a joke. It's the comedian—and I use that term loosely—in me.

I glance back at an unmoving Jaz. "Well . . . ?"

Her devious eyes narrow, and she sets her coffee down before cracking her fingers and shaking her hands out.

"I'm warning you, I'm not gentle."

"Do I look like a man who wants it gentle?" I ask.

"Given the way you moaned and groaned over eating 'the usual' at the diner, I'm going to say you won't be able to handle me if you could barely handle that."

"I handled it. I just wasn't mentally prepared for that entire morning. Trust me, I can handle you."

"Says the man who shivers in his skivvies when I'm in the same room as him," Jaz says to Fallon, rolling her eyes. And then Jaz crawls over to me and sits at my side. I stare up at her, challenging; she stares down at me, accepting.

She flexes her fingers one more time, just for good show, and then wiggles them in front of my face.

"Are you ready for the massage of your life?"

"I've been waiting. You're just stalling."

"I'm not stalling," she says, that temper igniting in her eyes. "I'm letting you mentally prepare, you know, so you don't have another Strawberry Fields moment. Last thing I need is for you to tell people around town that my massages didn't meet your standards because you weren't mentally prepared."

"I'm prepared. Have at it." I spread my legs a little farther apart and smile up at her. I'm calling her bluff.

"Okay, but just know, you'll probably fall in love with me after this, and I can guarantee the feeling won't be reciprocated. Especially since I have eyes for your brother."

"Try me," I say.

Her nostrils flare, and she brings her fingers up to her mouth, curled into her palm, and gives them a gentle blow before lowering them down to my—

"Enough," Fallon says, pushing Jaz away. "Good Lord, you two are acting like children."

"He started it." Jaz points to me.

Did I? I honestly can't remember . . . oh yeah, she was giving me sass for showing up late.

"No, you did by calling me Julia Dripping Balls."

Hands up in defense, Jaz scoots away. "I just state the facts."

Fallon rubs her temples. "We have a big workload today—"

"And no thanks to Julia, we're behind," Jaz says.

"He worked hard last night." Fallon comes to my defense, but I notice she doesn't look at me. Actually, has she really looked at me much since I arrived? I haven't caught a good glimpse of her eyes, nor have I really seen her smile.

Fear and embarrassment drive through me as I think about my bold touch last night. Is she mad? Is she regretting talking to me? Does she think I went too far?

"It's okay that he slept in," Fallon continues, "and arguing isn't going to get us anywhere." She rubs her eye, and that's when I notice just how tired she looks. Dark circles rest under her eyes, making me wonder if her obvious lack of sleep was from me. "Let's just get started on electrical work for the cabins and reattaching the moldings. Bathtub fitters are coming this weekend, as well as Tank's group. If we can prep these three cabins, we can give them a good idea what the others are supposed to look like. My dads are coming this weekend as well. It's all hands on deck to get the job done." She turns to Jaz. "Can you grab the new lights from the front office? I'll start with the moldings."

"Sure," Jaz says with a huff, but she stands and heads out of the cabin.

"What would you like me to do?" I ask.

"Eat something," Fallon says, standing as well. My eyes fall to her cutoff jean shorts that ride higher in the front than in the back. Frayed around her legs, there's a hole on the front left side that if any higher could be considered indecent. She paired the jeans with a red tank top, and her hair is pinned back, a red bandana rolled and tied around her hairline. She's wearing her work boots, which look hot on her, especially in those shorts. "Something wrong with the food?" Fallon asks, and I realize I've been staring at her instead of eating.

"No," I answer, smoothing my sweaty palms over my shorts. You'd think I've never been around a woman before with the way my body is reacting to a simple pair of cutoff shorts. "Is everything okay?" I ask. "You don't seem to be looking at me . . . at all."

"Everything is fine," she says, still evading my gaze. "Just trying to get it all done."

"Okay." I pick up a muffin but don't bite into it right away. "I'm sorry if I overstepped last night."

"You didn't overstep," she retorts, striding around in a flurry as she places the moldings against the correct walls.

"Are you sure, because things feel different—"

"Because they are different." Finally turning to face me, she leans against the wall, her hands behind her as she stares at me, still seated on the brand-new floors. "Last night made things different."

Oh.

What does she mean by that?

"Different in a bad way?" I ask, nerves filling me.

She lets out a deep sigh, and her eyes flit up to the window. "This is, God, this is so embarrassing." She presses her hand to her forehead. "But last night, when you pushed my hair behind my ear, I felt something." Her gaze connects with me. "I felt my heart beat faster, when I know it shouldn't. I felt my breath catch in my throat when your fingers grazed my skin." Her teeth tug at her lip. "And when you hugged me, I felt safe, protected, like I wanted to stay there longer than I should."

I . . .

Hell, I don't know what to say.

"So, I'm just trying to keep my distance, okay?" she says.

"Yeah . . . sure." I have no idea how to handle her honesty. I don't think I've ever had a woman tell me the problem right off the bat. Frankly, I'm shocked.

When she turns back around to work on the moldings, I say, "For what it's worth, I felt it too."

She pauses, and as she's bent over, I see the tension in the way her shoulders flex, the stiffness in her back when she stands all the way up.

And then her eyes connect with mine, and instead of their usual beautiful softness, they contain a worried edge. "We can't talk about this, Sawyer. I have a boyfriend."

"I know," I say quickly. "And I wouldn't ever want to be the person that gets in the way, especially since I've been cheated on. But . . . I don't know, I didn't want you overthinking anything."

"Don't you see?" she asks, turning around to face me. "I'm already overthinking everything. Every time I talk to Peter, he tells me he loves me, and do you think I can muster up those three little words in response? I can't." Her breath is erratic, her voice almost shrill. I stand and walk toward her but still keep a good distance between us. "And then you walk in"—she gestures to me—"graze my face, and I'm over here questioning my entire relationship with him. So yeah, I'm thinking, I'm overthinking, and I just need to get these renovations done so I can stop worrying if my grandpa can keep his cabins or not. I just need this all to be over, I need this to be—"

Before I can stop myself, I pull her into a hug and press her against my chest, holding her tightly.

"Shhh," I say as my hand cups the back of her head. "We'll get the renovations done, okay? There isn't much to do, and we'll have a lot of help this weekend. We got this. And that other stuff." I lean back so I can look her in the eyes. "Consider it a nonissue." I'm tempted to reach up and push another stray hair behind her ear, but I refrain.

"I can't just switch . . . that off," she says. Her arms are wrapped around me, and she's close enough that if I bend down, I could press my lips against hers. I could discover what she tastes like, how those perfectly plump lips feel drawn out in a long, intoxicating kiss.

"Should I talk about my sweaty balls some more—will that help?"

She laughs out loud and pushes me away, shaking her head. "No, that won't help; it only makes you more charming."

I scratch the side of my face. "Huh, if I only knew sweaty-ball talk is an attractive quality, maybe Annalisa wouldn't have left me."

"Annalisa left you because she's clearly self-absorbed." Fallon goes back to work, the air lighter between us, the tension broken for the time being. Instead of eating my muffin, I help her. We made a diagram for each room, marking the moldings in code, so we know exactly where they go. I've done my fair share of mixing up baseboards to know a diagram is necessary to make it a smooth process.

Fallon picks up a board and flashes me the number. I point to the wall to the right of the bathroom. "You know, when you say things like that, it makes me believe that we're friends."

She eyes me. "Don't push your luck."

"Wouldn't dare," I say just as Jaz walks in, Sully at her side carrying two boxes.

"We have an extra set of hands," Jaz says as she sets a few boxes down.

I glance at Fallon and see apprehension written all over her face at having Sully here. Given how last night went, I'm not quite sure how he's feeling today, which could add a large complication to our plans for the day.

"Sully, I thought you were going to go see Tank at Village Hardware?" Fallon says.

"Why would I do that when there's work to be done around here?" He sets down the boxes and places his hands on his hips. His posture reeks of authority, but the uneasiness in his eyes shows just how vulnerable he's feeling. Once he takes a moment to observe the floors, he says, "I like the floors." The comment nearly makes me laugh, since just yesterday he was bitching about how cheap he thought the floors looked.

"Thank you," Fallon says and then looks between us. I can sense she's strategizing a way to maneuver Sully out of here. "You know, Sully," Fallon starts again, "I was thinking that maybe you could go—"

"I'm not going anywhere," Sully says, a gruffness to his voice. "These are my cabins. I built them. I'm not an invalid, Fallon." He's brusque, feisty . . . borderline angry. Fallon shoots back, surprised at his tone, and I can see her struggling, not wanting him here because she doesn't want him to get hurt, but not wanting him to insult her either.

So, I decide to step in—hopefully it won't backfire on me.

"Sully, I actually have to install all of these lights, and I was hoping you could supervise me—you know, make sure I'm doing it to your standards." Sully glances at me, and I see the confusion in his eyes, so I add, "You know, your old pal Phil could really use some help."

Like flipping a switch, I see the snap of recognition, followed by a cocky rock back on his heels. "Can't have you messing up these lights and causing an electrical fire. It's best that I watch over you."

"Thank you," I say. "I really appreciate it. What, uh, what light should we start on?"

"Why don't we start in the bathroom so the girls can finish up with these baseboards."

"Great idea," I say, and Sully smiles proudly. "Meet you in the bathroom. I have to grab my electrical toolbox from the shed."

"Don't dawdle, we have a lot to get done," Sully says, picking up a light fixture and then bringing it into the bathroom.

"I wouldn't dream of it," I say, and I make my way out of the cabin. I head toward a shed where I put together an old toolbox for electrical needs only the other day. It was a practice I learned from Harmer a while back—always have an electrical toolbox handy—keeps things easy to find.

I'm halfway to the old, beaten-up shed when I hear footsteps jog up behind me. "Hey," Fallon calls out.

I turn around and catch her jogging the rest of the way. When she reaches me, she takes me by surprise by immediately putting her arms around me and giving me a hug.

"Thank you," she says when she pulls away. "I'm not sure if you realize how important you just made him feel. The way you phrased your request, making him feel valued. It was . . . it was perfect."

"I, uh, I've been doing some reading on Alzheimer's and remembered that the way you phrase things is really important. Sully's clearly proud and, if anything, wants to preserve his dignity. I figured asking him to supervise would make him feel involved without being too involved."

"You've been reading up on Alzheimer's?" Fallon asks, a hint of admiration in her voice.

"Yeah. Figured it would be helpful since I'm staying here for a while. I didn't want to do or say anything that would upset Sully or make your life more difficult."

"Wow, Sawyer, I don't know what to say." Her eyes well up, her lip trembling. The last thing I want is for her to cry. I don't ever want to see anguish in her expression—only joy.

"Please don't cry," I say. "I won't be able to handle it."

"I'm not going to cry." She takes a deep breath and steadies herself as she puts some distance between us, one step at a time. It's like she's erected a giant sign in front of me, not a merging lane: *Don't even think about coming any closer.*

"Okay." We stare awkwardly at each other, and after a few seconds, I point behind me. "Well, I think I'll go get that toolbox."

"Sure." But she doesn't move. An odd look crosses her face, and I know something's still on her mind.

"Is there something else?"

She shakes her head, twisting her hands in front of her. When our eyes connect, I see that softness return, her appreciation for what I did. Which seems so odd—I feel like I did nothing. It wasn't monumental, but maybe, in her world of confusion, it was. "No. Just . . ." She wets her lips. "Thank you, Sawyer, for everything."

I pull on the back of my neck, feeling incredibly uncomfortable. Not from her praise, but from the inability to scoop her up like I want. To take her in my arms and show her that she doesn't have to walk this path as a caregiver all alone, that I could be here, helping her. "You know, you keep thanking me, but I'm not too sure I deserve it." I meet her gaze now. "I should be the one thanking you."

"Me? What have I done other than tease you, be short with you, and recruit you to help me?"

How little she knows.

"The teasing is in good nature, the shortness I chalk up to you being under a load of stress, and recruiting me . . . sorry to say, but I volunteered." I wink, though the action doesn't pull a smirk from her like I hoped. "But all that aside, I don't think you realize how much I needed this escape. I wasn't necessarily in the greatest frame of mind, and getting out of LA, coming to a town that's so loyal and so *real* . . . it's been my saving grace. These projects, the conversations we've shared, they've meant something to me. They've helped me move away from a dark time in my life. So . . . no need to thank me when I owe just as much to you and this place."

Her eyes melt over me, and the desperation I feel to touch her again, to hold her . . . consumes me. The feeling is so deep, so palpable, that it has me in a vise, tightening around my lungs, making it feel next to impossible to breathe. The only solution, the only way to catch one tiny breath of air in this pressure chamber, is to touch her.

Feel her.

Hold her.

I know I said last night was it, that I wouldn't do it again. That I would keep my distance.

But a surge of gratitude floods me.

If it wasn't for Fallon and Jaz bringing me to the cabins the first night I was in Canoodle, I probably would have ended up somewhere else, a place that wouldn't have helped me muddle through the mess I've made of my life.

She might not see it, but Canoodle has replenished me in a way I never expected.

And I need her to know that.

I need her to feel that.

Before I can stop myself, I close the distance between us once more and pull her into a hug. Without hesitation, without waiting to see her reaction, I wrap my arms around her shoulders and hold her tight, letting my body relax into the embrace. And because I somehow lucked out, she sinks into the hug as well, and her head rests against my chest as her arms squeeze me tight.

Warmth spreads through my veins, like the sun is being injected directly into them. I can't remember the last time I had human touch, and yet here I am two days in a row, privileged to feel Fallon tight in my embrace. And the way her head rests against my chest, like . . . like she belongs to me. It makes me feel powerful, like I actually matter.

Like there could be something so incredible between us.

We stand still, holding each other as time passes by. It feels like minutes as the sun continues to rise into the sky and a pair of squirrels fight in the trees above us. In reality, I know it's only been seconds, but those seconds are precious. And I soak each one in. I don't ever want to let go.

But unfortunately, she releases me.

She takes a step back, pulling far enough away to look me in the eyes. "Okay, so . . . I guess we have work to do."

Work that I wish was just between us. Like last night, alone with her, talking.

"We do. Lots of work."

She points her thumb toward the cabins. "So, see you back at the cabin."

I rest my hands on my hips, nervous, unsure of how to act in this moment.

I wish she wasn't dating someone.

I wish there was an opportunity for me to make a move on a girl I should have made a move on a while ago.

I wish I hadn't been too engrossed with my own worries to recognize what was right in front of me.

A beautiful woman, with an even more beautiful heart that, as of this moment, has completely and irrevocably captivated me.

"See you at the cabin."

CHAPTER SIXTEEN
SAWYER

"How does that look, Sully?" I ask. This is my sixth fixture of the day, and I know it looks good, but to keep him feeling involved, I ask anyway. If I never have to see another gooseneck, urban-barn-style sconce again, I will be a happy man.

"Crooked," Sully grumbles. "I thought I told you to watch your angles. Where's that level?"

Crooked my ass. There is nothing crooked about this godforsaken light fixture.

From the corner of my eye, I catch Fallon glancing toward us and taking in the light fixture that hangs over the nightstand. There is no way it's crooked, not even close, but I patiently pick up the level and set it on the edge of the fixture to appease Sully. The bubbles in the tool state that it's level, but being a good sport, I say, "You know, I was off just a bit. Good eye, Sully."

I then pretend to adjust the light fixture, not moving it at all, just putting on one hell of a show until Sully gives me a nod of approval.

"Very well, well done. Shall we move on?" I hold back my smirk, because I don't need a tongue-lashing from him for finding light fixtures humorous. I learned very quickly after the first install that electricity is nothing to joke around about and, if I wasn't extra careful and focused, that I could be shocked to death. Yes, he used the phrase "shocked to death."

He also smacked me in the back of the head at one point and told me to stop staring at his granddaughter's legs.

I wasn't—at the time—but Jesus Christ, I don't think I've ever turned a deeper shade of red in my life, especially when Fallon glanced over at me.

"I think so," Sully says. I gather my tools and place them in the red toolbox. I know I said I didn't mind helping Fallon, and I really don't, but the light fixtures are starting to get to me. "On to the next cabin."

"Actually, I was thinking we go get something to eat," Fallon chimes in. When our eyes connect, I see her silently convey that she wants to give Sully a break. Little does she know, I'm the one in desperate need of a break. This could not have come at a better time.

So, I place my hand on my stomach and make a grand show of it; all the while, my body is grumbling, begging for more than just a muffin. "Yes, food. I'd love some. Do you have any good suggestions of where to eat?" I ask Sully.

"Of course I do. I've lived here all my life." He pushes me on the shoulder, shoving me toward the doorway of the cabin. For an old man, he still packs a good shove. "Let's get on with it."

"I have to get to the bar," Jaz says, checking the time on her phone. "I have some food prep to help with before we open."

"Cutting up extra tomatoes?" I ask.

"Nah, those are only for you, big boy." She winks, gives Fallon a high five, and heads out the door.

Fallon turns to Sully and gently places her hand on his shoulder. "What do you want to do for lunch?"

"Let's grab some wings, see what Phil here can handle in the spice department."

I move my hand over my jaw. "Not much—just a heads-up. I'm likely to disappoint."

"Can't handle the spice, son?" Sully asks, rocking on his heels.

"Not really. Can you?" He quirks his old-man eyebrow at me as if I just insulted him. "I'm guessing you can."

"Damn right I can. My stomach is made of steel."

Fallon slowly shakes her head behind him.

"Well, I'm ready for you to school me," I say, rubbing my hands together.

"Then wings it is. Meet me by my car—I'm going to change my shirt real quick," Fallon says as she takes off toward the residence.

Sully and I head up the pathway toward the employee parking lot, walking side by side. It's odd, I've only been here for a few weeks, and yet it feels like this is home. Walking next to Sully feels natural, and there's a comfort in falling in step with him, like I've known him my whole life—like he is my grumpy grandpa I can't help but love.

"You know, Sully, you never told me what you did to win Joan over. To steal her away from Earl."

Sully pauses on the pathway and turns toward me. Confusion rocks his eyes, and though he masks it with a veil of pride as he puffs his chest, I know him well enough to see through the facade. "Remind me where we left off," he says.

I match his confident strides toward the parking lot. "You were telling a great story about how Joan was living down in Palm Springs, dating Earl, and how she was helping you with the cabins, but she wasn't into you. You were just friends. You left me hanging. I've been wondering how the story ended between you and your sweetheart."

"Ah yes." The sweetest smile passes over his lips. "She wasn't into me; at least that's what I thought. We would work on the cabins together, decorating, setting up furniture, and at the end of the day, she'd walk away, completely indifferent to me."

"Bet that didn't settle well with you."

"It didn't," he says softly. "Because when she walked away, I felt that a little piece of me walked away with her. It was painful knowing she was going straight into another man's arms." He adjusts his glasses on his nose. God, does this feel so real right about now. "But it was the stolen moments with her that I clung on to. It was the teasing jokes we shared, the secret glances, the innocent touches when we accidentally bumped into each other. When she was here, I made sure to never put any moves on her out of respect for her relationship with Earl, but it didn't stop me from developing a friendship. And I grew that friendship to the point that she'd call me when she was upset or excited about a piece of furniture she'd sold to another customer. When she was here helping me, it felt like we were in our own little bubble, where no one else mattered—it was just me and her, and then . . . right before we opened, she brought Earl up here for a weekend getaway."

My heart drops from the sheer thought of that bubble bursting.

I wince. "Hell, I can't imagine the way you must have felt seeing him here, in your territory, where you developed such a bond with Joan. How did you handle it?"

"Not great," he answers with a shake of his head, as if it just happened yesterday. "Jealousy got the better of me. Seeing them hold hands, walking around the lake like I always dreamed of doing with her—it was like a punch to the gut. That night jealousy reared its ugly head, and I started an argument with Joan when she was checking into one of the cabins as a test run."

"Did you think she was going to test it on her own?"

"Yes," Sully answers as we reach the parking lot. Since there's only one car there, a dark-blue Jeep Wrangler, we walk over to it and lean against the doors. "I'd originally invited her up for the weekend test run, hoping that maybe something could spark between us. It was my chance to find out if she perhaps felt the same way I did about her. But then she brought Earl, and the only thing that sparked was a fight. It was not my finest moment, and the next morning, she and Earl left."

"You must have been heartbroken," I say softly.

"I was." Sully adjusts the glasses on his nose. "A lesser man would have thrown in the towel that night, but not me. I was determined. I knew how I acted was wrong. I knew what I said to her that night wasn't justified, and I owed her an apology."

"What did you do?" I can feel my pulse pick up as the image of a younger Sully chasing after his true love sparks a vivid story in my head. A story of true, unrequited devotion shining through the innocence of love at first sight. The type of love that makes your heart burn and your veins light on fire. A love that lasts a lifetime, that lasts until death do they part and beyond.

It's Sully's story, pure and simple, but I wonder if I'll ever have one like it.

Sully drags his hand over his wrinkled cheek, over the smallest of nicks from shaving this morning. "Drove down to Palm Springs and stood outside of her apartment with a single flower. I told her I was a jealous fool, and I was sorry for speaking to her so poorly when she didn't deserve it. I confessed my feelings and told her it was incredibly difficult for me to see her with Earl. But despite my bruised and battered heart, I promised to be the friend I always was to her, and that was never going to change."

"Were you the friend again?" I ask.

He nods. "I made a promise to her. I kept it."

"Wow." I shake my head. "That must have been hard, seeing her with Earl and only being her friend."

"One of the hardest things I've ever done."

Just then, Fallon pops out of the back door of the residence, wearing a large smile on her face as her ponytail swooshes behind her. As she approaches, my eyes fixate on her, and my heart skips a beat with every step she takes. A lonesome feeling hits me straight in the chest as I realize . . . my story with Fallon isn't very different from Sully and Joan's. And I'm cast in the role of the friend, the one she needs to rely on, not be involved with romantically. The pain I was feeling for Sully transfers to myself, settling over my heart.

One of the hardest things I've ever done.

I wish I could say I couldn't relate to the feeling, but when Fallon shoots me a wink, I realize just how real that pain is.

I want her, just like Sully wanted Joan.

And yet here I am, stuck in a role I don't want.

Sully places his hand on my shoulder, pulling my attention away from Fallon. When I glance down and meet his gaze, I'm not sure I've ever seen his eyes so clear or heard his voice so sincere as he says, "But sometimes, son, the best things are worth waiting for."

Fuck . . .

He squeezes my shoulder once more and shoots me a knowing smirk while opening the front passenger door to Fallon's car.

He can see it, written all over my face.

My yearning for his granddaughter.

My desperation to do something as simple as holding her hand.

My hopeless wish that she wasn't dating Peter, just like how Sully wished Joan wasn't dating Earl.

The stories collide, and yet I can sense how my story very well could end differently from Sully's—with my own heartache.

"You ready?" Fallon asks me, her infectious smile colliding with my fluttering stomach.

"Yeah." I swallow hard as Sully's words vibrate through me. "I'm ready."

Sometimes, son, the best things are worth waiting for.

I would wait for Fallon. I would move mountains to make her happy.

But unlike Sully and Joan, I don't think our story is written in the stars.

❖　❖　❖

"Sully, over here," Tank bellows from the corner booth where he's sitting with Rigatoni Roy.

The minute we walk into Put a Wing on It, I am hit by the thick scent of frying grease, followed by a distant hint of spice. Shit, I hope things aren't too spicy here—I might severely embarrass myself.

"Oh, that's right, the boys were meeting up here," Sully says before placing a kiss on Fallon's cheek and then pointing to me. "Be good to my granddaughter." And just like that, as if he was never diagnosed with Alzheimer's, he disappears into the depths of the exposed-brick building, leaving me alone with Fallon.

Funny how that worked out.

"Wow, ditched by my own grandfather—that doesn't feel great," Fallon says, humor in her voice. "Shall we take a seat?"

"Sure," I say, but my mind is reeling.

Classic move by a meddling family member. Getting the hero and the heroine together, unbeknownst to them. Usually such a move is performed by a zany mom who begs for forgiveness later, or an unapologetic best friend who knows what's best for the heroine in the story. But in this instance, it's a grumpy old-timer who just so happened to have a moment of clarity at the exact right time.

What are the chances?

Wait . . . what am I even talking about? I'm not the hero in this story, and even though I have feelings for Fallon—big, romantic, heart-pounding feelings—she sure as hell isn't the heroine.

We take a seat in the back, near the bathrooms—appetizing—at a bar-height table. The restaurant is quite dark, especially for the middle of the day. The dimmed hanging lights above each table offer only a faint hint of light, and the black floors and black chairs almost melt into the abyss, giving no dimension to the space. Menus are stuck between the napkin holder and the salt and pepper shakers, so I reach for them and hand one to Fallon once we're settled on our barstools.

"Have you been here before?" Fallon asks me.

I shake my head. "No, but my parents have been here a few times when passing through Canoodle to visit me in LA. It's one of their favorite places to stop, but they haven't exactly told me what they like to order." I glance up at her from over my menu. "Any suggestions?"

"Do you seriously have a hard time handling spice?"

"If I were trying to prove my manhood to you, I'd tell you I could eat a ghost pepper with no problem, but I think my manhood is a distant thought after you had to drag my drunk corpse into the cabin the first night I arrived."

"Yes, you didn't quite make a good . . . second impression."

"Two strikes on my character. I'm shocked you can even sit across from me at this table right now."

"You've made up for your lack of personality the first two times we ran into each other."

I set my menu down. "So, what you're telling me is that I have some redeeming qualities."

"A few." She smirks. "And just so you know, Sully orders the hot wings, but the kitchen knows to make his mild. I know it might not be right, but why hurt the guy's pride?"

"I get it. I think it's actually cute that you guys do that."

A small blush creeps over her cheeks—a blush I'm surprised I can see under the subtle lighting. "As for you," she says, pointing to the menu, "the original chicken sandwich is really good. It's not spicy at all, but since it's an original item on the menu, it won't look like you're unable to handle the heat of the kitchen."

"I like your way of thinking. Comes with fries—are they good?"

"They're the seasoned ones with the nice crisp on the outside."

"Dangerous, I'm sold." I stick my menu back in its slot. "What do you plan on getting?"

"A basket of their medium wings, side of blue cheese, a side of vegetable crudités, and I plan on snagging a few of your fries."

"Oh, you are? You think you have the right to my plate?"

"After the way you treated me on our blind date, I'd say I do."

I cross my arms and lean them on the table, drawing closer to her. From this distance, I can smell her sweet, heady perfume, a subtle floral scent that's been driving me crazy ever since I took a seat in her Jeep. It's fresh, and it makes me want to pull her in close and run my nose along the column of her neck.

"How long are you going to hold that date against me?"

Her lips turn up into a playful smirk, an expression I'm growing quite fond of. Annalisa never was much of a jokester. More serious than anything. She didn't quite understand the idea of teasing. It was a hard adjustment, but I made it work with Annalisa. I'm glad I don't have to fake it with Fallon.

With Fallon, there's a simple ease between us that I don't think I've ever had with a woman. We seem to just . . . understand each other.

And that's one of the main reasons why I'm struggling.

Because as I sit across from her at this table, her beautiful blue eyes glittering back at me, a hint of a smile playing at her lips, all I can think about is how I desperately wish I could reach across the diameter of this circular table and take her hand in mine.

A simple act. Holding her hand.

It's not much.

But to me, it would mean so much more.

It would mean that she's available, that I have an actual shot at having a second chance with her.

"I think for as long as you're staying at the cabins, I'm going to keep bringing up the blind date. I can hold a grudge, Sawyer."

"Apparently." Even though I can't have her, I can at least have this moment with her. "Tell me this—when we were on our blind date, was there anything you liked about me?"

She's caught off guard for a moment, and I watch her carefully process the question. Just when I think she's not going to answer, she goes with a safe response. "Your texting speed was quite impressive. I don't think I've ever seen someone work a phone like the way you did: accurate, precise jabs. And that's saying something because I once had a massage from a man who was texting with one hand the entire time."

"A one-handed massage." I shake my head. "Unfortunately, I'm far too familiar with that . . ."

Fallon's eyes widen before her head falls back and she lets out a loud laugh.

Her reaction is just enough of a return on admitting something far too embarrassing. Not sure why I even said it, but the words flew past my lips before I could stop them.

"I can't believe you just said that." She chuckles some more and then snags a napkin and dabs at her eyes. "At least you're honest."

"Can I get a recommendation to put on my dating résumé from you? 'Sawyer Walsh, honest about his one-handed massages. Highly recommend giving him a chance. Also quick with his fingers.'"

She laughs some more. "Both true things, but I'm not sure my star rating would be a great selling point."

"What do you mean?" I say just as the waitress appears at our table.

"What do you want?" she says, chewing a piece of gum and staring down at her notepad, pen poised.

Very abrasive and lacking "bedside" manner. A disinterested character who doesn't leave much of a mark on a story, other than breaking up the scene and leaving anticipation with the viewer. The perfect pause button for a screenwriter. Agora—according to her name tag—plays the role perfectly while also offering up a talking point for later if the screenwriter so chooses. It's always about setting up options, and Agora is just that . . . an option.

After we put in our order, Agora giving me a slight side-eye at my no-tomato request, I turn back to Fallon. "Star rating, what would it be?"

"I'm not sure your fragile man ego can take it." She leans on the table as well, bringing her just a few inches closer, inches I didn't have before. Inches I will gladly take.

"My fragile man ego is stronger than you—"

"Two stars."

"What?" I nearly shoot out of my stool. I glance around the restaurant and then playfully lean in closer. "You would give me a two-star rating? That's brutal. You're going to need to explain yourself because I don't think it's justified."

"And why don't you think it's justified?" she asks.

"Uh, because I feel like I've redeemed myself."

"You have redeemed your character, but that's different from 'Single Ready to Mingle' Sawyer. That Sawyer I only know as someone who doesn't pay attention to his date and runs out on an ex-girlfriend's wedding, sans one shoe. The reason you're not a one star is because I've shared a few meals with you since then, and from those interactions, I've been able to move your star rating up from a negative two deficit to a solid two. You should be thrilled."

"Positively ecstatic," I deadpan.

She chuckles. "But if I were to rate you as a nonfriend, I'd say five stars."

"Oh, now you're just trying to butter me up."

"Trust me, there's no benefit to me buttering you up. I know how men like you work."

"Men like me?" I point at myself. "Now this I have to hear. Please tell me, Fallon, how do men like me work?"

"If I go on some lengthy diatribe of how wonderfully thoughtful you are, two things will happen. One, you'll black out halfway through from so much pride that all you'll be able to think about is how you're 'the man.' And two, you'll make it your life's mission to bring up the compliments I toss your way as a reminder of this moment, the moment when I allowed you to enjoy some mediocre praise."

I pause.

I think on her response.

"Yeah, you're right about that."

She lets out a loud laugh just as Agora sets down our drinks without a word.

When she walks out of earshot, I lower my voice. "She has quite the personality." See, talking point. "Is her last name Phobe? You know . . . Agora *Phobe*."

Fallon shakes her head in mock disappointment. "Cheap joke, Sawyer. And offensive, since agoraphobia is a real thing."

"Yeah." I scratch my chin. "Not proud of myself."

"At least you can admit that."

I perk up. "Does that add to my star rating?"

"No," she answers, expressionless, and then takes a sip of her water. "Despite the lack of personality while waitressing, Agora is actually one of the lead actresses in this summer's play in the park."

"Play in the park? What's that?"

"Every summer, the town puts on a play voted on by the mayor, and they have a few summer night showings. This year I believe the chosen play, or musical, I guess, is *Hairspray*. Agora was cast as Penny, the upbeat best friend."

"Seriously? Upbeat?" I ask, chuckling. "She must be one hell of an actress."

"So I hear, and the whole town is excited to see it—word on the street is Roy is stealing the show."

"Roy? Who is he . . . wait." I raise an eyebrow, and Fallon smiles broadly. "Is Roy the mom?"

Fallon nods. "Edna Turnblad will be played by the incomparable Rigatoni Roy."

"Oh hell, now this is something I'm going to have to see. Roy decked out in a muumuu—that has to be a vision."

Fallon leans in and lowers her voice. "Jaz told me that she caught him in pantyhose the other day at the restaurant. He forgot to take them off. When she pointed them out to him, he said they kept his nuggets feeling comfortable."

I wince. "Oooh, not something I needed to envision." I shift on my stool, my mind landing on a key detail. "So, I have a question. How does a *cat* pick what the summer play in the park is?"

"How all decisions are made in this town. Two food bowls are presented to the mayor with the same amount of food, and underneath each bowl is a slip of paper with each choice written on it. Whichever bowl the mayor chooses to eat from is the winner."

"That is surprisingly diplomatic."

"It has worked very well, and not one person complains. Once the bowls have been chosen, the argument is over and respected. The mayor has spoken."

"There's never been a confrontation, or even anger, from the outcome?"

She shakes her head. "The only controversy that's come from a mayoral decision was when Beefy Boofcheck, the Saint Bernard from two terms ago, took a nap between the two bowls instead of choosing one."

"Scandal," I say. "What was the decision that had to be made, and how was it made?"

"They were deciding on what color the kitchen should be painted in the mayor's residence. Since no decision was made, the kitchen wasn't painted, despite needing a new paint job. If you visit the mayor's house, which is open for tours on Tuesdays and Thursdays—"

"Noted." My lips lift while I bring my water glass up to my lips.

"You can still see the old paint-color samples on the kitchen's back wall near the fridge. Both brilliantly ugly."

"They haven't painted it since? In two terms?"

"Nope. Because you see, Sawyer, the decision would have to default back to Beefy, since he was the one who originally chose a draw on the decision—it's in the bylaws—but unfortunately, Beefy was laid to rest a year after his term, therefore . . ."

"The kitchen will never be painted," I finish for her.

"Precisely. I'm sure there's some sort of amendment where the decision would fall to another mayor in the event of a death, but since the town is still reeling from losing Beefy, no one's even thought of bringing up the kitchen again."

"They were that attached to Beefy?"

Fallon brings her hand to her chest. "Oh, Sawyer, you have no idea of the love this town had for Beefy. Every morning he'd take walks and stop by every place of business to check in on the proprietor, who in return would toss him a treat. He also helped with Saturday deliveries by pulling a wagon along the sidewalk. He was truly a government official immersed with the people. Whenever you heard that squeaky wheel of his wagon come closer, it gave you a sense of comfort and reassurance that this town was well looked after. But when his term was up, a new era dawned, and the town chose a cat to serve as mayor." She shakes her head, as if she can't believe it. When her eyes connect with mine, my stomach twists in knots from how much I like this freaking girl. "It's never been the same since."

"Cats and dogs run the world very differently. Let me guess—the new mayor isn't making Saturday deliveries?"

"Nope, she's a show cat. More Instagram worthy than anything. All appearances. While Beefy was one with the people, Miss Daphne Lynn Pearlbottom delights the townspeople with her collection of fascinators that rival the queen's collection." Whispering, she adds, "Miss Pearlbottom has yet to wear a duplicate."

"Wow, impressive . . . that's quite the collection."

"One of the guest rooms in the house is dedicated entirely to Miss Pearlbottom's fascinators."

"Looks like I need to take a tour, specifically to see the famous color swatches in the kitchen."

"Worth the time, which you should have plenty of after this weekend. Hopefully, having Tank's guys helping, as well as my dads, will mean we can get everything done and start booking. Which reminds me: we're going to have to kick you out of your cabin for the renovations this weekend, but don't worry. Tank is taking Sully this weekend, and I can change the bedding. You can take Sully's bedroom. It'll be two nights, that's it."

"Sure, that's not a problem. As long as you turn off the monitors—I don't need you watching me while I sleep."

She rolls her eyes. "You say that as if it's something I'd enjoy doing."

"Wouldn't you?" I waggle my brows at her, and she reaches out and pushes my face away, laughing.

"I wouldn't, trust me—"

"Well, hello there."

Startled, I look past Fallon's shoulder and right into the deep-brown eyes of Peter, the boyfriend.

Holy shit, where did he come from?

"Peter," Fallon says as she turns in her stool to face him. Peter eyes me for a few more seconds before bringing his attention to her. His hand lifts up to her cheek and cups it tenderly as he leans down and places a kiss on her lips.

His movements are slow.

Deliberate.

Like he's making a statement right in front of me.

She's mine, back . . . away.

And it's fucking agonizing, watching his lips roam over hers.

He gets to touch her.

Caress her.

Claim her.

It's a tidal wave of truth crashing into me, reminding me that Fallon is attached.

When they part, she smiles up at him. "What are you doing here?" Fuck, that smile.

"Got a long weekend so I can help out with the renovations. Was I . . . interrupting anything?" Peter glances toward me.

"No," Fallon says quickly. "Just taking a break. Sit down, we can get some food for you."

The apprehension, almost . . . accusation in Peter's gaze is sounding off warning bells in my head. He doesn't like what he sees. Even though he doesn't have evidence of anything going awry, he doesn't like it. And I don't blame him.

Peter puffs his brawny chest. I can call it right now and classify him as the proud peacock in the story line—the overprotective, tentatively jealous boyfriend. Although, if this were a movie, there'd be something wrong with him, something that would make him unappealing. You know, the workaholic jerk who doesn't have time for his girlfriend. That's not the case here, because he clearly makes time for her by cutting out of work early.

Then there is the uninterested boyfriend, the one who makes viewers wonder why the heroine is even with the punk. But Peter is anything but uninterested. Every time I've seen them together, he's very interested. Always attentive. Always touching her. Making fucking googly eyes at her.

And lastly, there's the long-distance boyfriend who adds too much pressure, wanting them to be together but completely forgetting that the heroine has a life of her own. Goals. Dreams. Once again, not an issue here.

So . . . is Peter really the one? The story written in the stars is of Fallon and . . . Peter?

Hell, why do I care? It's enough that they're together, enough that she's off limits. I shouldn't care if they're meant to be together or not.

I snap out of my delirium. "You know, it must have been a long trip up the mountain. I'll go ask the hostess for another seat so you two can catch up."

I start to lift from my chair when Peter holds his hand out. "Not necessary. It would be good to get to know the person who's been helping Fallon out during these renovations." He gestures to my stool. "Take a seat, Samuel."

Ooooh, I was about to mentally congratulate him for being the bigger man before he pulled that classic power move—the old misname trick. You see, since he's in the presence of his woman, he doesn't want to come off as a jealous idiot at finding his girl eating a meal with another man, so he takes the under-the-table, backhanded-douchery route . . . using the wrong name.

Pulled that move straight from the polite-asshole toolbox.

I've borrowed a trick or two from there before. And I have most definitely misnamed someone before. Pretty sure I did it to Simon, the first time I had to have dinner with him and Annalisa.

Seeman, is it?

No, it's Simon, you tool.

Ah, that's right . . .

If I wasn't on the receiving end of Peter's misnaming, I'd stand up and applaud the man, because without Fallon knowing, he just put me in my place.

She's mine—back off, guy.

If there was a neon sign on his shirt, that's what it would say.

Either that or *This Dick Belongs to Her*. With an accompanying arrow that rotates when she moves around.

"Peter, his name is Sawyer," Fallon says to correct him, completely oblivious to the jab.

"Oh shoot." Peter snaps his fingers, moving seamlessly to the friendly-neighbor approach. "That's right, Sawyer. Sorry about that, my guy."

My guy.

Yeah . . . I'm not your guy. Not even close.

"Simple mistake." I give him a brief smile. "But seriously, I can take off."

"You stay seated," Fallon says. "After all the work you've done, there's no way you're going to go eat by yourself."

"She's right," Peter says. He takes his wallet out of his pocket and places it on the table before taking a seat next to Fallon. "Lunch is on me."

A few things:

One, his wallet on the table, fat and with obvious bills stashed on the inside, is, once again, another power move. He's flashing his money in my direction—though little does he know, I probably have investments that put his salary to shame.

Two, we're sitting at a round four-person table, a seat for each side of the table, and yet Peter scoots his chair right next to Fallon's so they're sitting shoulder to shoulder. Might as well have pulled his pants down and peed a circle all around her.

The man is embarrassing.

And yet I'm jealous of him.

I'm jealous of the way he angles his body toward Fallon, slipping his hand on her thigh and lending his lips to the column of her neck. Her face heats up with embarrassment from the public display of affection, but she also doesn't push him away, which means she might not welcome it, but she's not mad about it either.

Maybe a secret part of me wished that she would push him away, that she would comically slap him across the face out of pure mortification, only to apologize, and then slap him again because she doesn't know what's gotten into her.

A little slapstick humor wouldn't kill the mood for me.

"You don't have to pay for lunch," Fallon says. "I owe Sawyer. I can buy it."

"No, sweetheart, let me. I want to treat the man that's been helping out my girlfriend—it's the least I can do."

Did you see that . . . the marking his territory? Yeah, buddy, I get it.

Also . . . "sweetheart"? Ugh, gross, that's what parents call their children, at least in my writing experience. "Sweetheart" is reserved for the men who can't handle calling their woman "baby."

Sweetheart is not for the forever man.

Sweetheart is designated for the throwaway secondary hero.

"Thanks, man. That's kind of you," I say, wanting to stop the chatter of who's paying for lunch. "How was your drive up?"

"It was good." Peter shifts and moves in even closer to Fallon, if that's even possible. "I was listening to a rather fascinating podcast about medical procedures gone wrong. I think the situations that happen are every doctor's nightmare."

"Why do you listen to it?" I ask.

He shrugs. "To remind myself not to get lazy."

"That makes sense."

"Glad it does." His tone is clipped, but Fallon doesn't seem to notice because she's glancing over at Sully, who's chuckling at something Rigatoni Roy just said.

"Seems like he's doing well," I offer.

She turns back to me. "A big part of that is thanks to what you're doing with him."

"What's Sawyer doing with Sully?" Peter asks.

Fallon keeps her eyes on me. "He's been including Sully on the renovations, making him feel like he has purpose while protecting him from hurting himself. It's been . . . it's been mood changing for Sully." To my horror, Fallon reaches across the table and places her hand on mine.

I gulp.

Heat spikes up my spine as the air between the three of us becomes so palpable, so thick, that I'm struggling to find my next breath.

The glare of Peter's eyes on me is intense, like after a few more seconds his eyes will shoot out lasers, splitting me in half, leaving me to melt onto the floor, helpless against his inferno of anger.

"Uh, it's nothing." I—feebly—attempt to pull my hand away from hers, but she grips me even tighter.

"It isn't nothing. When I took Sully to the doctor, he said there was a change in his demeanor, and he asked what we were doing differently. For the life of me, I didn't know, but I had my theories, and after seeing the way you were with him, I know now exactly why he's been finding some moments of clarity from the fog that's taken over his brain." She tilts her head slightly to the side, her tongue wetting her lips. "It's you."

Hell . . .

She couldn't have saved this for when Peter wasn't around, staring me down and ready to take me outside and introduce me to the obvious boulders in his biceps? I'm a fit man, I even have muscles of my own, but Peter clearly has a vendetta against barbells, because he's been abusing them.

Unsure of how to react, I slowly pull my hand away and then grip the back of my neck. "It's nothing, really. He's been keeping me company, which has been nice because, well, you know, things have been lonely."

"That's right, your ex-girlfriend married your best friend," Peter says, losing his grip on civility. "How has *that* been going?"

"Peter," Fallon chastises. "Clearly that's none of our business."

"It's fine," I say. I glance over at Peter. "Being here in Canoodle has helped. I haven't been in love with Annalisa for a while, but the lack of loyalty hurt. Spending my time around people who have an abundance of loyalty has been refreshing. I told Fallon the other night that I'm grateful for her friendship, because it's really helped me."

"The other night, huh?" Peter asks, his tongue running over his teeth. Oh yeah, he wants to introduce me to his fist, no doubt about that.

"Here's your food," Agora says, slamming two baskets of food in front of us. She looks up at Peter and huffs. "Do you want food?"

"He can share with me," Fallon says.

Agora generates one of the heaviest, most annoyed eye rolls I believe I've ever seen. Call up the *Guinness Book of World Records*, because I think we have a leader in exasperation.

She turns on her heel, and I silently thank her impeccable timing.

"So, what's the plan for when we get back to the cabins?" I ask, wanting to divert from the "other night" as much as we can.

"I think since Tank's crew is coming tomorrow, I want to finish moving furniture into storage and ripping out the carpets so we can have all hands on deck with the floors and painting, which will be the biggest projects. Bathroom countertops and replacement sinks are also being brought up by one of Tank's guys—we got them at cost, which I'm still marveling about."

"Cost, really? That's amazing. I can't wait to see them."

"They're a really pretty white quartz that will look beautiful against the pewter-gray accent wall and the original red floor tiles, which I'm so glad we're able to preserve."

I nod, pleased as well. "Those tiles are a huge cost saver and offer some nostalgia to the cabin while also preserving Grandma Joan's memory."

Fallon smiles at me. "Yes, very true. Do you think it's okay if the cabins' exteriors stay the same?"

I pick up a fry from my basket and put one in my mouth. Just because I know she wants one, I take a large fry—the biggest in the basket—and I hold it out to Fallon. She takes it and thanks me with a smirk.

"I think the cabins will be fine as they are. They look stunning, maybe slightly weathered, but I don't think their outward design looks dated at all—they look retro if anything. They provide the kind of rugged mountain feel that visitors will want, especially on their social media. But yeah, those carpets." I shiver. "They have to go."

She chuckles. "I bet you'll be happy to have your cabin fixed."

261

"More like grateful." I wink and then pick up my chicken sandwich and take a large bite. Only then do I remember that Peter is sitting next to Fallon.

And let me just tell you, I'm meeting a new friend of his while escaping into the multitude of flavors bouncing off my tongue. It's called the left vein in his forehead, and it's pulsing with anger.

Throbbing.

Hammering so hard that I'm afraid it very well might burst.

Trying to break the tension, I hold a fry out to Peter. "Fry? They're yummy."

I envision him swatting the fry away, flipping the table over, and then gripping me by the neck before chucking me across the room with his boulder biceps, right into a wooden barrel of wing sauce.

But in reality, he takes the fry and chomps on it, staring me down.

Safe to say, I don't think we're going to be friends.

"You're stronger than I thought you'd be, Julia Dripping Balls," Jaz says as we maneuver a coffee table into one of the storage pods Fallon rented for the weekend.

"I have visible muscles."

Her eyes roam my arms. "You do, and they are very bulgy, especially when you're carrying something, but I wasn't sure if they were artificial."

"Artificial?"

"You know, implants. Isn't that a thing done over in LA? Fake muscles."

"I'd like to say it isn't, but I know quite a few guys who've gotten calf implants, so, yeah, it is. But these bulging meat arms are real."

"God, you're so corny. 'Meat arms.' Who honestly says that?"

"I didn't want to say 'muscles' because that would have been a word echo, and I wanted to keep the conversation fresh."

"Excuse me?" We set the table down, but Jaz doesn't move, waiting for an answer. I was paired with her to move furniture when Peter scooped in on Fallon. Of course they'd be paired up, but I thought I'd be moving furniture on my own—until Fallon said Tank closed the hardware store early and was taking over the bar for her with Sully so she could help us.

So, Jaz is my new partner.

How much you want to bet I'll be on the other end of her knife at some point?

"What the hell is a word echo? And why are you trying to craft our conversation?"

"A word echo is when you repeat a word within close proximity of the same word. Since we already used 'muscles,' I figured we could use something different, something with flavor. I realize this is not normal, but you're talking to someone who writes for a living—proper conversational flow is something I think about pretty much constantly."

"Ew, don't be creepy." She pushes past me, bumping my shoulder on the way out.

"It's not cree—"

"Fallon, Sawyer's being creepy," Jaz says as Fallon and Peter approach us, an accent chair in their hands.

"I'm not being creepy."

"I told you I didn't want to be partnered with him. He's trying to use word echoes on me."

"No," I retort, catching up. "I was attempting *not* to word echo—makes for a more interesting, less boring conversation. But with all the creepy talk and the repetitive mention of 'word echo,' we are in fact negating the whole purpose of what I was talking about."

"Oh great, now you're saying I'm boring. Wow, Julia, you really don't know how to make friends, do you?"

I press my fingers into my temples, massaging them. "I wasn't calling you boring; I was attempting to avoid 'boring.'"

"You know what, I'm attempting to avoid boring as well." Jaz bumps Fallon out of the way and grips the accent chair. "Peter is my new partner—I refuse to be subjected to his creepery."

"'Creepery' is not a word," I shoot back.

"You would know, Mr. Dictionary," Jaz says, pushing Peter down the path.

"Hey, I was enjoying some time with my girlfriend," he protests.

"You'll have plenty of time later to whisper doctor lingo into her ear as your form of foreplay. Now let's get a move on." She pushes again at Peter, who has no other option than to let Jaz take over.

I turn to Fallon. "I wasn't being creepy."

"I don't know—she paints a damning picture." Fallon smirks, and for the life of me, I can't help myself as I put my arm around her shoulder and guide her toward the cabin.

"I see where your loyalty is."

She doesn't pull away but instead bumps me with her shoulder playfully. "Best friends since we were five; saw each other every summer. Loyalty sticks with her."

"That's fair." I drop my arm—don't want to push my luck. "You know, if you and Peter want privacy tonight, I can try to find another place to stay, or just set a mattress on one of the floors in the cabins."

"Don't be ridiculous. I'm not going to make you sleep in an empty cabin. Besides, it's, uh . . . it's that time of the month for me, so nothing will be happening with Peter."

"Oh." I nervously laugh because I'm a twelve-year-old boy. "Uh, do you . . . do you need chocolate or anything?"

Fallon pauses and looks up at me. "Seriously? That's what you're going to say?"

"I don't know." I pull on my hair. "Not sure how to react to that. Do you need a break? A tampon? A cup of water to . . . help flush things out?" I pause and scratch the side of my cheek. "Jesus, maybe I am creepy."

She lets out a laugh and takes my arm, pulling me toward an empty cabin. "I wish it weren't true, but yeah, there might be a little creep in you."

"Perhaps there's a little creep in all of us . . ." I shake my head. "Why does that sound like I'm speaking of a mini alien?"

"You really have a disturbing mind, you realize that?"

"Yeah, it's why I started writing, to help let loose some of these ideas."

"Hence a martian falling in love with a human . . ."

Her lips tug at the corners, and I point at her with mock anger. "We are not to speak of my failures. I'm already logged in as creepy. You have to help a guy keep his dignity."

"Do I?"

"No, but it would be a nice gesture."

"Maybe I can find it in my heart. Come on, let's start on the carpets—Jaz and Peter can work on the furniture."

Together, we head into one of the empty cabins. The smell is musty, the carpet is a leopard print of gross stains, and there's a questionable hole in the wall where the bed's headboard used to be.

"What's that from?" I ask, pointing to the hole.

"Can't be sure. Possibly a blatant display of male fragility."

I let out a roar of a laugh. "That very well could be a reason. Should we frame it, add 'Artist unknown' at the bottom?"

"A novel idea, but not sure many would understand. Please tell me you can patch it."

"Pfft, of course I can patch it."

"That confident?"

"Fallon, please, that's child's work."

"Which means you can patch it tonight? So we can paint tomorrow."

"I don't know; do you have the supplies to patch it?" I ask with a raise of my brow.

"Do you really need supplies? If you're so good, I'd assume you could patch it using whatever is at your disposal."

"I'm good, Fallon, but I'm not MacGyver. I'll need at least some wall joint compound. Do you have any of that?"

She taps her chin. "Can't say that I do. I can check our supplies, though."

I laugh. "If you don't have any, I'll grab some from Tank in the morning. We can save this cabin last for painting, so it has time to dry. In the meantime, let's get this carpet torn out."

We slip on gloves, and I mentally prepare myself for the dust and grime that comes with ripping up these carpets.

It takes us a few minutes to get our footing, but once we start pulling and rolling, we're able to take it out in minutes.

I wipe my forearm across my forehead. "Ready to pull it out the door?"

"When you say 'pull,' you mean you're doing the pulling and I'm doing the pushing, right?"

"Right," I say. I hop over the roll and then maneuver out the door, where I grip the end of the carpet roll. "Ready?"

She gets into pushing position. "Ready."

"Three, two, one . . . go."

Together, we push and pull with such great force that we both surprise ourselves and pull the carpet right into the open grass field in front of the cabin, causing both of us to trip over our own feet. I fall backward into the grass, while Fallon falls forward against the carpet, only to roll off it and land face first in the planter by the door.

"Oh shit, are you okay?" I ask, springing up from the ground.

"Yes." She laughs.

She rolls to her back when I reach her, and I take her hand in mine and help her to her feet. When she's steady, I notice a dot of mud on her cheek. Before I can stop myself, I'm removing my glove and reaching up to wipe it away.

Her eyes snap to mine in confusion. "You have some mud on your cheek," I say quickly. "I'd say it looks good, but it really doesn't."

"Are you saying I can't pull mud off?"

"I'm saying it doesn't highlight your best features, which would be your eyes. It distracts anyone looking at you from getting lost in them," I say before I can stop myself.

My finger lingers on her cheeks as her gaze remains fixed on mine, as the breeze stands still, and the sun begins to set behind the mountain. Our eyes connect, and something passes between us. An appreciation? An understanding.

I'd be kidding myself if I said I wouldn't be overjoyed if Fallon acted on the attraction between us.

But something is there, a dangerous kind of emotion that gives me hope.

"Everything okay over here?" Peter's voice cuts right through us, sending a jolt of reality straight into my chest.

Fuck, pull away, man. "Yeah, she just fell," I say, turning to avoid eye contact as he strides past me.

"You okay, sweetheart?" Peter walks over to her, concern on his face.

"Yes, just tripped is all." Fallon's voice has a shake to it when she answers. I want to glance over my shoulder to see if I just imagined it, the rattle to her answer. I want to get one more look at her, see if her cheeks are stained in pink, if her eyes are cutting in my direction.

Did she feel it?

The zap between us?

The pull?

Or is it all me?

Knowing Peter caught us in an intimate position, I don't want to ruffle any feathers, so I let him coddle her as I turn back to the task at hand—the carpet. I grip the edge, and with all my pent-up frustration, I tug it toward the dumpster.

All the while, I remind myself: *She's not yours, Sawyer.*
She's not fucking yours.

❖   ❖   ❖

I thought I knew what being uncomfortable was until I stepped into Fallon's upstairs residence with her and Peter.

After the tumble, Peter claimed Fallon again while Jaz hacked away at the carpet with her knife. I stood over her, watching in horror. If Jaz ever ended up on the news, I'd know exactly why.

Finally, I coaxed her away from her carpet victim and rolled it up before carting it to the dumpster. Somewhere along the way, Peter lost his shirt and was walking around, sticking his chest out for the world to see. I would like to say that there was something wrong with the man, like a wonky nipple or a weird chest-hair pattern, but honestly, I couldn't pinpoint anything—which I found more irritating.

Because I know that if I'd taken my shirt off, I'd have exposed a freckle on my pec, close enough to resemble a third nipple if you only were allowed a quick glance. On closer study, it's obviously a freckle, but not everyone knows that.

Knowing my tumultuous relationship with Jaz, I didn't dare go shirtless. I knew she'd make some note of my freckle. She'd already seen me with my shirt off, but with my luck, she'd choose the worst moment to discover the offending freckle.

Once the carpets were torn out, we called it a night. Jaz went back to the bar, an extra pep in her step from being able to slash away, and I achingly followed behind Fallon and Peter, who were holding hands.

Showered and ready for bed, I had to navigate through the residence, heart heavy in my chest as Peter caressed Fallon on the arm, the back, pecked her with kisses here and there, made it absolutely known that even though she might have spent a portion of the day with me, he would be spending the entire night with her. The affection was too much for me, too painful, and instead of sticking around and sitting in the living room with them, I retired to my room.

"Are you comfortable?" Fallon asks. "I hope it's not weird being in Sully's bedroom." She's leaning against the doorframe of Sully's room, wearing a pair of red cotton shorts and a simple Canoodle T-shirt. From a quick glance—and I mean lightning speed—I can see that she's not wearing a bra, and that's all I'll say on that matter . . . except, God, she looks cuddle-able. Like she could melt right into my chest, legs tangled, arm around my waist.

"This is great," I say, hands on the mattress beneath me. I give it a little bounce, and the springs squeak. The mattress is old and lumpy, and I'm sure he's never once replaced it.

"I hope you're not someone who moves in their sleep, because with that squeak beneath you, you're going to be up all night."

"Lucky for me, I lie stiff as a board, on my back, hands at my side, like a pencil."

She laughs. "Why can I envision it?"

I press my hand to my chest, scandalized. "Fallon, how dare you envision me in bed."

She's laughing some more just as Peter walks up behind her and slips his arm around her waist so his hand rests on her stomach. He presses his lips to her neck, and jealousy skyrockets through me. "Ready for bed, sweetheart?"

"Yeah," she says. "Just making sure Sawyer's comfortable." She turns toward me, and I notice that she doesn't lean into Peter's grip, nor does she rest her hand on his, something a loving couple would do—he touches her, she touches him. Instead, he clings to her like a life float, while she stands tall, eyes trained on me, making me dare to hope I might actually have a chance. "You good?"

"I'm good. Thank you, Fallon."

"No, thank you, Sawyer. I'm honestly so grateful for everything you've done."

"Yes, thank you, Sawyer," Peter says from over Fallon's shoulder.

I catch his thumb rub her stomach. It's the lightest of movements, not something I think another person would observe, but it nabs my attention like a knife piercing into me. I know, from the perspective of writing romance and observing the little things about a relationship, that a stroke of a thumb is almost more intimate than a kiss.

Anyone can pucker up and press their mouths together.

But only a person in a devoted relationship would have the privilege of stroking their thumb over their partner's skin.

And that's what fucking breaks me.

That stroke of his thumb.

Like a tornado whipping through me, I'm swirled and consumed by jealousy, by anger, by longing.

Why the hell did I have to ignore her on our blind date? Why did I have to retreat to the one place where I'd run into someone I click with, someone I could see myself with, someone who is completely and irrevocably attached?

Why can't I be the man who holds her? Who caresses her?

Why does it feel like I've tossed myself into a self-induced purgatory with no way out?

"Okay, good night, Sawyer," Fallon says.

"Yes, good night, Sawyer," Peter says, bringing Fallon into his chest, and then I see it—she smooths her hand over his, and it's like a goddamn gut punch.

For a moment, the smallest, shortest of moments, I thought that maybe she wasn't feeling the same way about him that he does for her. From her smirks, to the playful way she jokes with me, to the stolen glances, my imagination conjured up hope, whispered in the back of my mind that I had a chance. But with that small, innocent touch, her loving body language toward Peter, those thoughts are banished.

I offer a soft smile through the pain. "Good night."

And then they take off, hand in hand, to Fallon's room on the other side of the residence, where they'll share a bed . . .

I flop back on the mattress and grip my head, agony ripping through me.

"Fuck."

CHAPTER SEVENTEEN

FALLON

"I'm exhausted," I say as I shut my bedroom door behind me.

"Me too," Peter replies as he corrals me against the door, his eyes heady as he slips his hand up my hip, to the hem of my shirt. He leans forward and presses a kiss to my neck. "I've missed you, sweetheart."

"Peter, I don't—"

"Didn't you miss me?" he asks, his mouth moving down my neck while his hand slowly moves up my shirt.

"I did," I say, and I grip his wandering hand and stop him. "But not right now."

He pulls away so our gazes connect. "Don't want to be with your boyfriend?" he asks, a stark anger behind his usually gentle eyes. "Why? Because *Sawyer* is in the other room?"

My brow creases from his assumption. "No, because I have my period, Peter." I push away from him and head to my side of the bed.

I feel his regret from across the room. "Shit, Fallon. I'm sorry."

That's the thing about Peter: he's always quick to apologize. I almost wish he would drag it out a bit, take a second to truly feel the meaning behind his apology.

"Are you sorry?" I ask him as I flip the covers to the bed down. "Or are you just saying that out of instinct?"

"What is that supposed to mean?"

"It means you've been parading around ever since you've gotten here"—I fling my arm out to the side—"acting like some kind of possessive . . . man, staking claim wherever I walked."

"Do you blame me?" he asks, his arms mimicking mine. "When I was driving up here, I was expecting to surprise my loving girlfriend, but instead, I find you with some other man."

"Oh my God, you say that as if I was cheating, like you caught us in bed." I remove the clip from my hair that's holding it into a loose bun and toss it on my nightstand. "We were just talking. He's been helping me with the renovations—I'm not going to act like a jerk to him."

"Well, you don't have to flirt with him."

"What? Are you insane? I'm not flirting with him."

"I'm not a moron, Fallon. I can see the way he looks at you. He likes you. And maybe you like the attention."

What an awfully bold statement.

Anger sears through me, and I attempt to keep my voice low so Sawyer can't hear anything. "He does not like me, and to assume that I enjoy another man's attention is insulting, Peter."

"He's infatuated with you," Peter says, stepping closer. "Trust me, I know when a man is interested, and he one hundred percent wants you."

"He doesn't," I say. "I know him better than you, and no, he does not see me like that. If anything, there's just friendship between us. He's a lost man, lonely, and looking for something other than the superficial life he was living. Plus, he was cheated on—do you really think he would do that to someone else?" And yes, we might have said there was attraction between us, but we both agreed to set it aside. That's nothing to even bring up, though, because Peter would lose his mind over it.

"Yes," Peter says without even thinking about it. "Yes, I do. Men don't have morals when it comes to something they want."

"He doesn't want me," I shout-whisper.

"But do you want him?" Peter asks.

I open my mouth to respond—and for some reason, the words are caught in my throat. My answer sticks to my tongue like a chewy taffy, unmoving, unwavering. It feels like minutes, but my pause is mere seconds before I say, "No, of course not."

But that pause, the second I take to gather myself, is all Peter needs to take a step backward, stunned. "You do," he says, as if he's stumbling upon this realization. "You want him."

"Peter, stop, I don't want him," I say. "I want you." I take a step toward him, but he backs up. "We're both tired. I think emotions are high right now; we should just—"

"Tell me you love me."

"What?" I freeze midstep.

"I love you, Fallon. You know that. But I can't sit by and wait for you to try to figure out if you love me back. We've been together for over a year—you either do or you don't."

I glance away. I can't seem to look him in the eyes. Not when I know the answer to his question.

He wants me to love him, and I've tried. I've tried so hard to dive deep into my feelings, to pull those emotions from the depth of my being, but anytime he utters those three little words, all I can think is . . . I don't.

"It's not that easy, Peter."

"Yes, it is," he says, walking up to me. He grips my cheek and forces me to look him in the eyes. "Tell me, right here, right now, how you feel about me."

"Peter, this . . . this isn't fair. You can't pressure me like this."

"Pressure you?" He laughs. "Fallon, I've been more than patient with you. I've driven up here almost every weekend to be with you. I've waited, I've put aside my needs, my wants, for you. I think it's fair for me to ask you if you love me or not."

"I never asked you to put aside anything for me."

"And that's what you don't get—because I love you, I do anything you want. Anything at all to make sure you're happy." I glance away because this is all too raw, all too much. The guilt consumes me, since I know he would. I know he'd do just about anything for me, and still, I can't muster up the type of love he wants me to. A sarcastic laugh pops out of his mouth as I take the coward's way out and glance away from him. "But that's not enough, is it?" He releases me and steps back. "My love, my promise to keep you happy. That's not enough for you." Turning away, he grips the top of his head and blows out a heavy breath. "Jesus Christ, have I been wasting my time?"

"What? No." I move toward him and touch his back, but he pulls away from my hand. A stark chill rushes through me. His denial cuts deep, deeper than I expected.

"How can I believe that?" He spins around. "How can I not think that I just wasted the better part of a year pining after someone who doesn't feel the same way toward me?"

His words knock me back on my heels. Wasting his time?

I fold my arms over my chest. "You truly believe you've wasted your time with me? Do you realize how insulting that is?"

"Do you realize how insulting it is that you can't mutter three little words to me?" he shoots back. "It's not that hard, Fallon."

"It is for me," I say. "We got together right before I moved up here. And yes, have you been amazing, driving up here and making our relationship work? Of course, but you need to realize something, Peter: I'm not the same person you met a year ago. And the fact that you can't see that tells me you don't know me at all. That maybe you're in love with the girl I used to be—not the girl I am right now."

"What do you mean you've changed?"

"The fact that you can't even see that speaks volumes."

"I'm not a mind reader, Fallon. I barely see you—how on earth can I tell if you've changed or not when we barely get a few days together?

Maybe one phone call a week with texts sprinkled throughout. I'm trying here, I really am, but you have to meet me halfway."

I feel my anger deflating in the face of his reason. Maybe he's right: maybe I do need to meet him halfway. Our communication isn't nearly as great as it should be for two people who've been together for over a year, and I know I have to take a great deal of responsibility for that.

"This is hard," I say. "Harder than I think I ever believed it would be. Before I moved here, before I found out about Sully, my life was so simple. Yes, I worked in the ER, but that was challenging, that kept my mind sharp. I spent my days off reading poolside, soaking in the Palm Springs sun, having game night with my dads and friends. Hell, I'd even enjoy a nice glass of wine and just relax. I don't have that privilege anymore. I'm bound to my grandfather, to these cabins. I don't know what a day off is anymore, but I don't care about that because my priorities are different. I know you mean well, but you keep wanting to take me away from here; you keep wanting to help me forget. But I don't want to," I say, my voice getting choked up with the real, deep truth pouring from my mouth. "I don't want to forget why I'm here, why I made the choice to help my ailing grandfather. This is a part of me now, a part of my soul, and even though you're patient with him, I know that you resent him as well—I can see it in your eyes." As I'm speaking, realization sets in as to why I've had a roadblock to loving this man. Why I can't say those three words. "How can I possibly love a man who resents the one person who makes me feel whole? Who makes me feel like I have purpose?"

Peter's lips twist to the side, and when his eyes drift past my shoulder, I know I'm right.

"I don't blame you, Peter. You met me when things were different, when I had all the time in the world to devote my energy to you. But I'm not that same person, and I don't want to be that same person. I want a partner in this life, here in Canoodle, not someone trying to pull me away from it. Not someone who is just counting down the days until Sully has no other choice but to be put into an assisted living facility." I motion toward the room. "This is my home. This is where I'm staying. These cabins, they're his legacy, and I'll be damned if I let anything happen to them. I know you think that maybe, one day, I'll come back to Palm Springs, and perhaps I thought that you'd come up here one day, but I think we both know that's not true."

He rubs his hand over his mouth, tension pulsing through his shoulders, wrapping all the way through his forearms.

"This isn't about Sawyer, Peter. This is about us."

And like a sunrise, the truth finally dawns on his face, transforming his anger into acceptance. He drops his hand and finally looks me in the eyes. "Shit," he mutters before walking up to me and pulling me into a hug. He cups the back of my head, and I twist in his arms so my cheek is resting against his chest. Tears spring to my eyes as I cling to him.

"I love you, Fallon. I truly do, but . . . fuck, I know when something isn't working, and this—you and me—we're not working."

I expect my watery eyes to leak, to drip and cascade down my cheeks. But the tears never fall. Not when Peter pulls away and grips my cheeks, locking our gazes. Not when he leans forward and presses a kiss to my forehead. And not when he packs up his overnight bag and puts his shoes on.

"You don't have to leave tonight. It's late, Peter."

"I can't stay here. I can't sleep in your bed, knowing it's over. It's too painful."

"I understand," I say, my heart twisting when he picks up his bag.

He motions with his hand. "Come here." I walk into his embrace and wrap my arms around him while he grips me tightly. "I'm sorry I couldn't be the man you needed right now."

"I'm sorry I couldn't be the woman you needed or deserve." I look up at him. "But I know you'll find someone. You're a beautiful soul, and I'm so happy I got to have this time with you."

"Same," he says, pressing a kiss to my forehead. "Can you do something for me?"

"Sure," I say.

"Can you tell Sawyer I'm sorry for acting like a possessive jerk? I know it wasn't my best moment."

"It was for sure a different side of you." I laugh. "I especially liked it when you took your shirt off and paraded around."

He groans. "Please, don't remind me."

I give him a squeeze. "Are you going to be okay?"

"I'm sure I will," he admits. "Need to nurse these wounds, but I'll survive. It's not easy getting over someone like you, Fallon." To my surprise, he lifts my chin and presses a very light kiss to my lips.

I remember the first time I ever kissed Peter—it was like a parade of fireworks went off in my head as his lips roamed mine. But that was the only time it happened. That very first kiss. After that, his kisses became routine, like I expected them rather than yearned for them.

And with this parting kiss, I don't feel anything other than regret, one niggling thought that nags at me.

When he pulls away, I can't help myself as I say, "I'm sorry, Peter. I'm sorry if I wasted your time."

He shakes his head. "I never should have said that. Time is never wasted when you try to find who you are with another human being. This is more of a stepping-stone in our lives. If anything, we've learned from it."

With that, together, we walk out to the living room, him carrying his bag, me holding his hand. When we reach the door, he turns toward me, eyes wide, face earnest. "If you ever need anything, you just let me know, okay?"

I nod. "Thank you."

He gives me a soft smile, and then, without another word, he leaves the residence, his footsteps trailing down the creaky stairs into the inky night. Quietly, I shut the door behind him and lock it.

When I turn around, I startle back into the door. Across the room, a dark figure stands by the kitchen sink.

"It's just me," Sawyer says, stepping into the moonlight streaming through the living room window. "Sorry, I wasn't spying, I swear, I was just getting water." He holds up a glass.

I take a deep breath, my racing heart not settling when my gaze locks in on Sawyer, wearing nothing but a pair of gym shorts that ride low on his narrow hips. His torso is endless, molded along his stomach, revealing his sculpted abdomen all the way down to the deep V in his hips. Whereas Peter was stockier, Sawyer has what feels like a surfer's frame, and even through my emotional turmoil, it makes me wonder—does he surf? My eyes travel up to his blond hair, now dark in the dim room.

"Do you surf?" I ask.

"Huh?" The confused look on his face is comical.

"It's a simple question—do you surf?"

His hand scratches his defined pec. "Well, yeah, when I get a chance. I'd like to say I'm good at it, but I'm barely better than some of the twelve-year-old kids I take lessons with." He studies me. "Is everything okay?"

"I . . . I don't know," I answer. "Peter and I just broke up."

His expression shifts from confusion and morphs to concern as he takes a step forward before stopping himself, as if he's reminding himself that he shouldn't come too close. He seems unsure of what to do. "Are you okay?"

"I think I am," I say. "Just a little sad, you know?"

"Yeah, I can understand that." He's silent but continues to lock gazes with me. "This is presumptuous, but I hope it had nothing to do with me."

I shake my head. "No, I think it was a long time coming. Peter actually wanted me to apologize to you. He said he was being a jerk and was sorry about it."

"He was fine. He wasn't doing anything I wouldn't have done—or haven't done in the past. When you truly like someone, the threat of another man is real. Not that, uh . . . not that I'm a threat or anything."

I almost smile at that. "Either way, he was sorry."

Sawyer nods. "That's awfully nice of him. I'm sorry to see him go."

"Are you?" I ask as Peter's accusations about Sawyer come to the forefront of my mind.

He's infatuated with you.

Trust me, I know when a man is interested, and he one hundred percent wants you.

I didn't want to believe it when Peter was saying it, and when Sawyer and I admitted our attraction, I didn't have time to put much thought into it, but now, standing in front of Sawyer, vulnerable and very fresh from a breakup, I'm curious.

"I mean, yeah, I don't want to see you hurt," Sawyer says, setting his glass of water down on the counter and crossing the room in a few easy strides. "I know what heartache can feel like—"

"I didn't love him," I say.

He pauses, absorbing that information.

"That doesn't mean you didn't care for him," he says finally, "that he wasn't an important part of your life."

"He mattered to me, but I'm not sure in the way I mattered to him." I bite down on my bottom lip, gut twisting. "Man . . . I feel really guilty." I glance behind me to the closed door, wondering if I should chase Peter down and tell him that, but then again, he probably needs some space.

"Hey, do you want to sit down, talk?" Sawyer asks.

I nod, and we both walk over to the navy-blue-and-red plaid love seat in the living area. The residence is one giant open living space with two bedrooms on either side. So the kitchen, dining room, and living room are all connected, separated only by furniture. We both take a seat and turn toward each other, our shoulders pressing into the back of the couch.

"Do you want to talk about Peter? Talk about something else? Listen to some mindless story about how I once got my finger stuck in a bottle?"

"You got your finger stuck in a bottle?"

"Early twenties. It wasn't my most intelligent decade. I did some pretty stupid shit, including writing a story about a martian falling in love with a human."

I let out a low chuckle. "I need to find that film and watch it, just from the number of times you've mentioned it. You never know: it might be one of those horrible movies that a TikTok influencer finds endearing, and after one dance move with the movie in the background, all of a sudden it's trending."

"So, what you're telling me is I'm one shoulder pop away from viral fame?"

"I think you already hit viral thanks to your double bird at the altar."

"Very true. I'd hate to see what kind of hashtags are trending over that move."

"Best you stay away from social media." I bring my legs up to my chest and curl into the side of the couch. "You know, with Peter, I think there was a disconnect. Well, I don't think—I know there was."

"What do you mean?" he asks with sincerity. That's how Sawyer always speaks, with true interest. He's not asking questions just to ask—he's asking because he's truly interested.

"I think he expected me to leave Canoodle at some point, and I expected him to maybe come up here, but neither of us spoke about it, and we weren't willing to change our minds."

"That can be tough."

"Yeah, and even though he was so sweet, I'm not sure he understands who I am now and what my priorities are."

"You mean making sure the cabins succeed and taking care of Sully?"

And just like that, without blinking an eye or stuttering over his words, Sawyer knows exactly what matters to me. How come Peter didn't see it? How is it that a man I've truly only known for a few weeks can understand me to my very core, but a man I've been dating for a year wore rose-colored glasses?

"Yeah," I answer, stunned. "You know, for someone who didn't pay attention to me on our first date, you sure know how to pay attention now."

"One of the biggest mistakes of my life," Sawyer says, his eyes cast down. "I've realized that ever since I came to Canoodle." His eyes meet mine. "I missed out on a big opportunity to get to know someone pretty damn amazing."

My cheeks heat up and my mouth goes as dry as a desert, looking, begging for any droplet of water. After our blind date, I really had the attitude of "good riddance." I never gave Sawyer another thought. If he didn't want to talk to me, that was his problem, so seeing him again never resurrected any feelings to earn his approval. But his confession strikes me so hard that I find myself struggling for words.

"I'm sorry, I shouldn't have said that," Sawyer adds.

"No, it's . . . uh, it's fine. We both kind of admitted to feeling something, and then Peter said he thought you might have had feelings for me. I, of course, told him he was wrong, and that wasn't the case at all. He truly thought you were trying to make a move. Can you believe that?" I ask, chuckling nervously.

He doesn't answer right away.

Instead, he stares at me, and I can see something running through his mind as his jaw clenches and unclenches. The awkward silence stretches to an unbearable length, at least unbearable for me. I hate awkward silences, but when it happens during a nerve-racking conversation,

I feel my fight-or-flight instinct start to kick in. Right now, the flight is going to win. I'm about to call it a night, extract myself from this moment so I can bury my head in my pillow and hope for the sweet release of forgetting this conversation ever happened.

Finally, he clears his throat. "I can believe it." Our eyes connect. "Because it's true, and hell, I shouldn't be saying that to you, not right now, not right after you broke up with your boyfriend, but yeah, I have feelings for you, and I would be lying to myself if I didn't admit it. I'm a fool for treating you the way I did on our blind date. You deserve so much better than anything I could offer, but yeah . . . there are feelings on my end, and they struck me hard when I saw you with Peter." He wets his lips. "Watching him touch you, kiss you, claim you . . ." He slowly nods. "Well, it just made me realize how much of a jealous asshole I was."

All of the air that was once pumping in my lungs has completely vanished, and now as I attempt to breathe, I can't seem to find any sort of oxygen.

He . . . he has feelings for me? Like actual feelings. Not just attraction or an offhand comment.

Peter was right?

Of course Peter was right—he's always right. And maybe a little piece of me, even though I denied it, knew Peter was all along.

But actually hearing Sawyer say it? It's hitting me on a whole other level. Deep down, if I want to really admit to myself what's been going on the last few weeks, my feelings for Sawyer have been surfacing as well. And this is more than a crush, a pounding heart when he touches my face. This is real.

"Hell, I'm sorry," Sawyer says. "This is the last thing you need right now, me acting like some chump, telling you how I feel. Just forget it, okay? Forget I ever said anything." He presses his palm to his eye and rubs it. "So, about getting my finger stuck in a bottle. I was in my twenties—"

I press my hand to his leg to stop him.

When his eyes meet mine again, I hold out my hand. He glances down and then looks back up at me, questioning. Wanting to help him understand, I reach out and I tug on his hand. He wets his lips as he once again checks for confirmation. When I nod, he tentatively places his hand in mine, and I entwine our fingers before resting my head on the back of the couch.

"Okay." I get comfortable. "Resume your story. You were in your twenties."

A small smile plays at his lips as he reaches out with his other hand and loops a strand of my hair with his finger, playing with it.

It's a simple touch, a small, intimate act letting me know that he's there for me, he's interested, and when I'm ready, he's ready.

If I didn't feel so guilty over Peter, I very well might lean in a little closer to him.

But holding his hand is good enough for me.

❖   ❖   ❖

"What on earth are you doing?" Jaz asks as I pull her inside the lobby's entryway closet, shut the door, and turn on the overhead light with one pull of the cord. The small space illuminates, and Jaz's irritated features come into view. "What exactly are you doing?" she asks, hand on her hip.

"Shhh." I hold my finger up to my lips. "Whisper." The Cove is crawling with Tank's motorcycle club, Sawyer is running from task to task, and I want to have this conversation in absolute privacy.

"Okay, why are we whispering?" she asks softly.

"I don't want anyone to know we're in here talking."

"Why not?" she whispers back.

"Because I need to tell you something, but I need it to be private, and I need you to not make any loud noises that would draw any attention to us."

It's the next morning after the breakup and the late-night hand-holding. Sawyer and I spent another hour on the couch before he walked me back to my room, gave me a gentle hug, and then walked over to Sully's bedroom. I woke up this morning to a note on the dining room table saying that he got an early run in and would start patching the wall as soon as he could with limited supplies. He also put a heart at the end of the note. I stuffed the note in my jean shorts and then came flying down the stairs to the lobby, where I found Jaz, and, without another thought, pulled her into the closet.

"Why aren't we drawing attention?"

I'm not quite sure how Jaz is going to react to the news. She was never consistent in her feelings about Peter. She had her moments when she really liked him, and then there were times when she could take him or leave him.

But when it comes to Sawyer, a.k.a. Julia . . . well, I'm pretty sure she's not going to be thrilled about that development at all—hence why I need to trap her in this closet and swear her to normalcy, so she doesn't create a scene in front of Tank, Sully, my dads, and all the guys from the motorcycle club.

"Now I'm going to tell you something, but you have to promise me you won't freak out."

She crosses her arms over her chest. "There's no way in hell I'm promising that."

"Please, Jaz. I need this weekend to go smoothly, but I have to tell you something as my best friend, and if I don't get it off my chest, I think I might combust. But it's something big. Something really, really big."

Her eyes widen, and she grips my shoulders. "Oh my God, you're pregnant."

"What? Good God, no."

"Oh." Her face falls. "Then what's so important that you have to stuff me in this old coat closet that honestly could use a clean out. What is that smell? Is that mothballs?"

"Peter and I broke up."

Her eyes flash to mine in a hurry. "You broke up? Why? Who did the breaking up? You or him? Is that why he's not here right now? I call dibs on the fritter I bought him—just calling it now so there isn't any confusion."

"That's what you're concerned about, the fritters?"

"I'm always concerned about fritters, but I'm concerned about you too." She robotically pats my shoulder, her lack of maternal instincts on full display. "But are you okay? Was he the one who broke it off?"

"Why'd you assume that?"

"Well, because he was all jealous yesterday. It was frankly a little embarrassing. He was throwing a tantrum when you went to do the carpet with Julia. He asked me if anything was going on between you two, and of course I said no, but that didn't seem to satisfy him. I just assumed it would have been too much for him, and he called it quits. Is that what happened?"

"Well, sort of. We both kind of called it off. It was amicable. And in the end, there was no tension. We just . . . we outgrew each other. We've changed a lot since we first met, and I think that set in last night, when we finally got it all out in the open."

"Makes sense. I've seen the downfall coming for quite some time, but I wasn't about to put that thought in your head. Better for you to realize it on your own."

"What do you mean you could see it coming? For how long?"

"Months," Jaz answers, sticking her hand out in front of her and examining her nails. "I could see you pulling away, talking about him less, not getting upset when he couldn't make it up for the weekend. The fact that you weren't able to tell him you love him. Just a culmination of small things."

"Oh . . . I wonder if Peter noticed those things."

"Clearly he noticed something if he was good with the breakup." She looks up from her nails, concern in her eyes. "Are you okay?"

"Yeah, I am. Surprisingly. I think you were right—it was coming for months now, and it finally happened last night. I feel guilty that I might have been stringing him along."

"You weren't stringing him along. I just don't think you understood your feelings, and that's okay—it takes time to work out those things. But I'll be honest, that news isn't really closet worthy. You could have told me that in front of Miss Daphne Lynn Pearlbottom, and we wouldn't have had an issue."

Yeah, she very well might be right, but that's not the big news. That's not why we're in the closet. It's what I have to tell her next.

"I held Sawyer's hand last night."

"What?" she shouts.

"Shhhhh." I clamp my hand over her mouth. I knew it was smart to hide away. "Come on, Jaz, I told you to be quiet."

She swats my hand away, and her eyes blaze with questions. I steel myself.

"You can't tell me that you held Julia's hand last night and expect me to act chill about it," she whispers, angrily. "That is not something to be chill about. That's something to . . . to . . ." Before I can decipher what she's going to do, her hands connect with my shoulders, and she pushes me into the wall of the closet.

I knock into it with a *clunk* and look at her, startled. "What was that for?"

"I don't know." She shakes her hands out, startled just as much as me. She pushed me . . . into a wall. "I don't know what's happening to me. Julia? You held Julia's hand? When? Was Peter still there? Is that really why you broke up?"

"Oh my God, no. I would never do that. It was after." I swallow hard. "Like right after. He was in the kitchen when I said bye to Peter, we started talking, he told me that he has feelings for me, and then—"

"He told you that? Right after you broke up with your boyfriend? What a chump. At least give her a second to breathe from the breakup, Julia. Jesus."

I wince. "He called himself that last night—a chump."

"And that's supposed to make it better?" she asks with a "get real" expression.

"No, but he did say he felt really bad about his confession and said it was terrible timing, but it just kind of came out."

"What the hell did you say to him?"

"Nothing. I just . . . I held his hand. Like fingers entwined, thumbs rubbing on backs of knuckles. Real hand-holding. And now that I have to see him this morning, I'm freaking out. What do I say? Do I mention the hand-holding? Do I mention how I liked when he twirled my hair with his finger? Because he did that—he picked up a single strand and just twirled. It took everything in me not to beat my leg on the floor like a dog. Or . . . do I tell him how I think he has a really nice, proportionate chest-to-muscle ratio. He was topless . . . wait, are men topless? Or do we say shirtless? Either way, there were no clothes on his body. Well, besides his shorts. I didn't see anything down south, so don't worry about that. But I mean . . ." I let out a pent-up breath. "Jaz, do I tell him how I have feelings for him too? Do I—"

"Wait. You have feelings for him too? Like legit feelings?"

I grip my cheeks. "I know, it's crazy. This is so crazy. I just broke up with Peter, but Peter and I have been drifting apart since before Sawyer even came along, and then when I started talking to Sawyer, I think I saw the difference between the two. Peter was holding on to the old me, but Sawyer embraces the new me. And I mean, the way he acts with Sully. How patient he is. It guts me. It makes me want to throw myself at him." Jaz doesn't say anything. She just stands there beneath the dim closet light, stoically, judging me with her piercing eyes, arms folded. "What? Say something. I didn't mean for this to happen—it just kind of did, and now that it has, I feel like a train wreck." I motion to the door, anxiety racketing through me. "I have to go out there, act normal, as if I didn't have a thousand butterflies shoot off in my stomach when he hugged me good night. God, Jaz, what is happening?"

She goes back to examining her nails. "Exactly what I assumed was going to happen when you realized who Julia was."

"What do you mean?"

"I saw it, that first night, the way you'd glance over at him. Even with my crooked-nose comments, you were interested."

"His nose is not that crooked, just a little, and it gives him character. He's quite handsome." I can't help but smile.

"And that right there"—Jaz points at my mouth—"is what I'm talking about. You've liked this guy from the moment he strolled into this town, even if you want to deny it. I'm just surprised you actually gave in, given how stubborn you are. And then of course there was the whole love triangle thing with Peter—and frankly it's upsetting that you can have two men fall for you and I can't even get Ralph, Roy's nephew, to walk into the bar."

"Because when he first met you, blood was dripping down the side of your face because you got so angry with the Chicago Rebels losing the first game in the World Series that you slammed your head into the wall. That would terrify even the strongest of men."

"Maddox Paige pitched an impeccable game, only for the relievers to blow it—that's worthy of a head slam. And you know what? Why should I settle for someone who doesn't appreciate my passions and my reactions when things don't go my way?"

"You shouldn't. That's why Ralph isn't right for you."

"Exactly." She tilts her chin up just a bit higher. "And maybe Julia's stupid brother will ask me out on a date one day, instead of just sending me ridiculous memes that make me laugh but mean absolutely nothing." She shakes her head and arms, almost to shake it all off. "But that's beside the point. You and Julia were bound to happen, whether you want to believe it or not. Now you just have to figure out if you're going to make something of it."

"That's just it, Jaz. I don't know what to do. I'm freaking out."

"I can tell, since we're currently in a coat closet, shout-whispering to each other."

"Just give me some advice, anything."

"Call him Julia; he seems to respond well to it."

"Jaz, that's not helping."

She sighs and then reaches out and grips my shoulders. "Are you listening to me? Because I'm only going to say this once—I'm not in the business of repeating myself, especially not over romantic involvements."

I blink a few times. "I'm listening."

"Good. Now, you are going to go out there, you are going to act like everything is normal, and when he says 'good morning'—because you know he will—you're going to tell him 'good morning' and then . . . go on with your day. Nothing to freak out about. The man liked you before last night; he liked you . . . for you. So, no need to overthink this. Just be you."

"But I don't know how to be me anymore," I say, my mind going cloudy with panic. "I've changed. I've morphed. I'm a woman—"

Smack.

Pain ricochets over my cheek as I stumble backward into the closet wall, blinking rapidly at a very pleased Jaz. I lift my hand to my offended cheek—hot from the slap of Jaz's hand. I wouldn't be surprised if there was a handprint, a permanent mark. This very well could be her way of branding, and yet . . .

"Th-thank you," I say, straightening up, my head clearing. "I needed that."

"I know. That's why I did it. Now get it together. We have renovations to do."

With that, she exits the closet and heads outside toward the cabins, though not before picking up her box of pastries and tucking them under her arm.

I step out of the closet and continue to rub my cheek until the sting of her hand is no longer there. I let out a deep breath. Just be myself?

Does that mean even though I'm feeling really awkward, really uncomfortable, that it's okay to let that show? That I don't have to be perfect the next time I see him?

Yeah, I guess that's exactly what it means.

With Jaz's advice propelling me forward, I exit the residence and walk the pathway to the cabins, the cement wet from the early-morning sprinklers. The rising sun will eat up the damp sidewalk in no time, though. There's only one cabin with its door open, which means Jaz has to be in there with him.

All I can hope is that she's not talking about what happened last night.

I hurry along the path and take a deep breath as I turn the corner into the cabin, ready to come upon Jaz saying something embarrassing—but stumble to a stop. She's nowhere to be found, and Sawyer is the only one in sight.

"Oh, sorry. I thought Jaz was in here," I say.

Sawyer looks up from where he's patching the hole in the wall we found yesterday, and when his eyes connect with mine, a flash of relief crosses them. Was he afraid I wasn't going to show up today? Ignore all the renovations and escape to the Harry Balls Trail, hiding out until it's all over and done with?

Although appealing, I'd never do that.

"I haven't seen her come by yet." He sets his spackling tool—whatever it's called—on the new bucket of spackle and stands.

"I, uh, I didn't think Tank opened this early," I say, making a sad attempt at conversation.

"He made an exception for me," Sawyer says, stuffing his hand in his paint-splattered khaki shorts. He's wearing his original Canoodle shirt that he bought when he first arrived and a plain red baseball cap that he has twisted to face backward, something I know he'll adjust when Sully shows up. "How did you sleep?"

"Okay, I guess," I say, and because I'm a fool and can't seem to act normal around a man when I realize I have feelings for him, I add, "I woke up in the middle of the night because I had to pee. Did you hear me?"

He chuckles and shakes his head. "No, you must be a stealth pee-er."

"I didn't flush. Well, I mean, I flushed this morning, but you know, if it's yellow, let it mellow, so I let it mellow because saving water is nice, and I also didn't want to wake you up. Sometimes if I go to the bathroom in the middle of the night, I'll wake up Sully, and getting him to go back to sleep is really hard, so I tried to be as quiet as possible."

"You were quiet." He smirks. The way his lips curl up like that, in a sexy, amused expression, makes me want to maul him with my mouth, but also melt into a slow, painful, liquid death.

"Good, guess a year of practice will do that to you." I glance away because God, what is wrong with me? I'm talking to him about peeing!

"Never know when the little things will come in handy, huh?"

"I guess not." I look up at him, and silence falls between us.

Him, smiling.

Me, nervously twitching.

And I don't know how long we stand there, how long we stare at each other as he waits for me to say something and I try to slowly morph into the wall, but it's too long.

And I can't take it.

So, I finally break the silence. "This is awkward. I don't know how to be around you."

Sawyer's playful smile turns endearing as he closes the space between us. When he's inches away, he reaches out and takes my hand in his, lacing our fingers together. Our palms collide, and I nearly moan from the innocent yet addicting feel of his hand in mine.

"Do you regret anything from last night?" he asks, his voice low as his thumb strokes over the back of my hand, just like it was last night.

Do I regret anything that happened last night?

Honestly . . .

Not even a little bit. I feel sad for Peter and for losing that relationship in my life. He was a solid confidant for a while, and his newfound absence from my life is sad. But I know breaking up with him was the right thing to do. I think we spent too long just pretending that it was working.

And then everything that happened with Sawyer, the confessions, the innocent touching . . .

I look up at him and shake my head gently. "No, I don't regret a thing."

"Good." He lifts our clasped hands and places a soft kiss on my knuckles. "Then there's nothing to be awkward about." He releases my hand and goes back to the wall just as Jaz pops in with her box of pastries.

"Aww, the lovebirds. Have you kissed yet?"

"Jaz," I say under my breath.

Sawyer glances at me. "You told her?"

"Of course she told me, Julia." Jaz takes a seat on the floor, her back to the wall. "She tells me everything."

"If she tells you everything, then why are you asking if we kissed yet?" Sawyer lifts a brow.

Jaz points at it. "You can lower that little quizzical brow of yours. I know you only held hands last night, and the mere touch made her pant—"

"Jazlyn," I say sternly.

"But I wasn't sure if this morning, while I took the long way to this cabin—on purpose—you finally made a move to mash lips."

What is wrong with her?

"I'm sorry, Sawyer. Jaz clearly has no decorum."

"No need to apologize." After walking over to Jaz, he takes a seat next to her before reaching into the box and pulling out a fritter. Without even an apologetic blink, he looks Jaz in the eyes and takes a bite. "I understand how Jazlyn works," he says, after swallowing. "This is her way of telling me she approves. She couldn't be happier that we . . . held hands last night."

"I'm not mad about it," Jaz admits, taking a fritter for herself and patting the floor in front of her for me to sit.

Uneasy, confused, and half believing the floor is about to split open and hell is about to boil over because Jaz and Sawyer seem to be . . . friendly, I take a seat on the floor in front of them. Sawyer shifts so he's next to me now and hands me the box of pastries. I reach in and grab myself a fritter as well.

I take a bite and look between the two of them. "So . . . this is happening? You two are getting along."

Jaz moans into her fritter, then pauses. "As long as he doesn't hurt you, we're good."

"Don't plan on it," Sawyer says just as his eyes connect with mine. "I know exactly what it means to be hurt."

Nerves rumble through my chest as he inconspicuously moves his hand along the floor and softly grazes my leg. A light touch, one you wouldn't notice unless you're the one being touched, and yet it evokes such a strong reaction in me it's as if he's just gripped my inner thigh. I close my eyes, savoring his skin on mine.

"What the hell are you doing?" Sully's voice booms from the doorway, startling all three of us. "I'm not paying you to sit around and eat doughnuts." Fritters, technically. "Get your asses up and moving." He stomps into the room.

"Well, good morning to you as well," I say, gathering my wits as Tank trails in behind him.

"The boys are on their way," he says, and his deep voice is so sooth- ing, like a sensual James Earl Jones. "Oh, fritters? Is there one for me?"

"Always," Jaz says as she pushes the box toward her grandpa, a loving look in her eye.

Tank picks up the box. "Slash any tires lately?" he asks her.

"Not yet," Jaz answers as she looks directly at Sawyer. "But I'm prepared."

Now that's the kind of animosity I'm comfortable with.

❖   ❖   ❖

Tank wasn't kidding when he said his boys were going to work hard. When their motorcycles rumbled into town, they didn't play around with hellos or jolly banter. Nope, they split into groups and attacked. Sully took charge, with assistance from Sawyer, of course. Watching them together just solidified exactly why I can't seem to tear my gaze off Sawyer, why I feel like an innocent schoolgirl with a deathly crush. Why, I wouldn't be surprised if I started a Sawyer fan club and served as president, vice president, and treasurer. He's very soft spoken with Sully, asking him questions even though he knows the answers, and then helping him find those answers when he needs them. But then, they also give each other crap, bantering back and forth like longtime friends.

Sully has a spark in his eye.

He looks more lively today than he has in weeks.

And the laugh I hear booming through the cabins, the laugh I grew up listening to, that turned into a source of comfort, I've heard it so many times today I've lost count. Sully is in his element, surrounded by people he loves, working on improving his legacy as one big family. It's been an absolute perfect day. And all hands have been on deck. The rest of the carpeted floors have been ripped out, and wood floors have been installed. Walls are being painted at the same time—it's like one large conveyor belt of work. Not one cabin has gone untouched, and from the smile on Sully's face, I not only feel like we're accomplishing a dream I've had for over a year, but we're also creating something special. We're building on the foundation Sully and Grandma Joan made, and we're guaranteeing a future.

My dads arrived a few hours ago and have been working hard on preparing a large dinner for the crew. When they first showed up, I greeted them and brought them to their newly renovated cabin. The tears in my dads' eyes had my heart beating even faster for the man who made this happen. Sawyer has no idea the kind of present this was for my entire family. When my dads asked me how I was able to get it all done, I told them about Sawyer and how he's been helping around the Cove. Apparently, I wasn't able to hide my infatuation with the man, because my affection toward him was written all over my face. So, I broke down and told them about Peter and then confessed my feelings for Sawyer, something I didn't want to do this weekend because I wanted to keep everything focused on the cabins. To my shock, they both said they'd seen it coming. Not Sawyer, but the breakup with Peter. And then Papa tried to scope out Sawyer among the crew but didn't get much of a chance because he's been putting in so much work that I've barely even seen him. But the dads are chomping at the bit, dying to meet Sawyer after all that I've told them.

And now that dinner is ready, the time has come.

I've rounded up all the men, but there's one last cabin at the far end of the pathway that I have to check, and I know that's where Sawyer has to be.

I walk up the two steps to the small porch and through the door, where I find Sawyer installing a black-finish light fixture. The muscles in his forearms fire off as he attempts to twist two wires together.

His shirt is off and tucked into the back of his shorts, which are riding low on his hips, showing off the elastic waistband of his black briefs. His back is broad and chiseled, just like the front of his chest, and as my eyes travel the length of him, I notice the adorable dimples right above his backside.

"Hey," I say gently, so as not to startle him. "Dinner is ready."

He glances over his shoulder, and when his eyes meet mine, his lips curl into an arresting smile.

"Hey you," he says before turning back to the fixture, where he caps off the wires and then twists. When he's done, he turns toward me, and I take in a shameless eyeful. I can't even count the number of times I've seen this man with his shirt off, but every time feels like the first. When my eyes return to his, I catch his pleased, almost devious expression. He's satisfied with my once-over.

I clear my throat and take a step back toward the door. "Yeah, so . . . you know, dinner." I gesture my thumb behind me. "My dads made what they're calling a 'summer soiree,' because it isn't a meal with them if it doesn't have a name."

"Sounds good." He retrieves his shirt from his shorts and removes his hat—which he's wearing backward—and dresses himself. Once his shirt is situated, he puts his hat back on, but according to Sully: "the right way." With Sawyer, it's the small things that really get me, like how he wears his hat as a nod of respect to my grandpa.

When he's ready to go, he walks toward me and gently places his hand on my lower back, guiding me out the door.

And it just about does me in.

Because it's not the first discreet touch of the day; it's one of many. Every time he's seen me, he's either given me a soul-searing look that splits me right down the middle, or a roll of his teeth over his lips. A once-over that tickles me to my core. A glance so palpable that it feels like his eyes are caressing me. And when it wasn't his eyes, it was his hand. His fingers trailing over my skin as he walks by. His hand smoothing over my lower back as he answers one of my questions. A small bump of his shoulder, which is normally anything but sexy, and yet I felt a small moan bubble up in my throat.

It's been like that all day, this constant awareness of my feelings for this man. And I'm not sure if he realizes what he's doing to me, but it's making me crazy with need. It's making me stop what I'm doing, right in the middle of wielding a hammer, to look up and just gaze at him. I'm distracted. I'm flustered. And I'm desperate for another fix.

"How are you doing?" he asks as we walk out of the cabin. Since we're at the far cabin, we're out of view of the picnic tables, which are just over the hill that slopes above us.

"Tired," I admit. "But very, very grateful. After tomorrow, I'll just have to set up the rooms. Jaz has already taken pictures and is working on uploading them to the website for me. We might be able to start booking on Monday."

"That's really great to hear." His palm slides off my back when we make our way to the path. "I can take care of the landscaping this week. I've noticed a few overgrown areas that won't take me long to fix."

"Sawyer, you don't have to do that. I can hire someone."

"I got it," he says with a wink just as his fingers brush against my hand. But before I can react and take his hand in mine, we're climbing over the hill and in view of everyone sitting at the picnic tables . . . which of course are decorated to the nines.

Black tablecloths cover the freshly painted red tables. Full eco-friendly place settings are at every seat, and in the middle for a center-piece—of course—are an array of pine cones scattered in bowls. The string lights are on despite the sun still shining above the crest of the mountain, and faint music plays in the background, creating the perfect ambiance.

Everyone is already seated at the tables, eating and chatting, while Papa strolls around, making sure everyone is set and comfortable.

There are two empty spots beside Dad, and I'm assuming that's where Sawyer and I are supposed to sit. I lead the way to the picnic table and smile when my eyes connect with his. "Hey, Dad, did Jaz leave?"

He nods. "Yes, but we set aside a meal for her like we promised. We'll bring it over to the bar after this."

"I can do that," I say, taking a seat.

Instead of sitting down, Sawyer walks up to my dad and lends out his hand. "I'm Sawyer—it's very nice to meet you, Mr. Long."

To my utter surprise, Dad's cheeks flush. "Please call me Izaak. And it's very lovely to meet you."

Just then Papa joins us and places his hand on Dad's shoulder. "This must be the Sawyer—or Phil—we've heard so much about."

Sawyer smiles broadly and shakes Papa's hand. "That would be me. It's very nice to meet you . . . can I call you Kordell?"

"Please." Papa waves his hand dismissively. "All that 'mister' stuff makes me feel like a seventy-year-old man, and I refuse to age."

"It's happening—we can see the laugh lines," Dad teases.

Papa presses his hand to his chest in mock horror. "How dare you!"

We all chuckle and take our seats. To my surprise, Sawyer sits right next to me, close enough that the sides of our bodies skim against each other. Normally I'd appreciate being this close to him, but I can feel my face heat up from the smell of his soap drifting so close to me. I'm nervous I'm going to make a fool of myself in front of my dads. You know, do something insane like leaning in and sniffing his neck, or heaving a heavy, dreamy sigh as I stare at him, or, even worse . . . relentlessly licking my lips over and over as I moan loudly. Not that I'd do that, ever, but there's a first time for everything, and Sawyer may be the kind of man who'd lead a woman to embarrassing herself with chapped lips and feral sounds.

"So," Dad says, a devious smile playing across his lips. I know that smile. It reeks of trouble. "You like our daughter."

Oh God. Yup, I was right.

It's going to be *that* kind of meal. The kind where I want to retreat halfway through and bury my head in the dirt.

"You don't have to answer that," I say, attempting to give my dads a warning glare.

But without skipping a beat, Sawyer looks toward me, his eyes blazing with promises. His expression is so sensual, so honest, that when he speaks, I hold my breath, waiting for his words to embrace me. "I do, Izaak. I like her a lot."

Pardon me . . . I need to go faint now.

Chapter Eighteen
SAWYER

Kordell lets out a roar of a laugh while flashing his phone to Izaak. They both watch what's on their screen, and right at the same time, they laugh again.

"Oh, that is priceless," Izaak says. "What I would have given to be there in person while you flipped your ex-girlfriend off at her wedding."

"Not my proudest moment," I say, pushing some beans around on my plate. Izaak and Kordell made quite the barbeque feast, full of corn on the cob, baked beans, watermelon slices, and a fresh strawberry, arugula, and feta salad, as well as pulled-chicken sandwiches with multiple sauce choices. I've devoured far too much, and yet I can't stop picking at my plate.

"It should be," Kordell says.

I wasn't quite sure what to expect from meeting Fallon's dads, but I definitely didn't expect them to welcome me into their family with open arms—not because they aren't nice people, but because I wasn't sure how close they were with Peter. I was apprehensive of meeting them under the label of Fallon's, uh . . . "love interest," but I'm not sure why I was worried at all. They're great. They remind me of the parents from *Meet the Fockers*. Open and welcoming, slightly dirty minded, but a really good time.

"Yes, I'd put that little episode on your résumé," Izaak says. "That, or turn it into a movie."

"Great opening to a movie," Kordell says. "I can see it now." He sweeps his hand across the sky. "Catchy rom-com song that makes your toe tap, aerial shots of Los Angeles, slowly sweeping into a quiet white chapel, where the camera pans down from the steeple, through the doors, and into the wedding ceremony, where the disgruntled grooms-man is standing."

"A voice-over commences," Izaak adds. "The groomsman tells the audience about his sour luck, turning the bride and groom instantly into the villains, so when the bride walks down the aisle, even though she looks angelic, the audience knows there's a demon beneath the white."

"Precisely," Kordell says, jumping in now. "And when the time is right, the disgruntled groomsman shows off his middle fingers with a bow, the audience gasps, and he takes off running down the aisle. And, like Cinderella herself, leaves behind one powder-blue shoe as evidence. Cue the Chicks' 'Ready to Run'—"

"No, no, no." Izaak holds his hand up. "We can't copy *Runaway Bride*. We need to have a song with the same impact, but won't make viewers think we're unoriginal."

"True," Kordell says, tapping his finger to his chin. "Aha, I got it." He lifts his finger to the sky. "'Make Way' by Aloe Blacc."

"What's that song?" Fallon asks as she leans in, looking adorably invested in her dads' narrative.

Kordell picks up his phone from the table and taps away on it. Smiling, he sets his phone down as a voice starts the song by saying "Legendary" and then breaks out into a bass beat, followed by clapping that hits with the drums. The song is fast paced, gives the vibe of fleeing from the scene, and also speaks of moving forward. I can see it, every-thing they've described. I can see it all.

"This song is absolutely perfect," Izaak says. "And while this is playing, you pan out to a montage of him driving away, the peeved bride and groom throwing their arms up in disgust. Credits roll, he blasts this song in the car and drives up to the mountains, more aerial shots, this time of his car weaving up the winding roads, the song slows down as he hits the bar, tie undone, top few buttons of his shirt unbuttoned, looking like he just got out of a bar fight . . . and that's when he runs into the small-town girl."

"Yes." Kordell pumps his fist in the air. "And from there, he navigates through the pits of his life while the small-town girl helps him see his worth. Then they fall in love, of course. Zany characters, two dads, a small town full of life and local color. Smells like a box office hit."

"And at the end, when they finally get together and kiss, the cameras do that classy spin-around-the-couple thing," Izaak adds, "while playing 'Love on Top' by Tim Halperin." He grabs Kordell's phone, does some typing, and then plays the song. It's slow at first, a cover of the original "Love on Top," and then, the song picks up . . .

"This right here," Izaak says, "when it really gets going, when the realization happens, this is when they confess their love and that they can't live without each other. This is where they kiss."

"Camera spins," Kordell says.

"And then we wipe away tears because we're so thrilled the couple has finally gotten together. And while credits roll, we're delighted with little updates about their lives."

"Like an epilogue," Kordell clarifies. "Like how they do that in *Maid in Manhattan*."

Izaak grips Kordell's hand and does the sign of the cross while looking up to the sky. "J-Lo in her prime. Bless us all, we'd be so lucky to have a brief glimpse of an epilogue like that." When Izaak gathers himself, they both turn toward me. "It could be called *Runaway Groomsman*." Izaak grins. "The title sells itself. What do you think?"

I scratch the side of my face, a bit stunned. "Well . . . can I hire you two? Because that was . . . that was incredible."

Kordell laughs, reaches over the table, and bops me in the nose. "Turn lemons into lemonade, baby." He presses his hand to his stomach and lets out a deep breath. "Now, I need to start cleaning up." He stands, snapping into host mode. "Izaak, start collecting plates."

"Yes, honey," Izaak answers with an eye roll and then maneuvers away from the picnic table and to the other tables, where he collects plates, piling them on his lap.

"I should get back to work too," I say to Fallon. "I have two more light fixtures to install in that last cabin."

"Why don't we help my dads and call it a night?" she asks. "The guys have already retired to the bar and set up their sleeping bags in the cabins. Tank has taken Sully back to his place. We should get some rest if we're going to tackle the rest tomorrow."

"Sure," I say. "If you don't mind that I finish tomorrow."

She sighs. "Sawyer, you've done so much already—please just take a second to breathe."

"Okay." I give her a smile and feel myself relaxing, grateful I can just enjoy the rest of the evening at her side.

We spent the next half hour cleaning the picnic tables. For the most part, the guys piled their empty plates together, but the corn on the cob made it tough for balancing. Fallon and I worked on the trash while Izaak and Kordell gathered any leftovers. Once the tables were cleaned, Fallon and I walked her dads to their cabin. They gave her hugs and kisses and she thanked them for coming up to visit before they turned toward me. Kordell brought me into a large hug and quietly thanked me for the cabin, for making Izaak feel comfortable. And then Izaak shook my hand with teary eyes before rolling up the ramp and inside. The entire time, I felt Fallon's adoring eyes on me.

After that, Fallon and I walked to the residence in silence. We both went our separate ways to take showers, and when I finished cleaning up, I decided to take a chance to see what she was doing and walked out into the main living space, where I found her curled on the couch, a cup of tea in hand, her wet hair braided into two braids, and dressed in a pair of black cotton shorts and a matching black shirt. I've seen her dressed down more than dressed up, and I can honestly say, I prefer her like this. Makeup-free, cozy, and content.

"Care for some company?" I ask.

She finishes taking a sip from her mug. "I hoped you'd join me."

"Did you now?" I ask with a raise of my brow. I take a seat on the couch next to her, and because I need to be closer to her, I pull her legs over mine and drape them over my lap. "What are you drinking?"

"Peppermint tea. Grandma Joan used to drink it before bed every night; picked up the habit from her." She offers me her cup. "Want to try it?"

"I would say yes, but I know I won't like it, and I don't want to insult your grandma like that, so I'm going to pass."

She chuckles. "Very honest answer." She takes another sip. "I hope my dads didn't freak you out with their whole movie-idea thing. They were just playing around. They wanted me to check with you, make sure you weren't mad."

"Mad?" I ask while I gently move my hand up and down her shin. "Are you kidding me? That was without a doubt one of the greatest pitches I've ever seen. I only wish I'd come up with it. Your dads very well might have a future in film."

"No way, they're just avid romantic comedy fans. They wouldn't know the first thing when it comes to writing a script. They did text me, though, and asked if I thought you were going to use the idea, because they would love to watch it."

"I don't know." I look her in the eyes. "Do you think the small-town girl and the disgruntled groomsman end up together?"

She smirks over the rim of her mug. "I think the chances are good."

I know humor is laced through our banter, but the meaning behind her answer doesn't escape me. She's giving me a second chance, the chance that I've been wishing for. And I'm going to take it. There is no way in hell I'm going to let this girl slip through my grasp again. I made that mistake once. Not again.

"If that's the case, can I ask you something?"

She tilts her head in question. "Sure."

"Monday, do you think I can take you out on a date?" I draw a small circle on her shin with my index finger.

"A date?" she asks, her lips tilting up. "Like, I dress up and you dress up and we go and enjoy an activity or meal together?"

"Yes, that would be the definition of a date." I chuckle.

Her eyes light up. "I can see if Tank can hang out with Sully," she says.

"Bring him with you."

Her nose scrunches up, and her hand reaches out and plays with a short strand of my hair. "It's really sweet that you'd invite my grandpa to go with us, but I would rather not have him on our first date—well, second date, technically. He can be rather grouchy and irritable, if you haven't noticed."

"So BYOG isn't sexy?"

"BYOG?"

"Bring your own grandpa."

She laughs and shakes her head. "Not the least bit sexy. Let me check with Tank, and I'll let you know. But yes, I would love to."

"Any day, really," I say. "I just want to take you out, you know . . . make up for that blind date."

"You have more than made up for the blind date," she says.

"Nah, doing work around the Cove isn't making it up to you— that's just showing you I'm not a dick. Taking you out on a proper date—that would be making up for it."

"Well, for what it's worth, I don't think you're a dick, not even close."

"No?" I ask, smoothing my hand up her leg to just above her knee. "Are you saying I've won you over?"

Her fingers continue to sift through my hair, and it's one of the most delicious feelings ever. "Let's see. I'm sitting on a love seat with you, my legs draped over your lap, and your hand is caressing my skin. I have no intention of moving anytime soon, so yeah, I would say you've won me over."

"Was it all those hot, shirtless summer days? Or did I win you over with my charm." I waggle my brows, and instead of laughing like I expect her to, she grows serious.

"Neither," she says before pressing her hand to my chest. "It was your heart."

I reach up and take her hand in mine. I kiss her knuckles, my eyes staying on her the entire time. "Some might say that answer is flirtatious. Is that what you're doing, Fallon? Flirting with me?"

"No. Just telling you the truth. If I were flirting, I would straddle your lap while saying it."

Playfully, I drop her hand and open my arms in invitation. "I'm all yours."

She chuckles and rests her head against the back of the couch. "I would, but I'm afraid of what might happen if I do. All those little touches today, the light brushes, the hand to my back, the piercing glances you gave me . . . it felt like the most intense foreplay of my life."

Her cheeks redden with her confession, and I find it so damn endearing.

"What you consider foreplay, I consider desperation—any moment I could steal today, just to be close to you, I took it."

"So, safe to say . . . we're into each other."

I chuckle. "Yeah, I've been into you for a while now, suffering on the sidelines, wishing I had one more chance with you." I push my hand through my damp hair. "I'm honestly shocked I actually get a second chance at taking you on a date."

"Where do you think you'll take me?"

"I have a few ideas," I say. "Depends on the night and the weather. It's supposed to rain this week."

"You already checked?"

"Oh yeah. I'm dedicated to taking you out. I've been planning it in my head for a while, just in case I ever got a chance, and now that I have one, I'm refining those ideas."

She lets out a deep sigh. "You're going to make it hard to even consider going out with anyone else, aren't you?"

"That's the plan."

❖   ❖   ❖

I stand up from a crouch and place my hand on my back as I straighten up.

Fuck.

My body has taken a beating the last few weeks, and it's finally catching up to me. My back is on absolute fire, and my hamstrings feel as though with one quick movement to the left, they might snap.

"You act like you're seventy-five," Sully barks as he strides into the cabin carrying the last piece of molding to be installed.

"Just a little sore," I say, taking the board. I hold back my groan as I bend down and line it up against the wall. It's the last piece of construction that needs to be done to the cabins—after that, we can start putting the furniture back and making beds. Everything else is complete: just a few paint touch-ups to cover nail holes, but that's it.

There's no way we could have done it without Tank's boys, who still wore their worn leather biker gear while hammering and painting away. The boys worked so hard that they were even able to build the new furniture pieces for some of the rooms. Even though they aren't my cabins, I still thanked each and every one of them for their help before they left.

I install the last board with the nail gun and then am slowly standing just as Fallon walks in.

I wince when I stand straight. I'm not good at hiding it, because she is quick to my side, hand on my back. "Are you okay?"

"Oh, he's fine," Sully says. "Just trying to get attention." He grumbles something under his breath, but I don't catch it.

"You know, Sully, I was wondering, would you be able to help me in the residence? There's a bunch of bedding in packaging, and I need to take it all out so I can wash it. Would you mind?"

"As if I haven't helped enough," he says, tossing his arms in the air—but he listens to his granddaughter and takes off toward the residence.

When he's gone, Fallon turns to me. "Hey, are you okay?"

"Just sore is all." I wince again as I move. "Pretty sure my thirty-five years are catching up to me."

She chuckles. "I guess so, old man. Since it's nine at night and the guys have all left, why don't you call it a night and head back to your cabin?"

"Normally I'd insist there's more work to be done, but I think you might be right this time." I set down the nail gun and then hobble toward the door.

"I don't think I've ever seen anything more pathetic," Fallon chuckles as she follows behind me.

"This does not bode well for my date plans. Please don't watch me as I head back to my cabin. It may involve limping, crawling, possibly rolling." I pause while she chuckles. "Oh shit, please tell me my cabin's been put back together."

"I just finished up. I even returned all your stuff."

I raise a brow at her. "Did you go through my things?"

"No." Her cheeks flush. "Well, maybe a bit. I smelled your cologne. But that was it."

"Uh-huh," I tease.

With Fallon at my side, we walk—slowly—back to my cabin, her hand around my waist, me trying not to put my weight on her. When we reach it, she opens the door for me, revealing the brand-new interior.

"Wow," I say, stepping inside. "What a difference."

We're surrounded by bright-white walls, with one rustic wood accent wall by the door and window. The beautiful pine flooring pops against the black wrought-iron bed with its white, fluffy comforter, red pillow, and black-and-white buffalo plaid blanket at its foot. The light fixtures I installed blend very well with the overall look, and the red accent rug on the floor adds a hint of warmth along with the black-and-white buffalo plaid curtains. For a moment, all my pain falls away and I just gape at all that we've accomplished together. "Man, Fallon, you really did a number on these cabins. It looks amazing in here."

"I did a number?" She pokes me in the arm. "More like you did. I couldn't have done this without you, seriously."

"Just remember that when I take you out on a date and I need to use a walker to get around."

She chuckles and carefully puts her arms around my waist, offering me a grateful hug. "You could take me and your walker out for the early-bird special, and I'd still date you."

"Be careful with what you say." I reach down and press a kiss to the top of her head. "I'm sure you have to get Sully in bed, and I need to attempt to take a warm bath. I know that will be an embarrassing journey with how sore I am, and I'd prefer you not experience that."

"Totally understand. Would it be okay if I check on you later?"

"Yeah," I say and then reach into my pocket for my phone. "Might be nice to get your number—you know, so I can text you sweet nothings about my aching sciatica and bristling bunions."

"Don't forget your sweaty balls."

A laugh rips out of me as I grip my lower back. "Damn, how could I forget those. It's a wonder you want to go out with me." She finishes entering her phone number in my phone, hands it back, and then offers me another hug.

Gratefully, I take it.

"I don't think you're giving yourself enough credit," she says as she pulls away. She lifts her hand up to my cheek. "Call me if you need anything—you know . . . like if you get stuck in the tub and can't get out."

"I'd rather die in that tub than call you for help. I need some shred of dignity."

She chuckles and squeezes my hand before taking off toward the residence.

I'm serious. There is no way I would call her. I don't need the first time she sees me naked to be in a tub as I flail about. I'd rather turn into a shriveled-up prune.

Still smiling, I hobble into the bathroom, which has been updated with a new counter, sink, and bathroom fixtures as well as a newly fitted tub. Sometimes, the small things really make a big difference.

I fill up the tub—which is going to be far too small for me, but I just need some warm water on my back—and undress. I consider playing some relaxing music from my phone, but I forgo that to play a word-search app. I slip into the tub. My six-foot-two frame is appallingly large for the size of this bath, but when the warm water hits my back, I don't care about the fact that my knees are bent and standing six inches out of the water, or that my penis is barely covered—which, let's face it, it's odd to be sitting in water, dick out—all I care about is the warm water on my lower back.

Comfortable—for now—I open my word-search app just as a text message from Roarick buzzes my phone.

Roarick: Are you dead? I haven't heard from you in a while and I'm starting to get worried. Should I drive up there just to check on you?

It's true, I've neglected my brother. I've neglected my agent. And most importantly, I've neglected the real world—for obvious reasons.

Sawyer: Alive, but barely. I've been doing renovations all week and my back just about gave out. I'm currently soaking in a bathtub and my penis is skimming the water, that's how small the tub is.

Roarick: Why do I find that way too comical? I legit snorted just thinking about the skimming penis.

Sawyer: Your support moves me.

Roarick: Hey, I checked to see if you were alive, didn't I?

Sawyer: I suppose.

Roarick: So . . . how is life? How is *says in annoying little brother tone* Fallon?

Sawyer: Specifying the tone is not necessary, I always think you're the annoying younger brother.

Roarick: You're avoiding the question.

Sawyer: Just adding suspense.

Roarick: Answer the damn question.

Sawyer: Why so impatient?

Roarick: I'm getting bored with this conversation.

Sawyer: I know you're not and if I don't tell you, you're going to stay up all night wondering.

Roarick: From your evasiveness and the absolute glee I can feel in your text messages, I'm going to assume something happened between you two. Just tell me she broke up with the boyfriend first.

Sawyer: She did. They broke up amicably and I'm going to take her out on a date this week. I really fucking like her, and I think she really likes me. She's said it more than once.

Roarick: Do I smell love in the air?

Sawyer: Not love, but a relationship, yeah.

Roarick: So, does this mean you will be staying in Canoodle longer than expected?

Sawyer: Yeah, and not just because of her, but because I like it here. It's calm. I've found peace here. Purpose. And the people are real.

Roarick: Are you thinking about making Canoodle your new home?

Sawyer: Haven't gotten that far yet, all I know is that I'll be staying longer.

Roarick: And what about the movie pitch?

I smile to myself and text him back.

Sawyer: I'm pretty sure I have an idea.

❖ ❖ ❖

Once I got out of the bathtub—more like rolled out over the side, because my back is still aching—I dried off and put on a pair of shorts before hobbling into bed.

Thank God for a new mattress. I don't think I would be able to survive on Sully's lumpy pile of springs anymore. How that man can stand it in his old age I have no idea. His back must be pure steel, completely impervious to the thorny entrapment he calls a mattress.

I open my word-search app, and I'm interrupted again, this time by a knock at the door.

I glance at the door and curse myself for locking it, or else I'd be able to shout "Come in."

Groaning quietly, I push off the bed and walk as gently as I can, trying not to create a spasm in my back. I flip the lock, and I open the door to find Fallon standing on the other side wearing her pajamas, her wet hair in its two customary braids.

"I told you I'd come check on you."

I smooth my hand on the door jamb and try to act like I'm not in pain. "I thought you were going to text me to check in."

"Oh, sorry. Should I have texted?"

I push the door open and step aside. "No, this is much better." She walks in, and I shut the door behind her. "Sully all tucked in?"

"Yes." She holds up her phone. "I'll be notified if he tries to leave."

As I walk over to my bed and take a seat—slowly—I ask, "Does he get up a lot?"

"Depends. Alzheimer's can be so cruel, because if he's startled awake, his brain doesn't quite grasp the concept of time, so it will be two in the morning, and he'll try to get ready for the day. Those are the roughest nights because he truly is confused."

"I can't imagine." I wince as I shift on the bed.

"Is your back still really sore?"

"Yeah. I think all the work, combined with Sully's mattress, has destroyed my muscles. I took some ibuprofen, so it should get better soon."

She moves toward me. "Lie down on your stomach."

"Why?"

"Because I'm going to help relieve some of the tension in your back."

"Oh, that's not necessary."

"I didn't ask you—I'm telling you. On your stomach, Sawyer."

Too tired to put up a fight, I roll onto my stomach and stretch out over the bed.

"Where's your lotion?"

"In the bathroom. I noticed you put it on my nightstand." I laugh.

"Well, you know . . . didn't know if that was where you used it."

"It's not," I say, chuckling into the pillow.

"Good to know." She goes to the bathroom and returns with lotion in hand before climbing on the bed and straddling my legs. "It's your lower back?" Her fingers drag across my skin, and, immediately, I'm hyperaware that the beautiful girl I'm crushing on is not only straddling me, but also touching my bare skin. Goose bumps erupt across my body.

"You know, this might not be a good idea."

"It will be fine—you need this," she says.

I'll need a lot *more* when she starts touching me.

"Yeah, but it's late, and I don't want to inconvenience you."

"You're not," she says as her slick hands knead into my lower back.

Fuck . . . that's . . . that feels so good.

"Oh, you're so tense right here." She rubs the muscle along my spine. "Can I pull your shorts down a little farther? I'll keep it decent, won't expose anything."

Not sure I can make the same promise.

"Uh, yeah."

She shimmies the waistband of my shorts down, and then her thumbs dig into me, pushing up to my midback, then repeating the movement. Pleasure and pain collide, and I grip the comforter beneath me as a low groan falls past my lips.

"Does that hurt?" she asks, stopping.

"No," I say, swallowing hard. "It feels really good."

"Oh, wonderful." She goes back to repeating the motion, a thumb on either side of my spine, dragging up and attempting to loosen the tension at the base—which she very well might be doing, though she's also driving the tension up in another region.

But I'm too addicted to her touch to stop her.

"I was wondering, do you think you'll stay here much longer?" she asks, rubbing all the way up to my shoulder blades and then starting back at the base again.

"I'm planning on staying for a while—is that okay?" I half groan into the sheets. "I can find a different place if you want to rent the cabin out to someone else."

"No," she says quickly. "No, I was just, you know, wondering. Since reservations are opening tomorrow, I wasn't sure if I should account for you to stay longer."

"Is that your roundabout way of finding out if I have any intention of leaving?"

"Maybe," she answers coyly.

"Nah, I'm good where I am. I kind of have a crush that I want to see through."

"A crush, huh? Tell me about her."

Her fingers dig circles into my lower back, and I swear, from just one circle, I grow hard, my cock pressing against the mattress with practically no room to spare.

"She, uh . . . she's really good at massages."

"An admirable quality."

"And she's resilient. Hardworking. Has a beautiful heart. Can be cranky at times, which gives her a sassy side, and I have to admit, I like it. She also tends to put on a tough exterior, a shield of armor she wears every day. Even though she can easily stand on her own, there are days when she needs someone to stand next to her, and I want to be that person for her."

Her hands slow down, and I glance over my shoulder to make sure everything is okay.

"Did I cross a line?" I ask, suddenly worried.

She shakes her head. "Not even a little. I'm just stunned." Her hands work my back again.

"Stunned about what?" I ask as her fingers approach the waistband of my shorts.

Jesus Christ.

I can't remember the last time I had a woman touch me. It's been a while, over a year I believe . . . yeah, that seems right. So having Fallon run her delicious fingers up and down my back has me harder than stone. And when she gets closer to my waistband, absolutely pathetic, but then again, I'm not sure any man in my position would be able to contain himself.

"Stunned that you already know me so well."

"It doesn't take much to read a person." Her fingers dig into the curve of my lower back and down to my ass. I grip onto the comforter harder and my pelvis shifts, letting my cock gain little relief. "Jesus," I breathe out heavily.

"That feel good?" she asks, repeating the process.

"Yeah, really good."

She moves from her thumbs to her palms and digs them in even harder. My eyes roll in the back of my head, a loud moan pouring out of me.

"Shit, I'm sorry," I say, chuckling.

"Don't be. It's . . . sexy."

Hell. I wonder what she'd think if I flipped over.

"Thanks, but I'd rather not moan in front of you like this. I prefer other . . . options."

Her palms move to the sides of my waist and then to my glutes—over my shorts—and I feel my hips grind into the mattress, my cock seeking more relief.

"Motherfucker," I whisper.

She doesn't say much after that but continues to drag her hands all over my back, digging in her thumbs, her knuckles, her palms. Her movements become melodic, and even though she's made me incredibly hard, I also start to relax, to the point that I feel my eyes drift shut—I can't stop them even if I wanted to.

I'm not sure how long I stay like that, drifting in and out of consciousness as she massages me, but the next thing I know she's pressing a kiss to my back as she climbs off me.

"I'm sorry," I mutter into my pillow.

"Don't be. You needed to relax, and I really enjoyed listening to you."

"Listening to me?" I ask sleepily, eyes still closed.

"Yes, it was really sexy, hearing your moans." She presses another kiss to my shoulder, and her hand slides down my back to the waistband of my shorts, tugging them up just an inch.

"I want to care about how humiliating my moans might have sounded, but I don't think I can even bring myself to worry about it."

"Don't." Her fingers graze over my back. "Do you feel slightly better?"

"I do." I open my eyes to find her standing above me, cheeks flushed. I reach my hand out, and as she takes it, I pull her in closer and press my lips to her knuckles. "Thank you."

She squats in front of me and sifts her fingers through my hair. "You're welcome. Get some sleep, okay?"

"Are we on for tomorrow?"

"We can worry about our date when your back is feeling better."

"I don't want to put it off. I'll be better tomorrow. Tell me I can take you out."

Her hand travels over my cheek, and she leans forward as she presses a kiss to my forehead. Her lips feel like soft petals caressing my skin, and I'm so tempted to pull her back to me and taste her mouth, like I've wanted to for a long time now. But I don't want our first kiss to be like this—me catatonic on the bed.

"You know I want nothing more than to go on a date with you," she says, her breath tickling my ear.

"Then it's official. Tomorrow, you and me."

"Please don't hurt your back doing anything special."

"Let me worry about the date and my back, okay?"

She nods and straightens back up. "Okay."

I give her knuckles one more kiss. "Thank you again for the massage. I'll see you tomorrow."

She smiles. "See you tomorrow, Sawyer."

Chapter Nineteen
FALLON

"How about this outfit?" I ask as I lay a purple pantsuit out on the bed.

Jaz is leaning against my headboard, legs crossed, chewing on a piece of black licorice. "I'm sorry, is this a date or an interview to be on the school board?"

Groaning, I flop back on the bed and drape my arm over my eyes. "Ugh, Jaz, I have nothing to wear."

"You have plenty to wear—you're just not making the right choices."

"I'm not wearing lingerie and only lingerie."

"Why not? I think we both know where the end of this date is headed, so just get a jump start."

I roll on the bed to face her. "We don't know that."

"Please, you two were eye-fucking each other the entire weekend. God, at one point I was starting to get turned on from the way he was looking at you."

"Right?" I say, sitting up on my elbow. "It was really . . . sensual, wasn't it?"

"Ew, don't say sensual. I'd say sexy. Invigorating. Intoxicating. Anything but sensual."

"Either way, I felt more seen than I have in a while. And I hate to compare Sawyer to Peter, but it just feels different from him. Right off the bat, it feels different."

"Peter was more reserved," Jaz says, biting off a chunk of her licorice. "Well, besides the last day he was here, but that was abnormal for him. Have you talked to him at all?"

I shake my head. "Not really. Just a quick text from him, letting me know he was okay. I thanked him." I shrug. "We both knew it was over."

Slowly, Jaz nods. "And what do you think it's going to be like with Julia? Aren't you worried he's only here for a bit? He has to go back home at some point, right? Doesn't that put you in the same position as you were in with Peter?"

"Possibly. But last night he mentioned that he wasn't going anywhere, and he knows what my intentions are—that moving is not an option. So, I think he's aware that if this continues between us, then it continues here, in Canoodle."

"That's right," Jaz says with a smile. "You make the man come to you."

"He's a good guy, Jaz."

She sighs heavily. "I hate to admit it, but he is. What he did for you this past weekend, the cabin for your fathers . . . God, I want to hate him, but it's hard."

"I know. He makes it impossible, which brings me back to the date. I don't know what to wear, and I'm going to lose my mind soon. He said plan for casual outside."

"So, you go with a purple pantsuit." She offers me a slow clap. "Yeah, that seems like a good pick."

"Jaz, please, the sarcasm isn't needed right now. I have to be ready in thirty minutes."

"Well, at least your hair and makeup are done. Maybe we consider the lingerie option one more time."

"Nooooo," I groan, annoyed.

"Fine," she huffs and then scoots off the bed. "But I'm sure he'd have appreciated it." Still snacking on licorice, she walks over to my closet and sifts through my things. Then she goes to my dresser and opens my pants drawers. She checks back at my closet. Back to my dresser and then . . . when I think she's going to sit back down, she pulls out a pair of black lace shorts and a simple black tank top. She tosses them on the bed. "Here. It looks like lingerie but doesn't reveal like lingerie. It's comfortable, won't make you sweat, and it's sexy too."

I stare down at the outfit and then back at her, relief flooding me. "This is exactly why I called you to help me. It's perfect."

"I know." She bites her licorice and sits back in her spot.

Not even caring about modesty, I strip down to my bra and underwear, and I'm about to put on the outfit when Jaz says, "Uh, what the hell kind of bra is that?" She uses her licorice to point at me.

I glance down at my nude cotton bra. "It's a comfortable bra."

"You're going to wear *that*? On your first date, where there's potential for it to be taken off, not by you, but by Julia? Are you insane?"

"It's newish," I protest. "And soft. I think he'd appreciate the soft . . . wait, what am I thinking? He's not taking it off. We're not going there tonight."

"Uh-huh, coming from the girl who said she wanted to flip him over last night and bounce on top of him."

"That is not what I said." Jaz challenges me with a glare. "Well, not word for word. But this is a date, it's classy. There will be no post-date . . . activities."

"Okay, even if that were the case, what if your tank top slips and he sees Miss Nude-Colored Bra's strap—is that a risk you're willing to take?" When I wince, she takes another bite of her licorice. "Told you. Now, let's check out your lingerie, and if you say you have none, you are going commando. That will be your punishment for being a grandma."

We spend the next five minutes picking out underwear options and then settle for a simple matching black set. I hate that she's right, but the lace bra makes me feel sexier and gives me an extra lift. I slip on a pair of cute sandals that pull the outfit together, and Jaz insists on swiping my deodorant on and spraying me with perfume. When I'm all set, she loops her arm through mine and escorts me down the stairs to the lobby, where Sawyer is sitting on the arm of the sofa, hands clasped in front of him, waiting for me.

He chose a pair of gray chino shorts and a navy-blue polo. It's a simple outfit, but he looks really good . . . impossibly good. When I approach, he stands, and I watch as his eyes eat me up and a smile spreads across his face.

"Oh God, he's giving you bedroom eyes," Jaz says as we reach the main lobby.

He lightly chuckles. "Good to see you too, Jaz."

"Jazlyn," she corrects him, but he doesn't care, because he takes a step forward and lifts my hand to his mouth, pressing a sweet kiss to my knuckles. "How's the back, old man?"

Sawyer smirks. "Good, *Jazlyn.*" Then he faces me. "You look beautiful."

"Thank you." A blush creeps up and over my cheeks.

"Is Sully good? Are you comfortable to take off?"

And this is exactly why I'm falling for this man—he's so considerate. He's not just pressing to get to our date; he wants to make sure everything is good on the home front first, and that means everything to me. He's putting Sully and my feelings first, and all I can think is . . . thank God I changed my underwear.

"He's great. He and Tank are watching *Dumb and Dumber,* one of their favorite movies."

"Classic," Jaz says, still standing next to us, offering zero privacy, but I guess I wouldn't expect anything else from her.

"But yes, I'm ready." I lace our fingers together and give his hand a squeeze.

"Perfect." He turns to Jaz. "Have a good night, *Jazlyn*, and thanks for letting me take your girl out."

"Don't fuck it up," she says, then reaches into her pocket and pulls out her switchblade. She flips the knife out and flashes the sharpened edge. "Or else . . ."

"Jesus," he mutters.

"I'd like to say she's all talk, but she isn't," I admit.

"I believe it. Don't worry, I'll be good to your girl."

With that, he guides me outside, and when I turn to head over to the parking lot, where I know his car has been this entire time, we continue on down the pathway, deeper into the Cove property.

"I know what you must be thinking . . . we're staying here? We're always here. And yes, that's true, but when I was thinking about a place to take you on a date, all I could think about was taking you to this specific spot."

"What spot?" I ask.

"Well, I've been thinking, you know how Sully and your grandma Joan have their bench?"

"Yes," I say softly, wondering where he's headed with this.

"I thought it would be nice if we could have a spot like that."

"So, my assumption is possibly true—you want to stay here long enough to establish a *spot*?" I'm unsure why the insecure question slips past me, but it does.

He pauses and turns toward me, mouth curving into a gentle smile. "I'm not going anywhere. Not only do I love it here, but I want to see where this goes between us. I know it's only our first date, but I like you a lot, Fallon. I like your life. I like Sully—grumpy attitude and all. And I can't imagine going back to my old life; it feels so empty at this point. Up here, I feel like I have purpose. You make me feel like I have purpose. So, no more questioning about my commitment to you, to this place. Got it?"

I nod, my stomach fluttering with butterflies. I can't pinpoint how this all happened, how in a blink of an eye, we've connected on such a deep level, but we have, and I can feel it. His commitment, his happiness, his purpose.

"Now, as I was saying, since Sully and Grandma Joan have a place, I wanted to find somewhere on the property that could be ours." He walks me past the picnic tables and the horseshoe pits, to the very back of the property, where the trees thicken, almost becoming a forest. Nestled among the pines is a small wooden covering. It looks like a hut, but with the front cut out so it's looking out over the distant lake. Inside, pillows cover the wood flooring, and a few strands of lights twinkle above us.

"What on earth is this?" I ask in awe.

"Something I put together this morning."

"You did? This morning?" I ask, incredulous. "But your back."

"My back is feeling much better. And yes, the building was easy. Finding the pillows was not. I had to make a trip down to Palm Springs, and I was cursing the entire time, not wanting to be late for our date. Thankfully, your dads hooked me up and met me at the bottom of the mountain."

"You spoke with my dads?"

He smirks. "Of course. They also gave me some cookies they made for dessert, as well as their full approval of my idea."

"I can't believe you asked them for help," I say, as emotions I can't even begin to parse out begin welling up inside me.

"I even recruited Sully before he went off to hang out with Tank. I needed him to hold the walls up for me while I nailed them together. He was grouchy about my lack of sanding, but I didn't have time to make it perfect. I can later."

"No." I place my hand on his forearm. "I want you to keep it as is. It's perfect."

"Yeah?"

I look up at him. "Yeah. Thank you, Sawyer. This is . . . this is magical."

"I'm glad you like it. I'm really hoping we'll be able to get a good look at the stars when it gets dark. I specifically chose this spot for that reason—it's private and wooded, but the trees won't overhang and block the view."

"You know, I didn't think you were this romantic," I say as he guides me to the quaint hut.

"I don't blame you. Your impression of me on a date is my head buried in my phone. But you need to remember that I write romantic screenplays for a living, and I believe in them. I'm not some martyr who doesn't believe in love, who just writes it to make money. Every story, every thought, every date idea—I create them all because I believe in them."

"Well, seems like I might be in for a whirlwind of a romance."

He smiles broadly. "This is just the start of it, Fallon. You might need to brace yourself—because it will only get better."

And I truly believe him.

❖   ❖   ❖

"I never expected the Pine Pantry to have such nice cheeses," I say as I lean back against one of the plush pillows in the hut. "But wow, when you pair them with the wine and the grapes—I'm addicted."

"I was surprised too. I was prepared to ask your dads to grab something good for me as well, but when I found the brie, I thought, why not give it a shot. Glad I did."

Sawyer pops another grape in his mouth and joins me, leaning against the pillows. But instead of holding my hand, like he has almost the entire night, he wraps his arm around me and pulls me into his chest so I'm using him as a cushion now. His hand draws light strokes along my arm. It's a straightforward touch, but it's lighting me up, putting me further and further in the mood to straddle this man. I hate to admit it, but thank God Jaz made me change my bra.

The sun is starting to set in front of us as light instrumentals play from a Bluetooth speaker Sawyer hooked up in the hut. He seriously thought of everything, from the cushions to the lights, to a small solar panel dish that's providing the electricity. How he did all of this in one day, I have no idea, but I'm very grateful he did. More than he'll ever know.

"How did you become so romantic?" I ask. "Did you spend hours upon hours watching romantic comedies until they were ingrained in your head?"

He chuckles. "I mean . . . my mom had two boys, and romance is her favorite genre. She drilled it into us that space sagas weren't the only movies available."

"Space sagas? Is that where the martian love came from?"

"Afraid so. I thought I would be the next George Lucas. When that clearly didn't happen, I thought I'd stick to what I knew best, and that was romance. But it wasn't just from watching movies with my mom—my dad is the biggest romantic you will ever meet. He set an example, a precedent for how men should treat their partners. My dad took my mom out on a date every Friday night, even if it was just to a place around the property, and he made an effort every week to remind her how much he loved her. He would also school me and Roarick on how to be romantic as we got older and started dating, and it just kind of . . . stuck. To me this isn't a grand gesture." He motions to the hut. "This is what should be expected."

This should be expected? This production?

I can't imagine being in a relationship where this is expected. It's so . . . swoony.

"Well then, I'm incredibly lucky that you chose to take me out, then."

"I'm the lucky one," he whispers as he presses a kiss to my head. "Grateful I get a second chance, and that you don't hate me for being a jerk on our first date. Hell, if my dad knew about that, he would have me hanging by the balls."

I laugh. "So, when I meet them, you don't want me to mention that."

"Not unless you don't care about my manhood."

"Oh, we wouldn't want anything happening to that. Precious equipment should always be guarded."

"Agreed, which is why you're no longer allowed to give me massages."

I snort. "I knew you were turned on last night—I could feel you squirming."

He pulls away slightly so he can look me in the eyes. "And yet you still kept going with those hands of yours."

"Because I found it fascinating. Plus, I really wanted to help your back."

"You found my painful hard-on fascinating?"

I cover my mouth as I chuckle. "I'm sorry, but . . . yes. It's hard not to. I mean, just with an amateur massage, I was able to get you up—imagine what would happen if I was naked."

His Adam's apple bobs up and down with a deep swallow.

His jaw grows tight as he clenches his teeth together.

And his grip around me tightens even more.

I know that look.

I know that feel of him needing to be closer.

Totally unmistakable.

He's turned on again.

I shouldn't feel this kind of pride for being able to do that to him, but I do.

"If you were naked . . . yeah, that would end this date immediately."

I drag my finger up his chest. "Would that be such a bad thing?"

"Yes," he answers. "And before you get any ideas, *that* won't be happening tonight."

"What?" I ask, pulling away from him.

Now it's his turn to laugh. "Were you looking forward to getting naked?"

"Well, sort of," I say, feeling my cheeks heat up. "I mean, Jaz made me change my bra and everything, so it was sexier."

He straightens up from his relaxed position and faces me before reaching out to my shoulder and threading my tank top strap to the side. He runs his fingers under the strap of my bra, and my breath catches in my throat from the brush of the back of his fingers over my skin. My mind dances with fantasies of him pushing the strap down my arm, exposing my bra, and flipping the cup over before bringing my breast to his mouth. He'd suck desperately on my nipple, and I'd thread my fingers through his soft hair.

"I never would have thought of you as a black bra kind of girl," he says before adjusting the strap of my tank top.

"What, uh, what did you expect?" My voice comes out breathless as I snap out of my fantasy. It's slightly embarrassing. *He touched the strap of your bra, Fallon. It's not like he stuck his hand down your pants. Get it together.*

"A one-piece suit of armor."

My eyes widen as he chuckles. I push at his chest, which only makes him laugh more. "Wow, good job killing the mood."

"I had to. You had lustful eyes. Nothing is happening tonight, so get that out of your head."

"Pfft, as if I wanted anything to happen tonight." I fold my arms across my chest, trying to ignore the pang of disappointment. "I don't even want you being near me. Yuck. Gross. Keep your hands to yourself."

"Was that supposed to be convincing?"

"I'm not here to convince anyone of anything. I'm just living my life."

"Is that so?"

"Yup," I answer, popping the *p* with a sharp snap of my lips.

"Okay." He scoots away and lounges back against the pillows, placing his hands behind his head so his shirt rises just enough so I catch a peek at his skin. Tan, taut skin.

My mouth waters.

My eyes travel up his torso, to his arms. His biceps are flexed, pulling against the sleeve of his shirt, showing off his strength. Strength that I'm all too familiar with. And then there's his face, his square jaw with just the lightest dusting of five-o'clock shadow caressing his skin. The adorable crook in his nose, and his devastating blue eyes that almost seem violet beneath the golden lights.

"Are you going to keep staring, or are you going to come lie here with me?" he asks.

A disgruntled sound falls out of me as I realize there is no way I'm going to be able to stay away from this man. Reluctantly—but also because I really want to—I curl into his side and rest my head against his chest. His arm falls to my waist, and he pulls me even closer.

"You're annoying me," I declare, though I can't fight the smile tugging at my lips.

"Already? Man, this relationship is moving along a lot faster than I expected. I feel scandalized." I poke him in the side, and he laughs as he turns toward me and places a kiss on my forehead.

❖ ❖ ❖

"When you were ten, what did you want to be when you grew up?" Sawyer asks as he twirls a strand of my hair around his finger, an act of affection I'm becoming quite addicted to.

We each ate two cookies from the basket my dads gave Sawyer. They were brownie marshmallow with chocolate chips, and they were too good to only eat one. We both agreed—one is too little, three is too much, but two . . . two is just perfect.

We turned the twinkle lights off so we could stare up at the stars, the moon being the only bright orb in the vicinity.

And of course, because I can't seem to keep my distance, I'm curled into the comfort of his arms.

"When I was ten? Hmm, I think I was still stuck in my rock phase, which means I still wanted to own my own rock store."

"A rock store?" he asks, surprise lacing his words.

"Oh yeah. I'd come up here to visit Sully and Grandma Joan, and I'd go on hikes and find these amazing rocks—well, I thought they were amazing. When I got home, I'd pull out my rock tumbler that Sully got me and tumble my rocks until they were polished, smooth, and beautiful. My dads hated it."

"Why?"

"Well, they didn't hate that I liked rocks. They thought it was kind of funny, actually, that the daughter they assumed would be their very own Elizabeth Taylor—I dressed up as her, by their choice, three Halloweens in a row—loved playing in the dirt and treating her rocks as her friends."

He chuckles. "Hell, that's adorable. Do you still have some of the rocks?"

"If I said yes, would you think I'm a dork?"

"No, I'd want you to introduce me to your friends." I needle his side, and he laughs some more. "Seriously, that's cute. So, what changed? When did the rock business get tossed from your future?"

"Oh, you know, some mean girl at school named Debra Lizowski said I was lame. In sixth grade, we had to present on what we wanted to do when we grow up, and I presented my rock store—which I spent a lot of time developing. I was over the moon with my design, so proud of myself, and I brought tons of polished rocks to show off. Blue, green, pink, purple gemstones, every color of the rainbow. Afterward, she told me I was lame and was going to be poor."

"Jesus, kids are fucking cruel."

"Yeah, that day, I put my rocks in storage and started thinking of other ideas. I decided to be a nurse when I was in high school."

"You're really hurting my heart." He pulls me in even closer. "What can we do to bring that rock store to life?"

I lightly laugh. "Nothing. No one wants to buy rocks."

"Not true. There are rock stores in touristy towns all the time. You live in a tourist town. I say you sell rocks."

I sit up and place a kiss on his jaw before saying, "You're sweet, but I'm pretty sure I have enough on my plate. Don't really have the bandwidth to open a rock store."

He heavily sighs. "Can I ask you one thing?"

"Sure."

"What was the name of your rock store?"

"Fallon's Rocks," I answer, remembering the sign I spent hours making.

"Huh." He pauses, thinking about it. "I can see why Debra Lizowski thought you were lame now. Show some creativity." When I glance up at him in shock, he's full-on smiling that playful smile of his.

"Yeah, you're right, nothing is happening between us tonight."

He chuckles even more and hugs me close. Smirking, I grip him tighter.

❖ ❖ ❖

"How does someone break their arm in a pool?" I ask. "It's full of water. Unless you have bird bones." I lift up to look him in the eyes. "Do you have bird bones, Sawyer?"

"I do. Please be gentle with me. I'm feeble and weak and can only handle feather-like touches."

"Does that account for your whole body?" I ask, glancing down at his crotch and then back up to his eyes.

"No, that's made of steel," he declares, his voice taking on a manlier tone. "But everything else is very feeble. I might need to be cuddled. I prefer bosoms to be cuddled into; they make me feel better."

"You're ridiculous." I chuckle. "But . . . how many *bosoms* have cuddled you?"

"Thirty-seven. You could be number thirty-eight."

"Thirty-seven?" My voice rises. "You've been with thirty-seven women?"

"Ohhh, been with? I thought you were just talking about a solid cuddle. If we're talking about women I've been with, an easy two hundred and seventy-nine. One month it was like a revolving door of females. But I have them to thank for my stamina."

It's clear he's joking. He's been joking this entire night, but I've really enjoyed all the teasing, the lightheartedness. I appreciate his sense of humor—there is so much in my life that's serious, sometimes heartbreaking. The idea of having someone beside me, holding my hand and making me laugh . . . it adds a light to my life that I was missing, even with Peter.

"Wow, two hundred and . . ."

"Seventy-nine."

"Yes, two hundred and seventy-nine, that's quite the harem. How are you even walking?"

"Having a third leg helps." He winks, and I push at his face, making him laugh out loud.

"And here I thought you were different from other men."

"I might be romantic and helpful and an obvious catch, but I'm still an idiot, so just mentally prepare yourself for that, moving forward."

"I guess so." I turn back to the stars. "So," I ask, after a few seconds, "how many women, really?"

"Eh, less than ten, probably. But none of them," he says in a dramatic voice, "and I mean none of them, compares to you, baby."

"Damn right."

"Have you ever walked the red carpet?" I ask Sawyer as we hold hands and make our way down the dimly lit pathway toward the residence.

"I have," he answers.

"Really? For the Oscars?"

He chuckles. "No. I walked the red carpet at a Lovemark screening. I'll admit, it's probably my least favorite thing about my job."

"Why?"

"Just not my thing. All the pictures and questions."

"Did anyone ask you who you were wearing?"

"Yes, but first, they asked me who I was and if I was trolling the red carpet."

"No!" I chuckle.

"Yup, and when I told them I was the screenwriter, they softened up a bit and asked who I was wearing. I replied with the solid answer of Men's Wearhouse, borrowed shoes from my father, and of course, Fruit of the Loom briefs."

"Oh my God, seriously?" I clutch his arm tight while the solar lights illuminate our path.

"Yeah. The interviewer was horrified, to say the least, and quickly moved me along."

"Did you do any other red-carpet events after that?"

"Yes, but I just power walked by the cameras from there on out. And of course, when Annalisa and I started dating, I was her arm candy and stood there while she posed."

"I'm guessing your suits weren't from Men's Wearhouse at that point."

"Not by my doing. Annalisa was very adamant about me spending money on a proper suit. So, I went out and bought a Tom Ford suit, and I've worn it to every event since . . . well, besides her wedding."

"No, you delighted everyone with that powder-blue ensemble."

"You liked it, didn't you?" He wiggles his eyebrows. "Got your gears grinding?"

I wave my hand in front of my face. "It's all I can think about—gets me all hot and bothered."

"Oh damn, if only I knew, I would have worn that tonight."

"But then again," I say as we approach the residence, "you don't want anything sexual happening tonight, so it's for the best."

We reach the front door, and he turns toward me, then places his hands on my hips. "True. But now I know what to wear when the time comes to have intercourse."

"What is wrong with you?"

He laughs the most hearty, sexy laugh I've ever heard. "Sooo . . . that's a no on the blue suit."

"That's a no on the blue suit and using the term 'intercourse.'"

"Got it." He chuckles and then sighs. "Hell, I've had a fucking good night with you, Fallon."

My body heats up, an inferno sweeping over every nerve and muscle. "I've had a really good night as well."

"Soo . . . we can do it again?"

"I would be mad if we didn't," I answer honestly, because I want him to know how I feel. I want him to see how happy he makes me. How much I love being near him, enveloped in his energy.

"Good." He sweeps his hand up to my jaw and cheek, pushing my hair behind my ear. "So then, I'll see you tomorrow?"

"Yes," I answer, wetting my lips.

"Okay." He tilts my head back, and I swear the air stills as I await a good night kiss.

It feels like a movie, the stars glittering above us, the faint sound of the wind rippling through the trees, and the distinct smell of his cologne, wrapping around us, pulling us closer.

His grip on my face is strong.

His eyes are set on mine.

And as he lowers his lips, I feel my heart beating, crawling up my throat as anticipation nearly eats me alive.

Before tonight even happened, I knew I wanted to kiss this man. I knew I wanted to feel his hands grip me tightly, feel the indent he leaves on my sides, because he's one of the most thoughtful and caring men I've ever met.

He makes me feel . . . special. He makes me feel like I matter, but also like the things I believe in matter. Without even knowing about the Cove and the problems we were facing, he took it upon himself to fix things. He's grown close to Sully, treating him like family. He's shown nothing but altruism toward my family, and he's embraced us as if we're his own.

And tonight, under the stars, he helped me relax, he showed me that in this crazy, stressful life I'm leading, I can let out a deep breath and have fun. That I'm not entirely alone on this journey of caring for my ailing grandparent.

Standing here, in his arms, looking into his soulful eyes, I know I want nothing more than to finally kiss this man.

I slide my hands up his strong, muscular chest and rest them on his pecs, near his collarbones.

He tilts my head just a little bit more.

He lowers his mouth.

Butterflies erupt in my stomach, shaking my nerves.

And then . . . he presses his lips to my forehead and pulls away.

"Good night, Fallon."

Uh, what?

Good night?

I'm stunned.

I stand there dazed.

Confused.

Unsure of what just happened.

He kissed me on the forehead. *The forehead.* You kiss a grandma on the forehead. A friend.

You don't kiss the girl you're interested in on the forehead, at least not in place of a good night kiss on the *lips*!

He must sense my irritation—instead of letting me go, he asks, "Are you okay?"

"No," I blurt out, making him rear back slightly. "I'm not okay, Sawyer."

"What's wrong?" He genuinely looks confused in the semidarkness.

"What's wrong is that I wanted you to kiss me, and instead, you said good night to me with a platonic peck to the forehead. I thought you said you enjoyed our evening."

"I did," he answers, a crease between his brows.

"Then why didn't you kiss me?"

"Because," he says, looking me in the eyes, "you just broke up with your boyfriend, and I don't want to be the rebound. I want to make sure that you're okay before we get into anything physical. I would rather we spend time getting to know each other better."

"Well, I wouldn't," I say before looping my hand behind his head and pulling him down to my mouth.

Before either of us realize what's happening, I move forward, closing the distance between us and connecting our mouths.

I'm expecting him to be stiff at first, to be caught off guard, but instead, he cups the back of my head with one hand, driving his fingers through my hair as his other hand splays across my lower back, pulling me closer.

With authority, he takes control of our kiss, deepening it as he parts his mouth.

I get lost.

In his touch.

In the taste of his lips.

In the press of his chest against mine.

In the low groan that falls past his lips when our tongues collide.

Nothing matters in this moment, nothing other than the way he cradles me into him, holding me in place, not letting me go anywhere.

I'm not sure if I've ever been kissed like this.

I've never felt a kiss to the tips of my toes, and I've never had this kind of visceral reaction. My hands are trembling, my legs are shaking beneath me, and with every swipe of his tongue against mine, I fall deeper and deeper into him.

I'm not naive to love, nor would I say I'm in love with him, but I know, with growing certainty, that this very well could be my last first kiss. I feel it, in every inch of my body. This could be it.

He could be it.

Slowly, he eases up, his mouth working mine for a few more seconds before he fully pulls away. His thumb strokes over my cheek, and he lets out a deep sigh. "Jesus, Fallon. That was . . ."

"Yeah," I say as I press my hand to his.

He leans down again and presses a final, quick kiss to my lips before he steps away and stuffs his hands in his pockets. "I should go."

"You don't have to, you know?"

"I do." He takes another step backward. "I really do." Another step back.

"Okay." My eyes drop because I'd give anything to extend this evening. And then I remember what he said, the reason he wouldn't kiss me at first. "Hey, Sawyer?"

"Hmm?"

"For what it's worth, you're not a rebound. Not even close to it."

"I hope not. After that kiss, not sure you're going to be able to shake me."

"Good." I smile. "Because I'm not going anywhere either."

CHAPTER TWENTY

FALLON

Jaz: How was last night?

Fallon: Amazing. 😍

Jaz: Amazing, huh, I didn't think Julia had it in him to deliver an amazing date. I thought he'd be at least slightly nervous.

Fallon: Not even a little. He was funny, sweet, considerate. He fed me, made us a little hut to lie in and look up at the stars—he said it could be like Sully and Grandma Joan's bench. And at the end of the night, we kissed. Jaz, it was the best kiss of my entire life. I know this is insane, but that one kiss made me believe that he could very well be the one.

Jaz: I feel as though I should respond with something along the lines of "YOU BARELY KNOW EACH OTHER" but since I know how strong your connection is when you're together, I could see it.

Fallon: Really?

Jaz: Easily.

Fallon: I wasn't expecting that at all.

Jaz: Never expect anything when it comes to me. So, only a kiss last night?

Fallon: Yes, but I intend on making sure that changes soon.

Jaz: Oh, Julia better watch out, you're coming for his dripping balls.

❖ ❖ ❖

"Jaz, look!" I gasp, pointing toward the computer screen.

She lifts her head from her phone, where she's been playing Candy Crush for the last hour, and stares at the screen. "What am I looking at?"

"The reservation queue. It's almost entirely full for opening weekend."

"Wait . . . really?" She leans in closer to get a better look. "Holy shit, it is." She lovingly swats at me. "Fallon, look at that, look at what you did. You turned this around."

I shake my head, so dizzy from relief that I almost fall out of my chair. "No way, this wasn't all me. This was a culmination of the community bringing Sully's vision to life. And so much help from Sawyer. So much help."

"With you as the driving force behind it. People follow those with passion. All you had to do was lead." Jaz leans over and hugs me just as the back door opens and Sawyer walks in, carrying a bag and looking crazy good in a pair of jeans and a tight-fitting black T-shirt.

He pauses. "Am I interrupting something?"

"The Cove is nearly booked up for opening weekend!" I exclaim, unable to hold back my glee.

"Wow, Fallon." He sets his bag down and hurries around the counter to pull me into a hug. "That's amazing. Congratulations. How do you feel?"

"Excited. Emotional. Relieved. Stressed. You know, just your typical set of emotions." I release him and take a step back, body thrumming with energy.

"She was just telling me how she couldn't have done it without you," Jaz says. "If you ask me, seems like my girl's smitten with you."

"Is that so?" Sawyer asks, smiling down at me. "If she's smitten from getting some help, then she should be smitten with you too, *Jazlyn*."

Jaz sits a little taller. "You know what, you're right." She reaches into her shorts pocket and pulls out some lip balm. She lines her lips and then puckers them in my direction. "Go ahead, I shall take my payment."

"Your payment is my friendship," I deadpan.

"Wow, seems like I'm getting the short end of the stick on that," she mumbles.

Sawyer gives me another squeeze and goes back to his bag on the other side of the counter. "I'm really happy for you, but . . . I have something I can't hold in anymore. I got you something." He places the bag in front of me.

"Oooh, presents," Jaz says. She nudges me with her foot. "This is important, pay attention. First gifts always matter. If he got you something dumb, I say get out now while you still can."

Sawyer shoots her a stern look. "It's not dumb."

"I'll be the judge of that."

He rolls his eyes but turns his attention back to me as he reaches into his bag and pulls out a box. But not just any box . . .

"You got me a rock tumbler?" I gape at him.

He grins. "I did. And . . ." He reaches down and pulls a bag of rocks from his bag and sets it on the counter. "Rocks. But that's not all—I got this as well." He sets a felt board with letters on the counter as well. "A sign, so you can sell your rocks here in the lobby once they've been tumbled. I also have a few store names written down that might be slightly more exciting than Fallon's Rocks."

He got me rocks. Oh my God.

He got me . . . rocks.

When he told me to get ready to be romanced, I didn't know it was going to be like this.

So thoughtful.

I don't think I've ever met someone like him, someone who can read me so easily and truly pick out the things that matter the most.

He's . . . he's so swoon worthy.

Jaz picks at the bag. "So you got her rocks, huh?"

Leave it to Jaz to squash the magic right out of a moment.

"There's a story—" Sawyer starts, but Jaz stops him.

"Oh, I know. Debra Lizowski is a real ho." She examines the rock tumbler, inspecting every inch. Once she's done, she turns to me. "We still have to hear the names he has to offer, but from just a quick overview, he's a keeper."

Wait . . . what?

For a second, I thought she was going to diminish this gift, cut it down, cut Sawyer down. Could it be that Sawyer is winning her over too?

"Does that mean we're friends now?" Sawyer asks Jaz.

"Ha, yeah . . . no. We'll be friends when I say we're friends. You're currently on a probation period—don't mess up, and your dreams might come true. Now, delight us with some names."

Seemingly resigned to that answer, Sawyer pulls his phone from his pocket and looks up at us. "These are my top three. I worked pretty hard on them." He clears his throat, and I find it far too adorable. "Option one is Rocks? Of Quartz." Smiling widely, he glances up at us.

I hold in my snort.

"Pass," Jaz says, catching him off guard.

"Yeah, that was my least favorite. But I think you might really like this one." He takes a deep breath. "Pass the Basalt."

Oooof, that one's rough.

"Oh, Sawyer." Jaz shakes her head. "This is getting embarrassing."

"Basalt is a type of rock," he says, looking between us.

"I understand the lame attempt at a pun," Jaz says, holding her hand up. "If those hit the top two, I'm afraid to ask what your third is."

Looking unsure now, he shifts on his feet and rubs his palm against his pant leg. "Well, the last is my favorite."

"This should be good," Jaz mutters sarcastically to me.

I'm hoping he saved a really good one for last.

Sawyer glances in my direction, and with the most enchanting smile, he says, "Coal as a Cucumber."

I wince, prepared for what's to come next . . .

"*That's* your best effort? *Coal* as a cucumber?" Jaz flits her hand in his direction. "And you call yourself a writer. Pathetic."

Even though coming up with names is the cutest thing and this entire gift is so sweet, I hate to admit it, but his store names weren't super great. The gift is overwhelmingly adorable, but I kind of expected better names from him.

"They aren't too terrible," I say, trying to be kind.

"Not too terrible?" Sawyer stuffs his phone in his pocket as his shoulders droop in disappointment. "How about this . . . Fallon's Rocks."

Oh, Sawyer. I adore him so much.

"Now that has a nice ring to it," Jaz says. She slaps the counter and walks toward the front door. "Consider those rocks sold." And as she exits, she throws the peace sign in the air, and the door swings shut behind her.

When she's gone, I walk around the counter and right into Sawyer's arms. "Thank you," I murmur into his chest. "This was the sweetest gift ever."

"You don't think I'm pathetic?" His voice is laced with humor, so I know Jaz had zero effect on him. A good sign because 80 percent of the stuff that comes out of her mouth is nonsense anyway.

"No. I think you're more than I deserve."

"Not true," he says, tilting my head back and then placing a soft kiss on my lips.

"Thank you," I say again when we part. "This was absolutely the most thoughtful thing I've received. Now I just need to start tumbling."

"You're welcome." He winks and pulls away. "Okay, I have to get some work done or my agent might kill me."

"Can't have you dead."

"I'll catch you later. Congratulations again on the reservations, Fallon. I know Sully has to be proud—Grandma Joan too." He gives me one last kiss and then takes off, and like the crush-struck girl that I am, I watch him walk away while letting out a deep sigh.

❖ ❖ ❖

"These seats are uncomfortable," Sully says, shifting on one of many plastic fold-out chairs lined up in the park.

"They're not bad, Sully," I say as I glance around, looking for Sawyer. He told us he was going to meet us here, and the play is about to start.

"Who's even in this thing?" Sully asks, flipping through a program that I know he can't read—he's lost that ability. It makes me sad because he really enjoyed reading. I can't remember a time when I'd visit him and Grandma Joan and not see him sitting in his chair with some sort of mystery or thriller.

"Roy's in it. He plays Edna."

"Edna?" Sully says loudly. "Isn't that a lady's name?"

"It is," I answer quietly. "But that's the usual casting in *Hairspray*. A man plays the mom's role."

Sully scoffs. "Men can't just let women have the spotlight, can they?"

"I think it's supposed to be funny."

"There's nothing funny about a man stealing a woman's role. Roy's going to get an earful from me about this."

Oh boy. I make a mental note to warn Roy before Sully gets ahold of him.

"Hey," Sawyer says, coming up to us. "Sorry I'm a bit late." He takes a seat next to me and leans in to place a kiss on my cheek. "Sully, I brought you this." He hands him a chair cushion.

Sully stares at the cushion and then eyes Sawyer. "Who the hell are you?"

I wince. "It's been one of those days," I whisper.

"Not a problem at all." Speaking directly to Sully, he says, "I'm Sawyer. I'm dating your granddaughter. I wanted to make sure you were comfortable, so I brought you a cushion. It's okay if you don't want to use it."

Sully snatches the cushion. "Of course I want to use it. These seats are an absolute joke." Sully slowly stands and sets the cushion on his seat, only to sit back down. He shifts a bit, and satisfaction passes over his face. He eyes Sawyer again. "So, you're dating my granddaughter?"

"Yes, sir."

He nods and turns back to the stage. "I approve."

I chuckle while Sully flits through the program. "You hear that? You have met the requirements to win my grandfather's affection. A cushion—who knew?"

Sawyer takes my hand in his. "I did. You know the saying 'happy wife, happy life'? Well, 'comfy behind, comfy mankind.'"

"How long have you been sitting on that rhyme?"

"Longer than I care to admit."

Just then, Roy steps out onstage in costume and greets the crowd by parading around, hand flitting against the air like the queen of England.

"What in Jesus Christ's name is this?" Sully asks, leaning forward, as if that will give him a better view of the beautiful catastrophe up onstage.

"Is he wearing torn pantyhose?" Sawyer asks, his lips close to my ear, which of course spreads goose bumps across my skin.

I nod. "Yes, he's been wearing them around for a month now."

Roy comes to a stop stage center and holds his hands in front of him, palms pressed together in prayer pose, thanking the not-so-energetic crowd. He's really milking this moment, and I don't blame him. He's a sturdy, rotund, hairy—very hairy—man wearing a blonde wig with accompanying bangs and fiercely owning the housedress that hits him midshin. The purple and pink plaid of the housedress—ahem, muumuu—doesn't distract from the runs in his pantyhose, nor does it divert your eyes from the purple Crocs he's wearing. Not sure they had Crocs in the sixties, but it wouldn't be a Canoodle play if it was completely authentic.

Just like the time in *Romeo and Juliet* when Romeo pulled out his phone to use as a flashlight instead of a lantern.

Or when *Singin' in the Rain* was chosen, and the tap dancing was far too advanced for everyone, especially the exertion-demanding "Moses supposes" number, so they wheeled in a TV—like they used to do in elementary school, the sacred TV that would give you a five-minute glimpse of what's going on in *The Voyage of the Mimi*—and they played the actual movie during the dance scenes while the actors clapped next to the TV. I'd never felt so embarrassed for another human before that.

So, the Crocs, just a minor risk of authenticity. But we have the entire play to go.

"Good evening," Roy calls out. "Thank you for joining us tonight. We have quite the play for you tonight, full of song and dance." His deep voice really does a number on your brain as you stare up at him in full-on drag. "But before we get started, we'd like to acknowledge the brilliant choice of play by our mayor." He gestures stage right, and

Faye walks on with Miss Daphne Lynn Pearlbottom perched on a pillow, wearing a brightly colored pink and green fascinator and looking less than amused. Frankly, it's surprising that she's not scrambling to go hide somewhere, but this is her public duty, and she's been trained for things like this.

"Whoa, I didn't know the mayor was going to be here," Sawyer whispers and then straightens up, adjusting his shirt. "You should have told me—I would have worn a suit and tie."

I chuckle while Faye parades Miss Daphne Lynn Pearlbottom—yes, you have to use her entire name—around as the crowd quietly claps using two fingers and their palms. The fancy clap: perfect for feline mayors, so their constituents don't scare them away.

"What's happening?" Sawyer asks.

"Just a typical Saturday in Canoodle—get used to it."

He crosses one leg over the other and wraps his arm around my chair, pulling me in close. "I can very much get used to this."

Smiling to myself, I lean into his hold and relax as the weirdness of my beloved town unfolds.

❖ ❖ ❖

"Why is Phil cooking?" Sully says as he stomps into the living room, a scowl etched into his face.

"He offered to cook for us tonight," I say gently.

Sully glances between me and Sawyer. "Is he any good?"

"I've fed myself for the last seventeen years," Sawyer says over his shoulder, stirring a pot on the stove, "so I'd say I'm pretty decent, since I've been able to live this long."

"Is that sass you're giving me?" Sully asks.

"Yup," Sawyer answers without even pausing to think about it.

This has been my life, these two, bantering back and forth. From the outside looking in, some might think you should be gentler when talking to an Alzheimer's patient, but what we've found is that Sully enjoys the barbing. It makes him feel whole. He doesn't like to be treated like some helpless, pitiful creature. He wants the give-and-take. It's why he loves hanging out with Tank and the boys, because they don't treat him any differently.

But we've noticed Sully has been grumpier lately, and it's showing right now. Since we finished the renovations a week and a half ago, his mood has definitely declined. Sawyer plans on doing some yardwork in the next few days, and he's going to bring Sully with him. We hope that helps improve the grump.

"Well, I'm not eating your swill," Sully says.

Sawyer spins around with a wooden spoonful of his homemade mac 'n' cheese and takes a large bite. "Are you sure?" he says, his mouth full. "It's really good."

"Where did you find this fool?" Sully asks me as he charges toward his room again. "An absolute animal."

"See you for dinner," Sawyer calls out.

"Yeah, see you at dinner," Sully mumbles before shutting the door to his bedroom.

Chuckling, I walk up to Sawyer and smooth my hand over his back and under his shirt as I lean into him. He curls his arm around me and pulls me in close while pressing a kiss to the top of my head. "He doesn't want to admit, but I know, deep down inside, he loves you," I say, rubbing his warm skin.

"Oh, I know. I'm the light of his life." He sets the wooden spoon down on the spoon rest and turns off the stove before facing me and leaning against the counter. "Just like I'm the light of yours."

I snort and shake my head. "You are so full of yourself."

"And yet your hands are under my shirt."

"Because your skin is always so warm." I bring my hands to the front of his shirt and drag them up past his abs to just below his pecs.

"Watcha doing there?"

I drag my finger over his nipple, and his eyes narrow on me. "Just feeling around."

"Feeling around for what? Lose something in my shirt that I'm not aware of?"

"Uh-huh, just can't pinpoint what it is," I say, running my fingers over his other nipple.

He lets out a low, guttural hiss as his hands fall to my hips. "Babe, stop, you're going to make me hard, and I'm not about to have dinner with your grandpa while sporting a boner."

"I think it might be fun." I playfully smile up at him, but he stops my hands and fishes them out of his shirt.

"For you, but not for me." He removes my hands.

"Sawyer—"

"I'm going to stop you right there," he says. "I know what you're going to say, and I'm pretty sure you know what I'm going to say."

"That you think I'm an ogress and that's why we haven't had sex yet—the mere thought of putting your hands on me disgusts you?" I ask.

He frowns. "Stop it with that shit." He has not been tolerant of my joking, but I don't know how to accept his denial of a physical connection without making light of it. He lifts my chin up, and our eyes meet, his beaming with sincerity. "Because I want to make sure you're ready."

It's the same answer every single time, and I'm not sure if he's asking if I'm ready . . . or if he's ready.

"I'm ready, Sawyer. I'm more than ready. We've spent so much time together these past couple of weeks that I don't think I could be more ready for anything else. I want you, and I think I've showed that time and time again." Insecurity wraps around me as I look away. "Maybe you don't feel the same way."

Grumbling something under his breath, Sawyer picks me up. I let out a surprised gasp as he spins me around and places me on the counter, only to spread my legs and move in close, resting his hands on my hips.

"Why are you questioning me?" he asks. His grip on me is domineering, possessive, like he's claiming me, right here on the counter. "I want you, Fallon. I do."

"Are you sure?" I ask. "Because sometimes it feels like you're using me as an excuse to not get intimate, and I'm wondering if it's you who's not ready. Which would be fine, but I'd like you to be honest about it."

"Why would you think that?" he asks.

"Because the whole Annalisa and Simon thing."

"I told you I haven't been in love with her for a while."

"Doesn't mean you still don't have some messed-up feelings from the whole situation."

The press has died down drastically surrounding Annalisa, Simon, and Sawyer. The public has lost interest in the jilted couple because you can only hear the same sob story so many times. And Annalisa—according to Jaz, who has been relentlessly keeping up on the drama—has worn out her welcome in the spotlight. There were talks that Annalisa and Simon were going to get their own reality show, but because Annalisa has taken on some negative press with her complaining and some less-than-stellar tweets, the show has been canceled.

But even so, he might still have complicated feelings toward the entire situation. I'm wondering if that's the reason he hasn't wanted to get intimate. The most we've done is kissing, and maybe a little groping from me while sitting on his lap, but that's it. Nothing more, and I'm going to lose it soon.

He shakes his head. "No. I have zero feelings toward the wedding. I honestly stopped caring a while ago."

"Are you sure? Because we haven't really talked about it much."

"Because there is nothing to talk about," he answers. "There's no use bringing it up when all we'd do is rehash what happened over and over again, and that doesn't help anything. But moving on, being able to be with you"—his hands slide up my side—"now, that is something I'm interested in. That's something I care about."

"Then why won't you be intimate with me?" I say, my eyes disconnecting from his. "Because I want you, Sawyer, and I really like you, and if you don't feel the same way, I'd rather—"

He grips my chin and forces me to look him in the eyes. "Listen closely, Fallon." His demanding tone sends a shiver of lust straight to my toes. "I want you, I've wanted you for a while, but I'm taking this slow because I don't want to mess it up. I royally screwed up my first chance at being with you, and I'll be damned if I make any mistakes again. Just trust me when I say it will happen. Until then, enjoy the small things like holding my hand, stealing glances, and, of course, late-night make-out sessions." He winks, and it makes me smile. "And for the love of God, don't call yourself an ogress again."

I chuckle and loop my arms around his neck, then pull him in even closer.

"Just wanted to make sure that's not how you felt."

"Trust me, I don't think you're an ogress. Quite the opposite." He presses a kiss to my nose. "Easily the most beautiful girl I've ever had the privilege to hold in my arms."

His hands move up to my back, and I know what he's saying isn't just a line to appease me. Sawyer is not that kind of guy. When he says something, he means it, and when it comes to romance . . . well, he wasn't kidding when he told me to expect the best. Every day, I feel like it's something new with him, even if it's the smallest of things, like he saw a flower on his walk that reminded him of me, so he took a picture. Or the time when he offered to hang with Sully for the night so Jaz and I could have some time together. Or how he built a display for the lobby where I can show off my tumbled rocks.

He cares. He really does.

So maybe I need to listen to him when he says he wants me. I just need to be patient, go at the pace that makes him comfortable. He's worth any wait.

I heave a sigh and look him in his cornflower blues. "I like you a lot, Sawyer."

"I like you too. A lot."

"You make me happy."

He smiles. "Same, babe." He leans in and is pressing a kiss to my mouth just as Sully's door flies open and he comes charging into the open space.

"Stop sucking face. I'm hungry."

Sawyer leans his forehead against mine and chuckles. "That's one way to kill the mood."

"What mood?" I whisper. "Remember, you're making us wait."

He glances up at me and whispers "Wiseass" before stepping away and grabbing bowls from the cabinets. "Your dinner's coming right up, you grumpy old coot."

"I'm grumpy, Phil, because instead of serving, you're over there trying to replace your lips with my granddaughter's."

"Sully," I say, embarrassed. "It was barely a kiss."

"Didn't seem like it from where I was standing. Are you even old enough to be kissing?"

"Plenty," I say. I walk over to him and place my arms on his shoulders. "And that's Sawyer, not Phil."

"I know," Sully grumbles.

I've made it a point to try—even though it might seem pointless—to instill in Sully who Sawyer really is.

"He was the one who fixed your bench. He also helped you with the picnic tables and repainting them. He did most of the renovations around the Cove. And he's my boyfriend."

Sawyer turns at the exact moment, carrying three bowls full of mac 'n' cheese with peas—one of Sully's favorites, recipe courtesy of

Grandma Joan—and when his eyes connect with mine, all I can see is absolute adoration.

I hate to compare the two, because they are so different, but I can tell you, from the depths of my being, that Peter never looked at me the way Sawyer does. It's as if every time Sawyer and I make eye contact, he can see to my very soul. He sees me for who I am, rather than who he hopes I'll be one day.

"Boyfriend?" Sully scoffs. "You're telling me you're dating Mr. Blond Hair, Blue Eyes?"

"I am." I smirk.

Sawyer sets Sully's bowl down in front of him. "I'm more of a dirty blond."

I chuckle as Sully points his spoon at Sawyer. "You're pushing your luck."

"Then I'm doing my job." He sets the other bowls down and lends his hand out to me. I take it, and he pulls my chair out for me before helping me down to my seat.

Sully watches every move, his eyes roaming in appreciation. When Sawyer goes to get drinks, Sully leans in. "He seems like a keeper."

I smile as soft fifties music plays over the Bluetooth speaker, Louis Armstrong's voice breaking through the silence. Sully's shoulders visibly relax as he sinks his spoon into the mac 'n' cheese.

Sawyer drops off glasses of water and then takes a seat across from me. When our eyes connect, I smile at him, and he winks in return before dipping his spoon into his bowl.

And this is why I'm falling for him, right here. Because as I'm taking care of Sully and attempting to prepare for the grand opening this Monday, the stress of it all is not resting solely on my shoulders. Sawyer is here, taking care of me. Giving me a respite when I need it the most.

He is a partner. Someone to walk at my side, and with every passing day, I realize that he very much could be the man I spend the rest of my life with.

I smile at him across the table and dig into my dinner.

No doubt about it, Sawyer drunkenly stumbled back into my life and quickly stole my heart.

❖   ❖   ❖

"Good morning," Sawyer says as he walks through the front doors of the lobby carrying three pastry boxes. "How are you feeling?"

I'm standing at the check-in counter, my hands sweating and my pulse beating—but not because of the man who's standing in front of me, freshly showered and looking like absolute perfection in a pair of khaki shorts and a black polo shirt.

"Like I'm going to throw up," I answer as Jaz pops into the lobby from the back office.

"She told me about how she dry-heaved into the toilet this morning." Jaz shivers. "Brutal."

Sawyer's brow creases. "You dry-heaved?"

"You didn't know?" Jaz asks. "What the hell were you doing? Still sleeping?"

"He was in his cabin," I answer, and the minute the words slip past me, I realize my mistake.

"Excuse me?" Jaz says, her palm landing flat on the counter as she glances between the two of us. "You're telling me that you're still sleeping in your cabin?"

Ignoring Jaz, Sawyer sets the pastry boxes down on the counter and takes my hand in his. "Are you okay?"

"I'm fine," I answer.

"Uh . . . I'm not fine," Jaz cuts in. "I'm not fine at all. I can barely get your brother to talk to me in more than meme form, but you're over here, in a relationship with my friend, and you aren't sleeping in the same bed?"

Sawyer reaches out and cups my cheeks, his thumb running over my skin. "Do you want me to get you any ginger ale? I'm assuming it's nerves for the grand opening today."

I nod. "Yeah, just want to make sure everything goes okay."

"Do you know what's not okay?" Jaz cuts in again and motions her finger between us. "You two not sleeping in the same bed. What's that about, Sawyer?"

"Everything will be great. But if it will make you feel better, I'll run another test in every cabin to make sure all is well."

I roll my teeth over my bottom lip. "Do you mind?"

"Not at all," he says with such sincerity that all I want to do is crawl over this counter and right into his arms. "Let me grab you some ginger ale first to settle your stomach."

"Not necessary." I shake my head. "I really think I'll be okay."

"You sure?"

I nod.

"Uhhhh . . . hello," Jaz says, her voice growing angrier. "You'd think you two would know by now not to ignore me if you don't want the rage to boil over."

Finally I turn to Jaz. "We're taking it slow."

"What for?" She gestures to Sawyer's body. "Why would you want to take it slow with that?"

"Are you complimenting me?" Sawyer asks playfully.

"No," Jaz says, jabbing her finger in his face before turning back to me. "Seriously, what's the issue?"

I awkwardly look toward Sawyer.

He clears his throat. "It's on me."

Jaz's eyes narrow in on him. "God, just like your brother. Annoyingly slow, with zero intentions."

"My intentions with Fallon are crystal clear, and she knows that."

"I do," I say, backing him up. "I'm good with waiting."

He brings me closer and places the sweetest kiss on my lips before pulling away. "I'll go check on the cabins. Pastries are for guests when they arrive. I stocked up the coffee and hot chocolate bar last night, so that's all ready to go. And I also added those opening day mugs to each cabin, along with the Cocoa Bombs and thank-you cards that tell people to tag you in their posts."

"Why are you so good to me?"

"Because I love you," he says offhandedly, then releases me and smiles at me before he heads out the back door, leaving me stunned.

I stare off at his retreating body through the glass back door, my mind stunned.

Shocked.

Absolutely infatuated.

"Uh . . . ," Jaz ventures, "did he just say he loves you?"

My mouth goes dry. "I think he did."

"Has he said that before?"

I shake my head. "No."

"Well . . ." Jaz picks up one of the pastry boxes and flips it open. "It seems as though you have a conundrum on your hands. Because once again, a man loves you, and the only question is, are you going to be able to tell him you love him back?"

As I take a seat on the stool next to the computer, still in shock, I consider Jaz's question. Would I say "I love you" back to Sawyer?

The answer almost feels too heavy, like it's sitting on the tip of my tongue.

Yes. I would.

CHAPTER

TWENTY-ONE

SAWYER

My nerves are still buzzing from telling Fallon I love her when I enter the last cabin to make sure everything is in working order. How the hell did I just let that slip past my lips? Probably because I couldn't hold it back anymore. I just hope I didn't just scare her away.

My phone vibrates, and I fish it out of my pocket as I turn on the lights to make sure they're working properly. I leave them on.

I lift the screen to see who's calling, and when Andy's name scrolls across the screen, I know exactly what this is about.

"Hey, Andy," I answer as I move to the bed. I switch on the nightstand lights and leave those on as well.

"Sawyer, do you have a second?"

"Yup, what's up?" I move around the room, examining all the details, checking on the floors, looking for any paint touch-ups we missed.

"Got your proposal. I have to say, it's very incriminating."

"In what way?" I ask as I walk to the bathroom and turn on the shower and faucet. I flush the toilet, making sure the pipes can handle all the movement. I check for leaks or anything out of place.

"For you. Everyone knows this movie is based off your experience."

"I realize that, Andy, and I don't care."

After Fallon's dads told me to make lemonade out of lemons, I sat down for the next few nights and worked on my proposal, fleshing out the plot of everything I've been through, all the way down to my drunken body being dragged through the cabins. Once I had a general idea of what I wanted the screenplay to look like, I brought it to Fallon and asked her how she felt about it. She read through it, and when she was done, she looked up at me with the most brilliant smile. She loved it but asked why I'd left Sully out. I told her I didn't think it would be right to include him. I didn't want to use his story line, since it wasn't mine. And because she's so fucking amazing, she told me the story wouldn't be right without Sully in it. So, I added him in.

I added it all. Every detail of Sully's love story with Joan.

When I was done with the proposal, I had Fallon approve it one more time, and when she said it was perfect, I emailed it over to Andy. I'd never felt more relieved to hit send.

"Are you sure? Because this would be exposing your life. I know how private you are, especially since you disappeared to get away from the public eye."

"But disappearing brought me to much more than I could ever have asked for, and this screenplay is an ode to that." I turn off the faucets and flush the toilet one more time to make sure it's good. When all is right, I exit the bathroom. "Do you not like it?" I ask, slightly worried because I'm not sure I have another screenplay in me, not now at least.

"No, I love it. It's perfect. It has everything Movieflix is looking for. But mainly, it's full of heart, and given the few pitches you've thrown at them with slasher scenes, I assume this will be a welcome change."

I chuckle. "Yeah, I figured."

"I have a few notes, which I'll send back to you, but overall, I think it's really good."

"Thank you, Andy."

"You know, I was worried about you, but it looks like I didn't have to worry at all. Maybe all this space and time to yourself is what you really needed."

"It was," I say as I take a seat in the accent chair situated in the back of the cabin. "I've come to really find a different side of me up here. I enjoyed writing the proposal, but I've been able to reawaken a side of me I forgot about. I feel at peace."

"I'm really happy to hear that." He pauses. "Are you planning on staying up there?"

I glance around the cabin, the stark white walls decorated in pictures of the Cove, courtesy of Jaz, the pops of red against the black-and-white buffalo plaid. It's cozy in here. It feels like home—like this is where I belong.

"I am," I answer honestly. "I've met someone who takes my breath away. I'm part of a community that makes me feel loved . . . needed. And I've found myself again. I'm enjoying the things I used to enjoy before the whirlwind of the movies took over."

"Does that mean you've turned in your last screenplay idea—are you leaving the industry?"

"No," I answer honestly. "But I do think I want to slow down a bit. I have a healthy balance here, and I want to keep that."

"I can understand that. Well, I truly believe you have a hit on your hands. And I think Movieflix will be very pleased."

"I hope so. I know everything went a little haywire there for a bit, but I hope this will help salvage that relationship."

"It will, I really think it will. And hey, all business aside, I'm really happy for you, Sawyer. I know going through the drama of Annalisa and Simon has taken a toll on you, and I'm truly glad you've been able to find happiness."

"Sometimes, when you think you've hit rock bottom, what you've really hit is the foundation for the next chapter in your life. This is my next chapter, and I'm excited to see where it takes me."

"Well, I'm ready to watch where it takes you as well. Happy for you, man. I'll talk to you later."

"Thanks, Andy," I say, equal parts touched and content.

I hang up the phone just as Fallon steps through the door.

When I glance up at her, she has a worried look on her face. "Everything okay?" she asks.

I stick my phone in my pocket and then reach my hand out to her. "Yeah, everything's great."

She walks up to me, and I pull her down on my lap, draping her legs over mine.

"That was my agent on the phone. He loved the pitch."

"Really?" she asks.

"Yeah. Thinks it could be a big hit. I owe your dads some sort of fruit basket."

"Trust me when I say the only thing they're going to want from you is a cameo."

I laugh out loud. "I think I can make that happen."

"Seriously?"

"Oh yeah." I wink. "I'll make sure they're in there. Since it takes place in Canoodle, we might even be able to shoot it here. No promises, but it's a possibility."

"Don't even joke about that. Everyone will freak out, even Jaz. And you know she pretends not to like you, but this very well might tip her over the edge."

I smooth my hand over Fallon's thigh. "Well, if that's the case, I better work hard at getting them to film it here. That's if they take the pitch, which I'm ninety-nine point nine percent sure they will. Andy had a few notes, but he's pretty sure it's ready to go, and they'll be more than happy."

"Wow. That's so incredible." She loops her arms around my neck. "I'm in awe, seeing you able to take a story like that and turn it into something." Her thumbs glide over the back of my neck. "Does that mean you're going to go back to LA?" Her voice trails off, and I can see the slight tension in her posture, possibly waiting on bad news.

"Funny you mention that," I say. "I was actually telling Andy that I planned on staying here, and not just indefinitely or for the time being—but permanently. It's only a little over two hours to LA, so when I do have to attend meetings, I can just drive in. But my priorities have changed, and there's no reason to stay in LA when I can be here, with you."

"You mean that?" she asks, a mix of surprise and appreciation on her face.

"Of course I mean it. I love it here, Fallon. I've truly found myself here, and a lot of that has to do with you."

"Me? What on earth did I do?"

"Remind me that the world doesn't revolve around me, but rather it revolves around the people near me, the community I live in, the love between family members and friends. Your selflessness and your need to carry on your grandfather's legacy were the gut punch I needed to open my eyes and shake off the selfishness I'd been carrying. I don't think I would have done that if I didn't stumble into this town. I'm grateful."

"Well, I'm grateful you did, because today never would have happened without you."

"Not true." I lean in and lightly press my lips to hers. "You would have found a way to make it happen. It might have been harder, and you certainly wouldn't have had the eye candy waltzing around the Cove shirtless, but you'd have made it happen."

The softest of chuckles passes her lips. "Well, I'm glad you feel that way, because I need to evict you."

"What?" I ask, pulling back just enough to look her in the eyes.

"Yeah, I just had someone call in hoping to score a reservation for the grand opening, and since you're not a paying customer, I'm going to need your cabin."

"What do you mean I'm not a paying customer? I've been paying this entire time."

She shakes her head. "I haven't been charging you for the last three weeks. You should really check your credit card statements."

"Fallon," I say, irritated. "I told you to charge me."

"And I decided not to. Are you really going to get mad at me about it?"

"Yes."

She sighs, and before I know it, she's straddling me and pushing me back against the chair, her hands on my chest.

"This changes nothing," I say, my hands falling to her backside. "I'm still mad at you."

Her hands sweep under my shirt and drag up over my skin.

"Still mad."

She lowers her mouth to my neck and peppers kisses up my jaw while her hands travel over my pecs.

Fuck . . .

"Still . . . mad." I gulp as she moves her hips over mine. It's the smallest amount of friction, but given how much I've wanted this woman, it feels like she just gave me a ten-minute lap dance.

"Don't be mad at me," she says, her lips traveling over to mine, delivering an open-mouth kiss that makes my goddamn toes curl.

Unable to stop myself, I grip the back of her head as I match her kiss with my own, keeping her firmly in place, just where I want her. In my arms.

I'm not sure how long we stay like that, our tongues dancing together, our need so palpable that it fills the air in the cabin, but when she finally pulls away, I feel dazed, unsure of my surroundings. The only thing that matters is the girl on my lap and the way she makes me feel.

"I didn't feel right charging you," she says as she draws circles over my half-exposed chest. "Please don't be mad about it. It felt like the only way I could pay you back for everything you did for my family and me."

"I told you, you helped me too, Fallon."

"I know, but it made me feel better, so don't be mad."

I sigh heavily and move my hands up and down her thighs. "Not sure I could actually be mad at you for long."

"I'm going to remember you said that." Her mouth descends and presses another kiss against my lips. "But I am going to need your cabin."

"For real?"

She nods. "Yes, for real. But don't worry—I have an alternative place for you to stay."

"If you say Jaz has a spare bedroom, I'll go to Village Hardware right now and buy myself a tent."

She chuckles and shakes her head. Her fingers dance across my chest. "You can stay with me."

"Is Sully going to be with Tank?" I ask. "If so, I'm going to switch out his mattress, and I pray to Jesus he doesn't realize it's different."

She heaves a heavy sigh. "Ugh, why are you making this so difficult."

"What?" I ask, confused.

She meets my gaze. "You won't be staying in Sully's bed—you'll be staying in mine."

"Ohh . . ." It hits me, and I let out a loud laugh at my stupidity.

"It's not funny." She pokes at me.

"I'm not laughing at you. I'm laughing at how idiotic I am for not picking up on what you're saying." I look her in the eyes. "Is this your way of trying to get in my pants?"

Her expression grows serious. "No, this is my way of telling you that I love you, and I want you near me, all the time."

My breath catches in my throat, and the world feels like it spins around me in slow motion. I shift on the chair and lower my shirt because this is a moment I want to remember, and I don't want half my chest exposed.

I know what those three words mean to her, and I know she never said them to Peter. So, for her to say them to me, to open her heart like this, I'm quite aware of the giant leap of faith she's taking.

I tread carefully as I take her hands in mine and entwine our fingers.

"You mean so much to me, Sawyer," she continues when our eyes connect. "You've made me feel like this complex and scary journey doesn't need to be traveled alone. How you interact with Sully, my dads, even Jaz, all the people that matter the most to me . . . you've adopted them as your own, and I can't tell you what that means. And beside all that, you treat me like I'm the most important person in your life."

"Fallon," I say softly. "You know you matter to me—"

"Oh God, wait, did I misunderstand you in the lobby?" she says, her eyes wide in embarrassment as she attempts to stand from my lap. "I'm so stupid—"

"Stop," I say as she struggles to get off my lap. "Let me finish." Her eyes well up with tears, and I quickly ask, "Why are you going to cry?"

"Because I just assumed when you said you loved me in the lobby, you meant you were *in love* with me. I read you wrong, and you're not there yet. I can hear it in your voice."

"Well, you're not hearing it correctly. I'm trying to tell you I love you too, very much." I pause, letting that sink into her beautiful, stubborn head. "But I don't want to ruin it by moving too fast."

"Don't you think saying 'I love you' is moving fast?" she asks.

"No. I think when you feel something for someone, you express it. We've spent a lot of time together, and those feelings have grown. I know mine were growing even before we were together. Now that we're together, those feelings have solidified. But I already messed things up with you, and I don't want to mess up again."

"You won't," she says, her voice almost desperate. "I promise you won't mess it up. I'm here, Sawyer. I'm not going anywhere. This is what

I want. Us. You. And we don't have to do anything—we can just cuddle, but at least stay with me. If you're uncomfortable, we can find you another place to stay in the meantime, but at least just give it a shot."

I lift my hand to her cheek and cup it gently. "Babe, I know I'll be anything but uncomfortable. I just don't want to push you too far."

"Don't worry about that." She grips my shoulders. "You're not pushing; you're slowing down the gratification of having all of you. Please just let me have every last inch of you."

A grin pulls at my lips. "Hell, how could I say no after that?"

"Really?" Her face lights up like a thousand suns, rays of joy beaming from her expression.

"Really."

And then, once again, her lips are on mine and her hands are up my shirt.

❖   ❖   ❖

"Do I smell cookies?" Sully says as he walks into the living room as I'm pulling a tray of snickerdoodles out of the oven.

Two weeks ago, when hanging out with Fallon, I found Grandma Joan's personal cookbook with all her favorite recipes and modifications. The pages were filled with printed-out recipes, handwritten ones, and extra notes, everything torn and splattered with ingredients. Well loved for sure. Ever since I found it, I've made it my mission to make everything in it, to bring a little bit of Grandma Joan back into the residence.

Tonight, I figured the best thing I could make for everyone was a batch of Grandma Joan's snickerdoodle cookies, especially since we had leftover pizza for dinner to keep things easy. I spent most of the day helping Fallon with check-ins and acting as a bellhop while escorting guests to their cabins, but once everyone was checked in, she sent me up to the residence to hang with Sully while she wrapped things up. I thought a snickerdoodle surprise would be nice for her.

"You do smell cookies," I say, turning around.

Sully glances at me, and confusion passes over his face. "Sawyer, right?" he says slowly.

"Yup, you got it." I smile.

Fallon printed a picture of me and put it on Sully's door, so when he exits, he knows I'm not an intruder, especially since she'll be spending more time at the desk. When check-ins slowed down, I spoke to her about hiring someone to run the front desk, and she said she was already on it—she's had quite a few inquiries from people around town about helping at the Cove, including a cleaning staff. But since she was in the middle of reservations and in need of funding, she held off. She believes that in a few weeks she can hire some people to help. In the meantime, it's me and her—and Sully, if he's doing okay. He's more entertainment than anything.

"Did Joan make these?" He walks up to the cookies and takes a sniff. "They look like she did."

Heartache grips my chest as I carefully place my hand on Sully's shoulder. "Joan has passed, Sully. I'm so sorry."

I brace myself for what's to come, but instead of breaking down like he normally does, he clears his throat. "Ah, right, I meant, uh, Fallon, did she make these?"

I tread carefully. "No, sir, I did. I found Grandma Joan's recipe and thought I'd make them as a surprise for you and Fallon. I hope that's okay."

He steps away and carefully observes me. It does make me sad to see him like this, completely confused, especially since we've shared some really good times together while fixing things up around the Cove. I can't imagine how Fallon must feel.

"Well, that was nice." He clears his throat and moves toward one of the cooled baking sheets. He picks a cookie up and examines it before taking a bite. As he chews, he examines the cookie, turning it over in his hand and thoroughly checking it out before he looks back up at me.

"Not like Joan's, but good enough." Without another word, he takes one more cookie and heads into his bedroom.

I chuckle to myself and put the cookies on cooling racks so I can wash the baking sheets. I already did the dishes and cleaned up around the house; I dropped my things off in Fallon's room, opting to not unpack so I could bake cookies instead. I have plenty of time to move in fully, so I'm not too worried.

Once I finish cleaning the pans and putting the cooled cookies in a Tupperware, I hear the stairs creak, indicating Fallon's approach. "I knew I smelled cookies." She pushes through the door and walks over to me. She places her hand on my chest before standing on her toes and giving me a chaste kiss. "Did you make these?"

"I did. Thought I could do something for you and Sully on grand reopening day. Sully charged in here, took two, and then retreated to his room. He did make sure to let me know that Grandma Joan's are better."

"Everything Grandma Joan did was better, according to Sully. Don't take it too personally."

"So, I shouldn't go cry myself to sleep?"

"No, don't waste a tear on it." She glances over at the cookies. "Can I have one?"

"I made them for you, so yes." I reach out and pick up one from the cooling rack. "Here."

She takes the cookie and nearly eats half of it in one large bite.

"Whoa, now that's a bite. Something I like to see in a woman."

"A biter?" she asks.

"No, being able to fit a lot in her mouth."

Both her eyebrows lift at the same time, and I realize what I said.

"Uh, not like that. I mean, sure, if you can take a lot, great, but it's not, like . . . required or anything." I drag my hand over my face in defeat. "Can we move past this conversation, please?"

Her hearty laugh fills me with ease as she takes my hand in hers. "Only because I want to go lie down."

Cookies in hand, we turn off the main lights and head into her bedroom. The first time I saw her bedroom, I was surprised by the lack of personalization. There's a picture of her and her dads on her dresser, along with a picture of her and Jaz on the Harry Balls Trail—in a very off-putting frame that has fake blood dribbled over it. But that's about it, minus a few of her toiletries and devices, as if she's kept it the same guest room that Grandma Joan must have set up years ago.

"Now that you've fully consumed the cookie, what's your final verdict?" I ask.

She licks the cinnamon sugar off her fingers—the way she sucks her finger in front of me doesn't go unseen. "Oh my. Really freaking good." Her finger pops out of her mouth, and my legs shiver from the thought of her mouth somewhere else.

I clear my throat. "Not better than Grandma Joan's, though."

"A close second." She winks and takes a seat in the corner armchair, near where my bag is. She toes it. "Stay for a while."

"I will." I take a seat on her bed, facing her. "Just wanted to make those cookies before you got back."

"It was very sweet of you. Thank you."

"You're welcome. So, everyone checked in and good?"

"Besides one person. A Margaret O'Hare. She called and said she won't be here until tomorrow. Other than that, everyone's in their cabins—well, some of them were down by the horseshoe pits, but yes, they're all good, and they have my number if they need anything." Her eyes water up, and she shakes her head in what I assume is disbelief. "I can't believe we have a full house. I can't remember the last time we had to light up the No Vacancy sign. And the guests are already tagging us in pictures." A tear falls down her cheek, and I stand from the bed. Lifting her from the chair, I take a seat so she's on my lap and I can hold her close. "We did it," she whispers. "Thank you, Sawyer. I'm sure you know by now how much this means to me."

"I do." I press my hand to her cheek so I can bring her close and press a kiss to her forehead. "I'm proud of you. People look for leaders to guide them through the dark. You lit a light, and people followed. You are incredible, Fallon."

She leans back to look me in the eyes. "I could not have done it without you." I wipe away her tear and push a stray piece of hair behind her ear. "This, you and me, it feels like we were meant to be all this time, but for some reason, in order for us to become a *we*, there were obstacles we had to face first. Like I had to be with Peter to understand the feeling of true love."

"And I had to be run over by Simon and Annalisa to comprehend the ideal of true loyalty, friendship, and the love of a pure woman."

She smirks. "Well, I'm anything but pure."

I chuckle. "I'm gathering that. But you know what I mean."

"I do." She leans in and presses a kiss to my lips. "I'm going to go check on Sully and then get ready for bed. Why don't you use the bathroom first, and I'll be in right after you?"

"Sounds good."

I press another kiss to her lips and lightly smack her ass as she gets off me. Her look of utter surprise makes me laugh out loud. "I'm anything but pure as well."

"Apparently," she says, rubbing her butt as she leaves the bedroom.

I lean down to my bag and unzip it. On top, I have a pair of shorts to wear to bed, my toothbrush, and deodorant. Simple. I grab all three things and take them to the bathroom, which is just off the main living space. I quietly close the door behind me and set my things down on the counter.

Sully's bedroom—the master—has a quaint adjoining bathroom that I was able to use last time, so this is my first time in this bathroom, and I have to say . . . we're going to need to make some updates. Hell, we'll need to make some updates to this entire living space.

Maybe that will be my next project. These dingy oak cabinets could use a face-lift, the yellowing counter is anything but appealing, and don't get me started on the tile. After a long day of working, Fallon deserves a place to relax, a sanctuary, and even though I know she probably wants to respect her grandparents and preserve what they built together, I think we could update some things, make the residence match the aesthetic of the cabins. At least in here.

I take care of my business, going to the bathroom, brushing my teeth, and, of course, reapplying deodorant—can't smell for my girl—and then I head out just as I see Fallon quietly shutting Sully's door.

"He all set?" I whisper, just in case he's trying to sleep.

She nods. "Yeah, he just lay down. He told me to tell the man in the kitchen thanks for the cookies."

I chuckle. "Well, he's more than welcome. I'm going to put those last ones on the cooling rack in the container, and then I'll meet you in the bedroom."

"Sounds good." She walks into the bathroom, but I snag her hand and place a quick kiss on her lips, making her giggle with my fumbled attempt. "Not much finesse there, Sawyer."

"Let's ignore that happened."

We part ways, and I go to the kitchen, where I put away the remaining cookies in the container and rinse down the cooling racks, and then I head back into the bedroom. I stare down at the bed—it's a double bed, not even a queen, which means we'll be on top of each other. No complaining here. What side is hers, though? I examine the nightstands, and when I see her phone cord on the right-hand side, I know I'll be on the left.

Since her phone is on the dresser, I plug it in for her, and then I'm setting up my phone on my side just as the bedroom door opens. I turn around, and I'm nearly knocked back into the wall from the sight in front of me.

Fallon shuts the door but remains in front of it, a huge smile on her face.

"What, uh . . . what are you wearing?" I ask her as I take her in.

If she says "pajamas," there's no way I'm going to be able to sleep in this small bed with her every night and not touch her. Because . . . *fuck*.

She's wearing a white silk top that barely touches the top of her thighs. Thin straps wrap around her delicate shoulders, and her hard nipples are pushing against the thin fabric of her top. And from what I can tell, she's wearing a matching thong to go with the ensemble.

"Oh, you know, just what I wear every night," she says, moving toward her side of the bed. "You plugged in my phone. Thank you."

I don't answer. I just stand there, stunned. "Uh, you didn't wear that when I was staying in Sully's room."

"Oh, really." She taps her chin. "Maybe I was being respectful of having a guest in the house." She flips the bedding down and climbs in. When I still don't move, she asks, "Are you going to lie down?"

I scratch the back of my head while I stare down at her. "You know, might be best if I go sleep on the couch."

"Oh my God, Sawyer, don't be ridiculous. Just lie down."

I still don't move.

"Are you really going to act like that? Do you need me to change?"

I mean, yeah . . . that would make things easier. But I'd never make her do that because I have self-control. I can do this. So what, she's wearing a white silky top that fits her body perfectly and makes her look incredible. Sure, do I want to touch her? Drag my hands over her breasts? Tear her thong down and find out what she tastes like? Yeah . . . but do I have self-control? Of course.

You must be thinking, Why are you holding back? Because . . . I think I've convinced myself I need more time. More time to dig deep into our connection.

371

Or maybe . . . fuck, maybe I'm just nervous because I truly love this woman and I'm waiting on the perfect moment.

"No, sorry. Just, uh . . . surprised." I climb into bed carefully, trying not to take up too much space. She flips off the light at her nightstand, blanketing us in darkness, the moon providing the only light in the room.

Her back is turned toward me as I lay there on my back, stiff as a board, staring up at the ceiling. See, I can do this. I can be a gentleman and keep my hands to myself.

"Are you going to spoon me?" she asks.

No.

That would require touching.

"Do you want me to spoon you?"

She chuckles. "I wouldn't have asked if I didn't."

True, very true.

Okay, so spooning can be simple—just put an arm over her.

I twist my body on the bed so I'm facing her back and drape my arm over her side. Not her ass, not her breasts, but her waist. A neutral zone. Mind you, my arm isn't curled around her stomach, nor is it romantically involved with her body at all. Just propped up on her side, dangling at the wrist.

"This is you spooning?" she asks.

"Is it not to your satisfaction?" I ask, my voice cracking with nerves.

"No." And then, to my despair, she throws—yes, throws—her body into mine, her ass lining up with my crotch, back to my chest, and her arm curls around mine, making me grip her tightly.

Lord, please fucking help me here, because Christ does she feel so good against me. Warm, soft, smells like a goddamn dream. And when she presses my hand to her stomach, I nearly choke out a plea, begging her to move away.

I want to take it slow with her. I mean that. I know we said "I love you," but I still have this notion in the back of my head that if I go at a snail's pace with her, then we'll be able to build and build on our foundation, so when we do start to have sex, it doesn't cloud the connection we're forming.

But she's making it hard—legitimately . . . she's making me hard.

"There," she says. "Was that so difficult?"

Yes.

Very.

When she notices just how stiff my body is still, she shimmies against me. "Loosen up, Sawyer, please."

Fuck, don't shimmy. Don't move. Just that slight movement sent a bolt of desire straight to my cock.

"I am loose," I lie.

"Wow, then you're terrible at snuggling." The disappointment in her voice cuts right through me, especially since this is the first time we're sharing a bed. I don't want her to regret inviting me, or think she made a mistake letting me into her world because I can't get it together enough to fucking spoon her.

Time to grow the fuck up.

"Sorry," I whisper as I loosen my limbs and truly bring her in close. My hand wraps around her stomach, where I hold her tight, and I bury my head close to hers. I kiss her bare shoulder. "Is that better?"

She sighs heavily. "Much better." Her fingers draw small circles on the back of my hand. "I was worried there for a second. Thought that I repulsed you."

"Stop it." I kiss her shoulder again. "Opposite, actually."

"Oh? So, I take it you like my pajamas?"

"You can say that," I say as I rub my thumb over her stomach. "But you know damn well this is not what you wear at night."

"It is when I want to impress my new boyfriend and let him know he's not dating a troll who walks around in jean shorts and T-shirts all day. I have a sexy side."

"You didn't need to wear this to show me you're not a troll. Trust me, I know you're not. Those jean shorts do just as much to me as this little number." I allow my hand to travel down the side of her leg and back up to the hem of her top. My fingers drag it a little higher and reach around her stomach again.

"So would you have preferred I wore jean shorts to bed?"

I chuckle against her hair. "No, this works. But you can't tell me this is what you wear every night."

"I have a few of these outfits. I actually find them comfortable and cooling, especially when it gets really hot here. So yeah, this is what you'll get most of the time—sometimes just underwear and a tank top. Other times . . . maybe just one of your shirts."

I grip her tighter at the thought of her wearing one of my shirts. "I like the idea of that."

And just as I'm getting comfortable, she twists to her back, my thumb dragging across the underside of her breast as she moves around. She looks up at me now as I hover over her, holding her in my embrace.

"Are you going to kiss me good night?"

I swallow hard because I can feel that her shirt has lifted from her twist, exposing a part of her stomach. I can feel her tempting me, trying to get me to crack, and she's doing a fucking good job.

"Yeah," I say, my pulse now pounding a mile a minute.

She touches my cheek. "Then kiss me, Sawyer."

A swirl of lust spins through my stomach as I drag my hand up her body, my palm skimming her tight nipple, and reach her cheek. Her breath catches, and I press my lips to hers. The delicious warmth of her lips consumes me, and I lose all thought of holding back as I press into her harder. My fingers curl into her hair, reveling in the silky strands as my mouth opens and my tongue swipes against her lips.

She groans as I move so I'm now halfway covering her body, granting us both a better angle. The hand that's not cupping my face goes to my back and travels down to my waistband. Her fingers slip past the elastic only an inch, but that inch feels like she's pulled my shorts all the way down.

I release my mouth from hers and breathe heavily as I stare down at her, collecting myself. I wet my lips, her taste branding my brain as I say, "Good night."

Her eyes search mine, and I can see the confusion in them. "Good night," she whispers.

I don't move right away. Instead, I continue to stare into her beautiful eyes. "You are so gorgeous," I murmur, stroking her face. "Truly breathtaking, Fallon."

Her lips curl into a blissful smile right before she reaches up and gives me one more kiss. "I love you."

"I love you too," I answer back, not a hitch in my voice, just pure truth.

Because I do, I love this woman. I love everything about her, from her heart to her sassiness, to her insecurities. I want them all.

I give her one more chaste kiss before moving off her. Her hand slides from my back, traveling across my waist and grazing my cock just before she turns around, offering me her back once again. I hold back the sharp hiss that wants to escape from that minor touch, but when she presses her ass right against my lap, I let out a full-blown groan.

"Babe, careful," I say, placing my hand on her hip and steadying her.

She doesn't say anything, but she takes my hand and curls it under her nightgown so my palm is touching her bare skin.

So warm.

Jesus.

My hand splays across her stomach, holding still, but when she shifts again, the tips of my fingers rub against the underside of her breast.

"Hell, Fallon. Stop moving."

She must hear the pain in my voice because she takes that opportunity to press her ass against my crotch again. This time, I can feel my inability to hold it together—my dick goes hard, and the groan of satisfaction that falls past her lips teases me.

"You're making me hard," I whisper, trying to adjust myself.

"Good," she says, right before she drags my hand to her breast. The combination of her soft, plump skin and her hard, pebbled nipple against my fingers has me unwinding.

I squeeze her, and she moans as her ass slides against me.

Shit. I'm losing it. Losing all control.

And is that so bad? Yes, I told myself I needed to wait longer—I needed to build more of a foundation, take her on more dates and really dive deep into our love before we get physical. But maybe I'm thinking too much about this, rationalizing my fear of being vulnerable with her. Maybe being intimate with her on this level is just another way to grow closer.

This is the next step, the perfect moment. Me and her, sealing the love we share.

I'm ready.

In a blink of an eye, my mouth collides with hers. All the energy I was using to hold back unleashes and is transferred into my grip on her and the force behind my kiss.

Her arms wrap around my neck, holding me close as I transfer my weight so I'm on top of her. My lips trail a path over her mouth, across her jaw, and down her neck as her chest arches into my palm and her legs part, making room for my body.

I crawl between her and unabashedly move my hips against hers.

"I want you," she says as my lips trail up to her mouth again. "Please tell me I can have all of you, Sawyer."

I pause my kisses, and I pull away just enough to look her in the eyes. I weigh my old fears against the desire beating through the both of us.

"I want you too," I say. "Really fucking bad. But I've been holding back because I don't want this to mess anything up. I feel like I've moved too fast in the past, and I don't want to do that with you."

"It's not too fast." She shakes her head while her fingers dive deeper into my hair. "It will only solidify why I love you so much." She wets her lips with her tongue. "Please, Sawyer."

The pleading in her voice does me in. I reach down to the hem of her nightgown and drag it up her body, pulling it over her head. I toss the garment to the side as I stare down at her.

"God, you're so beautiful." I take one of her breasts in my hand and lightly squeeze it while I lower my mouth to the other, sucking in her nipple between my lips.

Her moan grows a little louder as she presses into me, asking, begging for more. So, I move my mouth over to her other breast until she's writhing beneath me, her pelvis pleading for attention. I work my mouth down her stomach and to the waistband of her thong. I drag my tongue along the edge, around her belly button, and then I pull her thong down an inch and kiss the top of her pubic bone. Her legs spread even wider. Her need evident.

Wanting to tease this woman like she's teased me, I move my mouth to her inner thigh, pressing kisses along her skin until I reach the front seam of her thong and then move to the other side.

Her breathless pleas let me know I'm doing exactly what I should be doing, so instead of giving her what she wants, I move my mouth back up her stomach.

"Sawyer," she breathes heavily. "Stop teasing me."

I chuckle against her heated skin and lower my mouth back down between her legs. This time, I drag her thong down and toss it to the side before pressing my palms against her inner thighs and spreading her wide. And when I lower my head, I kiss just above her arousal, making her squirm in my arms.

"Why do you hate me?" she asks, her breath heavy.

"I love you, babe. This is how it will be with me, so get used to it." And then I drag my tongue up to her belly button and back down until

I hit her slit. I gently glide my tongue where she wants me but pull away and pay attention to her inner thigh again.

"Jesus," she whispers, her hands gripping the sheet beneath us.

I hold back my smile while I make my way to her other leg. I spend a few more minutes, yes, *minutes*, making sure she realizes just how serious I am about dragging this out, and when she's panting, her arm draped over her eyes in absolute surrender, I drag my tongue over her clit, pulling a feral sound past her lips.

All I can think about is how wet she is, how great she tastes, and how amazing she sounds. After that, I black out as I lose myself between her legs. Licking, sucking, kissing.

My breath hitches as I feel her clench around me. Her hips ride my tongue. Her moans are faster, more frequent. Her hand sifts through my hair, holding me in place. And as I flick my tongue across her clit, I feel her on the verge of her orgasm, closer and closer . . . until she pulls on my hair, her legs tightening around me as she comes, quietly calling out my name. I let her move against my tongue, riding it out until she's completely sated.

That's when I climb off her, remove my shorts, and grab a condom from my bag—guess Roarick was right about packing those for me. I roll the condom on, my cock so fucking eager to get inside her that there's no possible way I could stop at this point. Not with the sound of her orgasm ringing through my mind.

I climb back on the bed and take her hand in mine, entwining our fingers and pressing them against the mattress as I guide my cock to her entrance. "I love you," I say as our eyes connect.

Her hazy eyes smile up at me, and she loops her fingers around the back of my neck, bringing me to her mouth. As I enter her slowly, I work my lips over hers while I take in the absolute perfect feel of her wrapped around my cock.

I grab her other hand in mine and press that one against the mattress as well as I slowly kiss her and thrust my hips in and out.

It's intimate. It's indulgent. It's everything I've ever wanted with this woman.

A connection so strong, so great, that I don't believe for a moment that it could ever be broken.

My pulsing picks up when her tongue connects with mine, turning our lovemaking more feral, more needy. And before I know it, I release our hands and bring her legs up to my shoulders, creating a different angle, an angle that makes me bottom out. We both moan into the new position.

Her hands go above her head, pressing against the headboard as my thrusts become stronger, more forceful.

"Sawyer," she groans out. "Yes, more. Please, more."

I adjust myself, getting a better hold on her so when I thrust, I really can make it the best for the both of us as I bring my thumb to her clit and press down.

Her eyes shoot open, and her mouth parts in a silent cry. Her pussy clenches around me, and I break into a sweat as I feel the stirring of my climax claw up the backs of my legs to the base of my spine.

"Shit, baby. I'm getting close."

"Me . . . too," she says. "God, you're so good. So . . . good."

Her confession pours a sense of pride in me because I feel the same way about her. This, what's happening between us—nothing in my life has ever felt like this. I've never felt this connected, this in tune with someone.

My hips pulse, and she contracts around me.

My balls tighten with the sound of her whispered moans growing heavier.

And when her fingers grip my back and dig into my skin while she throbs around my cock, her orgasm seizing her, I fall right over the edge with her as white-hot pleasure rips through me.

"Fuck," I groan as I still inside her, my cock throbbing as she continues to pulse around me.

We stay like that for a few more seconds before I slowly lower my arms to either side of her head and drag my thumbs over her heated cheeks.

"Fallon . . . we might have a problem."

She chuckles. "I think you're right."

"Do you know what I'm about to say?"

She nods. "We just opened a part of our relationship we're not going to be able to control."

I nod. "Yeah. I hope you didn't plan on getting much sleep because we are doing that again."

She chuckles. "I was hoping you were going to say that."

I kiss the tip of her nose. "Love you, babe."

"Love you." She caresses my cheek, and I can honestly say that this moment is one of true happiness.

This is how I'm supposed to be living my life.

With this girl in it, stealing my heart.

CHAPTER

TWENTY-TWO

SAWYER

"Stop looking at me like that," Fallon says from her spot behind the check-in counter.

"Like what?" I ask. I'm lounging on the lobby couch, my computer on my lap, working on the notes from Andy while Fallon meticulously hand cleans the rocks she just pulled out of the tumbler.

"Like you're trying to convince me to strip down to nothing."

"Babe, I don't need to convince you—you do that on your own." I smirk while she rolls her eyes.

"Aren't you charming?"

"I believe I am," I answer as Sully comes downstairs, a grumpy look on his face as he stops behind the counter.

"Everything okay?" Fallon asks him.

"I can't find my socks. Have you seen my socks?"

Fallon glances down at Sully's classic high-waters and then back up at him. "Sully, they're on your feet. Along with your shoes." She gently presses her hand to his shoulder.

He looks down, and embarrassment crosses his face as he realizes his mistake. "I thought they went missing," he says while he moves around the counter and spots me. "What are you doing? Don't you have work to get done?"

"He is working, Sully," Fallon says. "He's working on his screenplay pitch."

"Screenplay? What's that balderdash? What happened to working on the firepit? There are people here—where are they going to roast marshmallows?"

"Sawyer finished that up a week ago," Fallon says. I did. It was a quick project that I had Tank and the utilities company help me with—we wanted to have a firepit that would ignite with the press of a button to keep any free-flying sparks from hitting the trees. "See, it's right outside."

Sully walks up to the back window and takes in the firepit, which is six by three in size, surrounded by two outdoor couches and two accent chairs.

Sully scratches the top of his head. "Well, the dishes need to be done. I'm going to go take care of them." Like the grump that he is, he stomps away, back upstairs, and slams the door behind him.

Fallon lets out a heavy sigh. "The dishes are done."

"I know," I say. "Do you want me to go check on him?"

Fallon shakes her head. "No. I'll go. It seems like it's going to be a rough day. I'm going to have Jaz come watch the desk for a bit while I'm up there."

"I can watch it."

She shakes her head and points to my computer. "No, you need to get that done. Andy is waiting on you, and you've helped enough. Jaz can easily cover for me."

"Fallon, I can do both at the same time."

"No, I'm serious. I'm going to text her right now, and when she gets here, she's going to kick you out. And I know you don't want to mess with Jaz and her switchblade." She's right about that. "Can you just man the desk until Jaz gets here? Margaret O'Hare is going to check in—not sure when. You just have to hand her the key, and I'll follow up later with her."

"Are you sure?"

She nods and walks around the counter and up to me. She leans over the back of the couch and lowers her mouth to mine. "Love you."

"Love you."

She kisses me for a few seconds before pulling away, making me groan.

"You can't just kiss me like that and leave."

"I can do whatever I want." She smirks and then takes off up the stairs. I watch, appreciating the view, until she's out of sight.

Talk about having it bad for someone.

I'm head over heels for that woman.

Last night just solidified it. Not that I needed to have sex with her to know that, but last night was way more than just sex—it was an example of the undeniable connection we have.

Because I don't want anyone walking in and thinking the counter is unattended, I bring my computer to Fallon's vacated spot and scoot her rocks to the side, gently placing them out of the reach of guests. She has a few on display in front of her sign, which I think is the cutest goddamn thing I've ever seen. We plan on hiking the Harry Balls Trail and looking for more rocks that we can polish this weekend. I find the whole process oddly soothing. The rocks tumble for a few days, we take them out, we add more grit, rinse, and repeat. And I love seeing how they turn out. Fallon was calling me a "rock nerd" the other day, and maybe I am, but it's just another thing we can bond over.

Just then, the front door opens. I assume this has to be Margaret O'Hare, but when my eyes land on the person walking through the door, I nearly fall right off my stool.

What the actual hell?

"Sawyer. You're here."

Cautiously, I stand from the stool, walk around the counter, and stick my hands in my pockets as I try to keep my voice calm. "Annalisa, what the hell are you doing here?"

The last time I saw her in person, she was the picture-perfect bride on her wedding day. Decked out in head-to-toe white with her nails done, eyelashes glued on, and hair covered with a veil. Now she's standing in front of me over a month later, clad in a loose-fitting red cardigan. She's a frail slice of the woman she was on that day.

Nervously, she says, "I caught wind that you might be up here, so I decided to check for myself."

"Who did you hear that from?" I ask her, my anger starting to boil. Was it Andy? Roarick? It would be tough to believe that either of them betrayed my trust.

"Some gossip site. There were pictures of you posted around town. But does that matter?"

Could have been anyone, even someone just passing through.

"No, what matters is, why the hell are you here?" I hiss-whisper at her, not wanting to draw any attention from upstairs. The last thing Fallon needs right now is to come downstairs and see Annalisa.

"Sawyer. I . . ." Her eyes well up with tears as her expression runs from relieved to apologetic in seconds. "I need to apologize."

Jesus Christ.

I'm not sure where this is coming from or why she finds it necessary to destroy my peace, but she sure as hell isn't about to disturb Fallon's happiness. That's for damn sure.

"Not here," I say, ushering her out of the lobby and toward the open grass. I glance around, looking for any spot to talk to her, any spot that's out of view.

"Should we sit at that bench?" Annalisa asks, pointing to Sully's bench.

Uh, over my dead body.

That's not fucking happening.

That bench, the Cove, those picnic tables, they will not be tainted by Annalisa.

Knowing cabin number one is currently waiting for Margaret O'Hare to show up, I point to it. "Go to that cabin; I'll be right there."

I jog back into the lobby and quickly grab the key to cabin number one that's hanging behind the check-in desk. Just as I'm retreating to the back door again, Jaz strolls through the front door. Fucking perfect.

"What's the hurry, Julia?"

Of course she shows up seconds after Fallon texts her for some help. Knowing Jaz's morning routine, she was probably already on her way over here, which doesn't bode well for me. I think we all know how temperamental Jaz is—pretty sure if she knew Annalisa was here, she'd unfurl her switchblade and start stabbing walls. Best she doesn't know. Best no one knows.

I'll listen to what Annalisa has to say and boot her ass out of here without a parting glance.

"Uh, just making sure cabin number one is ready for Margaret when she shows up. Want to double-check the pipes." I don't know why I say that—it's not like we changed the pipes at all, but Jaz falls for it.

"Okay, whatever. Just bring the key back when you're done."

"Sure thing," I say as I jog off toward the cabin, my hands sweaty from the thought of Jaz almost running into Annalisa. A few minutes earlier and we might have had bloodshed in the lobby.

Thankfully, cabin number one is shadowed by a tree, so Annalisa is out of view when I reach its front door. I quickly unlock the door and swing it open.

"Get in," I say angrily. To my surprise, Annalisa obeys, and I shut the door behind us. I toss the key on the dining table that sits two and push my hands through my hair. "What the actual hell, Annalisa? You can't just show up here like this."

"I know, I'm sure I'm the last person you expected to see today."

"Yeah, you could say that. You're the last person I really want to see, ever."

She nods solemnly. "I deserve that." She takes a seat at the table, while I sit across from her on the bed, my hands folded as I lean forward on my legs, in disbelief that I'm staring at Annalisa right now, the woman who's made my life absolute hell for the last year. And for God knows what reason—either expert acting or she's finally come to her senses—but she actually looks like the woman I met many years ago. The resting bitch face is gone, her brows aren't perfectly manicured, and there isn't a sneer to be found. Instead, her eyes seem brighter, like she's cleared the mud she's been flinging around and is actually acting sincerely.

"Can we just get on with this?" I ask. "Whatever you need to get off your chest, just say it so I can get on with my day."

She glances to the side. "Wow, you really hate me, don't you?"

"Uh . . . can you blame me?" I nearly shout. "Anna, you cheated on me with my best friend. You left me for him, and then I was forced to stand there and act like everything was okay while you traipsed around, telling the press, everyone who cared to listen, how he saved you, how he was your knight in a Tom Ford suit. Correct me if I'm wrong, but I'm pretty sure I didn't hold you hostage and treat you like a captive when we were together."

"You didn't."

"And yet you acted like I did. Jesus, Anna, you threw me under the bus every chance you had, and then after the wedding, it was like a goddamn witch hunt out there for my credibility. You realize the kind of damage you could have done to my career?"

"I know," she says. "I know everything that I did was wrong, and you didn't deserve any of it."

I half expect her to defend herself, to throw my misgivings in my face and blame me for my career mishaps—you know, since I was the one who flipped her off at the altar. But she doesn't. Instead, she looks up at me with such regret that I'm thrown off.

"I'd like to say that I was told to act that way. That the studio pressured me, or my agent advised me, but they didn't. What it comes down to is that the pressure of Hollywood got to me; it was eating me up inside for so long. But when I kissed Simon, it felt like I had power in the industry, something I didn't have before. People were paying attention to me. The media cared what I did, and for once, I actually felt like I mattered, stood out from all the other actors clamoring for parts."

"Yes, at someone else's expense."

"Which has taken me far too long to realize." Staring down at her hands, she adds, "I'm ashamed of my behavior, Sawyer, and I'm not asking you to forgive me because I frankly don't deserve it."

"Then why did you come here?" I ask.

"Because for some reason I thought it might be nice for you to see me like this."

"To gain sympathy?" I ask incredulously.

"No." Her eyes snap up to mine. "So that you can know that despite my attempts to trash your name, I'm the one who's been trashed. This whole charade, parading around from news outlet to news outlet, it's done nothing but damage my image. You should see what they're saying about me."

"About you?" I nearly fly off the bed. "Are you really trying to get sympathy from me? There are memes made of me with devil horns popping out of my head as I flip you off. You don't know what bad press is until you're in my shoes."

She sighs heavily. "I don't think I'm doing a good job explaining myself."

"Yeah, I think we could agree on that."

She leans forward. "I came here to apologize." I wait for her to continue, to hear that apology. "I'm sorry, Sawyer. For everything. I never should have treated you the way that I did, and I never should have cheated on you in the first place. In all honesty, you were the best thing to ever happen to me, and I threw that all away."

"Uh-huh, and how would Simon feel if he heard you say that?"

"He wouldn't care." She glances away. "He, uh, he and I have called it quits. I believe, as we speak, he's off to Tulum, Mexico, right now with his plastic surgeon's nurse." Not surprised. I quickly learned after he started dating Annalisa that Simon's loyalty was as valuable as a single penny.

I fold my arms across my chest. "Which means you're lonely, and that's why you came here. You say you want to apologize; is that the truth? Or do you really just want to get back together with me?"

"No. I don't." She shakes her head. "I know you won't want to take me back, and I also know I don't deserve you."

"Damn right on both accounts," I say as her eyes cast down. And I don't know why, you can say it's my conscience that took a moment to rear into high gear, but the defeat in her shoulders and her deflated expression actually make me feel bad for her.

I know. Crazy.

I should not have any sort of feelings toward her. I should be hoping she gets swept up by the winds that blow through the San Jacinto Mountains, never to be seen again. And yet I feel fucking sorry for her.

What is wrong with me?

I scrub my hand over my face. "I don't know how not to be mean to you right now. I'm just so . . . mad. And I thought I was over it. I've moved on. I found someone I truly love—"

"You moved on?" she asks, her eyes flashing up to mine.

"Yes, did you think I was just going to be single for the rest of my life?"

"No. I don't know what I thought." She smooths her hands over her legs, her white shorts barely covering the upper half of her legs. "I guess I'm just surprised. From your general attitude since the engagement, it seemed like you didn't believe in love anymore, and I know that's all because of me. I'm just shocked is all. I'm happy for you, though. I bet she is amazing."

"She is," I say softly. "She really fucking is." I pull on the back of my neck. "Okay, so you wanted to apologize, you did that—is that all?"

She stands and takes off her red cardigan.

"Whoa, what the hell are you doing?" I put my hands on her hips and move her backward.

"I'm just hot." She chuckles. "Don't worry, I'm not doing anything you need to worry about. I wouldn't."

Well, thank God for that.

"But I do have something I want to give you." She goes to her large purse and pulls out a powder-blue dress shoe and holds it out to me. "You left this on the steps of the church. I don't know why, but I thought you might like it, so, you know, you could burn the pair together."

I chuckle and take the shoe from her. "Yeah, this has potential for very good kindling."

"Figured as much." She clasps her hands in front of her. "You know, Sawyer, I really am sorry. I know there's no possible way to earn your forgiveness, and that's really okay. But I wanted to come here and see you in person, tell you that if I could go back in time and change things, I would. I never would have left you. I would have talked to you about my insecurities, and I would have leaned on you for support."

Touched at her honesty, I stand as well, and I take her hand in mine. "I would have supported you, Anna."

"I know." She quickly swipes away at a tear as she releases my hand. "Thank you. You're so much kinder than I deserve."

"Maybe in the future, you can learn to trust the people around you, the people with good intentions—Simon not included."

"Yeah," she says breathlessly.

We spend the next few minutes catching up. I tell her about the screenplay, which she's actually excited to see come to life. And she tells me about how her mom plays the video of me flipping the bird at the altar on repeat, laughing the whole time. It's a pleasant exchange. Does it make me think we can be friends? Never. But does it give me a slice of peace and the chance to shut the door on this part of my life? Yes.

"Well, I should get going."

"Yeah, a guest should be checking into this cabin at any time now."

Together, we exit the cabin, and when we're on the porch, she turns toward me. "I'm headed into Palm Springs for a mental health retreat. I thought you might want to know, since, well, you can see that I'm trying to make a positive change in my life. Not many people know about it, so please don't say anything. Not that I have any right to ask that of you."

"You can trust me. I wouldn't say anything. And I'm happy that you're doing something to help yourself."

"Thank you." Placing her hand on my arm, she reaches up and presses a kiss to my cheek. "That means a lot to me."

When she pulls away, she gives me a soft wave and heads up the path to the parking lot. She walks right past Jaz, who stands at the edge of the pathway, arms crossed, switchblade in hand.

Oh fuck.

Annalisa gives Jaz a quick once-over but doesn't say anything as she disappears behind the trees. Unfortunately for me, I won't be able to escape her as easily.

Not sure how to approach this, I gently hold up my hands. "Jaz, it's not what you think."

Her face remains neutral. Her pose, stoic. Commanding. Her silence is honestly more terrifying than her lashing out at me. Without uttering a word, she turns on her heel and heads into the lobby.

Double fuck.

I have no idea what she's thinking or why she was holding her switchblade like that, but what I do know is that the fear pulsing through me, sending all my nerves into high alert, is validated. And I need to catch up to her before she can say anything to Fallon. Jaz is a loose cannon. She's protective. Emotional. Reacts instead of thinks, and I can only imagine what she would say to Fallon. Hint: it won't look good for me. Not to mention, this is the last thing Fallon needs to deal with at the moment.

I jog after her, right up to the lobby. "Nothing happened," I announce, swinging the door open.

But she doesn't say anything; she doesn't even glance in my direction—she ignores me and types away on her phone. Fuck, is she texting Fallon? The panic in my chest feels overwhelming, to the point that I'm worried I might pass out.

"Jaz, did you hear me? Nothing happened." She continues to tap her screen. "Are you texting Fallon? You know I can just go upstairs to talk to her, right?"

She sets her phone down on the counter and crosses her arms over her chest. "Actually, you can't. Because she's on her way to the hospital with Sully."

"What?" I yell. I charge past Jaz and run up the stairs, taking two at a time until I reach the door to the residence. I swing it open and find nothing but silence. I glance around the room—no traces of them, not a single clue. Frantic, I run to the bedroom, snag my keys and wallet, and pat my pocket to make sure I have my phone. When everything is accounted for, I jog down the stairs, past Jaz, and straight out to my car, but I come to an abrupt halt when I catch a glimpse of my tires.

Slashed.

Every.

Single.

One.

Motherfucker.

I turn to find Jaz standing behind me, arms crossed.

"What the actual fuck, Jaz."

"It's Jazlyn to you." She nods toward my tires. "I saw you in that cabin with your *ex-girlfriend*. You thought you were being so stealthy. I warned you, you know. Do not fuck with my girl."

"I didn't!" I yell.

"Uh-huh, so these pictures I have of you on my phone embracing your ex mean nothing?"

"Yes!" I push my hand through my hair as my heart hammers in my chest. "They mean nothing. Christ, did you send them to Fallon?"

"What do you think?"

My anger boils over, my frustration hits its tipping point, and before I know what I'm doing, I'm screaming at Jaz. "You had no right to send her any goddamn photos. You might be her best friend, but I'm her goddamn boyfriend."

"Why are you getting so defensive? Screams guilty to me."

"What the actual fuck?" I say as I turn away from her, too distraught to even deal with her bullshit right now. I fish my phone out of my pocket and dial Roarick's number. The phone rings twice before he picks up.

"You know, I just found a smashed grape on the ground, and it oddly reminded me of you."

"I need you to come pick me up, right now."

"Huh?"

"Sully, he's in the hospital. Jaz slashed my tires, and I need a ride. Please, just hurry."

"Shit. Okay. Why did she slash your tires?"

"I'll explain later, just get here."

I hang up and turn back to Jaz, who's still standing there, tapping her foot. I don't bother talking to her. I move past her and head toward the residence while I shoot off a text to Fallon, who's most likely driving.

I'm not even sure what happened to Sully—my stomach twists at the thought—and I'm almost positive I won't find out from Jaz.

Sawyer: Fallon, just heard you're headed to the hospital with Sully. Long story, but I won't be there for two hours. I'm coming as quickly as I can. Whatever Jaz has said to you, ignore it. I love you.

Now let the waiting begin.

❖ ❖ ❖

"Why are you still holding that shoe?"

"Huh?" I ask as I look down at the powder-blue shoe clutched in my hand.

"I mean, when I first picked you up and saw it, I figured maybe you were too distraught to talk about it, but it's been a half hour, and you're still holding on to it. Should I be worried?"

I stare down at my phone, waiting for any sort of signal that Sully and Fallon are okay, but it's been radio silence. Which only means one thing—whatever photos Jaz sent must be pretty damning.

"Hello, earth to Sawyer. Are you going to talk to me, man?"

I slouch in the passenger seat and stare out the window as we head out of the mountains, coming closer to Palm Springs. The hospital's emergency room is the closest one to Canoodle, so I'm hoping this is where she's headed. I attempted to get more information from Jaz via text, but her response was a middle finger emoji followed by a knife emoji. I've always felt like I've gotten along with Jaz. We had a unique relationship where we pretended to not like each other, but Fallon even said she's been an advocate for us getting together. This lightning-fast switch has me wondering if I've been wrong this entire time.

"Dude, you need to talk to me."

"I'm just trying not to fucking lose it right now," I shoot back at him.

"I can see that, but it might help if you actually talk about it."

"You want to talk about it?" I say aggressively. "Fine. Annalisa came to visit me."

"Uh, say what?"

"Yeah, and because Sully was already having a bad day and Fallon was trying to calm him down, I didn't want to make her more upset with Annalisa—so I pulled her into a cabin to see what the hell she wanted."

"Oooh, that feels incriminating."

"She told me she was sorry, did all this bullshit apologizing, and then gave me this shoe. This stupid fucking shoe." I throw it to the floor of Roarick's Jeep Rubicon.

"An odd parting gift, but I can see the desire for a full-circle moment."

"And then, when we exited the cabin, Jaz was standing there with a murderous look on her face. Apparently, she saw us in the cabin and immediately thought the worst."

"Oh shit, now there's an unexpected twist. Usually, it's the girlfriend who sees the boyfriend with the ex. But the best friend—that's kind of a nice change."

"Why the fuck are you joking about this?"

"Oh, I'm sorry, did you not call me to lighten the mood? I must have missed the memo."

"What the fuck is actually wrong with you?" I ask.

"Dude, I'm trying to calm you down—usually this works."

"Well, read the goddamn room—"

"Technically, we're in a car."

"I'm going to fucking punch you in the goddamn eye."

He winces. "Yeah, that last one was pushing my luck. Okay, so Jaz finds out—what happens next?"

"She of course thought I was cheating, slashed my tires, and then told me Sully and Fallon were headed to the emergency room."

"Ah, and then you called me, your knight in shining armor. Makes sense. Well, did you clear the air with Jaz?"

"I tried. But she doesn't believe a goddamn word I said."

"Really?" Roarick asks, his brow pinched now. "That doesn't seem like her."

"Are you sure about that? Because it almost feels like she's had it in for me from the very beginning."

Roarick shakes his head. "No, she's told me a few times how she thinks you two are good for each other."

"Then what the hell? She has photos, and she sent them to Fallon."

"Seriously?" The disbelief in Roarick's voice actually makes me feel better. "I mean, clearly nothing happened between you and Annalisa, right?"

"Of course not. Christ. As if I would ever want to do anything with her, especially when I have Fallon, who is light-years ahead of anything Annalisa could ever strive to be. I let her clear the air for her conscience, but that was it. I told her about Fallon, how I love her, and she completely accepted all of that. She was actually on her way to some retreat. She wasn't here to win me back. And of course Jaz wouldn't let me explain any of that."

Instead of responding, Roarick just stares out the windshield, deep in thought. I join him, willing my phone to vibrate. Any news. Just anything so I can know that they're okay.

But the longer we drive and the closer we get to the hospital, the more I realize that I very well might be fucked.

Chapter

Twenty-Three

FALLON

All I can hear, over and over in my head, is Sully's body, thumping to the floor.

On repeat.

Thump.

Thump.

Thump.

Followed by a low groan.

I can still see him, on the floor, almost lifeless, unable to move. I left the room for a second, to check on his bedroom and make sure he didn't leave anything on the floor after getting dressed. I picked up his clothes to start a load of laundry, and then everything went to hell.

It's a miracle Jaz and I were able to carefully get him into my car. I realize moving someone who fell might not have been the best of ideas, but he fell after he injured himself, a large gash across his palm. My medical training kicked in, and I went right to work by cutting off the bleeding with a clean, tightly wrapped rag and fastening a sling to keep his hand at heart level. After that, I assessed the rest of him and realized he'd fallen on his right side, so we carefully got him in the car, the passenger seat reclined, and I rushed him down the mountain. It would have taken longer if I'd called for an ambulance—this was the best option.

My grip was so tight on the steering wheel as I drove that I felt my fingers melting into it as I begged Grandma Joan, over and over, to make sure he was okay. Because this happened on my watch. I never should have let him handle that knife on his own while cutting a bagel. I never should have left him alone like he asked me to. I know better than that, especially when he's not lucid.

Thankfully I still have friends at the hospital, because I called when I was five minutes away and begged them to have a stretcher at the entrance for him. When I pulled up, they were waiting. They carefully unloaded an unconscious Sully and wheeled him into the emergency room while I parked the car.

On the way in, I called my dads, who are just outside of Phoenix, scoping out some new properties to expand their Airbnb business. They got on the road immediately to come home.

And after I hung up with them, I saw all the text messages.

One from Sawyer, telling me he was on his way and to not listen to anything Jaz was saying. When I checked out the text messages from Jaz, I only found messages asking if Sully was okay. Telling me I was strong and she was there for me if I needed anything.

After that, I went up to the nurses' station, where I found Gardenia, the head nurse, and asked her if she knew anything on Sully. She said they were stitching him up, and then they were going to put him through some x-rays and a CT scan to determine if anything was wrong.

They got me a cup of the good coffee and helped me back to my seat, where I've been waiting ever since, rocking back and forth, willing the thumping to leave my head.

I consider texting Jaz back, asking her what the hell Sawyer is talking about, but I know whatever it is, I don't have the energy to deal with it right now. Those two are always getting into it with each other—the last thing I need to deal with is some small squabble.

The doors to the exam rooms open, and a familiar face appears.

Peter.

For the life of me, I didn't even consider running into him here. The thought never crossed my mind, but now that he's here, a friend in a sea of uncertainty, I burst into a fit of tears. Embarrassed, I bury my head in my hands, and in seconds, he's sitting beside me, his strong arm wrapped around my shoulders.

"It's going to be okay," Peter says as I lean into his embrace and rest my head against his shoulder. He pulls me in tight. "Shhh, it's okay, Fallon."

"I shouldn't have let him use the knife—that was beyond stupid of me. I was just so distracted with the cabins, I was thoughtless."

"Hey, this is not your fault," Peter says softly. "This is not your fault at all. These things happen with our older patients. As much as you want to protect him all the time, you can't."

"I always hide the knives, but I was so tired I forgot to put that one away after it dried. God, Peter, what was I thinking?"

"This is a lot to handle, Fallon. You can't be perfect."

"He's my grandfather; I have to be perfect for him. I have to be able to protect him. And the thump of him hitting the ground. That's all I can hear, over and over again. I know he hit his head as well—there was a bruise forming in the car."

"Hey." Peter presses his fingers to my chin and forces me to look at him. "This was an accident. No one's to blame. We're running all the tests, and I'll make sure he's okay."

My eyes search his, tears streaming down my cheeks as I slowly nod. "Thank you, Peter."

"Anything for you, Fallon. Anything." He smiles, but something catches his eyes from over my shoulder, and that smile fades. His gaze returns to mine. "I'll be back with more information. Okay?"

I nod and loop my hand behind his neck as I pull him in close for a hug, our cheeks pressing together. "Thank you, Peter."

"You're welcome." As he stands, our hands connect, and he gives mine a squeeze before taking off. I watch him walk away, through the electronic doors and down the hallway. When he's out of view, I turn back to my phone, but a movement catches my eye, and I look up to see Sawyer standing a few feet away.

And his expression is murderous.

"I see that you didn't take a second to even consider my text before moving on."

"What?" I ask, completely and utterly confused.

"I told Jaz, nothing happened between me and Annalisa. I asked you to trust me, and yet here you are, snuggling into your ex."

Annalisa?

He was with Annalisa? When?

My mind whirls, trying to remember a moment where we were apart long enough for him to even see her.

"Jesus Christ, Fallon, you couldn't have even waited an hour for me to explain."

The stress of Sully combined with his senseless accusation has me tipping over the edge with anger. "Don't tell me you are accusing me of being with Peter?"

"What the hell am I supposed to expect?" Insecurity is laced in his every word, squeezing the syllables extra tight. In the back of my mind, I can partially understand where this is coming from—his experience with Annalisa—but what he's saying is so insulting, during a moment when I don't need it, that all rational thought is thrown out the window.

Because I need him. I need him to put us first. To put me first, because I have no other option than to put Sully first in my life. I thought Sawyer understood that from the very beginning. He made it seem like I truly wasn't alone in this scary journey of being my grandfather's caretaker, but today . . . I've never felt more alone in my life.

I rise out of my chair and walk up to him. "I suggest you lower your voice and choose your words wisely."

"I know Jaz sent you the pictures of me and Annalisa at the cabins. But I'm telling you right now, nothing happened."

Uh . . . excuse me?

Call it stress.

Call it being mentally exhausted, but hearing she was at the Cove—the woman who broke him—sends me into a tailspin of doubt.

"And I didn't tell you she was there because I know you were dealing with Sully this morning. I took her into the cabin because she wanted to talk. Nothing else."

I take a step back, my mind whirling. "Hold on a goddamn second—she was here this morning? You were with her? So, when I screamed down the stairs for help, because Sully fell, the reason you weren't there was because you were with *Annalisa*?"

Pain flickers in his eyes. "I didn't . . . I didn't know. You know I would have—"

"And then, when I'm here in the waiting room of the hospital, worrying about my grandfather, instead of asking how he's doing, the first thing you do is accuse me of being with another man?"

"Fuck," he whispers while pulling on his hair. "Listen, Fallon, I—"

"No, you listen." I jab a finger into his chest. "Jaz never said a thing to me—all she's done is be supportive, so whatever this Annalisa bullshit is, it's news to me." His face blanches, his expression going stark with regret. "And not that I need to explain myself to you, but Peter was doing nothing other than consoling me as a friend and telling me that everything was going to be okay. So, you barging in here with the idea that I'm running back to my ex, when I have no idea what's going on with my grandfather, is disgusting."

"Fallon, I'm sorry."

"Save it, Sawyer." I move away from him and take a seat again. When he moves to sit next to me, I hold my hand up. "Unless you want to be dragged out of here by security—because I have friends here—then I suggest you leave on your own accord."

"Fallon," he says, his voice breaking. "Let me at least be here with you."

"Honestly, Sawyer, you're the last person I want around me right now." I grip my phone and look away. "Now leave, or I'll make sure you're escorted out of here."

I turn away so I don't have to be witness to the look of devastation on his face. I can't.

I can't shoulder the burden of his pain.

Not right now.

I need to focus on one thing—making sure Sully is okay. I will never forgive myself if he isn't.

❖   ❖   ❖

I am so grateful that the nursing staff loves me here. They've been taking care of me while I wait alone to hear about Sully. My friend Daniel sat with me on his break. We talked about his latest crush, Mark, an anesthesiologist in the OR, who is apparently a comedian in his spare time. Daniel has been to ten of his shows: two Mark knows about, eight where he hid in the back in disguise.

When Daniel's break was done, Mary Fran sat with me and shared her caramel M&M'S while she told me about the fortieth anniversary party she'd shared with her dear husband, Joe. There was a balloon artist for the grandkids, and one of the balloons popped in her sister's face, making her slightly pee her pants—I got a chuckle out of that.

And then Peter came and sat with me again. He didn't ask about Sawyer, and I didn't tell him. Instead, he told me about a spinach-artichoke dip recipe he'd made last week, only he used way too much spinach and the whole thing turned into a green brick. He left it in his trash, which was ransacked by raccoons. He was happy at least someone ate it.

They've all kept me busy, but in the back of my mind, all I could think about was Sully.

"Hey, Fallon," Peter says, pulling me from my thoughts. I glance up from my phone, where I've been mindlessly playing some brick game. "You can come back."

I launch out of my seat and hurry to Peter's side. He gently places his hand on my back. "Sully's doing okay. You were right about him hitting his head. He has some bruising that's spread pretty drastically, but as you know, that happens with our older patients. We're monitoring the head injury more carefully. There's no internal bleeding, which is a great sign, but given his condition, we're taking extra precautions. We scanned his body, looking for fractures, and he came out clear. He's a sturdy man."

That makes me smile in relief.

"His hand is bandaged up and looking good. There's a lot of bruising as well, but thank God his granddaughter was a nurse—you did all the right things to ensure he was safe and taken care of as you drove him down the mountain. He's very lucky to have you."

I shake my head. "He's not. This wouldn't have happened—"

Peter stops me in the hallway and grips my shoulder, his caring eyes looking in mine. "This was an accident. Do you hear me? You can't protect him every second of every day. As a caregiver to someone with Alzheimer's, this is going to happen. Frankly, the fact that this is the only occurrence in the time he's been in your care is astonishing. You should be very proud. I'd like to talk to you about the rugs I know are in your house, though. I think it might be smart to remove those, to avoid any other slipping."

I nod as I try to catch my breath.

"Hey." He tilts my chin up. "He's okay. You're okay. Everything is going to be fine. We'll keep him here for the next couple of days, just to make sure we didn't miss anything, but he'll be going home with you."

I nod again as tears stream down my cheeks. Peter pulls me into a hug, and I wrap my arms around him, burying my head into his chest.

There's nothing romantic about the hug, not one single spark lights up in my heart, but I need it all the same, the comfort I'm missing with Jaz watching over the cabins and my dads on their way here. I'm grateful for Peter.

I pull away. "Thank you, Peter."

"Just doing my job."

I shake my head. "No, thank you for being a friend when I needed one the most."

His expression softens. "I'll always be here for you, Fallon. We'll always have a piece of each other in our hearts, no matter where life takes us or who enters our lives." He doesn't mention Sawyer, but I know he's curious. A conversation for another day.

"Thank you. Can I see him?"

"Of course." Peter guides me down to Sully's room. "He's sleeping right now, but you can go in there. The nursing staff has set up the room for you to stay overnight."

"Thank you so much," I say as we reach Sully's room.

Peter opens the door for me. "I'll give you some alone time. Ring if you need anything."

I give him one more hug before entering the quiet private room. The lights are dimmed, offering just enough light for the medical staff to be able to see what they're doing when they come in to check on him. And cloaked in a white blanket, sleeping peacefully in bed, is Sully.

I know he's okay.

Peter said he'd be just fine.

And yet seeing him like this pierces my already-shattered heart, and I break down as I walk over to his bed. The nursing staff has already situated a chair next to him, so I take a seat and carefully grip his worn and weathered hand in mine. His bandaged hand is propped up in a sling, and just like Peter said, there's significant bruising around his head, which looks very alarming to the naked eye. Thank God I know better.

"Hey, you stubborn old man," I say as tears rain down my cheeks. "You realize you aged me about ten years today. My glowing skin is a pale green now. I hope you're happy." I lean down and press a kiss to the back of his hand. "I love you very much; I need you to know that. And I'm not sure how long we have together, but I'll tell you this—I will care for you as long as I can, as long as I can keep you safe and with your people and your town." I press the back of his hand to my cheek. "But . . . every single rug in the residence is going to be removed, whether you like it or not."

I chuckle and heave a sigh of relief as I rest my head on the edge of his bed, clutching his hand, silently thanking Grandma Joan for watching over him.

I know Sully's time is coming to a close; I realize he's not going to get better. We're just prolonging the inevitable, but I'm not ready to say goodbye either.

I need more memories.

I need the sweet smell of his soap to wrap me in a hug.

I need the comfort of his grumpy voice to cut through the silence.

I need to see him sitting at his bench, talking to his Joan.

And I need more of his stories, more of his love, more of . . . him.

Thankfully, I still have more time to capture all of that.

❖ ❖ ❖

"Why don't you go take a walk," Dad says as he places a hand on my shoulder.

They arrived about an hour ago, in a complete tizzy, then called Peter into the room and made him repeat everything he'd told me. It wasn't until he'd reassured them for the third time that Sully was going to be okay that they finally relaxed.

"Yes, you should probably stretch your legs," Papa adds.

"Fresh air might be nice. There's a bench just outside the hospital that looks comfortable."

"Very comfortable," Papa confirms as they exchange glances.

They're being weird.

"What's going on?" I ask.

Papa looks at Dad.

Dad looks at Papa, and then they both turn to me.

"Sweetie, Sawyer is sitting outside," Dad says. "Apparently he's been there for hours. I'm not sure what's going on with you two, but I do know he looks absolutely terrible."

As he should.

"Positively ghastly," Papa adds with a shiver. "Like a shell of a man." He takes a sip of his coffee. "Care to explain why?"

"No," I answer, my heart aching in my chest at the mention of Sawyer. There was nothing I wanted more today than to have Sawyer at my side, holding my hand, offering me a hug whenever I needed it. I really needed him, and he let me down. No, not only did he let me down, but he insulted me. He questioned my love for him, and that hurts more than anything.

"Ah, I see," Papa says. "You know, she gets that stubbornness from your side of the family."

Dad raises his hand. "Guilty." He then grows serious. "Whatever happened between you two, I can tell it's hit him hard. And if he's the one who screwed up, which I'm assuming is the case because men seem to have that bone in their body, you can tell he's extremely regretful."

I don't say anything because I honestly don't know what to say. Sawyer hurt me. Instead of being there for me, he stabbed me with an insult.

"He's been out there for a while," Papa adds.

Hours. I doubt he ever left. He probably exited the building and took up residence at his bench. Never once budging, because that's the type of guy he is.

"I think I'm going to take a walk," I say as I stand from my chair. "Do you guys need anything?"

"We're good," Dad says, offering me a knowing smile.

I excuse myself from the room, cell phone in hand, and pull up my text messages. I hover over Jaz's name, but instead I click on Sawyer's.

I don't bother rereading his previous text message; instead, I type up a text.

Fallon: Sully is going to be okay. My dads said you're sitting outside. The best thing you can do for yourself is leave. I can't even begin to think about you right now. Please just go home.

I send the text and continue to walk down the hallway to the elevators. When I press the down button, my phone buzzes in my hand. I brace myself.

Sawyer: I'm so glad he's okay. I'm so sorry, Fallon, that I fucked this up. I want you to know how much I love you.

I stare down at his text, my pulse picking up, my heart bleeding for this man. I want nothing more than to go outside and run into his arms, but the bruise on my soul is eating me alive. And I need to find out what the hell happened.

When I reach the cafeteria, instead of grabbing something to eat, I find my favorite table in the back—I used to sit here every day because it rests under a large indoor tree, offering peace in the hustle and bustle of the hospital. It reminded me so much of the Cove. I take a seat and dial up Jaz's number.

"Oh my God, how is he?" Jaz says in a panic.

"He's okay," I say. "Lots of bruising, but nothing is fractured or broken. And he's all stitched up. They're keeping him for monitoring, but hopefully he'll be out of here in a day or so."

"Thank Jesus," she says in relief. "Christ, I've been a goddamn wreck over here. I don't know how you're handling it."

"My dads are here now, and Peter's been a real help, along with the nursing staff. I'm really grateful."

"I'm glad."

Then silence falls over the phone.

"Sawyer showed up."

"I knew he would," Jaz says, a bite in her tone.

"What happened, Jaz?"

"He didn't tell you?"

"He did, but I want to hear it from you."

She clears her throat. "Maybe this isn't the best time."

"I need to know because honestly, the interaction I had with him was less than ideal, and it's going to eat away at me if I don't find out what's going on."

"Are you sure?"

"Yes."

"Okay." I can hear her shift around. "When I arrived, he was grabbing the key to cabin one. When I asked him what he was doing, he said he was checking on it before Margaret O'Hare arrived—which, by the way, the freaking potato of a woman just checked in. I didn't think much of it. I was passing the time with sharpening my switchblade when I heard you call up for help. So, I ran to get Sawyer and saw him with Annalisa through the window of the cabin. She was taking her sweater off, and he was gripping her hips. Pure rage took over my body. I ran back to the residence to help you get Sully in your car, and once you drove away I slashed his tires. When I went to go confront him, she was pressing a kiss to his cheek and taking off. She gave him that stupid blue shoe that he left behind. The whole thing was despicable."

"Hold on." I pause. "So, in the time between getting Sully into the car, you're assuming that Sawyer had some sort of . . . *affair* with Annalisa?"

"I mean, the evidence is there."

I think back to all the late-night conversations I've had with Sawyer, the multiple times he said he was over Annalisa. How he couldn't even fathom getting back together with her after everything she'd put him through. And I believed him.

I still do.

Because if anything, Sawyer has been sincere from the very beginning.

And despite the way he treated me today, he told me he loves me.

"Jaz, I'm not sure what you saw is what you think you saw."

"What do you mean? They were touching; they were in a cabin together. Why would he bring her into a cabin?"

"From what he told me, he knew I was having a rough morning with Sully, and he didn't want to make it worse."

"Uh-huh, and you believe that?"

I think about it. Even though I feel absolutely wrecked by his words, the way he treated me, accused me, I know deep down that he was telling the truth.

"I do."

"Seriously?"

"Jaz, you know I love you, deeply. But I also know you're still struggling with how Brad treated you. And even though you say you're over it, I think you're still upset over catching him with another woman—you might be projecting your feelings onto Sawyer."

There's silence on the other end of the phone.

"You there?" I ask.

"God damn it, Fallon. You know I don't ever like to be wrong, but I think . . . I think I messed up."

"It happens to the best of us."

"I'm so sorry. I hope I didn't ruin anything for you two."

I shake my head, even though she can't see me. "No, Sawyer did that on his own."

"Wait . . . what happened?"

I glance up at the tree stretching overhead, its small, dollar-size leaves providing much-needed life in such a sterile environment. "When he got here, he saw Peter consoling me, assumed the worst—you two are very much alike in that aspect—and accused me of turning to another man."

"What an idiot." I can hear the disappointment in her voice. "Then again, we knew he had idiot potential by the way he came storming into town with one shoe and the desire to forget." Normally a comment like that would make me laugh, but I just feel dead inside. "What are you going to do?"

"I don't know," I say. "He really hurt me. He didn't even ask how Sully was—just started accusing me. It was embarrassing and humiliating and . . . God, he broke me down. I thought we were stronger than that, you know?"

"I do." I can practically hear her thinking on the other side of the phone. "From personal experience, though, as someone who's been hurt like that, sometimes you sort of . . . black out, when you assume the worst and say things you don't mean."

"I can understand that," I reply. "But I just can't get over the fact that he assumed the worst. I thought we were in a much better place than that. And what about the countless hours we spent getting to know each other? He should understand my character at this point to know I would never do something like that." I wipe away at a stray tear that came out of nowhere. "And the worst of it is, he's the first man I said 'I love you' to, and despite it all . . . I still love him. Ache for him. Wish he was here."

"Then tell him that."

"I can't," I say, holding back a sob. "I'm too shattered, Jaz."

I tilt my head back, attempting to keep my tears in place, but it's no use—they free-fall down the side of my face as the pain of his words blisters my heart . . .

Chapter

Twenty-Four

SAWYER

"So . . . this feels awkward," Roarick says as he drives me back to our parents' vineyard. "You know, since I thought you cleared the air with Fallon."

"Can we not talk?" I stare out the window of Roarick's Jeep.

"Sure, we don't have to talk. We can just sit here and act like nothing of significance happened today. If that's what you want. I have other things to talk about, like how Mom and Dad took off to Italy, giving me a day's notice. Don't they know grape season is right around the corner? *Suuuuure*, we have staff, and *suuuuuure*, we don't technically need to be there, but what if there's a grape emergency—am I supposed to just handle that on my own? And if I were to be perfectly frank with you, I'm not even sure I like grapes anymore. I sure as hell don't like wine. So what am I really doing with my life, Sawyer? Huh, care to answer that?"

I press my fingers into my temples. "Jesus Christ, just stop talking."

"It's cute how you think I can just drive in silence. I gave you your silent time on the way down the mountain; now you have to deal with all that pent-up chatter. Hey, I'm hungry. Want some In-N-Out?" He points to the iconic yellow-and-red sign up on the left. "I could really see myself with a Double-Double and strawberry milkshake."

"I'm not hungry."

"Too bad, we have to eat." He veers off to the left, avoiding traffic, and pulls into a long drive-through lane. "Wow, looks like we have some time before we order. In-N-Out is always busy, for good reason, but man, what should we talk about. Hmmm . . . something to talk about, something to talk about . . ."

"Why are you the most annoying human to ever walk the planet?"

"You should be kind to the brother who's driven all around Southern California for you."

"It's hard to be kind when you won't leave me alone."

"For good reason." He grows serious. "You're clearly hurting, and I've seen you hurt before. I've seen the way you shrink into yourself, and I'm not going to let that happen again, so let's just get it all out in the open. Why aren't you currently back at the hospital with Fallon?"

He's right. After everything went down between Annalisa and Simon, I did sink into a dark hole. I drew the shades on my life and didn't come up for air until the studio pulled me out for press. And we all know how that went.

We move forward one car length in the drive-through line, and I know he chose this on purpose, to keep me in his car so I'm forced to talk. This In-N-Out is notorious for taking forever. We'll be here for at least the next half hour.

Guess there's only one thing I can do.

"When I arrived, I found Fallon, but she wasn't alone—she was with Peter."

"The ex-boyfriend?"

"Yeah." I smooth my hand over my mouth.

"Uh-oh, I'm guessing your jealousies roared to life in the nastiest of ways."

"You could say that," I say. "Accused her of moving on to another man." God, just thinking about the things I said to her makes me so goddamn sick to my stomach. And I know I projected my past relationship and mistrust onto Fallon when she least deserved it, when she's shown me nothing but loyalty. And here I thought I'd mentally recovered from the drama of Annalisa and Simon, but looks like I still have some work to do.

Roarick lets out a low whistle. "Oh yeah, that hurts."

"Didn't even ask her how Sully was."

"Yikes, dude."

"And then in a panic apologized after she told me to choose my words carefully."

Roarick rubs his chest. "Damn, I think I'm having secondary chest pains. Is that a thing?"

"No." I shake my head. "But if you want an example of a massive fuckup, this would be it."

"Oh yeah, easily. This goes down in history as one of man's greatest idiotic moments, because you and I both know she wasn't getting back with Peter."

"Yeah, I know."

"He was probably just a friendly face, someone to lean on."

"Yup," I answer.

"And when she saw you, she was probably so relieved—until you opened your mouth."

"Can't argue there."

"So, we agree, you're a moron."

I slowly nod my head. "Yeah."

"And that you dumped all your past trauma on Fallon, accusing her of something she'd never do because your brain decided she must be acting exactly like Annalisa did when you were with her."

I heave out a "Yup."

"Ah, classic damaged-hero mistake. Instead of pausing, taking a breath, and using his brain, he reacts like a fool, creating the dark moment that everyone dreads but also looks forward to—who doesn't enjoy dancing in someone else's pain? I do. honestly, I could bust out in a Frank Sinatra–inspired tap number, cane and top hat included. Kind of funny how you write these romantic movies that everyone fawns over, and now you're living it, making the same dumb mistakes."

"Have you been studying up on screenplays or something? Jesus."

"No." He pulls forward another spot. "Just watching a lot of movies lately. You'd be surprised to hear Jaz is a closet rom-com fan, so I've been watching her favorites."

"I thought you only spoke to her in meme form."

"Yeah, for the most part—there's something so special about picking the right meme to convey how you're feeling."

"It's lazy."

"Romantic advice . . . *really, Sawyer?*"

"Fuck off," I say, crossing my arms over my chest.

"Mature, very mature." He falls silent for a few seconds, and I welcome it, but it doesn't last long. "You need to apologize to her."

"I know."

"Sooner rather than later."

"Plan on it."

"Maybe include some sort of grand gesture."

I shake my head. "That's where you're wrong. I've already performed the grand gestures. This isn't a moment where I knock down the community center like in *Two Weeks Notice* or proclaim my love in front of the entire company like in *The Proposal*. This needs to be an intimate apology, a meaningful one."

"Sooo, you don't want me to call up my friend Huxley Cane who owns Cane Enterprises in LA and ask him if he can connect me with his billboard guy? Set up a fivefold campaign that shows how apologetic you are so when she drives home, she'll see your face on every corner?"

"I honestly can't stand you."

He chuckles. "Sad, because I fucking love myself."

It's obvious.

❖   ❖   ❖

Roarick leans back in his chair and pats his stomach. "Fucking animal-style—does it get any better than that?"

We're sitting out on the patio of our parents' house, looking out over the lush green vineyard. As I watched my brother devour his food like a goddamn beast, all I could think about was how much I wished Fallon was with me here instead. She'd love this view—the sun setting over the endless rows upon rows of vines that disappear over the hill.

"You're gross."

"Please, as if you didn't burp while taking down your single cheeseburger. Sorry about the tomato, by the way; In-N-Out always gets the order correct."

It's just my luck that they didn't remove the tomato on my burger. That's the universe telling me I deserve it after today.

I took my penance and flicked it into the to-go bag.

"So, what's the plan?" Roarick asks.

"I don't know."

"Wow, can't wait to see you win her back with that. Call the Nobel Peace Prize committee—I think we have an entry based merely on thought."

The snarky comments. The sarcasm. The annoying wit of my brother is tipping me over the edge. I'm about to toss my chair at him when I hear someone clearing their voice behind us.

In tandem, both Roarick and I turn around to find Jaz standing behind us, hands folded in front of her, looking . . . nervous.

Actually nervous.

I'm not sure I've ever seen this side of Jaz. She's either aggressive, sarcastic, or barely tolerating my presence. But this side, this uneasiness, is new. She's showing a vulnerable side that I didn't think existed.

"Sugarplum, what are you doing here?" Roarick asks.

Sugarplum? What the hell is that?

"I need to talk to Sawyer."

"Sure," Roarick says, standing. His voice has morphed from that of sarcastic asshole to concerned loved one. "You can have my seat." When Jaz walks over to us, Roarick places his hand on her hip and leans down, pressing a kiss to her cheek. "You look good."

Uh, what the hell is happening? I thought they were just texting—I didn't think there was anything actually going on.

"Thank you," she murmurs before taking a seat.

Roarick gathers our trash and leaves us to ourselves. Once he's out of earshot, Jaz's eyes connect with mine. "I need to tell you how sorry I am, Sawyer."

Well. She just shocked the hell out of me.

I'm tempted to make a scene by wiggling my finger in my ear to see if I heard her right, but I refrain. No one likes a gloater. Jaz most likely doesn't tolerate them.

"I should have given you a chance to explain before jumping to conclusions," she continues. "Miscommunication never helps anyone, and here I was, participating in it. Not that it's an excuse, but I was frazzled that Sully was hurt, and when I saw you with Annalisa, I could only think that you were cheating on my best friend. I just . . . lost my cool."

"I understand the feeling," I say before sighing and slouching in my chair. "I did the same thing to Fallon."

"So I heard." She glances out toward the vineyard. "I don't want to admit it, but I think we have a lot more in common than I like to let on. We've both been hurt, we've both had our trust broken, and we both hold insecurities that were brought on by others." She turns toward me now, eyes wide and concerned, and I realize this is the most real I've ever seen Jaz. Yes, she's fun, she's kind of crazy, and that can be charming in a friendship, but there's no doubt in my mind that this side of Jaz—the vulnerable side—is why Fallon is friends with her. "Let's make a promise to each other, moving forward, that we won't let other people's short-comings ruin our lives." She lends out her hand, and without giving it a second thought, I take it.

"Deal," I say, shaking on it.

When we release hands, she says, "I really am sorry, and I'll do everything I can to help you fix this."

I take a deep breath, feeling relieved for the first time since Fallon banished me from the hospital. "Does this mean we're past the probation period and are now officially friends?"

She smirks. "It does." She points her finger at me. "But you'll always be Julia to me."

I shrug. "I've kind of grown fond of the name."

"Good." She leans back in her seat. "Now, let's formulate a plan, because I'm never going to be able to forgive myself if you two don't make up."

"Same, *Jaz* . . . same."

She smiles at my use of her nickname, and to my surprise, she doesn't say anything. Instead, she pulls out her phone and starts hashing out a plan with me.

CHAPTER

TWENTY-FIVE
FALLON

"Will you stop fussing over me?" Sully shoos my hand away as I'm fluffing his pillow.

"I just want to make sure you're comfortable."

"I'm perfectly fine, other than the fact that you've rolled up every rug in this godforsaken place. The wood is cold on my feet."

"I'll get you slippers, with grips. You'll be fine. No more slipping hazards."

"You treat me like a child," he grumbles.

I take a seat on the edge of his bed, the overhead light shining above us. We weren't released from the hospital until late—and after two days there, we were itching to leave. My dads wanted to take Sully back to their place for a few days, but Sully pitched a fit, insisting he wanted to be in his own home, where he could be with Joan. We all decided it would be best to just bring him back to Canoodle.

"I don't mean to treat you like a child—I'm just trying to make things safe for you, because I love you so much and I don't want you to get hurt again. Can you understand that?" I place my hand in his good hand.

The scowl in his brow eases as he nods.

"Thank you. Now, if you're comfortable, I'm going to go check on the Cove. Faye's granddaughter, Minnie, has been running the front desk, and I want to make sure everything is good. Jaz gave her a quick and dirty rundown, but I'm sure it wasn't enough."

"Okay. I'm comfortable." He squeezes my hand. "Thank you, Fallon. I'm sorry I scared you."

"Please don't apologize. I'm just happy you're okay."

"I am."

I lean in and give him a kiss on the cheek before standing and heading to the door.

"You know, I feel very honored that you're my granddaughter," he says as I reach the door. When I turn to meet his gaze, his eyes are wet, and the sight nearly brings me to my knees. "You could have chosen a different life, but you chose me." He wipes at his eyes. I start to move toward him, but he holds up his hand, stopping me. "Grandma Joan would be very proud to call you her granddaughter, proud of all the love and patience you've given me. I'm not sure if I say this enough, but I'm very grateful for you, Fallon." He sucks in a sharp breath. "I love you."

"I love you too," I say, my voice catching in my throat.

He nods and closes his eyes as he rests his hands on his stomach. "You know, sometimes the best things in life are worth waiting for."

Huh?

Where did that come from?

"There were multiple times I messed up with Grandma Joan," he continues, "but I knew in the long run we built our love off a foundation of friendship, and that was a love worth waiting for. You waited for true love, so don't let it slip through your fingers because of your partner's self-doubt. If Grandma Joan let that happen to me, we never would have grown the kind of love that lasts a lifetime."

I stand there, aghast. How on earth . . . ?

He peeks one eye open and smirks. "I'm not completely inept. I heard you speaking to your fathers. Not sure who this man is, but if he can cause you such pain, there's a reason. Like I said, Fallon, sometimes the best things are worth waiting for . . . even if you have to sift through the mud while waiting for them."

Is that what Sawyer and I are going through? Some muddy waters?

He shifts on the bed. "Good night, Fallon."

"Good night," I reply softly as I close the door to his room, my mind swirling with what Sully is trying to convey. His words hold truth, a heaviness to them that I wasn't quite expecting. Grandma Joan told me many years ago that Sully drove her nuts at times. That there were more than enough occasions when he was "in the doghouse"—and then I remember her reaching over and squeezing my arm, a smile on her face as she told me it was just part of the joy that came with loving someone.

Love isn't perfect.

Love is a challenge, and Grandma Joan and Sully were the perfect example of that.

I check my phone to make sure the monitor notifications are on and then slink into my room. I change out of my clothes and into a pair of cotton shorts and a simple white T-shirt in an attempt to shed the memory of the hospital. When I toss my clothes in the hamper, I spot Sawyer's suitcase, open, his clothes still neatly tucked inside.

Unable to stop myself, I slide down to the floor and pull out one of his shirts. I bring it to my nose and take in a deep sniff. Memories flash through my mind at the scent.

Sawyer walking into the bar in that hideous powder-blue suit, missing one shoe.

Sawyer filling up his water bottle, a smirk on his face, knowing damn well I can't stop looking at him with his shirt off.

Sawyer holding my hand on our first date, staring up at the stars in the hut he built just for us.

Sawyer telling me how much he loves me, making me feel the meaning of those words to my very core.

He might have hurt me, but Sully's right: self-doubt can drive us to do and say stupid things. Things we don't mean.

I need to talk to him. I reach for my phone but realize I can't talk to him until I settle things with Minnie, who's been more than a trooper about handling things during this mess.

Pulling myself together, I head downstairs and catch Minnie sitting at the desk, creating an Excel sheet on the computer of all the reservations and notes about each guest, notes she must have taken when talking to them.

"Hey," I say as I walk up behind her.

"Oh, hey." Minnie saves the sheet and exits out of it. "How's Sully?"

"He's good. Thank you so much for your help. I can't tell you how grateful I am."

"Please, what are small towns for? Plus, this has been an amazing experience. I've been looking for an internship with a small business. I love my grandma and all, but the trolls . . . too much. This is perfect. I can't thank Jaz enough for setting it up."

Internship? Oh, that clever, clever Jaz.

"Not a problem at all. Once things settle down, maybe we can speak more about the internship and make it official."

"That would be great." She hops off the stool. "The lights at the picnic table are still on—I wasn't sure how to turn them off."

"No worries, I can go turn them off."

"Oh, and I took it upon myself to do some Instagram posts for you. They seem to be picking up traction. It's something we can talk about during our meeting."

I smile despite the ache in my heart. "Sounds great. Thank you, Minnie."

"You're welcome." She tosses her small backpack over her shoulder and heads toward the front door. With her mom jeans and platform shoes, she has Gen Z written all over her. She might be exactly what we need to keep modernizing the Cove.

The night is still and quiet as I make my way down the pathway and past the cabins. It seems like everyone is either tucked in for the night or enjoying a few more drinks down at Beggar's Hole. I'm sure Jaz is there, slinging drinks as usual. I spoke to her before we left the hospital—she kept insisting she'd messed up and begged me not to be mad at Sawyer. And she actually called him Sawyer. I could hear the regret in her voice. The pleading. The hope that she hadn't messed up anything.

I can feel her pain. As I make my way past the bench Sawyer fixed, all I can think about is how I was unfair to him, not letting him explain, sending him away when all he wanted was to make sure I was okay.

Stress and fear really do a number on your emotions, your thoughts, and your heart.

I round the corner to the picnic tables, and the whole area glows golden, the string lights shining brightly against the dark night sky. I stop in my tracks, because sitting on one of them, holding a single daisy, is Sawyer.

My pulse picks up at just the sight of him, but when his gaze meets mine and those soulful eyes cut right through me with a pleading stare, I nearly lose all the air in my lungs.

He hops off the picnic table as I draw closer. When we're a few feet apart, he holds out the daisy, and I take it, amazed that he remembered my favorite flower, the same flower Grandma Joan used to love.

"How's Sully?" he asks as he stuffs his hands in his jeans pockets, his black T-shirt bunching in the center as his shoulders turn inward.

"He's good. Settled. Tired."

"I can only imagine how exhausted he is." He shifts on his feet. "And how about you? How are you?"

"Been better," I admit.

"Yeah, no thanks to me." He heaves a heavy sigh. "Can I speak with you?"

"Sure."

He nods toward the picnic tables, and I follow him over to one. We both take a seat, me on one side, him on the other. In other circumstances, before all of this happened, there's no doubt that we would be sitting next to each other rather than apart.

Once we're settled on our benches, his eyes connect with mine. "I've spent the last two days thinking about this moment, when I'd get to see you again. When I had a chance to apologize for the awful way I treated you. I thought of these film-worthy apologies. The ones where the world stops around the characters, and the hero organized an all-hands-on-deck-style apology with fanfare, a live band, and a parade. That's what Roarick wanted me to do—the typical grand gesture—but I realized you don't need that kind of apology. Not that you don't deserve it, because you do, but I thought you'd appreciate this more. Intimacy, under the dim yellow lights of the picnic table area, the place where your grandfather first told me about the love of his life."

Anxiety, nerves . . . *love* bounce and ping through my chest, making my stomach flip and my breath come out in short spurts as I stare into his sorrowful eyes.

"So, beneath the stars and where I fell in love with you, I want to tell you how sorry I am for assuming the worst about you and Peter. Instead of getting jealous and throwing around accusations, I should have been grateful for his friendship, for being there for you. The words I spoke to you were inexcusable, and the only thing I can do is grow from the moment and do better. Try better. Continue to strive to be the man you deserve." He swallows hard as he nervously reaches his hand out to me. Needing to feel his touch, I take his hand, and his shoulders visibly relax. "My father once told me a smart man is a man who can admit when he's wrong. I was wrong, Fallon. And I can only hope that you'll be able to forgive me enough that I can make things right."

And this is why I love him—because I know deep in my very soul that he'd do anything, and I mean anything, to make me happy. He'd move mountains, he'd part seas, he'd trudge through a foot of sludge wearing one powder-blue shoe in order to give me the world.

I drag my thumb over the back of his hand. "What you said, Sawyer, it was hurtful. I'm not going to deny it. With all the distress of the day, the anxiety, the fear of the unknown, I can see where it was coming from, but I need you to know something." I stand, still holding his hand, and walk over to his side of the table, straddling the bench so I'm facing him. He does the same. "I've told one man, and only one man, that I love him. That man is you." I reach up and stroke his cheek softly. "I can't imagine a moment in time when I'd ever stop loving you, because this feels eternal, you and me. You don't need to worry." I press my hand against his chest. "I'll protect the beautiful heart that beats beneath my hand, and I will make sure it's never hurt again."

He brings our entwined hands up to his mouth and kisses my knuckles before bringing them to his cheek, hugging them close. "I'm not sure you understand the kind of impact that has on me, how that makes me feel protected . . . cared for."

"I have an idea, because it's the same way you make me feel." I lean in close and press my forehead to his. "I love you, Sawyer."

His hand comes behind my neck as he holds me in place. "I love you, Fallon. To my dying day, it will be you and me. I promise you."

I bring my hand to the back of his neck as well. "To our dying day."

And then he nudges me with his nose, lifting my chin slightly and placing a sweet kiss on my lips. Before he can go any deeper, I ask, "Is this when the camera starts spinning like Dad suggested?"

He lets out a low chuckle. "Nah, this isn't a spinning moment; this is a zoom-in moment."

"Both are fine with me." And then he leaves no space between us as he pulls me onto his lap and presses me into his body, his mouth on mine.

As I savor this beautiful moment with Sawyer under the lights, Sully's words echo through my mind. *Sometimes the best things in life are worth waiting for.*

Sawyer was worth the wait.

Epilogue
SAWYER

I stare at Fallon, the most beautiful person in this entire chapel. She's dressed in white lace, her chestnut-brown hair curled into soft waves and my ring on her finger to let everyone know she's mine—and I can't think of anything other than how goddamn lucky I am.

And as everyone stares up at the altar, the pastor droning on with some marital diatribe that goes in one ear and out the other, I connect eyes with the woman who has brought me so much joy.

"With the power vested in me by the beautiful state of California," the pastor says, finally finishing his monologue, "I now pronounce you husband and wife. You may kiss the bride."

I smile.

Fallon smiles back at me.

And together, we watch as Jaz and Roarick seal their marriage with a kiss. The whole town of Canoodle—Tank's motorcycle club included—cheers while Roarick dips Jaz backward in her stark black dress, putting on a show for everyone.

When they come up for air, they both hold their hands up, triumphant. The pastor introduces them as Mr. and Mrs. Roarick Walsh, and a song by Cat in Heat plays as they walk down the aisle.

Their relationship started off slowly, built on a foundation of meticulously chosen memes, until it grew into weekend visits. Those weekend visits turned into my brother making more frequent trips up the mountain, which then morphed into daily visits as they both went back and forth, until one day when Roarick pulled me to the side and said he had fallen in love with the tire slasher. It was after I'd married Fallon in an intimate ceremony next to Sully and Grandma Joan's bench that Roarick told me he was going to propose.

Strange as it is to say, I couldn't imagine him with anyone else. They're a menace to society in the best way possible.

As they travel down the aisle, I move toward the center and hold my arm out to my beaming, pregnant wife. She grips me gently, and I press a kiss to the top of her head as we walk down the aisle, the town still cheering. When we pass Sully, I give his shoulder a squeeze.

He's aged drastically in the last year. It got to the point that we needed a full-time nurse to help us with his care. Because he thrives in this town—where he's lived his life and loved his Joan—we expanded the back cabin where her fathers stay, converting it into a three-bedroom ranch with a small kitchen and living space for Sully and his live-in nurse.

With all the extra help, we've been able to expand the cabins and add a few more to the property in the very back, past the horseshoe pits; and, as my greatest accomplishment, we added a pool. Trust me when I say summers will never be the same.

Thanks to the success of *Runaway Groomsman*, Movieflix signed me on for three more screenplays, a seven-figure deal that absolutely helped pay for that pool. The next project will take place in Greece. It's about a girl who falls in love with a local while attending her sister's wedding. Total *Mamma Mia!* vibes.

To keep Sully busy during the days, my parents—who are obsessed with Fallon, by the way—helped move my kayak up to the Cove, where Sully and I work on it together every day. We took it for a test float the other day in the pool, to see how it would hold up. The kayak floated, but according to Sully, it needed much more work. Typical.

As for Annalisa, well, the damage was done to her career, and she ended up leaving show business to escape the pressure. She moved to upstate New York, where she's helping an old friend with her wedding-planning business. A small town called Binghamton. Never heard of it, but given the wedding she threw for her and Simon, she has pretty flawless taste, and her friend, Georgie, was more than happy to help her out.

Ahh . . . and Simon. What's he doing, you ask? He's currently the spokesperson for erectile dysfunction and the happy pill that man needs in his life. Whenever the commercial comes on the TV, Fallon and I turn it up so we can hear our favorite part: "Blurg, why isn't my penis getting hard? There's got to be a better way." Cut to the magic pill. Kills me every goddamn time.

In other news, Faye finally got the nerve to ask out Tank, and he immediately said yes because, as he put it, he likes a little freakiness in his life. Rigatoni Roy won so many accolades from the town for his portrayal of Edna Turnblad that he's now reprising his role every July 28 in his restaurant—pantyhose and muumuu included. Izaak and Kordell invested in some properties in Phoenix and were featured in *Architectural Digest*. Izaak announced he could die a happy man. And of course, because I'm a man of his word, both Izaak and Kordell were granted their cameos. Agora was hired full time at Beggar's Hole, where she's carried on the tradition of berating customers, just the way Jaz likes it. And Minnie, well, she's come to work for us full time, which has really helped give Fallon and me the time to build a cabin of our own, on the far right side of the property, nursery included. In case you were wondering—because I know you are—we're having a baby girl, and yes, her name will be Joannie.

And last but certainly not least, Jaz never adopted that pet. When Miss Daphne Lynn Pearlbottom's term came to an end, she attempted one more shot at reelection with a dazzling display of sequined fascinators, but no amount of glittery headpieces could beat the unexpected entry that rocked the town to its core. Beefy 2.0, a.k.a. Beefinator—the great-grandchild of the beloved late mayor—appeared out of nowhere and kicked that cat right to the curb.

Which brings me to this, the age-old question I'm sure you've been chomping at the bit to find out . . . was there EVER a color chosen for the mayor's kitchen? And the answer is, yes . . . Beefinator chose a sunshine yellow. Town conspiracy theorists argue that was the color Beefy had wanted all along.

I think that about covers it . . .

Oh wait, there is one more thing. You have to be wondering, What about Sully and Joan? How did their epic romance finally materialize? That was a story I was gladly told one early morning while sharing a seat with Sully on his bench. The fog was lifting off the lake, the air was eerily quiet, and I asked him how long he'd waited for Joan after he'd apologized. It took him a whole year from that moment to finally cross over from friends to lovers. It happened on a rainy night, after she'd driven up the mountain to yell at him for not visiting her over the weekend. He asked why she was so mad, she stuttered with her answer, and then finally she said . . . because she was in love with him. Sully said he experienced the most life-changing kiss in that moment, as the heavens parted and rain soaked them to their core. But the torrential downpour didn't stop them; instead, they continued to kiss until it was pitch black and they were trembling. That moment, that instant when he captured Joan in his arms, he said that was when his life had truly started.

I felt that confession to my very soul. On the day of my wedding, Sully gave me a watch; it was once his but it wasn't working. I pointed that out to him, and he told me that the moment I kissed Fallon, he turned it back on, because up until then, time stood still, and now that Fallon was mine, our lives could truly begin.

And that, my friends, is what they call in showbiz an epic, full-circle epilogue.

ACKNOWLEDGMENTS

Runaway Groomsman was not a planned book for me. I was actually supposed to write something else that was based in Boston, but when I sat down to start writing, I was so not into it. Being that I had no time to sit in my feelings and see what I wanted to write, I decided to come up with a story at 11:30 at night. With a single light on and an annoyed wife next to me, I came up with the idea of *Runaway Groomsman*. I went back and forth with Steph, asking her if this was a good idea, if I should add a dog to the story, if I should base it in California or somewhere else. She had some opinions, grumbled some sentences, and begged me to turn off the light, but I didn't until I had an email ready to go to my agent to see if we could make the change happen.

Thankfully, Montlake was very thrilled about the new idea, and I started writing.

When I was in high school, my mom booked us a long weekend getaway in this small mountain town called Idyllwild. It was one of my favorite vacations of all time. When writing this book, I based everything off that small mountain town, and it felt like I was revisiting it all over again. The words flowed, the plotline came to me in the moment, and the characters are all pulled from people I know. It's a book that truly came from the heart. I hope you enjoyed it just as much as I did.

Aimee Ashcraft, my agent, thank you for putting up with my "spontaneity" with this book. It was a brutal schedule, but you were accommodating and made it easier with your positivity and what felt like daily affirmations. Couldn't have done it without you.

Lauren Plude, I know that I possibly broke your heart with moving the book out of New England, but I will get you back there soon. Thank you for taking a chance on this "on a whim" plot and having faith in my abilities.

Lindsey Faber, I feel like this was the easiest book we've edited together. Maybe I need to make more plot holes so we work longer together. Kidding! Less work, the better.

To all the bloggers and readers out there, I don't even know how to express my deepest love for you. You take a chance on my books every time I release one, which is something I can never show enough gratitude for. Thank you for being the best fans a girl could ask for. You make this job so much fun!

And lastly, thank you to my wife, Steph. I know that late-night plotting session was painful, but it truly paid off. Didn't put the dog in there like you said, but I think I made it all work. Thank you for always taking care of me, our family, and our business. You are the reason I can continue to do what I do. I love you.

READ ON FOR AN EXCERPT
OF *A NOT SO MEET CUTE*
BY MEGHAN QUINN

PROLOGUE

LOTTIE

"Hey, girl."

Hmm, I don't like the cheeriness in her voice.

The smirk on her lips.

The overuse of her toxic, throat-choking perfume.

"Hey, Angela," I answer with wary trepidation as I take a seat at the table in her office.

With a flip of her bright blonde hair over her shoulder, she clasps her hands together, her body language conveying interest as she leans forward and asks, "How are you?"

I smooth my hands over my bright red pencil skirt and answer, "Doing fine. Thank you."

"That's so wonderful to hear." She leans back and smiles at me, but doesn't say another word.

Ohh-kay, what the hell is going on?

I glance behind me to the row of suited men, sitting upright in chairs, folders on their laps, staring at our interaction. I've known Angela since middle school. We've had one of those on-again, off-again friendships, me being the victim of the intermittent camaraderie. I was her main squeeze one day, the next it was Blair—who works in finance, or Lauren—who works over in sales, and then the friendship would come back to me. We're constantly interchangeable. Who's the bestie this week? I'd always wonder, and in some sick, demented way, I'd have a hiccup of excitement when the bestie card landed on me.

Why stick around in such a toxic friendship, you ask?

The answer is threefold.

One—when I first met Angela, I was young. I had no idea what the hell to do during such a vibrant roller coaster ride. I just gripped the handles and held on for dear life, because frankly, hanging with Angela was exciting. Different. Bold, at times.

Two—when she was nice to me, when we were deep into our friendship, I had some of the best times of my life. Growing up in Beverly Hills as the poor girl didn't lend its hand to many adventures, but with the rich friend who looked past your empty wallet and welcomed you into her world—yeah, it was fun. Call me shallow, but I had fun in high school, despite the ups and downs.

Three—I'm weak. I'm confrontation's bitch and avoid it at all costs, therefore—raises hand—here I am, doormat, at your service.

"Angela?" I whisper.

"Hmm?" She smiles at me.

"Can I ask why you called me in here and why the FBI seems to be lined up behind me?"

Angela tilts her head back and lets out a hearty laugh as her hand lands on mine. "Oh, Lottie. God, I'm going to miss your humor."

"Miss?" I ask, my spine stiffening. "What do you mean, *miss*? Are you going on vacation?"

Please let that be the case. Please let that be the case. I can't afford to lose this job.

"I am."

Oh, thank God.

"Ken and I are headed to Bora Bora. I have a spray tan scheduled in about ten minutes so we need to get on with this."

Wait, what?

"Get on with what?" I ask.

Her jovial face morphs into something serious, the type of serious I don't see very often from Angela. Because, yes, she might be the head of her lifestyle blog, but she's not the one who does the work—everyone else does. So, she never has to be serious.

She sits taller, her jaw grows tight, and through her thick, fake eyelashes, she says, "Lottie, you're a true pioneer for Angeloop. Your mastery behind the keyboard has been positively unmatched by anyone in this company, and the humor you bring to this thriving, money-dripping lifestyle blog has made this trip to Bora Bora a reality."

Did I hear that right? Because of me, she's able to go on her vacation?

"But, unfortunately, we're going to have to let you go."

Hold up . . . what?

Let me go?

As in, no more job for me?

Like a bolt of lightning, three of the men come up behind me, two on either side, flanking me like security. With their heavy-set shoulders blocking me in, one of them drops a folder on the table in front of me and flips it open, revealing a piece of paper. My eyes are too unfocused to even consider reading what it says, but taking a simple guess, I'm thinking it's a termination paper.

"Sign here." The man holds a pen out to me.

"Wait, what?" I move the man's hand away, only for it to bounce back right where it was. "You're firing me?"

Angela winces. "Lottie, please don't make this a thing. You must know how difficult this has been for me." She snaps her fingers and an assistant magically pops up. Angela rubs her throat and says, "This conversation has truly taken it out of me. Water, please. Room temperature. Lemon and lime, but take them out before you give it to me." And like that, the assistant is gone. When Angela turns back around, she sees me and clutches her chest. "Oh, you're still here."

Uhhh . . .

Yeah.

Blinking a few times, I ask, "Angela, what is going on? You just said I make you a ton of money—"

"Did I? I don't recall making such a statement. Boys, did I say anything like that?"

They all shake their head.

"See? I didn't say that."

I think . . . yup, mmm-hmm, do you smell that? That's my brain smoking, working overtime, trying to not LOSE IT!

Calmly, and I mean . . . calmly, I ask, "Angela, can you please explain to me why you're letting me go?"

"Ohh." She laughs. "You've always been such a nosey little thing." The assistant brings Angela her water and then rushes away. Sucking from an unnecessary straw, Angela takes a long sip and then says, "Your one-year anniversary is on Friday."

"Yes. That's correct."

"Well, per your contract, it says that after a year, you're no longer under restricted pay, but instead receive your actual salary." She shrugs. "Why pay you more when I can find someone to do your job for less? Simple bottom-line thinking. You understand."

"No, I don't." My voice rises and two large hands land on my shoulder in warning.

Oh, for fuck's sake.

"Angela, this is my life, this isn't some game you get to play. You told me when you begged me to work for you that this job was going to be life-changing."

"And hasn't it been?" She holds her arms out. "Angeloop is life-changing for everyone." She glances at her watch. "Oh, I have to get naked in five. Spray tans don't wait." She twirls her finger at the guys beside me. "Wrap it up, boys."

Two sets of hands grip me and help me up from my chair.

"You can't be serious," I say, still not quite grasping what's going on. "You're having security drag me out of your office?"

"Not by my choice," Angela says, the picture of innocence. "Your hostile attitude is making me use security."

"Hostile?" I ask. "I'm hostile because you're firing me for no reason."

"Oh, honey, I can't believe you see it that way," she says in that condescending voice of hers. "This is nothing personal. You know I love you and still plan on your monthly invitation to brunch. This is just business." She blows me a kiss. "Still my bestie."

She's lost her goddamn mind.

I'm pulled toward the door but I dig in my two-seasons-ago Jimmy Choo heels. "Angela, seriously. You can't be firing me."

She looks up at me, tilts her head to the side, and then presses her hand to her heart. "Ahh, look at you, fighting for your job. God, you've always been scrappy." She blows me another kiss, waves, and calls out, "I'll call you. You can tell me about your horrible boss later. Oh . . . and don't forget to RSVP to our high school reunion. Two months away. We need a head count."

And just like that, defeat whips through me, my heels let up in total shock, my body goes limp, and I'm dragged by my underarms through the offices of Angeloop, the most idiotic and absurd lifestyle blog on the Internet, a place where I didn't want to work in the first place.

Peers watch me.

Security doesn't skip a beat as they drag me all the way through the tall, glass front door.

And before I can take my next breath, I'm staring at the obscenely large Angeloop sign outside of the office, box of my office things in hand.

How the hell did this all happen?

CHAPTER ONE

HUXLEY

"I'm going to fucking murder someone," I shout as I throw my suit jacket across my office and slam my door.

"Seems as though the meeting went well," JP says from where he's leaning against the expansive wall of windows in my office.

"Seems as though it went incredibly well," Breaker offers from where he's lying across my leather couch.

Ignoring my brothers' sarcasm, I grip my hair and turn toward the view of Los Angeles. It's a clear day today, fresh rain from the night before eliminating some of the smog in the air. Palm trees reach high to the sky, lining the roads, but look small compared to where my office sits above the rest.

"Care to gab about it?" JP asks while taking a seat in a chair.

I turn toward them, my brothers, the two idiots who have been by my side through thick and thin. Who have ridden the ups and downs of our lives. Who have dropped everything to join me in this crazy idea of taking over the real estate market in Los Angeles with the money Dad left us when he passed. We've built this empire together.

But the smarmy looks on their faces makes me want to punt their goddamn dicks out of my office.

"Does it look like I want to *gab* about it?"

"No." Breaker smirks. "But fuck do we want to hear all about it."

Of course they do.

Because they were the ones who said I shouldn't meet with Dave Toney.

They were the ones who said it was going to be a waste of my time.

They were the ones who laughed when I said I had a meeting with him today.

And they were the ones who sarcastically said good luck as I walked out the door.

But I wanted to prove them wrong.

I wanted to show them that I could convince Dave Toney that he needed to work with Cane Enterprises.

Spoiler alert—I did not convince him.

Capitulating to my brothers' stares, I take a seat as well and let out a long sigh. "Fuck," I mutter.

"Let me guess, he didn't fall for your charm?" Breaker asks. "But you're so personable."

"That shit shouldn't matter." I slam my finger into the armrest of my plush leather chair. "This is business, not some goddamn parade of nurturing friendships and coddling one another."

"I think he missed something in business school," JP says to Breaker. "Because wasn't fostering business relationships an entire course?" His sarcasm is grating on my nerves.

"I believe it was," Breaker says.

"I went in there and kissed his ass—what more does he want?"

"Did you wear lipstick? Not sure his girlfriend would appreciate finding another pair of lips on her man's ass cheeks." Breaker smirks.

"I hate you. I really fucking hate you."

Breaker lets out a bark of a laugh while JP says, "Hate to say it, but . . . we told you so, bro. Dave Toney doesn't work with just anyone. He's a different breed in this city. Many have tried to break into the vast amount of real estate he owns; many have failed. Why did you think you'd be any different?"

"Because we're Cane Enterprises," I shout. "Everyone wants to fucking work with us. Because we have the largest real estate portfolio in Los Angeles. Because we can turn a broken-down building into a million-dollar business in a year. We know what the fuck we're doing, and Dave Toney, although successful, has some dead pieces of land on his hands that's hurting his business. He knows it, I fucking know it, and I want to take those pieces of land off his hands."

JP grips his chin and asks, "What precisely did you say to him? I hope not that? Because, although your little speech made my nipples hard, I doubt he'd appreciate the tone."

I roll my eyes. "I said something along those lines."

"You realize Dave Toney is a prideful man, right?" Breaker asks. "If you insult him, he's not going to want to work with you."

"I didn't insult him," I shout. "I was trying to get on an even playing field, you know, let him see that I'm a pretty normal guy."

Both of my brothers scoff.

"I am a normal guy."

JP and Breaker exchange glances and then both lean forward, and I know what's coming: a classic come-to-Jesus moment. They like to perform them on me from time to time.

"You know we love you, right?" Breaker asks. And so it begins.

"We're here for you, whenever you need us," JP adds.

I drag my hand over my face. "Just get the fuck on with it."

"You're not normal. You're anything but normal. None of us are. We live in Beverly Hills, are constantly invited to premieres and celebrity gatherings, and have been in the headlines on Page Six many times. There's nothing normal about us. Dave Toney, now . . . he's normal."

"How the fuck so?" I ask. "Because he doesn't get invited to celebrity after-parties?"

Breaker shakes his head. "No, because he's down-to-earth. Approachable. You could easily grab a beer with him in a bar and not feel the least bit intimidated. You're the exact opposite. You're flashy."

"I'm not flashy."

JP nods at my watch. "Nice Movado—is it new?"

I glance down at it. "Got it last week—" I raise my eyes to meet my brothers' knowing looks. "Am I not allowed to spend my hard-earned money?"

"You are," JP says. "The way you live your life is completely acceptable. The house, the car . . . the watch, all earned and rightfully so, but if you want to connect with Dave Toney, then you're going to have to get on a different level. And that doesn't mean dressing down, because he'll see right through that. He already knows you're a flashy guy. But he needs to see you in a different light."

"Ooo, I like that," Breaker says. "A different light. That's what he needs." He taps his chin. "But what would that light be?"

Irritated, I get up from my chair and grab my suit jacket from where I tossed it. "While you two morons think about it, I'm going to grab lunch."

"If only Toney could see this moment, where Huxley Cane doesn't ask his assistant to grab him lunch but, like a mere peasant, walks the streets of Los Angeles to fetch his own food," JP says.

I slip on my jacket, despite the heat outside. Ignoring them, I cross toward my door.

"Could you grab us something?" Breaker calls out.

Sighing, I call back, "Text me what you want from the deli."

"Pickles. All the goddamn pickles," JP yells as I make my way down the office hallway to the elevator. Luckily, the doors slide open for me, so I step in, press the lobby button, and lean against the wall, hands stuffed in my pants pockets.

Get on a different level. I don't even know what that means. And I know I'm a businessman who's made deals with people I've gotten along with, but I've also made deals with people I absolutely despise. The difference between me and Dave Toney—I don't give a fuck who takes my money or who I sell to. Business is business, and if it's a good deal, I'm going to take it.

I offered Dave a fucking good-as-shit deal today, better than what he deserves, if I'm honest. And instead of shaking my hand and accepting it, he sat back in his office chair, scratched the side of his cheek, and said, "I don't know. I'm going to have to sit on this."

Sit on it.

Sit on my goddamn deal.

No one sits on my deals; they take them and thank Jesus Christ Himself for doing business with Cane Enterprises.

I push through the elevator doors when they part, weave my way through the busy lobby, and then head out of the office building toward the hole-in-the-wall deli that's just down the road. Two blocks. I don't usually send my assistant, Karla, to grab me food, because it makes me feel like an asshole—despite what people might think of me—and I also enjoy the second to get out and breathe some fresh air. *Well, it's LA, so fresh air is an overstatement.* But it gives me a second to reset before I get back behind my desk, where I control our billion-dollar operation with my keyboard.

My phone beeps in my pocket and I don't bother looking at it because I know it's JP and Breaker's orders. I don't even know why I told them to text me, because they get the same thing every time. Same as me. Philly cheesesteak with extra mushrooms. And, of course, pickles. It's our go-to sandwich. Something that we don't eat often, but when we do head to the deli, it's our usual.

The sidewalk is more crowded than normal. Summer has hit Los Angeles, meaning tourists are sweeping in, celebrity bus tours will be at their max, and driving on the 101 is going to be a hellish nightmare. Lucky for me, I only live thirty minutes from the office.

As I approach the deli, a familiar black SUV pulls up in front of it. When the door opens, I catch sight of Dave Toney—speak of the devil—stepping out of the vehicle. What are the odds?

Whatever they are, they look like they're in my favor. Nothing like a good follow-up to try to secure the deal. Maybe JP was right, Dave Toney might change his mind when he sees me picking up lunch. That's definitely *on a different level.*

I button my suit jacket and pick up my pace. Never miss an opportunity in business. Never. As I grow closer, I'm dangerously caught off guard when I see a feminine hand pop out of the vehicle behind Dave. I slow down and zero in on the hand . . . the small hand with a VERY big engagement ring on it.

Holy shit, Dave is engaged?

I'm assuming he is, since he's holding the woman's hand.

But engaged . . . hell, how did I miss that?

Usually I'm aware of such—

My thoughts pause and I blink a few times as the fiancée turns, giving me a profile view.

Holy . . . fuck.

Looks like the engagement isn't the biggest surprise of the day.

Thanks to her tight-fitting dress and slender frame, there's no doubt in my mind that Dave Toney's fiancée is pregnant.

Dave Toney, engaged with a baby on the way. How . . . when?

He waves to the driver, shuts the door, and then glances behind him, just enough for us to make eye contact. His eyebrows lift in surprise and then he turns all the way around and waves to me. "Cane, didn't expect to see you on the streets."

Yeah, neither of us expected to see each other, but I'm not going to let the shock of this new development rattle me.

Showtime.

I plaster on a smile.

"Just enjoying the sultry California sun while on my way to get lunch for me and my brothers." I walk up to him and extend my hand. He gives it a brief shake. "This deli is our favorite."

"Is that right?" Dave asks in surprise. "It's Ellie's too. I've never been, but she was telling me they have the best pickles."

"My brothers are a sucker for the pickles as well." I hold my hand out to his fiancée. "You must be Ellie."

"Shit, that's rude of me," Dave says with an awkward laugh. "Yes, this is Ellie. Ellie, this is Huxley Cane."

"It's a pleasure to meet you," Ellie says in a very sweet southern voice. One that I've heard before.

I shake her hand and then let go, only to say, "Let me guess, you're from Georgia?"

Her smile brightens. "I am. You could tell?"

Yup, this bodes well for me.

"My grandma is a self-proclaimed Georgia Peach. I spent many brutal, humidity-filled summers out on her screened in porch, rocking on chairs with her as she filled me in on the latest town gossip."

"Really? Whereabout?"

"Peachtree City."

Her eyes widen in delight. She presses her hand to her chest. "I grew up in Fayetteville, just east of Peachtree. Wow, what a small world."

Yes. Yes, indeed. Especially since my grandma actually resides in San Diego, and I've never been to Georgia, actually, but they don't need to know that. They also don't need to know I recognize her accent because I dated a girl in college from Peachtree City. All semantics.

Delighted with the small connection I'm making in Dave's world, I turn toward him, only to be met by a very territorial-looking man. Uh-oh. Jaw clenched, brows narrowed, his eyes find no humor in our small . . . very small world.

Dude is practically marking his territory with that angry snarl. I wouldn't be surprised if he started circling Ellie and peeing all around her.

Given what he knows about me, flashy, a flirt, Mr. Page Six—not recently, thank God—he must think I'm a threat. Which, I'm not. I mean, yeah, Ellie is a petite bundle of blonde. Pretty, with blue eyes, but she's also pregnant—total nightmare—and she's engaged, therefore, completely off the market.

But given what my brothers said, Dave probably doesn't see it that way when it comes to me.

Which means, I need to salvage this and fast.

But how . . .

How can I possibly make it—

Light bulb

Did you see that brilliant flash of light? Yeah, an idea has emerged. It might not be smart. It's definitely not the most intelligent thing I've ever thought of, but Dave seems to be growing more and more tense by the second, so . . .

Here goes nothing.

Please don't come back to bite me in the ass—famous last words.

"Fayetteville, huh?" I wet my lips. Here goes. "Wow, crazy. I think my fiancée's parents are from Palmetto. Isn't that just north?"

Yeah, fiancée. Told you it wasn't intelligent, but it's the best I've got.

"Yes, Palmetto is just north of it," Ellie says with such joy, while Dave moves his hand around her waist in a protective embrace.

"Fiancée?" he asks after clearing his throat. "You're engaged, Cane?" There's genuine interest in his eyes and the tension that was collecting in his shoulders is slowly easing.

"Yup."

"Huh, I'm surprised."

I can't read him. Does he believe me? Is he testing me? Am I making this exponentially worse? I hope to fuck not. I don't want to lose this deal.

I refuse to let it slip through my fingers, not when I'm so close. To have those properties would be exponentially more beneficial to our portfolio, especially with what we have planned for them. And to snag a deal with the illusive Dave Toney would make me that much more victorious. My business mind takes over, leaving my common sense to the wind.

So, before I can change my mind on what's about to come out of my mouth, I swallow hard and say, "Yup, engaged and . . . expecting."

The minute the lie leaves my lips, a gross feeling takes over, because fuck, I know how hard some women try to get pregnant, and to lie about something like that . . . hell, it doesn't feel right. But like I said, common sense is nowhere to be found at this moment, it's pure idiotic instinct.

"Really?" Ellie cheers. "Oh my gosh." She rubs her belly. "So are we. Dave, isn't that exciting?"

"That really is." Dave's face morphs from unsure, protective boyfriend to . . . to a look I haven't seen on him before. Compassion.

Understanding.

Dare I say—camaraderie?

I stick my hands in my suit pants pockets to keep them from fidgeting as I tell the biggest goddamn lie of my life.

"Yeah, my grandma introduced me to her back in Peachtree. It was one of those love-at-first-sight meet-cutes."

Ellie clasps her hands together. "Oh, I love meet-cutes."

I shrug. "Yeah, and we hit it off quickly." I attempt to gaze off toward the sky as I think about my imaginary pregnant fiancée and how much I *gulp* love her. "We did things a little backwards, with getting pregnant first, but I guess we've never done anything right, according to society's timelines."

"Same," Dave says, and I see it, right there in his eyes. A new appreciation for me. This is what the boys were talking about. This was what Dave needed, to see me as a "human."

This is me, meeting Dave on a new level. Connecting on a new level. In this moment, he doesn't see me as the flashy, take-no-prisoners businessman, but rather, someone he can ask out for a beer and talk through his worries about becoming a father.

This might very well be exactly the kind of in I needed. A little chit-chat, an acute white lie that isn't going to hurt anyone. He doesn't have to actually meet this imaginary girl. He doesn't even need to know much about her. Just the idea of her makes me that much more appealing.

Huh, maybe this wasn't such a bad idea after all.

Maybe this was actually pure brilliancy at its finest.

Mark my words—by this time tomorrow, he'll be calling me up, no longer willing to sit on my offer, but more likely willing to take it.

Huxley Cane, you're an absolute genius.

"Dave, wouldn't it be absolutely divine to have Huxley and his fiancée over for dinner?"

Ehhh, what now?

Dinner?

Ellie clasps her hands together and continues, "It would be so lovely to talk with people in our same situation." Leaning forward, Ellie says, "Family has been less than thrilled about us waiting to get married until after the baby is born. My parents are quite traditional."

Sweat breaks out on my upper lip as I try to keep my face neutral.

A dinner date.

With my "fiancée."

Oh . . . fuck.

Abort, Cane. ABORT!

"That would be wonderful," Dave says with a jovial smile.

FUCK!

"How does Saturday night work?" he continues.

Saturday night?

Double fuck!

That's four days from now.

Four fucking days to not only find a fiancée, but a pregnant fiancée.

Huxley Cane, you're no genius, you're an absolute moron.

"Oh, give him a second to talk about it with his girl," Ellie says. I'd say thank God for Ellie, but the anxiety-ridden dinner date was her idea. "Why don't you get back to Dave and then let me know if it's a go. I love cooking. I could make us a real southern meal if you'd like."

My mind is already formulating excuses as to why my fiancée and I won't be able to make Saturday work.

"And maybe we can talk about the deal some more," Dave says with a genuine smile.

Fuck.

Fuck. Fuck. Fuck.

Can't say no, now. Not at the risk of securing the deal.

Christ.

Despite the desert that is my mouth, I swallow hard and nod. "Yup." My voice cracks. "Saturday sounds great."

"Wonderful." Ellie claps her hands. "Oh, I can't wait. I'm going to make my best peach cobbler and collard greens. Dave will exchange information with you."

"Perfect," I say with a shaky smile. What the hell am I getting myself into?

About the Author

Photo © 2019 Milana Schaffer

USA Today bestselling author, wife, adoptive mother, peanut butter lover, and creator of romantic comedies and contemporary romance, Meghan Quinn brings readers the perfect combination of heart, humor, and heat in every book.

Text "READ" to 474747 to never miss another one of Meghan Quinn's releases. Message and data rates may apply.